Camp Club Girls

Elizabeth

4-in-1 Mystery Collection

Camp Club Girls

Elizabeth

Renae Brumbaugh Green

BARBOUR BOOKS
An Imprint of Barbour Publishing, Inc.

Print ISBN 978-1-68322-767-0

eBook Editions:
Adobe Digital Edition (.epub) 978-1-68322-972-8
Kindle and MobiPocket Edition (.prc) 978-1-68322-973-5

Published by Barbour Books, an imprint of Barbour Publishing, Inc., 1810 Barbour Drive, Uhrichsville, Ohio 44683, www.barbourbooks.com

Our mission is to inspire the world with the life-changing message of the Bible.

ecpa Member of the Evangelical Christian Publishers Association

Printed in the United States of America.
06328 1218 BP

Camp Club Girls and the Mystery at Discovery Lake

Cabin 12B

"*Shhhhhhh!*" Sydney told Bailey. "What was that noise?"

"What noise?" asked Bailey.

"*Shhhhhhhhhhhhhh!*" commanded her new friend.

The two listened with all their focused energy. Then, there it was. Footsteps. Large, heavy footsteps.

The girls stood in terrified uncertainty.

Aaaaaaaaarrrrrrkkkkk!

Sydney gasped as the eerie shriek filled the air.

Yahahoho-ho-ho!

Bailey trembled uncontrollably as the crazy, other-worldly laugh followed.

"Run!" Sydney screamed. The two dashed as fast as their legs could carry them back toward the camp. Sydney stopped twice, waiting for Bailey's shorter legs to catch up.

•—•—•

Fourteen-year-old Elizabeth sat in the middle of the dusty road, trying to cram her undergarments back into her suitcase before anyone saw. *I thought wheels were supposed to make a suitcase easier,* she thought. Instead, the rolling blue luggage had tipped over three times before it finally popped open, leaving her belongings strewn in the street.

Suddenly, she was nearly barreled over by two girls running frantically. "Run for your life!" the smaller one cried. "It's after us!"

"Whoa, calm down." Elizabeth focused on the terrified girls.

The taller one panted. "Something's back there!"

Elizabeth looked toward the golf course but saw nothing. She noticed that the smaller girl seemed to struggle for air, and her protective instincts took over. "Calm down. You'll be okay."

"Need. . .inhaler," the girl gasped.

Elizabeth sprang into action, digging through the girl's backpack until she found a small blue inhaler. Then she helped hold it steady while the slight girl puffed in the medication. The taller girl kept looking toward the miniature golf course they'd just left. "Sorry," the small girl whispered. "I'm supposed to keep that in my pocket, but I got so excited I forgot."

"I'm Elizabeth. Why don't you tell me what happened?"

"I'm Bailey," said the short, dark-haired girl. "Bailey Chang."

"And I'm Sydney Lincoln," said the tall, dark-skinned girl with beaded braids. "We were at the golf course, and. . .and. . ."

"And something came after us!" exclaimed Bailey.

Elizabeth looked skeptical as she tucked a strand of long blond hair into the clip at the base of her neck.

"Is this your first year here? This is my third year here, and the most dangerous thing I've seen is a skunk."

The girls giggled but didn't look convinced. "Come with us. We'll show you." Bailey pulled Elizabeth back toward the golf course.

"I thought you were afraid of whatever it was! Why do you want to go back there?" Elizabeth asked.

The young girl stood to her full height. "Because I am going to be a professional golfer. And I'm not going to let whatever that was bully me. I plan to practice my golf strokes while I'm here."

"Will you tell me exactly what happened?" Elizabeth asked Sydney.

Sydney looked each girl in the eye and spoke slowly. "Something or someone is in the woods by the golf course. And it wasn't friendly." She paused for dramatic effect. "And. . .it came after us."

•—•—•

Kate Oliver leaned back on her bed and smiled. *Yes! I got the bed by the window!* she thought. *Hopefully, I'll be able to get good reception for my laptop and cell phone.* She tucked a strand of blond hair behind her ear. It was too short to stay there and just long enough to drive her crazy.

Bam! The cabin's outer door slammed, and Kate heard voices. Pushing her black-framed glasses up on her nose, she sat up. Two girls entered the room giggling and talking.

"I can't believe I'm finally here! This is so cool. And look at this cute little dorm room! It's just like the cabin in *The Parent Trap*! Oh, hello!" The fun-looking brunette with piercing blue eyes greeted Kate. "I'm Alex Howell. Alexis, really, but nobody calls me that except my mother. I am so excited!

This will be the best two weeks ever!"

Kate smiled and reached to shake the girl's hand. "Kate Oliver," she said. "Welcome to cabin 12B." She looked at the other girl.

The girl's freckles matched her curly auburn hair, and she offered a friendly smile. "Hi there. I'm McKenzie Phillips."

•—•—•

The two girls looked at Elizabeth stubbornly, as if needing to prove their story to her. Hearing another bus pull up, Elizabeth remembered her belongings, which were still lying in the middle of the road.

"I'll tell you what. You help me get this awful suitcase to cabin 12B, and then I'll walk to the golf course with you. Deal?"

Bailey's mouth dropped open, and Sydney's eyes widened.

"You're in cabin 12B?" asked Sydney.

"That's our cabin!" exclaimed Bailey.

Now it was Elizabeth's turn to be surprised. "You're kidding! Wow. It is a small world. Okay, roomies, help me hide my underwear before the entire camp sees, and we'll be on our way."

The girls gathered the strewn articles of clothing. Bailey held up one particular article of clothing and giggled. "Tinkerbell? Seriously, you have Tinkerbell on your. . ."

Elizabeth snatched the unmentionables from Bailey, crammed them in her suitcase, and snapped it shut. "Not another word, shorty!" Elizabeth scolded, but with a twinkle in her eye. The three girls chattered all the way to cabin 12B. As they approached the cabin, the two younger girls pulled their luggage out from behind some bushes.

"We sat together on the bus from the airport, and we both wanted to see the golf course before we did anything else. So we stowed our suitcases here until we got back," explained Sydney.

Elizabeth laughed. With these two as roommates, this year's camp experience would be far from dull.

The girls entered the cabin and located room B to the right. Three girls were already there, smiling and laughing.

"Hello, I'm Elizabeth. I guess we'll be roommates!" She tossed her things on the lower bunk closest to the door, and Sydney placed her things on the bunk above that. Bailey took the top bunk next to Sydney. After an awkward pause, McKenzie stepped forward.

"I'm McKenzie Phillips," she said. "I'm thirteen, and I'm from White Sulphur Springs, Montana."

Alex bounced forward. "I'm Alexis Howell, Alex for short. I'm twelve, and I'm from Sacramento."

"Sydney. Twelve. Washington, DC."

"Oh, that is so cool. Do you know the president?" asked Bailey, and everyone laughed. "I'm Bailey Chang. I'm nine, and I'm from Peoria, Illinois. And just so you'll all know, I plan to be the next Tiger Woods. I'll be glad to sign autographs, if you want. They'll be worth money some day."

Elizabeth stepped forward. "I'll take one, Bailey. I'll sell it and use the money for college. I'm Elizabeth Anderson, fourteen, from Amarillo, Texas."

"Well, I guess that leaves me," said Kate. "Kate Oliver, eleven, Philadelphia."

Alexis jumped up and down. "Oh, this will be so much fun! Kate brought her laptop with her. I have the coolest roommates ever!"

Everyone's attention turned to Kate's bed, which was covered with a laptop and several small gadgets. "What is all that stuff?" asked Sydney. The girls gathered around Kate's bed and watched her pull items out of a black backpack.

"It's like a magician's bag. It has no bottom," mused McKenzie.

Kate laughed. "My dad teaches robotics at Penn State, so he's always bringing home little devices to test out. Some of them are really helpful. Some of them are just fun to play with."

One by one, she pulled the oddly shaped gadgets out of her bag, describing the functions of each.

"This is my cell phone. It can take pictures and short video clips, has a GPS tracker, a satellite map, internet access, a motion sensor, a voice recorder, and about a zillion other things!" Aiming it at the others, she said, "Say cheese!"

The other girls leaned together and smiled. "Cheeeeeeeeeeeeese!"

Kate saved the picture then passed the phone to the others and dug through her backpack again. "This digital recorder can record conversations up to thirty feet away."

Sydney squinted her eyes. "You're kidding! That thing is the size of a contact lens! Let me see!" Kate handed her the recorder and kept digging.

"This is a reader," she continued, holding up a small penlike device.

"A what?" asked McKenzie.

"A reader. You run it across words on a page, and it records them to memory. Like a small scanner."

"That is so cool! I had no idea stuff like this existed!" McKenzie examined the reader.

"Here, I have my Bible. Will you show us how the reader works?" Elizabeth grabbed a worn Bible from her bag and handed it to Kate.

"Sure. You turn it on by pressing this button, and. . ." She ran the pen over a page in Psalms.

Elizabeth giggled. "I've heard of hiding God's Word in your heart, but never in your pen!"

The gadget girl suddenly stopped her display to announce, "Hey, I'm starved. Is anybody else hungry?"

"It's almost dinnertime," announced Elizabeth. "But first, we have some business to take care of at the golf course."

The girls listened as Sydney and Bailey described their experience.

"Whoa, cool!" exclaimed Alex. "We have a mystery on our hands! Why don't we go right now and check it out?"

"Why don't we eat first?" called out Kate. "Starving girl here, remember?" The others laughed when the petite girl's stomach growled loudly.

Since it was almost dinnertime, the group decided to head to the dining hall first. Bailey led the way, taking over as tour guide.

"Wait for me," called Alex. "I need to grab my lip gloss!" She shoved a strawberry Lip Smacker into her pocket.

The group wandered through the camp, with Bailey pointing out different sites. Suddenly, she stopped. "Well guys, I hate to tell you this. . .but I have no idea how to get to the dining hall from here."

"It's this way," stated Elizabeth. "You'll get your bearings. My first year here, it took me the whole time before I could find my way around. But I get lost in a closet."

McKenzie spoke up. "Come on, girls, let's go. Remember, Kate's about to starve. We wouldn't want her to waste away to nothing."

Everyone laughed at Kate, who pretended to be nearly fainting. "I need sustenance, and I need it now!"

The group arrived at the dining hall with seven minutes to spare. They stood near the front of the line, and Elizabeth said, "Get ready for a long meal. The camp director will explain all the camp rules, introduce the counselors, and tell us more than we want to know about Camp Discovery Lake."

"Terrific." Bailey sighed. "I wanted to visit the golf course before dark."

"Don't worry," said Alex. "After the story you and Sydney told, I think we all want to find out what's down there."

"Really?" Bailey asked. "You'll all come?"

"You bet!" said McKenzie. "The girls of cabin 12B stick together!"

•—•—•

The sun was dipping behind the horizon by the time the girls left the dining hall.

"Hooray! We can finally go to the golf course!" Bailey called.

"We'd better hurry. It's getting dark," said Elizabeth.

"Yeah, and after the story you and Sydney told, I certainly don't want to be there after dark," added Kate.

The girls scurried while chattering about the different camp activities they wanted to try. Before they knew it, the sun was gone and they could barely see the road. "Why is the golf course so far away from the main camp?" asked Alex nervously.

Sydney laughed. "So nobody will get hit on the head with a stray golf ball!"

Suddenly, a voice called out from the woods.

"Who? Who? Who?"

"What was that?" whispered Bailey.

"Who?" came the voice again.

McKenzie giggled. "You city girls don't know much about the country, do you? That was an owl!"

The others burst into laughter as the voice called again, *"Who?"*

"I'm Sydney! Who are you?" Sydney shouted, and the laughter continued.

"It sure does get dark here, doesn't it?" said Kate. "It never gets this dark in the city."

"Are we close to the golf course?" Alex asked.

"It doesn't seem nearly as far in the daytime," Elizabeth told her.

They continued, each trying to seem brave. The trees that had seemed friendly and protecting in the daytime now loomed like angry giants. The girls' steps became slower and slower as they struggled to see where they were stepping.

Finally, Kate stopped and looked at the sky through the trees. "Look, everybody! It's the Big Dipper!" The other five girls looked to where she pointed.

"Wow, the sky is beautiful. It's so dark, and the stars are so bright," whispered Sydney.

"The stars are never this bright in Sacramento," Alex commented. "The city lights are brighter. Hey, this reminds me of an episode of *Charlie's Angels,* where the Angels' car broke down in the middle of nowhere, and they had to use the stars to find their way home."

The girls were so focused on the sky that they didn't notice the image moving toward them. Kate was the first to lower her eyes, and she blinked in confusion. Adjusting her eyeglasses, she whispered, "Uh, guys?"

The girls continued pointing out the brightest stars.

Kate tried to make her voice louder, but terror kept it to a soft squeak. "G–g–guys?" The image moved closer, but still no one heard her. Finally, Kate grabbed Sydney's sleeve. "Wh–wh–what is that?" she squeaked.

Sydney looked. "Oh my word! What in the world is that?"

The girls saw a white stripe in the road, moving slowly, steadily toward them. They were frozen, until Elizabeth yelled, "Skunk!"

Camp Discovery Lake resounded with shrieks and squeals as the girls ran back toward the cabins. McKenzie led the way with Alex close on her heels.

The girls didn't slow down until they had burst through the door of cabin 12B. They fell onto the beds, panting and giggling.

"Can you believe it? A skunk! We were scared of a little bitty skunk!" McKenzie howled.

"I don't know about you, McKenzie, but I wasn't about to smell like Pepé Le Pew out there!" Alex held her nose, and the girls laughed even harder.

"Hey, Sydney, is that what scared you today? Some forest creature?"

Sydney and Bailey stopped giggling and looked at one another. "No," they replied.

"Whatever we heard was not small," said Bailey. "And it wasn't friendly."

"And it definitely came after us," added Sydney.

Dan Ger?

"No! Make that noise go away!" Bailey groaned, pulling the covers over her head as a loud trumpet sounded reveille over the loudspeaker the next morning. "It's still dark outside!"

The wretched music continued. Apparently, the unknown trumpet player was committed to torturing the entire camp.

Sydney threw back her covers. "I'm taking a shower before all the hot water is gone," she told her roommates.

"Good idea. I'm coming too," called Kate. Alex sat up and stretched, while Elizabeth began making her bed. McKenzie remained a motionless lump.

Alex tossed her dark curls, smiled, and began singing with an off-key voice. "It's time to get up. Get out of bed. It's time to get up, you sleepyheads!"

A pillow flew at her from Bailey's bed, but this only encouraged the perky brunette. She stood to her feet and stretched close to Bailey's ear. "It's time to get up. Get out of bed. It's time to get up, you slee—"

"Okay! Okay! Promise me you will *never, ever* sing again, and I'll get up!" Bailey sat up and rubbed her eyes.

Elizabeth, spotting McKenzie's motionless form, laughed. "Alex, I think your services may be needed elsewhere."

The vivacious songbird stooped to McKenzie's level. Just as she poised her mouth to sing, McKenzie's eyes popped open. "Don't even think about it!"

They all laughed, and soon they headed toward the dining hall.

"Food at last!" Kate exclaimed as they took their places in the long line. "I feel like I haven't eaten for days!"

"You look like it too!" announced a sneering voice. "What's the matter? Don't your parents feed you?"

The whole group turned around. "And those glasses. . . Maybe if you'd eat a carrot once in a while you could get rid of those," the very pretty, very mean-looking girl announced.

Sydney stepped forward, towering inches over the girl. "Excuse me?"

"It's okay, Sydney. I can handle this." Kate stepped forward, adjusted her glasses, and stared into the eyes of her unpleasant opponent. "It's a common misconception that small people don't eat much. However, the genealogical consequences of the high metabolic rates of both of my parents have resulted in similar metabolism in each of their offspring."

The girl stared at Kate, clearly baffled by her words. Kate triumphantly smiled.

Ever the peacemaker, Elizabeth stepped forward. "Hi! Aren't you Amberlie Crewelin? You were here last year. I'm Elizabeth, and these are my roommates, Sydney, Kate, McKenzie, Bailey, and Alex. It's nice to see you again. Oh look! They've opened a new line. I guess we'll see you later!" Elizabeth guided the group to the other line. "We probably want to steer clear of her," she murmured to the others. "She has some. . .issues."

"Don't let her get to you," McKenzie added. "People like that are miserable, and they want to make everyone else miserable."

"Well, I don't know about the rest of you, but I'm not hungry. All I can think about is that miniature golf course and those noises we heard last night!" Bailey announced.

"Not hungry? Speak for yourself," said Kate.

Alex jumped up and down. "Let's check it out after breakfast! If we hurry, we'll have almost an hour before our first session begins. Oh! I just love a good mystery!"

"And I just love a good meal," Kate stated.

The small band of detectives moved hastily through the line and chose foods they could eat quickly. Kate loaded her plate with five fluffy biscuits and five sausage patties, drawing amused stares from her roommates. She grabbed two cartons of chocolate milk, a carton of apple juice, and a banana. She started toward the table but paused again to add an orange to her tray.

The girls settled at a table by the door and ate quickly. Kate was only half finished when the others began picking up their trays. "Hey! I'm not done yet!" she protested.

"Bring it with you," replied Elizabeth. "Here, wrap it in this napkin and stuff it in your pocket. The golf course is at the other end of the camp, so we need to hustle."

The group hurried past the chapel and around the stables on their way to the site of last night's mystery noise.

"Hello, girls!" called a man from the stables.

"Hello, Mr. Anzer," Elizabeth called back. "You all will love him," she told her friends. "He's the camp grandpa." Then, looking at her watch, she said, "We have forty-seven minutes. Last year a group was late to the first session, and the camp director made them clean the kitchen in their free time!"

"Hmm. Did they get to eat the leftovers?" Kate asked.

"Shhhhhh!" Alex hushed them as they neared their destination. "Listen! I think I hear something!"

The young sleuths stopped in their tracks, afraid to move. Sure enough, they heard a distant howling noise.

"Is that what you heard last night?" Alex asked.

Sydney and Bailey both shook their heads. "No. What we heard was more. . ." Sydney searched for the correct word.

"Creepy!" Bailey interjected. "What we heard was like creepy laughter."

"That noise sounded pretty creepy to me," whispered McKenzie.

"Well, I don't know why we're standing here. Nancy Drew would already be investigating!" Alex exclaimed.

No one moved. "Okay. I'll go first!" said Alex. The young investigator led the way, and the other detectives reluctantly followed.

Elizabeth stopped the group as they reached the gate to the miniature golf course. "We need to stay together. We don't know what we'll find, and we're a long way from the main camp."

The girls all nodded their heads. Bailey unlatched the gate, and it swung open with a low creak. The girls moved inside and slowly approached the howling noise, which was getting louder.

"It sounds like a wounded animal," said Sydney. "Not scary, just. . .sad."

As the girls tiptoed through the golf course, they noticed the worn attractions.

"Wow! Look at this place! We don't have anything like this back in Peoria." Bailey said. "Look, there's a windmill, and a clown, and a castle. . . . It's not nearly as scary in the daylight. I'm going to come here every day to practice my Tiger Woods strokes."

Suddenly, a high-pitched, mechanical-sounding laugh came from the direction of the clown.

The girls squealed and banded together more tightly. "Or maybe I won't," continued the group's youngest member.

"What was that?" asked McKenzie. "It sounded so. . .fake."

The howling turned to a whimper, and the group froze. "That doesn't sound fake!" said Kate. Forgetting her promise to stay with her friends, she ran ahead. "Hey, get over here! Come look at this!"

The girls ran to join Kate at the windmill. They found a skinny puppy caked in mud. His paw was caught in the golf hole, and he whimpered pitifully.

Kate knelt to help the puppy. With the help of the others, he was soon free of the trap.

"Here you go, little fellow! You're okay now." Kate held the small dog close, then at arm's length. "Whoa! You stink!"

"Awww, look at him! He's hungry," said Elizabeth. "Kate, where's the rest of your breakfast?"

Kate pulled a biscuit from her pocket, and the dog swallowed it in two bites. Then, tail wagging, he attacked his rescuer with puppy kisses, knocking her glasses askew. She offered him half of a sausage patty and another biscuit.

"Look at that. He loves you, Kate! You're his hero," said McKenzie.

"He sure ate those biscuits in a hurry. I think we should name him Biscuit!" suggested Bailey.

Biscuit wagged his tail in agreement.

Suddenly, the girls were startled by a man's voice.

"Hey! What are you girls doing? Get away from that mutt!"

An angry-looking man walked toward them. His green collared shirt showed that he was a Camp Discovery Lake staff member.

McKenzie stepped forward. "Oh, we were just looking around, and we found him. His paw was stuck in a—"

"You girls need to stay away from here. Give me that dog, and get to class!" He reached for Biscuit, but the small dog wiggled out of Kate's arms and ran toward the woods.

"But sir, he's just a puppy! He was stuck, and hungry, and we had to help him," Elizabeth told the man.

He glared at her. "You girls aren't here to rescue dogs or to poke around an old golf course. Stay away from here, you understand?" The girls backed away a few steps.

"What are you waiting for?" he shouted. "Get out of here!"

The girls turned and ran through an open side gate, into the woods.

"And don't come back!" the angry man yelled.

They ran frantically, not stopping until they were deep in the woods. Finally, out of breath, they halted.

"Why was. . .he so angry? . . . We weren't. . .doing anything wrong," said Sydney, catching her breath.

"He seems like a. . .very unhappy. . .person to me," replied McKenzie.

Alex sank to her knees, while Bailey propped herself against a tree. Gradually, their breathing slowed, and they began to look at their surroundings.

Elizabeth leaned toward Bailey. "You okay, Bales? Got your inhaler?"

"It's in my pocket. Umm, does anybody know where we are?" asked Bailey.

"Does anybody know where Biscuit is?" asked Kate, her voice shaking.

"Biscuit! We've got to find him!" exclaimed Elizabeth. "If we don't, that horrible man will probably send him to the pound!"

The girls started yelling, "Biscuit! Come here, Biscuit!"

"Wait!" Elizabeth stopped them. "We have to stay together. The last thing we need is for one of us to get even more lost!"

"Yes, Mother," teased Bailey.

All of a sudden, a bloodcurdling scream pierced the air, followed by a rustling sound in the trees above them. The girls shrieked and huddled together.

"Wh–wh–what was that?" whispered Bailey.

"I don't know, and I d–don't want to find out!" McKenzie responded.

Elizabeth craned her neck, trying to determine the source of the alarming sound. "It sounded like a woman. A terrified woman!"

"It sounded like a cougar," said Sydney. "We studied them in my Wilderness Girls class."

"A cougar! Yikes! Let's scram!" exclaimed Alex.

"We do need to stay together," Sydney continued. "Cougars probably won't attack a group, but they sometimes attack individuals. I think we scared it."

"But Sydney, what about Biscuit?" asked Kate.

A worried silence fell over the group. Then they began calling for the lost puppy again. Just a few minutes later, they heard the rustling of dead leaves, followed by a whimper.

"Biscuit!" Kate followed the sound and pulled the bedraggled puppy from a pile of leaves. "I'm so glad you're safe!"

The girls surrounded their wiggly, smelly treasure and took turns holding him. Then the cougar screamed again in the distance.

"Let's get out of here," McKenzie urged, wide-eyed. "We may have scared that cougar, but it scared me too!"

"You and me both," agreed Alex. "But we have a problem. I have no idea where we are or how we got here!"

The frightened young campers all looked to Elizabeth, the oldest. "Don't look at me!" she told them. "I'm directionally disabled."

"I have a compass," Kate told the group as she struggled with her wiggling bundle. They all looked at her hopefully until she added, "In my backpack. Back at the room."

"We can figure this out," asserted Sydney. "Let's think about this. The golf course is south of the main camp. We came into the woods from the right, which would be east. So, we were heading west."

"Maybe so, but we've turned around so many times, I don't remember which way is which," said McKenzie.

Five pairs of eyes remained glued to Sydney's face as she continued to work things out in her mind. She muttered under her breath, reminding herself of things she had learned in her nature studies. The others listened, not wanting to interrupt the girl who seemed to be their only hope for escape from these dark, menacing woods.

Sydney walked around trees, examining the bark, scrutinizing the branches. Her beaded braids jangled as she moved from tree to tree. Finally, she addressed her fellow campers. "To get back to the golf course, we need to head east. Look for moss growing at the base of the trees, and that will be north. Also look for spiderwebs, which are often found on the south sides of trees."

The group began to examine the details of their surroundings.

"This is fun," said Bailey. "It's sort of like a treasure hunt!"

Elizabeth stopped her search and looked thoughtful. "That reminds me of something in the Bible. Several times in Deuteronomy, God said His people are His treasured possession."

Just then, the girls heard the screaming once more in the distance. "Will you hurry up, already?" Bailey urged Sydney. The other girls tried to remain calm.

"You sure know a lot of Bible verses," McKenzie said to Elizabeth. "Let me guess. . .I'll bet your dad is a preacher!"

"Close," Elizabeth said, smiling at the insightful redhead. "My grandpa's a preacher. My dad teaches Bible at the local seminary."

"This way!" Sydney called, and the group anxiously followed her. "I see the windmill up ahead!"

Moments later, they approached the now-abandoned golf course.

"Any sign of Oscar the Grouch?" asked Bailey.

The group chuckled, and McKenzie stood on her tiptoes and scanned the area. "I don't see anyone."

"Probably couldn't find a job anywhere else," muttered Sydney. "But look—someone has been digging over there, by the castle!"

The amateur sleuths walked to the fresh pile of dirt.

"It had to be the Grouch! Why would he dig here?" Alex knelt for a closer look.

"I don't know, but we'll have to figure it out another time. We'll be late for our first session," Elizabeth informed them, looking at her watch.

"What can we do with Biscuit?" asked Kate.

"If we hurry, we can take him back to the room. We'll hide him there for right now," Elizabeth told her.

As the group headed out the gate, Alex and McKenzie lagged behind.

"I have a feeling there's more to the Grouch than meets the eye," McKenzie told her friend.

The two began to follow the others until Alex spotted a small piece of paper near the pile of dirt.

"Oh my!" she exclaimed as she read it. She held it out to McKenzie.

The torn paper issued a warning: *"Dan Ger".*

The girls looked at each other, then took off running, full speed ahead.

Keep Out!

The two girls caught up with their friends in no time.

"Look what we found. By that pile of dirt," Alex panted. She passed around the wrinkled piece of paper.

Then they all spoke at once.

"What does this mean?"

"Who is this for?"

"Do you think this was meant for us?"

"I wonder if the Grouch had anything to do with this."

Sydney paced back and forth, hand to her chin. "Why do you think he was so mad at us? We weren't doing anything. That was our free time. We haven't been told to stay away from the golf course."

Elizabeth jumped in. "Speaking of free time, we may not have any if we're late. We can talk about this later. Let's go! Kate, I'll go with you to take Biscuit back to the cabin, and the rest of you get to class."

The small group of sleuths scattered.

In the cabin, Kate laid Biscuit gently on her bed. He licked her hand, curled into a ball, and promptly went to sleep. "Poor little fellow," she said. "He's had a rough morning."

"Let's just hope he stays asleep while we're gone," said Elizabeth. She grabbed Kate by the arm and led her out the door. "I'll meet you back here as soon as this first session ends."

The two girls hurried to their classes and scooted into their seats without a moment to spare.

•—•—•

A while later, Elizabeth sat in the end chair in the back row, trying to focus on the camp counselor's words. Her mind was crowded with thoughts of puppies and cougars and cryptic warnings.

"My name is Miss Rebecca. For the next two weeks of camp, you will compete with your other five roommates as a team. Each group needs to create a team name, and whoever has the best name will receive points. You will also earn points for cleanliness, punctuality, and attitude. These points will be given at the discretion of the counselors.

"Your team will also compete in various categories in a camp-wide competition. The categories are scripture memory, nature studies, horseback riding, rowing, and a few others we'll tell you about in the next few days. On the last day of camp, the team with the most points wins the title Team Discovery Lake. Each girl on the winning team will receive a blue ribbon and a partial scholarship to next year's camp."

Elizabeth looked around at the other girls. There, in the front row, smiling sweetly at the counselor, was Amberlie.

Now that girl is trouble! Elizabeth had never gotten to know her very well, but she knew enough. All sugar and spice and everything nice around the counselors. But the minute she was away from adults, her sugar and spice turned to vinegar.

Amberlie's hand shot high into the air. "Will there be *daily* winners?" she asked.

"Good question, and yes. Each day, the team with the most points earned on the previous day will be first in all meal lines. Teams will receive daily points for attitude and for the cleanest rooms."

This announcement was followed by an enthusiastic buzz from the campers. First at mealtime—now *that* was worth competing for.

Miss Rebecca smiled as she gave the girls time to absorb the information. "Now that we've got that out of the way, let's begin our Bible Explorers class! We'll memorize a lot of scripture in the next two weeks. Let's start with a game. . . ."

Elizabeth settled back in her seat and smiled. She was good at scripture memory. This class was right up her alley.

•—•—•

McKenzie and Sydney stood with the other girls by the stable door, listening to the counselor talk about basic horsemanship. The horses all seemed gentle and trustworthy, unlike some of the stallions back at McKenzie's ranch in White Sulphur Springs.

"During your time here, you will learn basic horse care and riding techniques. These horses are used to young ladies and are calm, so you don't need to be afraid of them. However, they are very large animals, so you need to be gentle with them as well."

Sydney elbowed McKenzie. The auburn-haired girl looked at her new friend and saw her motioning to a large oak tree at the edge of the paddock. In the shade of the tree was the grouchy man from the golf course talking to the older man Elizabeth had pointed out earlier in the day. From the abrupt gestures of the grouchy man, Sydney guessed he wasn't too happy.

The girls watched and strained to hear the words, but it was no use. The men were too far away, and the counselor's words drowned out any chance of eavesdropping.

They continued to observe the exchange. The older man—Mr. Anzer—put his arm around the Grouch's shoulders, and the Grouch seemed to calm a bit. The two then walked away, continuing their conversation as they moved toward the offices at the east end of the stables.

•—•—•

Kate had signed up for the nature studies class right away. In her concrete world of Philadelphia, she didn't get much exposure to the rugged outdoors. The closest thing she had back home was the well-groomed city park or the beautiful college campus where her dad taught. She had been excited to learn about various trees and flowers and wildlife. She had even brought her cell phone so she could take pictures.

But now she could only think of the muddy black-and-white puppy asleep on her bed. *He likes me,* she thought. *I've never had a dog. I wonder if Mom and Dad would let me keep him.*

"That's about it for today, girls. As you're walking around the camp, remember to pay attention to the shapes of the leaves you see. Try to identify the ones we talked about."

Kate jerked to attention. Had she really daydreamed the whole class away? Staring at her blank phone screen, she wondered how the hour could have passed so quickly. She couldn't remember a single thing the counselor had said.

Snapping her phone closed, she remembered Elizabeth's request to meet back at the cabin. *Immediately after class.* Besides, she was eager to check on Biscuit.

Slipping the small phone into her pocket, she ran as fast as she could, nearly crashing into Bailey and Alex as she reached the crossroad that led to their cabin.

"Whoa, Kate! Slow down! At that rate, you'll have a major collision!" Alex laughed.

Kate caught her balance and smiled. "Sorry! I just can't wait to get back to the cabin. Biscuit was asleep when we left him, and I. . ." She was interrupted by a low, mournful howl.

The three girls looked at each other and exclaimed, "Biscuit!"

They ran to cabin 12B in record time. Bursting through the door, they stopped short at the sight before them.

The dirty, round-eyed puppy sat in the center of the room, tail wagging with excitement. A pair of green shorts hung off his back, and he held a dirty sock in his mouth. Undergarments, nightgowns, and T-shirts were scattered from one end of the room to the other.

"Oh Biscuit. What have you done?" Kate scooped up the puppy, and he licked her face. "Hey, stop that!" She laughed and held him out of face range. "I don't mind the kisses, but we've gotta do something about your breath!"

"Uh, girls. . .we'd better clean up this mess. The counselors are coming before lunch to check our rooms!" said Alex.

"But first. . ." Bailey dug through her pockets. "Look what we made for Biscuit!" She pulled out a colorful ribbon-braided rope and attached it around the dog's neck. "Alex and I worked on it in class. Now he has a collar!"

"Perfect!" exclaimed Kate. Alex and Bailey looked pleased.

"What in the. . .world?" The girls turned as Elizabeth stepped into the room. "Oh my." The older girl just stood there, taking in every detail of the disastrous room. "Oh my, oh my."

•—•—•

Sydney and McKenzie lingered after class, pretending to admire the horses. "Do you think we should go find out what they're talking about?"

"I think we should at least see if the Grouch has an office over here or something," Sydney urged.

"That older man he was talking to, Mr. Anzer, seemed nice. Elizabeth seemed to really like him. Surely he's not like. . ." McKenzie paused. "No, it looked more like he was trying to calm the Grouch down, didn't it?"

The two girls walked toward the office area, pausing to look at the horses when a counselor passed.

"I want to ride the bay over there," exclaimed McKenzie.

"I think I'll stick with the pony," replied Sydney.

When the coast was clear, the girls continued to the east end of the building, pausing outside an open window. Hearing voices inside, they grew still, straining to hear the conversation.

"I'm telling you, Dan, you can't post a KEEP OUT sign at the golf course. It may be old, but the kids still love it. You can't keep them from playing a few rounds of miniature golf if they want to."

"But William, I'm trying to get my work done. I can't make the repairs if a bunch of little girls are running around everywhere."

This was followed by a long pause.

Finally, Mr. Anzer spoke again. "Just do what you can while the girls are in their classes. I'll see if I can come help you."

"No! That won't be necessary!" Dan spoke up quickly. "I'll just figure out a way to make it work."

The two girls looked at each other, wide-eyed, but didn't move. Suddenly, the man they now knew as Dan burst through the door and nearly barreled over them. He stopped, clearly surprised to see the sleuths, and opened his mouth as if to speak.

McKenzie spoke first. "Pardon us, sir! We didn't mean to get in your way. We were just headed back to our cabin. You have a very nice day, sir! Umm. . .goodbye!"

The two girls dashed toward the cabins.

As soon as they were out of earshot, Sydney spoke up. "Whew. That was close. I wonder if he knows we were listening."

"I don't know. I just can't figure out why he doesn't want anyone at the golf course. I mean, this is a kids' camp," McKenzie responded.

Sydney's voice rose. "Yeah. Of course kids will be running around—that's kind of the point. If it weren't for us, he wouldn't have a job here in the first place!"

"Shhhhh. We don't want the whole camp to know. Something tells me that the Grouch doesn't care much about his job. He doesn't keep the golf course tidy. He must have some other reason why he doesn't want anybody down there," McKenzie told her friend.

"I think you're right. Let's go tell the others what we heard."

The girls jogged back to the cabin, where they found the others making piles of clothing. "What in the world? What are you all doing with my shorts? And my headband? And my. . ." Sydney's bewildered gaze landed on the innocent-looking puppy sitting at Kate's feet. "Biscuit! What did you do?"

The puppy answered her with a bark and a wag of his tail.

•—•—•

The young detectives sat in a circle on the floor examining the wrinkled piece of paper.

Dan Ger.

"Why is it written that way? You know, with a space in between, and the *D* and the *G* capitalized?" asked Bailey.

"I think the way it's written must be a clue of some sort. Maybe the space in the *middle* means we are in the middle of danger!" Sydney added.

The girls passed around the small paper, trying to find further clues. Elizabeth held the paper up to the light. "This looks like envelope paper. If you hold it up, it has a pattern, kind of like the business envelopes my parents use."

Alex reached for the paper. "May I see that?" Then, holding it up, she said, "Elizabeth is right! This may be. . . Hey! Maybe Dan is someone's name!"

McKenzie and Sydney began talking at once. "I can't believe we haven't told you yet!"

"We got so caught up in cleaning up Biscuit's mess that we forgot to tell you what happened!"

The other four sat up straight, all ears, listening to the two girls tell what they knew.

"So. . ." Alex stood, still holding the paper. "We know that the Grouch's name is Dan, so maybe this paper belongs to him. Elizabeth, can you find out Dan's last name?"

"Sure. I'll go talk to Mr. Anzer. I've been meaning to visit with him, anyway."

"Great!" Alex continued. "Kate, what else do you have in that bag of yours? Surely you have some kind of gadget to help us get to the bottom of this."

Kate sprang into action, going through her treasures and evaluating each one for its possible mystery-solving potential.

"Here's my robot spy-cam." Kate held up what looked like a remote-control four-wheeler. "We can hide and make this baby go wherever we want. The only problem is, the sound isn't that great. So we can watch what happens, but we might not be able to hear it."

"What about the tiny recorder you brought?" asked Sydney.

"I've tried that. It will work, sort of. But it's hard to get the recorder to play at the same time the video plays. So you end up watching something happen while listening to the thing that happened a minute or two before, and it gets confusing."

Elizabeth laughed. "Sort of like watching a foreign film with the words at the bottom of the screen! I can never keep up with those movies."

Alex seemed a natural fit for the role of lead detective, and the other girls listened to her instructions. "Okay, here's what we'll do. Elizabeth, you and McKenzie go back to the stables. See what more you can find about this Dan fellow. The rest of you come with me. Kate, bring the robot."

"Sounds like a plan," said Elizabeth. "Let's go!"

Kate quickly put Biscuit into her oversize backpack and zipped it, leaving a small air hole.

Just then, Miss Rebecca poked her head around the door. "Hi, girls! I'm Miss Rebecca—oh, hi, Elizabeth! Good to see you! I'm the counselor for cabin 12. My room's at the end of the hall, in case you need anything."

"Thanks!" the girls replied, trying not to look guilty.

Miss Rebecca stood looking at the group. "Umm. . .okay then. Don't forget that now is your Discovery Time. For the next half hour, find a quiet place and study today's Bible lesson."

"Yes, ma'am," said the angelic-looking group. Biscuit whimpered, and Bailey began sneezing to cover the sound while Kate used her foot to gently push the wiggling backpack under her bed. The counselor stepped into the room and looked around with a suspicious gaze.

Discovery Time

Bailey sneezed several more times.

"Bless you," Miss Rebecca said. She lingered a few moments, looking each camper directly in the eye. Then, with one last look around the room, she said, "Remember, I'm right at the end of the hall!" With a smile and a wave, she was gone.

"Whew! That was close!" exclaimed McKenzie as she closed the door.

Once again, Alex took charge. "Okay, you heard her! It's *discovery* time. And we have a lot of discovering to do. . . ."

"Wait! Before we go, let's read our Discovery Scripture. That way we can talk about it while we're walking. Then we'll be doing what we're supposed to be doing," Elizabeth said as she grabbed her Bible. "Today's verse talks about wisdom. Hmm. . .let me find it. . . . Here it is! Proverbs 2:4–5 says, 'If you look for it as for silver and search for it as for hidden treasure, then you will understand the fear of the Lord and find the knowledge of God.' "

"That's perfect!" Alex exclaimed. "We are going on a treasure hunt to find clues, which will give us wisdom and knowledge about what is going on around here!"

The group laughed at Alex's enthusiasm. Elizabeth smiled at the girl as she put her Bible away. "Or something like that. . ." She chuckled. "Just remember, if any camp counselors ask what you're doing, talk about that verse."

"Okay, let's go!" The group split up, with McKenzie and Elizabeth headed toward the stables and the others toward the golf course. Biscuit poked his head out of Kate's backpack and enjoyed the ride.

As they approached the golf course for the second time that day, the girls walked cautiously and stayed in the shadows of the trees lining the road. Sure enough, Dan the Grouch was digging away.

"Why is he digging?" whispered Alex. "It looks like he's trying to find something."

"He should be trying to clean up, not making a bigger mess," added Sydney.

"Here. I brought my robot-cam. Maybe we can get a closer look," said Kate, setting down her backpack. Biscuit, glad to be free, began sniffing around the trees. The other three watched as Kate pulled out the small remote-control gadget. "I have it set to deliver the images to my phone, so we can watch from here. I'll drive, and you all can hold the phone."

"Okay, but be careful. We don't want Grouchy Dan to catch us. I've been yelled at enough for one day. He scares me," added Bailey.

The girls crouched at the edge of the golf course, hidden behind an overgrown bush. Kate held the remote, flipped the On switch, and pressed buttons. Slowly the car moved forward.

The other girls started whispering, giving Kate directions.

"To the left!"

"No, to the right!"

"All we can see is dirt and leaves!"

"Hold it!" Kate whispered with a hint of frustration. "One person at a time, please. Sydney, you direct me."

The other girls remained quiet, and the only sound was Sydney's soft whisper, "Left. Now forward. A little to the right. . ."

Finally, she whispered, "Stop! That's perfect. We can see him. What is he looking for? He shovels, then stops and digs with his hands, then shovels some more. What does he think he's going to find?"

"Maybe he's looking for electrical wires or water pipes or something," said Kate.

"It looks like he's. . .he's. . .he's moving."

"Where did he go?" The girls didn't look up until it was too late. An angry-looking Mr. Dan glowered at them. "I thought I told you girls to stay away from here! Aren't you supposed to be somewhere right now?"

The girls sat frozen, not knowing how to respond. Finally, Bailey, remembering the Bible verse, spoke up in her sweetest voice. "We're searching for treasure, sir."

Elizabeth and McKenzie approached the stables, stopping to admire the horses. "That one reminds me of Sahara, my horse back home. I can't wait until I can ride the trails here," McKenzie said.

"I've always wanted horses," Elizabeth responded. "I look forward to coming here every summer just so I can ride."

"I thought everyone in Texas had horses!" said McKenzie with a laugh.

The girls continued around the stables, heading toward the office area. "This is where Sydney and I overheard the two men talking. The Grouch, or whatever his name is, seemed determined to keep people away from the golf course."

"Well, I don't know anything about him, but I know Mr. Anzer has a heart of gold. He would never let anything bad happen here at Discovery Lake," said Elizabeth.

"Did I hear my name?" Mr. Anzer asked as he walked around the corner. "Oh, hello, Elizabeth! Who is your friend?"

"Hi, Mr. Anzer!" said Elizabeth with a smile. "This is McKenzie. She's one of my roommates, and she has her own horse!"

"Is that right?" asked Mr. Anzer. "Well, feel free to hang out at the stables while you're here. We can always use an extra stable hand!"

McKenzie laughed, and Mr. Anzer motioned the two girls to join him on a long, low bench.

"Mr. Anzer"—Elizabeth looked at the gray-haired gentleman—"McKenzie and I wanted to ask you something. This morning we got in trouble by one of the staff members for being at the golf course. We didn't think we were doing anything wrong. Have the rules changed? Are we not allowed at the golf course anymore?"

Mr. Anzer looked concerned. He leaned back against the rough wooden wall. Finally, he answered, "Mr. Gerhardt is the groundskeeper for the golf course. He's a new staff member. I suppose he's just trying to figure out his job. I'm sure he didn't mean any harm."

McKenzie spoke up. "Mr. Gerhardt. . . Is his first name *Dan,* by any chance?"

"Why yes, it is," answered the old man.

Elizabeth spoke up. "Well, he seemed very upset that we were there. To tell you the truth, he was pretty scary."

"Mr. Gerhardt is a good man. He just has a lot on his mind. I'm sure he didn't mean to scare you," said Mr. Anzer.

Elizabeth and McKenzie looked at each other but said nothing. Standing up, Elizabeth told her old friend, "Thanks, Mr. Anzer. It's always great to talk to you. Maybe I'll come by for a ride this afternoon."

"That would be nice, Elizabeth. You girls go have fun. And stay out of trouble!" he said with a twinkle in his eye.

•—•—•

At the mention of the word *treasure*, Mr. Gerhardt's face went white, his eyes grew wide, and his hands balled into fists. "What do you know about a treasure? Have you found something? If so, you need to tell me about it right now!"

The girls scrambled backward.

"Tell me what you know!" the man yelled.

"Bailey was just talking about our Bible verse for today. God's wisdom is like treasure, and we have to search for it," said Kate. The other girls nodded.

Mr. Dan seemed to calm down a bit. He looked into the distance and ran his fingers through his hair. Taking a deep breath, he spoke slowly. "I didn't mean to yell at you. But you girls need to be careful around here. You shouldn't be down here yet; free time isn't until this afternoon. You need to stay in the main part of the camp until your free time. You never know what might happen."

The girls stared at the man, not knowing what to say. He looked at them a moment longer then turned, walked to his golf cart, and drove away.

The girls collectively let out their deep breaths. "Something is definitely going on down here," said Alex.

"Yeah, that was strange. Why did he get so mad?" asked Sydney.

"He seemed almost normal until. . .until. . ." Bailey stopped. "Until I mentioned treasure!"

The other girls looked at Bailey. "Think about it," she continued. "We were hiding and spying on him. He asked us what we were doing, but he didn't freak out until I mentioned—"

"Treasure!" they exclaimed.

"That's it!" said Sydney. "He must be looking for treasure!"

"But why would he look for treasure in an old miniature golf course at a kids' camp?" asked Kate.

"That's what we're going to find out." Alex looked to be deep in thought. "I remember watching an episode of *Murder, She Wrote*, where—"

"Murder!" Sydney exclaimed. "Who said anything about murder?"

"Don't be silly. Nobody is going to murder anybody. Just listen to what happened in this episode, okay?" Alex continued. The girls leaned in to listen to the animated brunette describe the television mystery. "In the episode, 'Dead Man's Gold,' all of the suspects are searching for buried treasure. One of the suspects owes money to a loan shark, and he doesn't want anyone else to find the money before he does!"

"You think Mr. Gerhardt owes money to a loan shark?" asked Sydney.

"I think he's a suspect and doesn't want anyone else to find whatever treasure he's seeking," said Alex.

•—•—•

McKenzie and Elizabeth headed toward the golf course to meet the others, each absorbed in her own thoughts. Finally, Elizabeth spoke. "Well, at least now we know what the *Dan Ger* paper meant. It was just part of Mr. Gerhardt's name."

"Yeah. But Elizabeth, I don't care what Mr. Anzer says. That man gives me the creeps!"

"Me too. Something definitely isn't right. But I also trust Mr. Anzer. I think he'd know if we were in any danger. I guess we should just stay away from Mr. Gerhardt."

"That will be hard, since Bailey's determined to be a golf pro by the time she leaves camp!" McKenzie said. The girls laughed.

Suddenly, Biscuit loped toward them with what looked like a large metal stick in his mouth. "Biscuit!" cried Elizabeth. "Where did you come from?" She bent and retrieved a small golf club from his mouth.

"That's funny," said McKenzie. "He wants to play fetch."

Elizabeth picked up the puppy and turned her face away. "Oh Biscuit! You seriously need a bath!" The girls continued on the path to the golf course and met the other four girls coming around the curve.

"Oh good, you found Biscuit!" exclaimed Kate. "We thought he'd gotten away!"

"He was carrying this golf club, like he wanted to play! Isn't that funny?" McKenzie held up the club. "I'll just go put this by the fence. I'm sure Mr. Gerhardt will find it."

The four spies looked at each other, and then Sydney said, "Mr. Gerhardt?"

"Yeah, that's the Grouch's name. Dan Gerhardt."

The six sleuths exchanged information and tried to fit the clues together. They didn't notice that Biscuit had gotten ahead of them. They also didn't notice the group of girls headed right toward Biscuit.

Suddenly, their conversation was interrupted by screeches. "*Eeeee-www!* Get off of me, you filthy creature! *Help!* This dog is attacking me! Help!"

The girls ran forward, Kate in the lead, and pulled Biscuit off Amberlie Crewelin. "Sorry about that," Kate told the terrified girl.

Amberlie's fear quickly turned to disdain as she said, "Is that *your* dog? Pets aren't allowed here. I'm going to report you."

Kate dropped Biscuit. "Oh no, he's not mine. I guess he's just a stray. Go away, little dog!" she yelled at Biscuit.

Confused, the poor dog headed toward the woods. Elizabeth spoke up. "We should go report this. Don't worry, Amberlie. We'll take care of everything. I can see you've been through enough. . .trauma."

With a snort, Amberlie gathered her group and turned. "Come on! I'll have to go back and change clothes now. That horrible creature got me all muddy."

As soon as the girls were out of sight, Kate ran toward the woods, her five roommates close behind her. "Biscuit!" they called. "Biscuit, come back!" Within moments, the puppy charged back at Kate, bounded into her arms, and gave her his slobbery greeting.

"Oh Biscuit, can you ever forgive me?" asked Kate.

"It looks like he already has," said McKenzie.

Elizabeth looked at her watch. "Come on. We need to give this dog a bath, and if we go now, nobody will be in the showers at the cabin."

•—•—•

Sydney and Bailey peered around the cabin door to see if it was safe to exit. After a group of laughing girls wandered out of sight, they gave the signal. "Take him to the back of the cabin before you put him down," suggested Sydney.

Kate held a wet, clean Biscuit at arm's length, and the other five girls circled her to shield the dog from view. Once out of sight of the main road, Kate let Biscuit go. The dog immediately shook himself, splashing his protectors and causing them to squeal.

The puppy took their squeals as an invitation to play and began running. He ran a few yards, then stopped to see if they were chasing him. Satisfied that his playmates were following, he ran more. This continued as the girls tried to catch the damp puppy without drawing attention to themselves.

They finally cornered the dog, dried him, and combed his hair. Then they stood back to admire the handsome dog before them. No one would ever recognize him as the muddy stray they had found that morning.

Biscuit took their looks of approval to mean that they wanted to play some more, and with a bark and a wag of his tail, he was off. The girls kept him cornered, but no one could catch him.

Finally, Kate disappeared into the cabin and returned with a handful of cheese crackers. "Here, Biscuit! Here, boy! I don't have a biscuit, but trust me—you'll love these!"

Instantly, the dog bounded to her, and she knelt to feed him. "That's a good boy! Now, we have to leave you behind while we go to our next classes. If you're good, we'll have more food for you!"

The girls once again hovered close together to hide their new pet from view. They placed him inside the room and closed the door. Almost immediately, the howling started.

"Shhhhhhh! Make him stop!" Alex whispered. "I think I see Miss Rebecca coming up the road!"

Elizabeth opened the door, and the howling stopped. She closed it, and the noise started again. She and Kate slipped inside.

"What are we going to do?" whispered Kate. "We can't leave him here! We'll have the whole camp investigating our cabin!"

"I know," said Elizabeth. "We'll just have to take turns taking him with us. I know you're pretty attached to him, and he fits perfectly in your backpack, so you take him with you now."

"Uh, I don't think that will work," responded Kate.

"Why not?" asked Elizabeth, surprised.

"Because my next class is a cooking class. He will never stay still and quiet if he smells food!"

"Hmm. . .you're right about that. I'm going on a nature walk, so I guess I'll take him with me. I think Bailey is in that class too. We'll stay at the back of the line. Here, let me borrow your backpack."

Outside, the girls greeted their counselor, chatting to cover their nervousness.

"Hi, Miss Rebecca! How are you?"

"Do you like being a counselor here?"

"We're so glad you're in our cabin. You're the coolest counselor."

The pretty young woman laughed and again eyed the group with gentle suspicion. "What are you girls up to? Don't you need to get to your next classes?"

Then she noticed that they were all water splashed. "What in the world have you been doing? Swimming isn't until this afternoon! And, ew! What is that smell?"

The girls exchanged panicked looks. Would Miss Rebecca figure out their secret?

Moans, Howls, and Growls

The girls stood in silent guilt, wondering how to respond.

Miss Rebecca laughed. "I'll tell you what, girls. I don't even want to know what you've been up to. But I want you all to march right back into your rooms and get some clean clothes on. Come with me."

Sydney began speaking loudly, hoping that Elizabeth and Kate, still inside the room, would hear. "Yes, Miss Rebecca! We'll go inside this very minute to change our clothes! We are coming inside right now!"

The girls stood in front of their door, none of them wanting to open it while Miss Rebecca was with them. The counselor, with an expression of confused amusement, stepped forward and opened the door herself.

As the door groaned open, Kate and Elizabeth stood there innocently, ready to head out the door. "Oh, hello everyone! We were just leaving. See you all later!" Elizabeth called as she and Kate left the room. The counselor just shook her head and continued down the hall. The girls all sighed in relief that she didn't notice what the rest of them saw clearly. The backpack draped over Elizabeth's shoulders was *moving*.

The four girls quickly changed their clothes and hurried to their next classes.

The next few days passed in a whirlwind of camping activity and Biscuit training. Before long, the young dog knew how to sit, stay, fetch, and roll over. The girls learned that as long as he wasn't left alone, he wouldn't howl. But keeping him with someone at all times was becoming more and more difficult.

"I have an idea," said Bailey one evening as the girls prepared for bed. "I've visited the golf course several times a day to practice, and I haven't seen Mr. Gerhardt there since that first day. But every time I go, I see new places where someone has been digging. He must dig at night. . . . Anyway, why don't we leave Biscuit at the golf course during the day? It's far enough away from the camp that if he howls no one will think anything of it."

"That's a great idea, Bailey!" said Elizabeth, combing out her blond tresses. "That would sure make things easier. I don't know about the rest of you, but I've had some pretty close calls with the little guy."

"Me too!" said the other five girls.

"Hmm. . ." Alex fluffed her pillow and crawled under her covers. "I wonder why the Grouch has disappeared during the day. And why in the world would he dig at night?"

"I don't know, and I don't care," said Bailey. "I kind of like having the golf course to myself. I stay away from him, he stays away from me, and everything's good."

The girls turned the light out and stopped talking, until Bailey broke the silence. "But then, there are still those noises."

Sydney sat up, flipped on the lamp by her bed, and asked, "Noises?"

Bailey covered her eyes with the pillow and said, "Turn that thing off!"

"Bailey, what noises?" McKenzie asked.

Bailey rubbed her eyes. "Well, there's that weird laughing thing that happened on the first day. And sometimes I hear moans and howls and a deep, low growly thing."

The other girls were wide-awake. "Bailey, what are you talking about? Why on earth would you keep going down there?" Elizabeth asked her.

"Well, the first couple of times it happened, it scared me. Good thing I had my inhaler with me! But I finally figured out that it must just be the golf course. Those noises are wired up somehow—probably to make the course more interesting. They don't even bother me anymore."

Alex dangled her feet from her bunk and asked, "Do you hear the noises every time?"

"No," Bailey answered. "A couple of times I've been there and nothing has happened. But I think the digging must have tripped a wire or something."

"Why do you say that?" asked Kate.

"Because every time I go near a hole, I hear one of those freaky noises. As long as I stay clear of the holes, everything stays quiet."

The girls thought about that for a moment, and then Alex piped up. "I remember an episode of *Scooby-Doo* where—"

The other five moaned, and Kate threw her pillow at the pretty brunette. "Not again, Alex! You and your Hollywood mystery solving. . ."

"Seriously, you guys! Listen to me! In one episode. . .actually, in several episodes, there were these spooky noises! They almost always turn out to be someone hiding and making the noises go off when the characters are close to solving the mystery! The noises are a fear tactic. Whoever is causing them doesn't want Bailey near those holes!"

The room grew silent as each girl digested Alex's information. Once again, Bailey broke the silence. "Well, that's just great. I was getting used to the noises. Now I'm going to have to use my inhaler again."

"You could just stay away from the golf course," Elizabeth told her.

"Are you kidding? I have to practice my strokes! You'll be glad too when I'm rich and famous. You'll be able to say, 'I knew her when. . .' "

The girls laughed, and Sydney turned off the lamp. "We'd better get some sleep," she said. "We'll talk about this more in the morning."

•—•—•

Early the next morning, before the trumpet wake-up call, Alex sat up in bed. "I have a great idea!" she called to her roommates.

The girls groaned and moaned, but Alex didn't let that stop her. She hopped out of bed and continued chattering. "We can attach Kate's tiny recorder to Biscuit's collar, and we'll leave him at the golf course. Then, we can hear the noises Bailey told us about. If they go on and off all day, we'll know they're just random. But if they only sound when people are there, we'll know someone is making them go off."

"Yes, but what if it's Bailey making them go off? What if she's just accidentally stepping on something?" asked Sydney.

"We'll figure that out later. First, let's just find out if they happen all the time or just when people are around," Alex told her.

"Uh, guys, you're forgetting one thing." Everyone looked at Kate, who was still in bed. Her muffled voice came from under the covers. "If we leave Biscuit alone at the golf course, he will howl all day. That's all we will hear."

Alex sighed. "You're right. I didn't think about that."

The conversation was interrupted by the wretched trumpet music, and the rest of the girls began crawling from their beds. When the song ended, Elizabeth spoke. "We could try it anyway. Maybe we'll hear something in the background, even over Biscuit's howling. It can't hurt to try."

Hearing his name, the puppy poked his head from beneath the covers at Kate's feet and barked.

"Come on, boy. I'll take you outside." Elizabeth scooped up the small dog and tucked him into the folds of her robe. She carried him outside, behind the small cabin, and waited for him to do his business. Biscuit had just disappeared behind some trees when she was startled by a voice behind her.

"Elizabeth, what are you doing out here?" Mr. Anzer called from the road. He was making his morning golf-cart drive through the camp.

"Oh! Mr. Anzer, you startled me! I was, uh. . .I was just out enjoying the sunrise!" Elizabeth smiled at her old friend.

Mr. Anzer gave her a puzzled look. "Elizabeth, how many years have you come to this camp?"

"This is my third year, sir."

"Then you should know that the sun rises in the east. You are facing west."

Elizabeth giggled nervously. "Oh, I guess that's why I missed it. I never was very good with directions."

Mr. Anzer shook his head, waved goodbye, and drove away. The girl breathed a sigh of relief and scooped up the puppy, who was now at her feet. "Biscuit, you are a lot of trouble, you know that?" she scolded the dog, then kissed him on his cold, wet nose. "But I suppose you're worth it."

•—•—•

The girls hurried to the old golf course before breakfast. When they arrived there, Kate knelt to check Biscuit's collar. "The recorder is attached securely, and. . .there. I turned it on. So now, we'll just wait and see what happens." She gave the little dog one last hug, placed him inside the gate, and closed the latch.

Sydney and Alex jogged around the course to make sure no other gates were open. When they were convinced that all was secure, they called goodbye to the little dog, who had retrieved a golf club and sat expectantly wagging his tail. When the girls turned to walk away, his tail sank. He dropped the golf club, gazed after them with sad eyes, and began howling.

"Just keep walking," said Elizabeth as Kate and Bailey paused. "Going back will just make it harder."

"This is breaking my heart," said McKenzie, trying not to turn around. Somehow, they ignored the dog's soulful cries and kept walking to the dining hall.

As the six roommates stepped into line, they were rudely pushed aside by Amberlie and her crew. "Pardon me, excuse me, step aside, please," said Amberlie in a commanding voice. "Make way for the

Princess Pack. We won the clean cabin award yesterday, so we go first. Move out of the way."

Elizabeth stifled a laugh, Bailey let out an exasperated moan, and Sydney tried to keep from rolling her eyes. "Oh my, my," said Sydney. "The *Princess Pack*? We cannot, and I repeat, *cannot* let Amberlie win this competition. What are those counselors thinking, awarding her more points than the rest of us?"

"Don't worry, we can catch up," Elizabeth told her friends. "So far, the only real points awarded are for clean cabins. Let's just make sure ours is really clean today. But first we need to come up with a team name."

"I've been thinking about that," said Bailey. "I think it should have something to do with the fact that we're at camp."

"Let's make it a name to reveal that we are members of an elite group," said Alex.

"How about the Discovery Lake Discoverers?" suggested McKenzie. "No, it's too much of a tongue twister."

"I think we should keep it simple," said Elizabeth. "Something easy for everyone to remember."

"So. . .we want to have a camp club, or something like that," said Kate.

"I've got it!" said Bailey. "We can be the Camp Club Girls!"

"I like it! It's simple and to the point," said Sydney.

"Very well then. We are the Camp Club Girls!" said Elizabeth, and the group let out a cheer.

After breakfast, the Camp Club Girls hurried back to their cabin and cleaned it to a high shine. "I love Biscuit, but he sure is messy! It's a lot easier to clean without him dragging everybody's socks out!" said McKenzie.

"Tell me about it! He thinks my panda is an intruder! Every time I take it off my bed to make it up, he attacks it!" said Bailey.

"We need to decide who will compete in which camp event," Elizabeth told them. "McKenzie is the natural choice for horseback riding. We'll also need a team for the canoe races and someone to compete in the nature studies quiz. And, of course, the talent competition."

The girls talked at once, discussing who wanted to do what.

"Kate, why don't you do the nature studies quiz, and I'll do the scripture memory competition," Elizabeth suggested as she helped Bailey straighten the covers on her bed.

"I think this competition is in the bag!" exclaimed Bailey, heaving her giant panda back onto her bed.

"I do think we have a good chance, but it will be tough. Amberlie seems pretty competitive. She really wants to win," McKenzie told her friends.

"She can want it all she wants," said Sydney, "but we want it more. And we're gonna win!"

•—•—•

Kate left her nature studies class, pressing past campers returning to their cabins. When she was halfway to the golf course, Elizabeth caught up with her.

"I'll bet I know where you're headed," said the fourteen-year-old.

Kate sighed. "I feel guilty about leaving Biscuit alone. But I know it's best this way. I've just never had a pet before. I wish I could talk Mom and Dad into letting me keep Biscuit."

Elizabeth smiled. " 'Take delight in the Lord, and he will give you the desires of your heart,' Psalm 37:4. That's today's Discovery verse. I guess you could say that a dog is one of the desires of your heart."

"Yes, it is. I guess I'll have to think more about that verse. Maybe there is hope, after all," Kate responded. "Come on, let's go. I miss Biscuit!"

They jogged the rest of the way to the golf course. As they approached, they heard the low, mournful howls that told them two things: Biscuit was safe, and Biscuit was very, very sad.

The little dog lunged at Kate, nearly knocking her to the ground as soon as she slipped inside the gate. "Biscuit!" she exclaimed. "I've missed you too, boy! I'm sad when we're apart!"

The dog attacked her with slobbery kisses and muddy paws.

"Hey! Stop that!" Kate laughed at the dog's enthusiasm.

Elizabeth smiled at the girl and dog who were so in love with each other. "Boy, that bath didn't last very long," she said. "Now be still, Biscuit, and let us listen to your collar."

•—•—•

Alex and Bailey returned from their crafts class, each holding a small wooden treasure box. Bailey's sparkled with glitter and plastic jewels, while Alex's was painted with bold stripes. Arriving at their room, they stopped. They stared. Then the girls jumped up and down, cheering.

A cardboard trophy with the glittered words CLEAN DORM WINNER—25 POINTS hung on their door.

"We won!" The two girls squealed.

That is how Kate and Elizabeth found their two friends moments later. They had run all the way from the golf course, and now they were panting. "Girls, listen. . ."

Kate stopped and fell onto her bed, trying to catch her breath. Holding up the small recorder, she said, "Listen."

They were interrupted by Sydney and McKenzie, who had seen the trophy on their way in the door.

"Hey, cool! We won! Now, unless Amberlie can rack up some serious character points, we'll be first in line all day tomorrow," said McKenzie with a grin.

"I can't wait to see Amberlie's face when we pass her," Sydney said.

"Well, don't act too smug. The Princess Pack is still way ahead of us in overall points. Remember, they've won three days in a row! We still have some serious catching up to do," said Elizabeth.

Kate, now recuperated from her run, waved her arms. "Guys," she called out. "I think this is more important than standing first in line. Listen to what was on Biscuit's recorder!"

The girls gathered around Kate's bed and leaned in to hear the tiny device.

"Sounds like howling, just like you said," McKenzie told her.

"Shhhh! Just listen."

The girls strained to hear something, anything, over Biscuit's desperate howling. Then, after about thirty seconds, the howling stopped.

Digging for Treasure

The girls looked at each other and continued listening. In the background, they heard what sounded like the low rumble of a truck's engine. Then the engine died. They heard a door slam and heavy footsteps approach.

The footsteps ended with what sounded like a cell phone ringing then a man's voice. "Hello? Oh, hi, Dad. Yeah, I've been digging. No, I haven't found anything. No, no sign of any treasure. But I'm not giving up. Don't worry, I'll find it. I'll call you as soon as I know something."

The talking ended, and then the footsteps started again. Only this time, they seemed to be going away from the recorder. A car door slammed, an engine revved, and then it seemed the truck drove away. When the noise from the vehicle faded, Biscuit started howling again.

The girls sat in silence.

Finally, Alex spoke up. "Well girls, the plot thickens."

"I'll say," said Bailey. "I guess that explains all the holes."

"So, Mr. Gerhardt *is* digging for treasure. . . ." McKenzie looked thoughtful. "I wonder what his dad has to do with all of this."

"Yeah," said Sydney. "And if his dad is in on it, does he come here and help his son?"

Elizabeth just sat quietly, soaking it all in. Finally, she spoke up. "Well, we have a full-blown mystery on our hands. And it's up to us to get to the bottom of it. But for now, let's only go to the golf course in groups of two or more. No more going down there alone, okay Bales?"

"No problem! I almost needed my inhaler just listening to the recording!"

•—•—•

Elizabeth dangled her feet over the side of the dock and watched the ripples from the rock she had just thrown. Her Bible was open on the dock beside her, and her eyes focused on the verse she had read three or four times. She read it out loud, as she often did when trying to memorize something:

"Matthew 6:19–20. 'Do not store up for yourselves treasures on earth, where moths and vermin destroy, and where thieves break in and steal. But store up for yourselves treasures in heaven, where moths and vermin do not destroy, and where thieves do not break in and steal.' "

Lord, there sure is a lot of talk about treasure here at camp this year. I want to have the right kind of treasure—the kind that will make You happy. But what about the mystery at the golf course? Is a treasure really buried there or somewhere around the camp?

When she heard the soft murmur of a golf cart drawing near, she knew it was Mr. Anzer. He faithfully made the rounds in that golf cart, watching over the camp, making sure everything was running smoothly. She smiled at the man who reminded her so much of her grandpa.

"Hello, Elizabeth. I had a feeling I'd find you here in your old spot. Don't let me disturb you. I'm just going to check the pedals on these paddleboats. They've been sticking. I'll bet they just need some oil." The old man pulled an oil can from the toolbox in the back of the cart.

"Oh, you're not disturbing me. I was just thinking about this morning's verse. I've noticed all of our verses so far have talked about treasure, and I think it's funny."

"Funny?" Mr. Anzer's eyebrows lifted.

"Oh, not funny, ha-ha. The other kind of funny."

The old man began examining the pedals of a boat banked along the edge of the lake. "Tell me why it's funny," he said.

Elizabeth leaned back and looked at the sunlight glistening through the branches. She didn't want to reveal too much of the mystery, but she did want some answers. Something told her that Mr. Anzer was a good source of information.

"Oh, my roommates and I have just been playing sort of a. . .a mystery game. We're pretending a treasure is buried somewhere in the camp. It's silly, really. But we're having fun."

The old man stood and looked at her. "Well that is funny. Just where do you think this treasure may be hidden?"

Elizabeth laughed nervously. "Oh, it could be anywhere—the stables, the nature trail. . .the golf course. . ."

Mr. Anzer turned his attention back to the pedals. "I've been working here for a long time, and I've never run across any buried treasure.

But that doesn't mean it's not here!" The man chuckled. "If anybody can find treasure in this old camp, I'm sure it will be you."

Elizabeth smiled. "How long have you worked here, Mr. Anzer?"

"Oh, longer than you've been alive. Years ago, I was the manager of camp operations. All three of my children attended this camp every summer, and my wife used to oversee the cafeteria. She died a few years back, and my kids are all grown and married. I just can't bring myself to leave this old place. . . ." He paused and smiled. "So now, I just putter around and fix things."

"It sounds like a fun job to me," Elizabeth told him, and he smiled at her. "I have a question, though. This is such a great camp, and everything is kept in top shape—except for the golf course. It seems kind of run-down, and that doesn't fit in with the rest of the camp. Why?"

Mr. Anzer moved to the next paddleboat and knelt to check the pedals. "The golf course was a main attraction when the camp was new. But years ago, it turned out that a gang of thieves had their hideout on the old Wilson farm—just on the other side of the golf course. When they were discovered, we increased the security here at the camp. For a couple of years, we didn't let any campers go down that way—the golf course was off-limits. Then, even when we reopened it, most of the campers were a little spooked by the idea that thieves might have hidden there. It just never became a popular attraction again. And with a tight budget, maintaining the golf course never seems to become a priority."

"Wow, that is kind of scary. Any chance the gang is still there?" Elizabeth asked.

"No. This happened a long time ago. I don't know what happened to the thieves, but I'm sure they wouldn't come back to the same place where they got caught," he told her.

Elizabeth picked up her Bible and stood. "I need to do something before my next class, Mr. Anzer. It's been really nice talking to you."

The old man waved goodbye and continued on to the next paddleboat. "See ya later," he called.

Elizabeth hurried toward the cabins. *Wait till the others hear about this!* she thought. *This is more complicated than we thought.*

A few minutes later, she flung open the door to find her roommates getting ready to leave for their next classes. "You will never believe what I just found out!" Elizabeth announced.

•—•—•

That afternoon, the girls used their free time to explore the golf course.

They greeted a very excited, muddy Biscuit, and slipped through a small opening in the far side of the fence.

"The old farmhouse has to be this way," said Sydney. The six young detectives, with their four-legged sidekick, tromped through thick trees and brush until they arrived at a clearing. There, just beyond a trickling creek, was an old farmhouse.

"This is it!" said Alex. "This is just like in *Dragnet*! I watch those reruns all the time with my grandpa. Once they were looking for—"

"Shhhh!" whispered the other girls in unison.

"We don't know what we'll find," said Elizabeth in a hushed voice. "Whatever happens, let's stay together."

The girls nodded, gingerly walked through the shallow creek, and approached the old house that was falling apart. The only sounds were the gentle rustle of trees swaying in the breeze and Biscuit's steady panting.

They noiselessly drew closer to the old farmhouse until they were close enough to peek through a broken window. Old newspapers and discarded fast food containers littered the floor, and tattered furniture was flipped this way and that in careless disarray.

Biscuit began to growl, and the girls froze. The dog's growl grew louder, until finally he dashed toward the trees. Standing on his hind legs, he looked ready to scale the tree.

A squirrel chattered angrily from its branches. The girls sighed with relief and continued exploring.

Alex motioned for the group to follow her. "This way," she whispered, and the band of detectives stepped carefully around the corner of the house, onto the steps of the wide porch, and through the door, which hung only partially on its hinges.

"Wow, this looks like something out of a scary movie," said Bailey.

The girls spread out through the small downstairs area, turning chairs upright and peering in closets.

"Whoa! Bad move!" they heard Sydney call from the kitchen. She had opened the refrigerator, and the foul stench spread through the rest of the house in moments.

"Ugh! Gross!" The other girls covered their noses. Kate and McKenzie pulled their T-shirts up over their faces, leaving only their eyes visible.

Elizabeth rushed to open a window, but she found it painted shut. Then, spying a back door in a corner of the kitchen, she opened it wide. "At least there's a breeze. Maybe it will blow the smell away." Sure enough, the odor began to die down.

Alex stood at the foot of the stairs, looking into the shadowy hallway above. "Hey, let's go upstairs and look around."

The girls looked at each other, waiting for someone else to go first.

"Uh, you go on ahead, Alex," said Sydney.

"Awww, come on, guys. You're not scared, are you?" she prodded them.

"I'm not scared. Are you scared?" Sydney retorted.

"No, I'm not scared," Alex shot back. She remained glued to her spot.

Finally, Kate led the way. "Okay, Alex. Come with me." Then she said, "If we're not back in ten minutes, run for your lives!"

The other girls laughed nervously then followed Alex and Kate up the stairs. "We might as well stick together," said Elizabeth, bringing up the rear. Biscuit bounded up the stairs ahead of them and rushed into a dark room.

The girls followed their beloved mascot into a dusty bedroom. McKenzie pulled back the curtains and lifted the shades, and sunlight flooded into the room. Biscuit sniffed here and there and then dove under the bed. A moment later, he reappeared with an old sock in his mouth.

"What is it with you and socks, boy?" asked Kate, kneeling to scratch him behind the ears. The girls opened drawers and closets, finding a moth-eaten coat, a muddy pair of brown work boots, and more old newspapers. The small connected bathroom revealed a rusty drain, a dried-up cake of soap, and a roll of yellowed toilet paper.

Together, the girls moved to the next bedroom, and this time Elizabeth opened the curtains. As the other girls snooped around, Elizabeth stood at the window. She noticed a ladder propped up against one side of the window. Then her gaze went to the driveway leading to the farmhouse. The mud showed fresh tire tracks, but she saw no vehicles. Funny, she hadn't noticed those earlier. The house certainly looked like no one had been inside for a very long time, so why the tire tracks?

She turned from the window, not wanting to frighten the younger girls. "I think we should head back," she told the others. *I'll tell them about the tire tracks after we're safely back at camp,* she thought.

"Hey, look at this!" said Kate, pulling a faded spiral notebook from a drawer in the bedside table. "It looks like an old journal of some sort. But it must have gotten wet, because most of the words are washed out."

The girls crowded around, looking at the cryptic notebook. Biscuit, still carrying the old sock, hopped onto the bed beside Kate and made himself comfortable.

Bang! The girls jumped at the noise from downstairs. Their eyes filled with panic as they heard heavy footsteps. Bailey opened her mouth to scream, but McKenzie clasped her hand over Bailey's mouth. The girls remained frozen as the footsteps got louder. Quietly, Elizabeth tiptoed to the door, shut it softly, and turned the lock. Then she looked at the girls, held a shushing finger over her lips, and tiptoed to the window.

No one moved except Elizabeth, who skillfully opened the window. In a soft whisper, Elizabeth said, "We need to stay calm. Here's a ladder, but we have to be extra quiet, or whoever is downstairs will catch us. Sydney, you go first and help the others down. I'll stay here and go last."

Sydney's eyes widened, but she tiptoed to the window, slipped over the ledge, and scurried down the ladder. Bailey went next, then Kate, holding the notebook. After that, McKenzie descended with Biscuit. Alex grabbed an old newspaper before heading down. Finally, with one last look around, Elizabeth started out the window.

Just after Elizabeth's feet hit the ground, the ladder tipped. Before the girls could catch it—*crash!*—it landed on the ground.

"Hey!" a man's voice yelled.

"Run!" shouted Elizabeth. The girls took off. Through the creek they splashed as heavy footsteps followed.

Just when it seemed they would escape, Bailey tripped over a large root. The others stopped to help her, but Elizabeth shouted, "Go, go, go!" She helped Bailey to her feet.

The girl gasped for air. Elizabeth felt in her friend's pockets until she located the inhaler. She looked around but saw no one. She stood with Bailey, holding the inhaler in place and coaxing her friend to breathe slowly.

Finally, Bailey pushed the inhaler away. "I'm okay," she said. "Come on, let's get out of here."

The girls jogged after the others. As they reached the fence line for the golf course, Elizabeth stepped into the shadows of a large tree, turned, and looked.

Missing Jewels!

Elizabeth caught up with the other girls. They lingered by the golf course gate, making sure Bailey was okay, all talking at once and trying to make sense of what had just happened.

Biscuit stood patiently with a golf club in his mouth until Kate finally threw it. He immediately retrieved the club and begged her with soulful eyes to throw it again. The other girls chattered on with frightened, excited exclamations.

"Did you get a look at him?"

"No, but he sounded big!"

"How do you know it was a man?"

"Well, the footsteps sounded big. I don't think a woman would walk that loudly."

"Well, I think it was the Grouch," said Bailey.

Finally, Elizabeth spoke. "I saw him."

Everyone looked at her. "Bailey is right. It was Mr. Gerhardt."

"I knew that man was trouble! He is definitely up to no good," exclaimed Alex.

"I don't know," Elizabeth mused. "He walked back toward the farmhouse, but he didn't look angry or scary. His shoulders were down, and he just looked. . .I don't know. I thought he looked sad."

"Well, I think you have too much compassion. He nearly scared us to death, remember?" Sydney reminded her.

"Yes, but perhaps he didn't mean to scare us. He couldn't have known we were there. Maybe we scared him!" Elizabeth countered.

The other girls stared at Elizabeth as if she'd lost her mind. Finally, McKenzie spoke. "Let's get back to the cabin. I need some time to relax. I think I'll change into my swimsuit and head down to the pool."

"Now that sounds like a great idea!" Alex agreed. The group said goodbye to their puppy and headed back toward the main camp.

•—•—•

That evening, Sydney and Alex wandered to the front of the dinner line, where Elizabeth was holding their place. They smiled in response to congratulations and good-natured "Just wait until tomorrow! We'll win!" from other campers.

They were almost to the front when Amberlie blocked their path. "Enjoy your short-lived victory, girls," she sneered. "Tomorrow, you all are toast!"

The two girls scooted around their ill-tempered rival and greeted Elizabeth at the front of the line.

"What was that about?" Elizabeth asked.

"Oh, nothing. Just Amberlie being herself," said Sydney.

When the girls had their food and sat down, talk quickly turned to business. "We have to get to the bottom of this mystery," said Alex. "Elizabeth, I know you think Mr. Gerhardt is some poor, sweet man, but I think he's looking for something. I think he's one of the thieves!"

"I didn't say he is poor or sweet! I just think there is more to him than meets the eye," said Elizabeth.

"I agree with Elizabeth," McKenzie announced. "And I agree with Alex. Mr. Gerhardt definitely has something to do with this mystery, but we need to find out more facts before we accuse him of anything."

The conversation halted as a shadow fell over the table. The girls looked up to find—of all people—Mr. Gerhardt. He stood at the end of their table, looking at Bailey, not saying a word.

They all remained still, waiting for him to say something. Bailey squirmed.

Finally, the man spoke. "Are you enjoying camp?" he asked.

They nodded.

"That's nice," he said. Then he turned and walked away.

No one spoke for a moment.

"What in the world was that about?" Sydney asked.

"That man gives me the creeps," said Bailey.

"My point exactly," said Alex, picking up where the conversation left off. "Let's hurry and go back to the room. Kate, can you google something for me?"

Kate, mouth full, looked longingly at her heaping plate. She swallowed, then answered. "I'll do anything you ask. Just don't rush me!"

Later that evening, Elizabeth leaned over Kate's shoulder, watching her type various phrases into the search engine. "Try 'thieves near Camp Discovery Lake,' " she suggested.

Kate typed in the phrase. The words *"Sorry, but there are no results for that term"* appeared on the screen.

Kate breathed a frustrated sigh. "The problem is that all of this took place before everyone had access to the internet. So, unless someone has written about it on the web, we won't find anything."

Bailey and McKenzie lay on the floor, flipping through the water-stained notebook Kate had found. "This is useless too. The ink is too faded to read," complained McKenzie.

Alex and Sydney had divided the old newspaper, and each scanned through the stories. "This newspaper is over twenty years old. It's crumbling in my hands," said Sydney.

"Surely we'll find some kind of clue here. Let's keep looking," Alex encouraged the group. She gently turned the pages, reading headlines.

"Wait, I think I found something!" exclaimed Sydney. "Look! It's only one paragraph, but it says that a jewel thief has been convicted. And, oh my goodness. You are not gonna believe this. . . ." Sydney continued to stare at the page.

"What? Tell us!" the girls urged her on.

"The name of the man who was convicted. . ." Sydney looked at her roommates.

"Come on, spill it!" Alex nearly shouted.

"William Gerhardt!"

"I knew it, I knew it, I knew it!" exclaimed Bailey. "I knew that the Grouch was no good!"

"There's more," continued Sydney. "It says the jewels were never found."

"Maybe the thief was Gerhardt's father!" said Alex. "And now Dan is trying to recover the jewels!"

Kate began typing on her computer again.

"Jackpot!" she cried, and the girls gathered around her. "The search for 'William Gerhardt, jewel thief,' turned up six, seven, eight different articles! Looks like we may solve the mystery, after all!"

"And look what I just found," said McKenzie. "It's hard to read, but it looks to me like an address. And right above, it says, 'Manchester Jewels.' Is that the name of the jewelry store that was robbed?"

Kate clicked on an article and lifted her arms in victory. "Mystery solved. It says right here—William Gerhardt was convicted of grand theft for robbing Manchester Jewels, a large jewelry store in Springfield. That's about an hour from here."

They all chattered at once, celebrating this new information. Then Kate lifted her hand. "Not so fast. It says here that the jewels were never found. He was convicted by a jury with a seven-to-five vote. Nearly half of the jurors didn't think he was guilty."

"Of course he was guilty. Why else would his son be digging for the jewels? He must know they were hidden somewhere at the golf course," said Sydney.

The girls sat in puzzled silence. Finally, Alex spoke. "Kate, you come with me. We need to go get Biscuit. And we have a little more discovering to do."

"I'll come too," said Elizabeth.

"Not me," said Bailey. "I'll save my trips to the golf course for the broad daylight!"

Sydney and McKenzie, tired from a long day, decided to stay with Bailey.

•—•—•

The three girls approached the golf course, using Kate's cell phone as a flashlight.

"Shhhh! Listen," Kate whispered just before they rounded the curve leading to the gate.

"What is it?" asked Alex.

Kate motioned for them to scoot into the woods behind a thick crop of trees. "Biscuit is either gone or he's not alone. He's not howling."

"You're right," whispered Elizabeth.

"Well, we can't just stand here. I'll tell you what. . .I'll go on around through the gate, and you two stay here in case something happens," suggested Alex.

"No, I don't like that idea. We need to stay together," said Elizabeth.

"Shhhh! What's that?" Kate interrupted.

The girls quieted, straining to pinpoint the sound. "It sounds like digging," said Elizabeth. "Let's sneak to the fence and see what we find. Kate, snap your cell phone shut, or whoever that is will see us for sure."

Kate closed the phone, and the only light left was the soft moonlight. Slowly, the girls crept through the brush until they arrived at the fence line. A twig snapped beneath Elizabeth's feet, and the girls froze. Then a soft whimpering moved toward them. "Biscuit!" whispered Kate, and the little dog lunged at her face, kissing her with wet, sloppy kisses. She stifled a giggle, and the other two girls shushed her.

"Be quiet! I think I see someone," Alex whispered. Sure enough, the girls could just make out the figure of a man. The digging had stopped, and the man stood still, looking their way.

"Who's there?" he called.

The girls crouched in the shadows, holding their breath and praying Biscuit didn't make any sudden moves. The dog wiggled in Kate's arms, but his preoccupation with kissing her kept him from making much noise.

"Hello?" the figure called again. Suddenly, a bright flashlight snapped on. The girls remained still as statues, praying the man wouldn't see them. Slowly, the beam passed through the woods to their left, traveled in front of them, then continued to the right.

Finally, after many long moments, the light was snapped off, and eventually the digging resumed. Still, the girls remained, partly because they were too frightened to move, and partly because they wanted a better look at the man's face. They thought they knew who it was. They just wanted to be sure.

A cloud passed in front of the moon, leaving them in complete darkness. Then the cloud moved away and rays of moonbeams fell directly on the man's face.

Mr. Gerhardt was digging.

Noiselessly, the girls tiptoed back through the brush to the road. As soon as they were out of sight of the golf course, Kate snapped her cell phone back on, casting a soft blue glow around their path. They remained silent all the way back to the cabin.

An hour later, the girls were still awake, talking about the mystery.

"Well, we know Mr. Gerhardt is guilty. We just have to prove it," said Sydney.

"I'm not sure I agree," said Elizabeth. "Sure, he's looking for the jewels. Sure, he has some kind of interest in this case. But I keep thinking about that internet article Kate found. Surely, there must have been some reason why the jury was so divided."

"I'll research more tomorrow," said Kate. "But I'm tired of thinking about it. Biscuit and I want to go to sleep." She pulled the covers over her head then started giggling. "Biscuit, stop it! Biscuit, quit licking my toes! Stop!"

Before long, the whole group was laughing at Kate and the small dog.

"Well, I do have one more thing I want to talk about before we go to sleep," said Bailey. "Who wants to be in the talent show?"

The giggles turned to groans, and Bailey sat up. "Come on, you guys. We need those points!"

"I think you should do it, Bales. You have Hollywood written all over you," said Alex.

Bailey's face lit up with a smile. "Well, okay, if you insist! I was in the spring talent show back home in Peoria, and I can do my singing and dancing act. I did happen to bring the music and props with me in case they had talent shows here. But I need someone to play the piano for me," she said.

No response.

"I need someone to play the piano for me," she repeated.

Silence.

"Elizabeth, don't you play the piano?" Bailey continued.

Elizabeth leaned up on her elbows. "I don't like to play in front of people."

"Awww, come on, Beth! Pleeeeeeeaaase? Pretty please with a cherry on top? For me?" Bailey begged.

More silence.

Finally, Elizabeth sighed. "Okay."

"Hooray! Oh thank you, thank you, thank you! You're the greatest! I know we'll win. We have to start practicing tomorrow. Isn't there a piano in the dining hall? I wonder if they'll let us use that. How about during our free time? Or maybe sooner. Maybe we should wake up early and go practice. I have this great tap dance I do, and the song is so fun. It goes like—"

"Go to sleep, Bailey!" chimed five voices in unison.

•—•—•

Early the next morning, Bailey and Elizabeth walked to the dining hall. The sun was barely peeking over the trees, and Bailey was humming and singing her song so Elizabeth could learn it.

"It goes like this, Beth:

"I love being beautiful,
Being beautiful is grand,
With my hair just so, and my eyes all aglow,
A new dress, and my nail-polished hands!

"I have some pink spongy rollers for my hair and some of my mom's face cream! Won't that be hilarious? I'll be out there, my face all creamed up, rollers in my hair, tap-dancing and singing about being beautiful!" Bailey's excitement grew as they entered the dining hall.

Elizabeth laughed at Bailey's enthusiasm. "You will be the star of the show," she told her. "Now, where is the music?"

Bailey pulled the sheet music out of her backpack and handed it to Elizabeth.

Sitting down at the old piano stationed to one side of the stage, Elizabeth began flipping through the pages, becoming familiar with the chords and the key changes. "This music has several key changes. I'm not sure I can play it like it's written; I'd need to practice this for weeks. But the chords are listed, so in some parts I'll just play those. I'll jazz it up here and there. I think it will be fine."

Bailey smiled. "I know you can do it!" she encouraged.

Elizabeth began playing with Bailey singing along. After a few rough starts, she finally sang through the piece.

"Okay, now let's try it with me on stage. We'll go all the way through without stopping," Bailey instructed. Elizabeth began to play, and Bailey began singing and dancing her heart out. She performed to the empty room as if it were an audience of hundreds. At the close, she held out her last note, arms high in the air, and then finished with a grand curtsy.

Both girls were surprised when applause came from a corner of the room. Amberlie stepped out of the shadows.

"Very nice, for an amateur. Your little act will add some good variety to the show. But you certainly won't win the grand prize. Your talent doesn't even come close to mine. Sorry to break it to you, kiddo, but you don't have a chance."

Bailey's smile turned into a frown as she responded, "How dare you! You are so. . ."

"Amberlie! We didn't know anyone was here. So great to see you. Did you want to practice? Here, we were just finishing. Come on, Bales. Let's go." Elizabeth gathered the music, grabbed Bailey by the arm, and walked past Amberlie.

When they were outside, Bailey let loose. "How could you just let her talk to us like that? She is so mean! I'd like to give her a piece of my mind!"

"Bailey, that's exactly what she wanted us to do. If we act like her, she wins. She knows she got to us. Sometimes it's best just to play dumb," Elizabeth said.

"Play dumb?" Bailey questioned.

"Pretend you don't know she's being mean. And keep being nice. Then she looks bad, and you look like a saint. Eventually, she'll go away and be mean to someone else," Elizabeth explained.

"But then she wins!" complained Bailey.

Elizabeth laughed. "That's where you're wrong. Right now, she's back there trying to figure out why she didn't intimidate us. We won."

As they rounded the corner leading to the cabins, they nearly collided with Sydney, who was running at full speed. "Elizabeth! Bailey! Come quick!"

Into the Darkness

The girls rushed back to their cabin, where Alex and McKenzie leaned over Kate's shoulder, reading something on the internet. "Unbelievable," Kate was saying.

"But that doesn't mean anything. I still say he's guilty," Alex responded.

"I don't know. I just don't know," said McKenzie.

Elizabeth jumped in. "Would somebody please tell us what is going on?"

"Yeah," added Bailey. "What's so unbelievable?"

Kate looked over her shoulder and said, "Listen. 'William Gerhardt was convicted of grand felony theft and sentenced to twenty-five years in prison,' " she read aloud. " 'The conviction came beneath a shroud of doubt and questionable evidence, with a seven-to-five jury convicting him. Gerhardt, an employee of Manchester Jewels, is accused of selling the jewels on the black market. The jewels have not been found. In a post-trial interview, jurors continue to debate the legitimacy of the evidence presented.' "

The girls listened eagerly.

"If he sold them, why is Mr. Gerhardt looking for them?" asked Elizabeth.

"Well, I still say Gerhardt is guilty. I mean, look at his son, the Grouch. That man is digging, breaking into abandoned houses, chasing little girls. . . That's not exactly normal, innocent behavior," said Sydney.

"Perhaps we should wait until we know more before we make up our minds," Elizabeth told her friends.

"I agree with you," said Alex as she smoothed on her strawberry lip gloss. "As a matter of fact, I think we should do a little more investigating of our own as soon as possible."

"Well, I think we should eat," said Kate. "It's time for breakfast, and if we don't hurry, they'll start without us. That would be a waste of a perfectly good front-of-the-line pass."

"You're right," said Bailey. "Is the room ready for inspection? I'd love to win again today."

"Yep," said Sydney. We delivered Biscuit to the golf course and made sure everything was perfect before we started the internet search."

"Hello! Starving girl here, remember?" called Kate. "You all stay here and gab all morning if you want. I'm leaving!"

The other girls laughed, and then they followed their tiny, hungry roommate to the dining hall.

•—•—•

During breakfast, Alex brought up the mystery again. "Nancy Drew always says, 'Drastic times call for drastic measures.' I think we need to snoop around Mr. Gerhardt's office."

Elizabeth held her fork in midair, deep in thought. "When did Nancy Drew say that?" she asked.

Alex giggled. "Well, come to think of it, I'm not sure she did say it. But somebody said it, and I agree."

"Okay, Miss Hollywood. What do you think we should do? Just waltz into Mr. Gerhardt's office and snoop through file cabinets and desk drawers?" asked Bailey.

Alex smiled. "Yes, that's exactly what I'm suggesting. And I think I may have the perfect plan. . . ."

The girls leaned together and began making plans, when suddenly Amberlie fell in front of their table, sending scrambled eggs, orange juice, and dishes in every direction. The girl began crying in a loud, dramatic voice, "They tripped me! Those mean girls tripped me!" She pointed at the Camp Club Girls.

The girls were caught off guard, and when a counselor rushed over to help Amberlie, she looked at the six roommates with a disappointed expression. "Is this true?" she asked.

"Yes, it's true. I saw it," said one of Amberlie's sidekicks.

"I saw it too," testified another of Amberlie's friends.

"I'm not sure which girl it was, but I definitely saw a leg stick out just as Amberlie walked by," said one of the girls.

"Yes, and just before that, they were all whispering together, like they were planning something," said the other girl.

"I saw that too," said the counselor. She turned to the six roommates and asked, "Which one of you tripped Amberlie?"

The girls just looked at her in stunned silence.

"Okay then, if none of you will tell the truth, I'll have to punish all of you." Then, zoning in on Elizabeth, she said, "I'm disappointed in you. You know we don't put up with that kind of behavior here."

Elizabeth found her voice. "But we didn't trip her! We were talking about something totally different!"

The counselor looked at her. "Then tell me what you were talking about."

The six girls looked at each other. They certainly couldn't tell her they were planning to sneak into Mr. Gerhardt's office and snoop.

Their silence sent the wrong message. "That's what I thought," said the counselor. "All six of you will be on clean-up duty for two days. You can start right now."

The girls began gathering their trays as Amberlie and her two buddies stood looking innocent. As the counselor walked away, Amberlie gave the group a smug grin.

Sleuthing would have to wait. It looked as if the girls would spend every free moment of their next two days in the dining hall.

•—•—•

After lunch on the second day of their punishment, Elizabeth scrubbed burned goo from the bottom of a pot with furious determination. Her roommates worked around her, talking, laughing, and flicking soapsuds on each other. But Elizabeth worked in silence.

She was too angry to speak.

I don't understand, Lord, she prayed silently. *We didn't do anything, and Amberlie is so awful. Didn't You say You would not let the guilty go unpunished? So why are we scrubbing pots and mopping floors, when the guilty one is probably out riding horses and having fun right now? It's not fair. We should be enjoying our camp experience. Instead, we are stuck here.*

Bailey interrupted her thoughts. "Elizabeth? Did you hear me?"

Elizabeth jerked to attention. "I'm sorry. Were you talking to me?" she asked.

The other girls laughed. "That pot doesn't have a chance against you," McKenzie said. "You're attacking it like it is your worst enemy."

Elizabeth smiled, but inside she still felt mad. She knew she had to forgive Amberlie. But she wasn't quite ready to do that.

"They want to hear our song, Beth. I was asking if you'd play for me. C'mon. We need the practice, and it'll be fun. We are allowed to take breaks, you know." Bailey spoke with a pleading voice. "Pleeeeeeeeeeeee-aase?" she begged.

Elizabeth nodded, set down the pot, and wiped her hands on a dish towel. She walked to the piano and sat down.

Bailey scrambled to get the sheet music out of her backpack then placed it on the music stand. She described her crazy costume to the girls then nodded at Elizabeth to begin.

Before the song was halfway through, each member of the four-person audience was on the floor in fits of giggles. "That's the funniest thing I've ever seen!" laughed Alex. "I think you two should go to Hollywood for an audition!"

Sydney held her side; she was laughing so hard she couldn't speak. Tears streamed down Kate's cheeks, and McKenzie let out a giggling sound that sounded partially like a monkey and partially like a chicken. The silliness of it all, paired with the girls' tiredness, made everything funnier. Before long, Elizabeth and Bailey had joined the laughter.

This was how Miss Rebecca found them. She silently stood in the doorway, and one by one, the Camp Club Girls noticed her. Slowly, the laughter died as the girls waited to see what their counselor had to say.

An amused smile spread across the young woman's face. "Carry on," she told them, then turned and walked away.

After a few moments of stunned silence, the silliness continued. After all, Miss Rebecca had told them to carry on. Who were they to disobey a camp counselor?

•—•—•

After dinner that night, the girls moved slowly, mopping, sweeping, and scrubbing dishes. Bailey stifled a yawn and brushed a wisp of hair out of her eyes. "I am going to sleep well tonight," she said.

"I still can't believe we've been stuck working here for two days," said McKenzie. Then she chuckled. "It has been kind of fun, though."

"Yeah, sort of like in those *Facts of Life* reruns, when Jo, Blaire, Tootie, and Natalie had to paint the dorms," said Alex. "Or when they had to work in the cafeteria serving line."

"Oh, I remember seeing that show. Yeah, I guess we are kind of like those girls," said Sydney.

Once again, Elizabeth remained quiet. Yes, she'd enjoyed some fun moments during the two days of clean-up duty. But she was still angry at Amberlie. She would need a little more time to get over this injustice.

The room fell into a comfortable silence as the tired girls finished their final duties. Suddenly, they heard voices from the office next to the dining hall. They didn't think much of it—counselors came and went from the office all the time. They had a special area there where they could relax away from the campers.

Then the name "Gerhardt" caught their attention. They looked at each other then strained to hear the words.

"Such a shame, really. It has taken over his entire life," said a high-pitched voice.

"How much longer until he gets out of prison?" asked a lower female voice.

"I don't know. He must be getting close to the end of his time. But Dan is still obsessed with finding new evidence."

"Do you think his dad is really innocent?" asked the lower voice.

"Who knows. But it's sad. Dan talks to his father every chance he gets. And Tiffany said he gets a letter almost every week postmarked from the prison. She delivers them to his office, and he keeps them all in a desk drawer, tied with brown string."

"What if his dad is guilty, and Dan's trying to. . ."

"Don't even say it. I've said too much as it is."

With that, the distant conversation turned to which flavors of ice cream were stored in the lounge freezer.

•—•—•

Back at the cabin, the girls practically fell into bed. "I don't think I've ever been this tired!" groaned Bailey.

"Me neither. But now I won't be able to sleep. We've got to get our hands on those letters!" said Alex.

"I'm starving." Kate sighed. "All that work has really built my appetite."

Elizabeth reached under her bed. "Well, I have just the cure. I've saved these for an emergency. After all we've been through, I'd say we've earned them." She pulled out three boxes of Ding Dongs, and the girls suddenly found new energy as they pounced on her bed.

"You've been holding out on us!" chided Kate. "I'm surprised Biscuit didn't find these."

Elizabeth laughed and passed out the treats. "I had them zipped inside two plastic baggies, then locked inside my suitcase."

Kate sat up suddenly. "Biscuit! We were so tired we forgot him! We can't leave him there all night!"

"Kate, don't you think he'll be okay? I love the little guy, but I'm sooooo tired!" said Bailey.

Kate reached for her flashlight and stood. "It's okay. I'll get him."

"Oh no you don't," said Elizabeth and Alex together.

"You can't go out there alone at night. I'll go with you," said Elizabeth.

"And this is the perfect time to snoop around Gerhardt's office. I'm coming too," said Alex. "Kate, grab that reader-pen-thingy of yours, the one you showed us on the first day of camp."

The other girls looked at Alex as if she'd lost her mind. "Are you kidding?" asked Sydney.

"No, I'm not. We're going down there anyway, so why not make the most of it? It's dark, so no one will see us," Alex persuaded. "If Gerhardt shows up, well. . .we'll just cross that bridge when we come to it."

The other girls stared at her. Finally, Kate dug through her backpack. "She's right. We might as well kill two birds with one stone," Kate told them.

Elizabeth spoke up. "We don't all need to go. That will just increase our chances of getting caught. Sydney, McKenzie, and Bai—" Stopping, she looked at Bailey's bed. "Look. She's out like a light."

Elizabeth continued. "Sydney and McKenzie, you stay here. My cell phone is in my suitcase, and we'll take Kate's cell phone. If we get into trouble, we'll call."

The girls looked at each other with fear and excitement. Finally, McKenzie spoke. "Be careful."

With a wave, the three girls stepped through the door and into the darkness.

•—•—•

The howling got louder the closer they got to the golf course. "Well, at least we know he's okay," said Alex.

"Poor little guy. We've really neglected him the last couple of days," said Kate around a mouthful of Ding Dong. "Remind me to bring him an extra sausage in the morning."

The little dog pounced on them as they entered the gate. Kate scooped him into her arms. "We're so sorry, boy. We'll make it up to you, we promise."

Suddenly, Biscuit jumped out of her arms and bounded into the darkness. He returned a moment later carrying a golf club in his mouth, and the girls laughed.

"He likes to play fetch more than any dog I've ever known," said Elizabeth.

"Well, we'd better get down to business and get out of here. Let's see if Mr. Gerhardt's office is unlocked," said Alex, drawing them back into detective mode.

Kate shined the light of her cell phone, and the girls tiptoed to the small building that housed the golf clubs, balls, and a small office for the groundskeeper. Rattling the door, they discovered it was locked.

"Let's try the window," Alex suggested. They moved to the side of the building. Biscuit stayed close to their feet, sniffing the area protectively.

The window was small and high off the ground. Elizabeth, the tallest, pushed on the windowpane, and it easily opened.

"You're the smallest," Alex told Kate. "We'll push you through, and you can look around."

"Okay, but you guys are gonna owe me big-time for this," Kate said. Then, looking straight at Elizabeth, she said, "I'll take my payment in Ding Dongs."

The two taller girls hefted Kate through the window. She landed on the floor with a loud thud. "I'm okay," she reassured.

"What do you see?" asked Alex.

"Nothing," Kate replied. "You still have my light."

"Oh, sorry," called Elizabeth, standing on her tiptoes. "Here, I'll drop it down." She held the phone through the window and released it.

"Owwww!" came Kate's voice. "Right on my head!"

"Sorry!" Elizabeth called out.

They heard Kate moving inside. "Okay, here is the desk. Now, I just have to—"

Her voice was cut off by the sound of a truck's motor. Elizabeth and Alex ducked behind a bush just before two headlights flashed onto the building. The motor died. A door opened and closed. The girls heard footsteps and then keys jangling. They heard a click, a door opening, and then the window lit up as the person inside switched on the light.

"Prince"

Kate had just removed the stack of letters from the desk drawer when she heard the truck's motor then saw a flash of headlights through the window. Thinking quickly, she noticed a small closet in the corner of the room. Clutching the letters, she moved around a couple of large storage boxes, slipped into the closet, and shut the door. Her cell phone light revealed a large pair of men's boots with a long overcoat hanging above them. A couple of dirty shovels rested in the opposite corner. She stepped into the boots and slid her body into the middle of the coat, hoping to disguise herself in case someone opened the closet door.

She tried to quiet her breathing and wished she could soften the pounding of her heart. She heard the click of the office door opening, then saw light beneath the crack in the closet door. Heavy footsteps were accompanied by whistling. . .was that a praise song?

The footsteps came toward the closet, and the door creaked open. Kate held her breath and prayed like she had never prayed before. *Please, Jesus, don't let me die. I'm too young to die.*

Large hands reached into the closet, grabbed the shovels, then shut the door. She then heard rustling outside the door and assumed the person was searching through the boxes. She heard a scooting sound, and the light from the crack in the door was covered. After more rustling, the footsteps retreated. The light clicked off and she heard the outer door close. Slowly, quietly, she let herself breathe.

Thank You, God; thank You, God; thank You, God, she prayed. Then she reached for the door handle and pushed. The door wouldn't budge. Apparently, one of the boxes had been moved in front of the closet door. She was stuck!

Kate took a deep breath and told herself not to panic. She slid to the floor and pulled out the letters. If she was going to be stuck in a dark closet, she might as well make the most of it.

•—•—•

Elizabeth reached for Alex's hand in the dark. Biscuit nuzzled between the two girls, and Alex scooped him up. Neither girl made a sound as they peered through the small shrub. They watched the truck park. The headlights died. They heard the truck door open, then footsteps, accompanied by whistling. Elizabeth recognized the tune—the campers had sung it that afternoon at the worship service.

The girls heard a door opening. Suddenly, light flooded out of the window above them, and Alex gasped. Elizabeth held a finger to her lips. The girls remained still as opossums, staring at each other and squeezing hands.

After what seemed an eternity, the light disappeared, the office door opened and closed again, and the footsteps retreated. The two girls sat, afraid to move. Finally, Alex whispered, "What do you think happened to Kate?"

"I don't know. I guess she found a place to hide," Elizabeth spoke softly. Then she stood to her toes and strained toward the window. "Kate!" she whispered urgently.

No answer.

"Kate! Answer me!" Elizabeth urged.

Still no answer.

The clouds shifted, casting moonlight on the area. Elizabeth looked at Alex and said, "I'm going in. Help me up."

"What? You can't leave me out here alone!" whispered Alex.

"I have to. We have to find out if Kate is okay!" Elizabeth answered.

"Well, let's both go," Alex whispered back.

"We can't both get in. Besides, one of us needs to stay here in case something happens," Elizabeth said firmly. "Now help me up. Please."

"Okay," said Alex. "But this is not going like I thought it would." She clasped her hands and held them down so Elizabeth could use them as a step.

Struggling, Elizabeth wiggled through the window, landing with a thud on the other side. She stood, rubbed her sore backside, and groped through the dark.

"Kate!" she called desperately.

"Elizabeth! Is that you?" Kate's muffled voice came through the darkness.

Elizabeth stumbled around the room, feeling the wall, trying to find her friend. "Kate, where are you?" she called.

"I'm in the closet. Something is in front of the door!" she called out.

Elizabeth felt around until she located the boxes and the door. It took all of her strength to push aside the large box, but soon the closet door was free. Kate stepped out, and the light of her cell phone cast a soft glow around the room. The girls peeked in the box to see hammers, wrenches, and a pile of oddly shaped metal tools. The girls breathed deep sighs of relief.

"What ha—"

"I was so sca—"

Both girls started whispering at once, and this started them in a series of nervous giggles.

"I can't believe this is happening. Did you get the letters?" Elizabeth asked.

"Yes, but we need to put them back and get out of here. I used my reader pen and recorded about a dozen pages, but it was dark, and I had a hard time seeing the lines. We may end up with a bunch of gibberish, but hopefully we'll have something we can use," Kate told her.

The girls jumped when they heard a voice through the window. "Hey! Are you two okay?" Alex frantically whispered.

"Yes, we're fine. We'll be right out," Elizabeth told her.

Elizabeth turned to Kate, "We'd better go out the window so no one knows we've been here."

Kate hurried to the desk and replaced the letters. They scooted the desk chair beneath the window and climbed back through the opening. Each of them stifled cries of pain as they landed on the scratchy branches of the small shrub.

"Finally!" Alex exclaimed. "I was starting to think you were going to have a slumber party in there!"

In the excitement, they hadn't heard the sound of footsteps drawing closer. Suddenly, a flash of light shined through the window. "Hey! Is somebody in here?" Mr. Gerhardt demanded from inside the office.

The girls paused. Then, without saying a word, they ran full speed through the darkness. Alex still clung to Biscuit, and they were just rounding the corner when they heard, "Hey! You girls! Come back here!"

The girls ran faster than any of them had ever run in their lives. They were too afraid of what might happen if they stopped!

Finally, they arrived back at cabin 12B. Sydney and McKenzie sat on the front steps in their pajamas.

"Oh, thank goodness you're back! We were just trying to decide if we should come after you!" whispered McKenzie. The five girls entered the cabin, three of them holding their sides from the pain of the long sprint. The clock read 12:33 a.m. when the whispers stopped and the girls finally slept.

•—•—•

During Discovery Time the next morning, all six girls dangled their feet from the dock. They had elected Elizabeth to lead them in their devotions, and now they listened to her read the scripture from her Bible.

"Proverbs 10:2, 'Ill-gotten treasures have no lasting value, but righteousness delivers from death,' " she read.

"I definitely agree with the first part!" said Kate.

"Why?" asked Elizabeth.

"I guess you could call those letters last night, 'ill-gotten treasures.' We could have been arrested for breaking and entering! We had no business going through Mr. Gerhardt's letters, and now they have no value."

The girls nodded. They had been disappointed that the reader pen hadn't delivered more information. The closet had been too dark for Kate to run the pen evenly along the lines. Most of the lines were scrambled, and what little they could read was just about prison life.

"Well, we may not have acted in 'righteousness,' but it sure felt like we got delivered from death!" exclaimed Alex.

"Oh, I know it! I was so scared! I just knew we were going to. . ." Kate was interrupted by loud squeals from Bailey.

"Eeew! Gross! Get that thing away from me!" she yelled. The other girls laughed when they saw the source of panic. It was a tiny green lizard that had climbed onto the dock and almost into Bailey's lap.

"Awww, look at him! He's cute," said McKenzie. She scooped up the lizard and held him for the others to see.

"Step back, Mac!" squealed Bailey to McKenzie.

Alex, Elizabeth, Sydney, and Kate crowded near McKenzie for a better look, while Bailey kept her distance.

"I wish we could keep him," sighed Kate.

"No!" said all five roommates. But Elizabeth took the lizard from McKenzie and studied it.

"We can't keep him. But maybe we should hang on to him for a few hours. I have an idea. . . ," she said with a mischievous grin.

•—•—•

McKenzie helped Sydney into the saddle of a gentle-looking mare. "This will be fun," she told her friend. "This will be the first time I've gotten to ride the trails since camp started."

Sydney looked at her freckle-faced friend. "He seems pretty gentle. I've always wanted to ride a horse."

McKenzie chuckled. "She. The horse is a she. Her name is Sugar. I've helped Mr. Anzer a few times with the grooming, and she's a sweetie. You'll like her." She then adjusted the saddle on a strong black quarter horse, stepped into the stirrup, and pulled herself into place. "This is Spirit. He's well trained and full of energy. He reminds me of Sahara, my horse back home."

The two girls were about to hit the trails when Mr. Anzer and Mr. Gerhardt rounded the corner and approached them. The girls avoided Gerhardt's eyes and focused on Mr. Anzer.

"Hello, girls," Mr. Anzer said. "Headed out?"

"Yes, sir," they responded.

"That's nice. It's a lovely day for a ride," he said with a smile. Then, his expression changed to one of concern. "Say, girls, Mr. Gerhardt told me that some campers were fooling around at the golf course late last night. He said he thought it might have been some cabin 12 girls, though he didn't get a good look. Were you at the golf course after dark last night?" He looked straight at McKenzie then at Sydney.

The two girls looked at each other then back at Mr. Anzer. "No, sir," they answered.

He eyed them steadily, then said, "That's good to know. You two be careful, and have fun!" The smile returned to his face, and he waved as they rode through the gate and toward the trails.

"That was close," said McKenzie as they got out of earshot. "I wouldn't have lied to him."

"Me neither," said Sydney. "My mom says withholding information can be like lying, though."

The girls grew quiet, enjoying the beauty of the trails. Suddenly, they heard giggling from the trees. Out of nowhere, a fat water balloon exploded on the trail in front of them, spooking Spirit and causing the horse to whinny, rear back, then take off in a full-speed run. Red hair streamed in the wind as the horse rounded the curve and sped out of sight.

Sydney turned to see Amberlie and her friends running away. She decided she would deal with them later. Right now she had to help her friend.

•—•—•

McKenzie clutched the reins. After a brief scare, she realized the horse was staying to the trails. Eventually, they would circle back to the stables. She held her head back, enjoyed the wind on her face, and let the horse run. After a few minutes of a thrilling ride, she felt the horse getting winded. Tugging gently on his reins, she guided him to slow down.

"I don't know where that balloon came from, Spirit! I'm sorry it scared you," she told the horse, rubbing him gently behind the ears. "Sydney will be worried. We'd better go find her."

She gently guided the horse to turn around and head in the opposite direction. Before long, she met Sydney, who was coaxing Sugar into a slow, labored gallop. McKenzie had to chuckle at the sight of her friend bravely coming after her on the slow horse. "I'm okay," she announced.

"Well, that's good," said Sydney. "I didn't know whether to come after you or to go back and get help. Either way, Sugar doesn't know the meaning of 'Hurry up'!"

McKenzie guided Spirit to turn around once again, and the girls continued down the trail. "Did you see who threw the balloon?" McKenzie asked.

"Do you even have to ask?" Sydney responded.

McKenzie nodded. "It's a good thing Spirit is well trained. That could have been really dangerous."

"I don't understand that girl. She's so fake around the counselors. But she's the meanest girl I've ever seen. I almost feel sorry for her," said Sydney.

"Yeah, I'd love to know what's going on inside that head of hers. She obviously has some problems." McKenzie looked thoughtful.

The two girls settled into a comfortable silence; then Sydney started laughing.

"What's so funny?" McKenzie asked.

"Elizabeth's plan. Never in a million years would I have thought Elizabeth was capable of coming up with something so. . .so. . ." Sydney searched for the word.

"Naughty?" McKenzie helped her out.

The girls chuckled and talked about the plan for the rest of the trail ride.

•—•—•

The campers had just been released from the evening meeting, and groups of girls were ambling toward the cabins. No one was ever in a hurry to get ready for bed. Amberlie and her roommates were about to turn down the path leading to cabin 8 when Bailey and Alex stopped them. "Amberlie, could I talk with you for a minute?" Alex asked sweetly.

Amberlie looked at the two with a mix of curiosity and suspicion. "What do you want?" she asked. Amberlie's roommates stood by, listening.

"I was just wondering if you are a cheerleader," asked Alex.

Amberlie was taken off guard. "A what?" she asked.

"A cheerleader. Are you a cheerleader at your school?"

Amberlie paused. "No," she said.

"Oh, that's a shame. You've got the perfect build to be a cheerleader. And you're so pretty. You should think about trying out," Alex told her.

"Uh, okay," Amberlie responded. She clearly wasn't sure how to take the compliment.

"If you'd like, I can show you some moves. Here, watch this," Alex continued, then demonstrated a double forward handspring. "It's really not as hard as it looks," she continued.

During this conversation, Elizabeth, Sydney, Kate, and McKenzie watched from behind the trees at the side of the road. When Alex had Amberlie's full attention, the four Camp Club Girls, along with the lizard, sneaked toward cabin 8.

"Shhhhhh!" Elizabeth told her giggling friends, but she had a hard time controlling her own giggles. She removed a small jar with holes poked in the lid from her tote bag. "You all stay here and keep watch. I'll go in and put Prince under Amberlie's covers. She always brings a pillowcase with her name on it, so I shouldn't have any problem finding her bed."

"Okay, but hurry!" McKenzie told her. "I'm not sure how long Alex can keep them entertained!"

Elizabeth surprised them by standing tall and walking right into cabin 8 as if she had every right to be there. It took her only a moment to locate the pink ribboned pillowcase with the name AMBERLIE embroidered across the top. Carefully, she turned back the covers, then gently removed the small lizard and kissed him on the head. "Do your job, Prince," she said. She tucked the creature under the blankets and smoothed them back into place.

The other three girls stood in the road, trying to act casual. A few moments later, Elizabeth darted out of the building then slowed down. The four girls walked toward their own cabin, trying to control the laughter that bubbled up inside them.

Alex and Bailey caught up with them at their cabin door, and the girls circled toward cabin 8 again. They hid in the bushes outside the windows of Amberlie's cabin. This would be a show they didn't want to miss.

Missing Biscuit

The Camp Club Girls could hear the conversation from Amberlie's room drifting through the open window.

"We're going to beat those girls from cabin 12. And it's going to start tomorrow night at the talent show. After that, we'll win the horse-riding match and the canoe races, no problem," said Amberlie.

"What about the scripture memory competition? That Elizabeth is good. She's won all the practice competitions in class," said a voice Elizabeth couldn't place.

Amberlie laughed. "Yes, but she hasn't been up against me yet. My dad's a preacher, and I've memorized scripture since before I could walk. No way she'll beat me."

The girls looked at one another. "A preacher's kid? Amberlie's dad is a. . ." Bailey felt Elizabeth's hand cover her mouth.

"Shhhhh!" The other girl whispered. The light went out in cabin 8, leaving only the soft glow of a lamp. Slowly, the Camp Club Girls peeked in the window, just in time to see Amberlie pull back her covers.

The girl was wearing pink satin pajamas, and her head was covered in pink hair curlers. She slid leisurely beneath the covers and reached for the lamp. She clicked it off, and all went black. Not a sound.

The six girls outside the window waited for several minutes then looked at each other in the moonlight. Disappointed, they turned to go back to their cabin. They had just stepped into the shadows of the trees when they heard the loudest, shrillest, most chilling scream.

"Help! Help me! Heeeeelp! Get it off, get it off, get it off! Eeeeek! It's in my hair! Get it off! Ew, ew, ew! Heeeeelp!"

The cabin door flew open, and Amberlie dashed outside, jumping up and down and smacking herself in the head, yanking out her curlers and screaming.

The girls of cabin 12 didn't know whether to run or stay and enjoy the show. They backed a little farther into the shadows but stayed to watch the scene play out.

A counselor soon emerged, saying, "Amberlie, be still or I can't help you."

"I can't be still! There's a giant snake, or a big spider, or something crawling in my hair! *Get it off!*"

The girls saw that Amberlie was truly terrified. They almost felt sorry for her.

Almost.

Later, after the Camp Club Girls had climbed into their own beds and switched off the lamp, Elizabeth said, "I feel kind of bad."

"Yeah, me too," said McKenzie.

Silence filled the room. It was interrupted first by Bailey's giggles, then Kate's, and soon they were all lost in an uncontrollable combination of guilt and giggles.

•—•—•

Elizabeth was awakened early the next morning by Bailey, who was shaking her back and forth. "Beth! Psssst! Beth, wake up!"

Elizabeth opened one eye. It was still dark outside. "This better be an emergency, Bales," she mumbled.

"It is, Beth! It's a big emergency!"

Elizabeth sat up groggily. "What is it?" she asked.

"The talent show is tonight! We have to practice. Now."

Elizabeth dropped back down and pulled the covers over her head again. "Go to sleep, Bailey," she grumbled.

"But we have to practice, and everyone else who is in the talent show will want to practice today too. That means the piano and the stage will be taken all day long. If we don't go now, we may not get a chance later, Beth!"

Elizabeth moaned. Bailey had a point. But sleep was more important to her at that moment.

Unfortunately, winning was more important to Bailey, and she wasn't giving up easily. "Beth, please? Pretty please, Beth? Don't you want to beat Amberlie?"

Reluctantly, Elizabeth sat up once again. "Okay. But you owe me," she mumbled.

The two girls dressed quickly, left a note to let the others know where they were headed, and were halfway to the dining hall when the trumpet began to warble reveille. They pushed open the doors to the quiet building without paying much attention to where they were going. As they entered, someone else was exiting. A very tall someone with muddy boots and a large cup of coffee. The two girls collided with the man, spilling coffee all over the boots and the freshly mopped floor.

"Oh, I'm sorry!" both girls cried out before they realized who they were speaking to.

Mr. Gerhardt pulled a handkerchief out of his pocket and knelt to clean up the mess. "You girls are up early. Do you always wander around in the dark?" he asked.

"Oh, no, sir," said Elizabeth. "We just need the piano to practice for tonight's talent show."

Mr. Gerhardt gave them each a long, steely look then turned back to refill his coffee.

"We only have a couple of days of camp left," Elizabeth told Bailey, who stared after the man.

"Yeah," Bailey said. "If we're going to solve this mystery, we need to move!"

The girls were now wide-awake and scurried through the inner doors of the dining hall. Elizabeth sat at the piano and began warming up with some scales. Bailey sat next to her and sang, "Do, re, mi, fa, so, la, ti, do." When both girls were warmed up, Bailey took the stage and began smiling at the tables and chairs.

"What are you doing?" asked Elizabeth.

"I'm practicing my smile," Bailey replied, as if it were the most obvious thing in the world.

Elizabeth chuckled and began playing the song. They ran through it three times before a line formed outside. "We'd better go," she told Bailey. "Come on, we can hold a place for the others."

The two stepped outside and took their places at the end of the short line. Before long, the rest of the Camp Club Girls joined them. "I can't believe you two got up so early," mumbled Kate. "The rest of us overslept. Biscuit is still in the room. We didn't have time to take him to the golf course, so we'll have to do that after breakfast."

"Oh, and tell her about the socks," Sydney urged.

"Oh yeah, the room is a wreck. Biscuit got into the socks again," Kate told them. "The alarm clock didn't go off, and we woke up to Biscuit slinging Alex's smelly sock onto my head."

"Hey!" Alex protested. "My socks aren't any smellier than yours!"

"He got into the socks again? Great. What is the deal with that dog and dirty socks?" Bailey groaned.

"We need a plan. Why don't we get our breakfast to go? Kate, you and Alex take Biscuit to the golf course, and the rest of us will clean up the room."

"No, let me go instead of Alex," urged Bailey. "Maybe I can practice a few strokes!"

The other girls laughed at their youngest roommate. "Bailey, I don't know where you get all that energy, but you should bottle it and sell it," said Elizabeth.

The girls followed the rest of the line into the dining hall.

•—•—•

Kate, Bailey, and Biscuit entered the empty golf course, and Biscuit immediately ran for the pile of golf clubs stacked on the office porch. He returned with his favorite club. The handle was marked up and down with his teeth marks.

He dropped it at Bailey's feet and looked at her longingly. "Ew, sorry boy. I have to practice, and I'm not gonna do it with your slobbery club. I think I'll get a fresh one," she told him with a pat on the head. She headed over to select her own club.

Kate picked up the chewed-up golf club and looked at it. "I've never known of a dog who likes golf." She laughed. "My dad plays golf. If only I could convince him to let you be his caddy, you could come home with me." She threw the golf club, and Biscuit bounded after it.

Bailey was on her third stroke when the sound of a golf cart interrupted them. Biscuit, who seemed afraid of Mr. Gerhardt, slipped behind the clown attraction, tripping the wire and causing the loud, silly laughter the girls had grown used to. Kate and Bailey were relieved to see that Mr. Anzer was with Gerhardt.

"You girls sure spend a lot of time down here," said Mr. Anzer as he climbed out of the cart.

The girls laughed nervously. "Yeah, I wanna be the next Tiger Woods," Bailey told him.

The old man smiled. "Sounds great. Then the rest of us will be able to say, 'We knew her when. . .' "

Kate glanced nervously over her shoulder, looking for Biscuit. Since that first day at the golf course, the little dog disappeared every time

Gerhardt came around. But he had drawn attention to himself with the clown's laughter. Gerhardt looked toward the clown then started walking that way.

"Is that the dog I ran off last week?" he asked. "I keep seeing his paw prints around, but I can never catch him. I've called the pound. They should be out sometime today or tomorrow."

Suddenly, Biscuit took off.

"Hey, mutt! Come back here!" yelled Gerhardt, chasing the little dog. Biscuit slipped through the gate, and he was gone. Gerhardt examined the gate then walked toward his office. "I'll fix this problem. That back gate is going to be fastened for good."

The color drained out of Kate's face, and she looked like she was going to be sick. Bailey gently touched her friend's arm and whispered, "It's okay. We'll find him. He'll probably find us first."

Kate gulped then nodded. She couldn't do anything about it now.

"You girls need to get to class, don't you? You'll be late," said Mr. Anzer.

The girls nodded then headed out the gate. When they were out of earshot, Kate said, "What will we do now? Gerhardt said the pound is coming. We've got to find Biscuit before they do, or he'll be lost to us forever!"

"Well, I'd rather the pound find him than that cougar! At least they won't hurt him," said Bailey. "Come on. If we hurry, we might be able to catch the others before class. Let's see if they have any ideas."

The two girls ran back to the cabin and arrived just as the others were leaving. "Biscuit!" Kate said, stopping to catch her breath.

The girls could read the pain in Kate's eyes. "What's wrong?" McKenzie asked.

"He's gone!" exclaimed Bailey. "And the pound is coming for him today!"

Kate and Bailey took turns explaining what had happened, and the others listened with concern.

"What can we do?" asked Kate in a worried voice.

"We'll divide up right now and search the woods," suggested Alex.

"We can't miss class. We'll get in trouble," said Elizabeth.

"I know what we'll do," offered Sydney. "Mac and I go on a nature walk with our class this morning. We'll walk right through the woods where Biscuit is hiding. Why don't we each carry a backpack filled with treats. . .something he'll smell. Maybe then he'll find us. If he does, we can slip him into the backpack."

The others agreed that this sounded like a good plan—at least until later when they could search more freely.

"What kind of treat should we put in your backpacks?" Bailey asked.

The girls offered suggestions, from stale cheese crackers to leftover biscuits. But Elizabeth offered the winning solution.

Minutes later, Sydney and McKenzie left the cabin, each with a backpack filled with dirty socks.

•—•—•

"Today is our last day to practice before the big contest," Miss Rebecca told her students. "I am very pleased with how much scripture you have memorized. As you know, memorizing God's Word is one of the most important things you can do. That's why the winner of this competition will receive double points for her team. So, who's ready to get started?"

Hands shot up around the room until the counselor called on Elizabeth. Then all hands went down. "Oh, come on, doesn't anybody want to compete with Elizabeth?" Miss Rebecca asked with a smile.

The class laughed. Elizabeth had a reputation for being a scriptural encyclopedia.

Finally, Amberlie raised her hand. "I'll do it, Miss Rebecca," she said sweetly.

"Wonderful! Come to the front. For this first part, I'll give the reference, and then you say the complete verse with the reference at the end. Every once in a while, I may stop and ask what the verse means. Ready?"

Both girls nodded.

"Elizabeth, you first. Proverbs 20:15."

Elizabeth smiled. " 'Gold there is, and rubies in abundance, but lips that speak knowledge are a rare jewel,' Proverbs 20:15."

Good job. Amberlie, Proverbs 3:13–14."

Amberlie smiled sweetly. "Certainly, Miss Rebecca. 'Blessed are those who find wisdom, those who gain understanding, for she is more profitable than silver and yields better returns than gold,' Proverbs 3:13–14."

"Very good, Amberlie. I'm impressed! You've been holding out on us," said the counselor.

Amberlie beamed. But when Miss Rebecca turned to address the class, the girl leaned toward Elizabeth and whispered, "You're toast, Anderson."

Elizabeth smiled. "Bring it on," she whispered back.

•—•—•

The nature hike provided some interesting clues in the search for Biscuit, but the girls couldn't find the little dog. At one point, Sydney spotted paw prints in the mud, which looked the size of Biscuit's. But the girls couldn't disrupt class by calling out for the little dog, so they just kept hiking. They tried to mark the spot in their minds so they could come back and search later.

The girls gathered at the cabin for Discovery Time, and Elizabeth said a special prayer. "Dear Lord, please keep Biscuit safe! Please help us to find him before the pound does. And please help us to solve the mystery of Mr. Gerhardt's digging. Amen."

"Amen," the girls echoed.

"We have two goals for today," said Alex. "We have to find Biscuit. And we have to find out why Mr. Gerhardt is digging at the golf course every night. We know he's probably looking for the missing jewels that were never found when his father was convicted."

McKenzie jumped in. "Perhaps we should stop concentrating on why he's digging, and start digging ourselves."

The rest of the girls looked at McKenzie. "You're brilliant!" exclaimed Sydney. "Why didn't we think of that before?"

The girls divided into two teams. Kate, Sydney, and Elizabeth would search for Biscuit, and the other three would search the golf course for hidden treasure.

Kate would take her cell phone into the woods, and the other three would carry Elizabeth's cell phone with them. That way they could maintain contact in case the jewels were found.

Or in case any cougars showed up.

•—•—•

When they arrived at the golf course, Alex, Sydney, and McKenzie heard Mr. Gerhardt's voice from inside the office building. Sneaking to the window, they listened to the man talking frantically. There were no other voices, so he must have been talking on the phone.

"I know, I know. The golf course is a mess. But I'm. . ."

He stopped to listen to the other person. Then he started again. "I know. But trust me, I have a good reason for digging things up. I'll fix it before the next camp begins, I promise."

More silence.

"I can't tell you why."

Quiet.

"I know I can trust you, but. . ."

There was a long pause, and then Gerhardt sighed. "Okay. I'll tell you everything, but it will take awhile. I'll meet you in your office at two o'clock."

More silence.

Then he said, "Okay. I'll see you at the stables at two o'clock." They heard the man hang up. "Oh, dear God," he said, "if those jewels are here, please let me find them. Please help me prove my father's innocence."

The girls looked at one another, wide-eyed, then headed back toward the main camp. As soon as they were out of earshot, Sydney spoke. "It sounds like he's going to spill the beans to Mr. Anzer. We've got to figure out a way to listen in on that conversation!"

Golf Clubs and Socks

Alex, Sydney, and McKenzie were halfway back to the cabins when they remembered the cell phone. "Let's call and check on the others," McKenzie said.

Kate answered the phone right away. "Did you find the jewels?" she asked without saying hello.

"No, but we may be very close to solving the mystery. How about you all? Any sign of Biscuit?" asked McKenzie.

"We saw signs of him but no Biscuit. Sydney led us to where you two found his paw prints this morning. We've called and called, but we can't find him. We're headed back now. We'll search some more after lunch." Kate sounded sad.

"Don't worry, we'll find him. Meet us back at the cabin. We have a lot to discuss," McKenzie told her.

All six girls were back at the cabin within ten minutes, discussing Gerhardt's phone conversation.

"How can we listen in on that conversation? The stables are busier than the golf course. We can't just stand by the window; that would look suspicious," said Elizabeth.

"I have an idea," said Kate. "Let me see Elizabeth's phone. . . ."

•—•—•

After lunch, the girls headed to the stables. They had talked about splitting up again to search for Biscuit, but only Kate was willing to miss the conversation. And they agreed it wasn't safe for Kate to search the woods alone.

"We'll all go search as soon as we hear what Mr. Gerhardt says," Elizabeth promised.

The girls walked casually into the stable area, admiring the horses and talking about riding the trails. They each played their parts well.

"Hello, girls!" greeted Mr. Anzer. "What can I do for you today?"

"Well, um, I actually have a question," said Kate. "Could I talk to you in your office?"

The old man smiled. "Certainly, young lady." He held the door open for her then followed her inside. "What can I do for you?"

Kate took a deep breath then began talking. She fingered the telephone in her pocket, ready to press Elizabeth's number on the speed dial. "I live in the city—Philadelphia—but I'd really like to spend more time around animals. Are there any clubs I could join that would let me be around horses even though I don't have room for one at my house?"

"Why, certainly! I'm sure an equestrian organization is near you. I'll check into it and get back to you before you leave camp." Mr. Anzer smiled. "Was that all you wanted?"

Um, yes, sir. Thank you so much," she answered. As the gray-haired man stood, she pressed the button. She heard Elizabeth's phone ringing just outside the door. Suddenly, she heard Amberlie's voice.

"You think you're so smart, Elizabeth! But you just wait. I'm gonna smear you in that scripture memory competition, and every other competition. You and your little team will wish you never came to Camp Discovery Lake!"

Mr. Anzer was out the door in a moment, and Kate quickly slid her phone under a corner of his desk, then followed him out. Elizabeth's phone was still ringing.

"Amberlie, may I see you in my office, please?" Mr. Anzer said sternly.

Amberlie, clearly surprised, turned syrupy sweet. "Oh, hello, Mr. Anzer. Elizabeth and I were just. . ."

"I heard you, Amberlie. Now step into my office, please," he told her.

Her face held a mixture of defiance and fear as she stepped into the room. Elizabeth answered her phone just as Mr. Anzer shut the door.

The six girls didn't know what to do. They had meant to plant the phone for Gerhardt's conversation. Now they could hear Mr. Anzer's conversation with Amberlie. Sydney took the phone from Elizabeth, held her finger to her lips, and pressed the button for the speakerphone. Alex kept watch at the stable entry as the conversation was broadcast for them all to hear.

"Amberlie, I don't understand you," came Mr. Anzer's voice through the phone. "You're a smart, beautiful, talented girl. You act sweet around adults, but you don't have any of us fooled. You are mean and spiteful to the other girls your age. Why?"

"I don't know," Amberlie said softly.

There was a long silence. Then Mr. Anzer said, "You know, Amberlie, my father was a pastor. When I was a little boy, I felt like everyone expected me to be perfect. I wasn't allowed to act silly or get into mischief or make the normal mistakes that most kids made. I felt like I had to be perfect. Sometimes I envied the other kids because their lives seemed so. . .normal."

The girls heard sniffles. Then sobs. Finally, Amberlie spoke. "It's not fair! Those other girls get to do whatever they want, and nobody expects anything of them! Everyone expects me to be polite, to make good grades, to be clean and tidy. I feel like I'm being judged all the time by everyone."

Mr. Anzer said, "Here is a box of tissues. I know exactly how you feel. But you know what I finally learned?"

"What?" the girl asked.

"Most people weren't judging me at all. Oh, a few were. But most of them just loved me and wanted me to be happy."

Amberlie sniffled. "Really?" she asked.

The girls outside the door were silent. None felt right about eavesdropping on this conversation. But they needed to keep the phone on so they could hear Gerhardt. Finally, Elizabeth took the phone from Sydney and flipped it shut. "This is wrong," she said. "We'll just have to forget about Gerhardt. We don't need to eavesdrop. I feel almost like we're stealing something. . . ."

The other girls nodded.

"We were stealing a conversation that didn't belong to us," said McKenzie.The girls were just leaving when the office door opened again. No one looked at Amberlie as she walked past them.

Kate approached the office door as Mr. Anzer was leaving. "I left something in your office," she said and retrieved the phone. The girls left the stables in silence. They had a lot to think about.

The girls spent the next hour in the woods searching for Biscuit. But either the little dog had escaped to the other side of the woods, or else. . . well, they didn't want to think about the "or else."

Finally, tired and sweaty, they gave up. Bailey and Elizabeth decided to go back to the cabin to shower and prepare for the talent show. The others decided to snoop around the golf course and perhaps do some digging of their own.

When they arrived at the golf course, Sydney, McKenzie, and Alex started examining the piles of dirt. Kate sat on the office porch and looked at the pile of golf clubs. Biscuit's chewed-up club was on top of the pile, and she picked it up. She sat holding the club and thinking of her little lost dog when her phone rang. It was her father.

"Hello, Katy-kins! Are you still having fun at camp? Do you miss your ol' dad at all? I can't wait to see you tomorrow evening!" Her dad's voice was loving and familiar. The sound of it brought the tears that had threatened all day. Before she knew it, she was pouring out her heart.

"Daddy! I found a dog, and I named him Biscuit, and he has been my dog for the whole camp, and I taught him to sit and to stay, and he sleeps at my feet, and he's the best dog in the whole world, and. . . and. . .he's gone!"

"Whoa, there! Slow down! Why don't you back up and tell me what you're talking about," her father told her.

She sat on the porch, holding the tooth-marked golf club and telling her daddy the whole story of Biscuit. When she finished, he remained quiet.

Finally, he said, "You say he's been sleeping with you in your bed?"

"Yes, sir," she answered.

"And he's not bitten or hurt you or the other girls?"

"Oh no, sir! He's the sweetest, gentlest, smartest dog in the world!" she told him.

"Well, your mother and I have talked about letting you have a dog. I'll call the camp director. If they find him, as long as he is healthy, you can keep him," her father told her.

"Really? You mean it?" Kate asked, hardly believing her ears.

As Kate hung up the phone, her spirits were lifted, but only for a moment. Right now, she had no idea where Biscuit was. She didn't know if she'd ever see him again. She picked up the golf club, walked to the fence, and tossed it into the woods. If Biscuit came back, maybe he'd find the club and bring it to her, wanting to play fetch.

•—•—•

The crowd was growing, and Bailey was getting nervous. She stood with Elizabeth behind the curtain, watching the chairs fill. "We just have to win, Elizabeth! We just have to! This could be my big break, you know?"

Elizabeth smiled at her friend, who looked ridiculous in her pink curlers and face cream. "You'll be great, Bales. Just relax. If you don't make it to Hollywood, you always have golfing to fall back on."

"Yeah," said Bailey. "Too bad there wasn't more interest in the golf course. I would have won a golfing competition for sure."

Soon, the camp director was on stage testing the microphones. When she was certain all was working properly, she began her speech. "Good evening, ladies. As you know, Camp Discovery Lake is almost over. Tonight's talent competition marks the beginning of the final competitions, which will continue all day tomorrow.

"Before we begin, I want to tell you how proud I am and how proud all the counselors are of all of you. You have been a wonderful group of ladies, and I believe you have experienced real growth here during the last two weeks. You've learned about all sorts of things, but the most important thing we've tried to teach you is that nothing is more important than your relationship with God."

The woman continued with a reminder about being supportive and polite to all the contestants, and before long, the first act was introduced.

Elizabeth and Bailey were third on the program, just after a baton twirler and before a tap-dancing duet. When their act was introduced, they were surprised by loud cheers and applause. The Camp Club Girls had a reputation for being friendly to everyone, and it was paying off.

Elizabeth began playing, and Bailey performed. The audience laughed in all the right places. When she finished, she bowed, and the room erupted in more applause. Then she gestured toward Elizabeth, who also bowed, and the girls left the stage.

They were nearly knocked over by their four roommates. "You were awesome! Bailey, you're a natural! And Elizabeth, you can really play! We'll win this for sure!"

The group was hushed by a counselor as the next act was introduced. The girls sat and politely applauded when the dance number was finished. The next act was Amberlie, and the girls held their breaths. They had a feeling she would be their main competition.

Amberlie took the stage and held the microphone. The music began, and the girl began to sing. Her voice was pure and sweet, and she sang a popular Christian song almost better than the original artist. The audience leaned forward, drinking in her voice.

Then, at a climactic point in the song, a dreadful howling noise sounded from outside the window. It got louder and louder, and more and more dreadful. At first the audience thought Amberlie had really messed up. But the Camp Club Girls knew that howl. Without thinking, Kate jumped to her feet and ran out the door, yelling, "Biscuit! You're okay!"

Her five roommates followed, creating quite a stir in the room. Amberlie, who had just sounded like an angel from heaven, stopped the song. "I can't believe this!" she yelled. "Those girls did this on purpose so they would win! This isn't fair!" She slammed her microphone into its stand and stormed off the stage.

The girls exited the dining hall just in time to see two men getting out of a large white van. It had the words ANIMAL CONTROL painted on the side. Gerhardt spoke to the men, one with a long stick and the other with a net.

"Oh no! What will we do now?" whispered Kate. The howling continued as campers and counselors poured out of the building.

Elizabeth thought quickly. "Kate, you and Sydney come with me. Alex, Bailey, and McKenzie, create a distraction."

"A distraction?" questioned McKenzie.

Alex grabbed her with one hand, Bailey with the other, and said, "Come with me!" She led them to the men beside the white truck. "Excuse me?" she interrupted.

The men looked at the girls, their eyes resting on Bailey and her silly costume.

"That howling has interrupted our talent show. What kind of animal is that?" Alex asked.

"We believe it's a dog, miss. Now if you'll. . ."

"You have such a dangerous job. It must be scary to have to catch these animals. I mean, you don't know if they have rabies or if they will attack you. Have you ever been bitten?" she continued.

As the men looked at Alex with annoyance and confusion, Kate, Elizabeth, and Sydney moved toward the howls. Biscuit seemed to be in the woods across from the dining hall. As they moved into the shadows, Kate flipped open her cell phone for light.

"Biscuit!" they called. The howls were getting closer, but they couldn't find the little dog.

"He must be stuck," said Sydney, "or he would have come to us by now."

The girls continued the search but soon heard men's voices behind them. A large spotlight shined on them, and Mr. Gerhardt called out, "You girls get back to the dining hall. You could get hurt out here!"

Suddenly, they heard one of the men yell, "I found him! He's stuck in this hole. Poor little guy! Good thing he didn't get stuck out here a few days ago, before we hauled off that cougar. He would have eaten this little fellow for lunch!"

The man walked into the spotlight holding a very wiggly, very dirty Biscuit in his arms. When Biscuit saw Kate, he lunged out of the man's grip and ran for his beloved owner.

But Gerhardt was too quick for the dog. He stepped in front of Kate, saying, "Oh no you don't. You're not getting away again!"

Biscuit changed directions and dashed toward the dining hall. Campers and counselors squealed as the filthy dog ran into the building, followed by three men and six girls, all yelling, "Come back!"

The man with the net cornered the dog on the stage, but just as the net was coming down on him, Biscuit took off again and headed back out the door. The big man leaped for the dog and crashed into a row of chairs.

Out the door came the little dog, then Gerhardt, then Kate and Sydney, then the man with the pole, then Bailey with her curlers and face cream, then the other three Camp Club Girls. The man with the net followed, limping.

Biscuit led the group toward the golf course. The men gradually slowed, holding their sides and breathing heavily. The girls raced ahead, and as they reached the fence, they found Biscuit, tail wagging, with his favorite golf club in his mouth.

"Biscuit!" Kate yelled, and scooped the filthy dog into her arms. "I'm so glad you're safe!"

The dog clung to the golf club, and the girls laughed. "Bailey, I know you want to be the next Tiger Woods, but I think Biscuit may give you a run for your money," said Elizabeth.

Just then, Mr. Anzer's golf cart pulled up. Gerhardt sat beside him, and the two Animal Control men were in the backseat. Several of the counselors followed, including Miss Rebecca. Gerhardt jumped out of the cart and stepped toward Kate. "You need to put the dog down," he said sternly. He grabbed the golf club, but Biscuit growled and refused to let go.

The tug-of-war continued, Kate holding Biscuit, Biscuit holding one end of the golf club, and Mr. Gerhardt pulling on the other end of the club.

Suddenly, the club broke apart, and out spilled an old sock.

Everyone gasped as the contents of the sock tumbled out!

Real Treasure

No one moved. They stood in the moonlight, with the golf cart headlights casting a soft glow on the broken golf club, the old sock, and the sparkly, shiny jewels that had fallen from it.

Then Mr. Gerhardt sank to his knees. Tears trickled down his cheeks as he gathered the colorful treasures. "Thank You, God! We found them!"

The girls jumped up and down and cheered, and the man looked confused. Elizabeth stepped forward. "We know all about your father, Mr. Gerhardt. We know he was convicted of stealing these jewels and selling them on the black market. And we know he didn't do it."

The man stood up. "But. . .but how did you—"

Alex spoke up. "We were curious about your digging. We figured that the spooky sounds weren't real, and we figured you were behind them. So we decided to do a little investigating of our own."

"When Mr. Anzer told me about the thieves that used to hide in that old house, we put two and two together. You looked pretty suspicious for a while," Elizabeth told the man.

The adults who had followed them to the golf course were now gathered around, listening intently.

"We went to the house, as you know. There we found an old newspaper with an article about the stolen jewels. I did an internet search and found out your father was convicted for stealing them," said Kate.

"Yeah," Sydney interjected. "But we also learned that the jury was divided. That there wasn't real proof of his guilt."

"It didn't make sense," McKenzie added her two cents. "If your father was guilty, he would have just told you where the jewels were hidden. You wouldn't have been digging those holes everywhere!"

"That's when we decided the thieves must have hidden them

somewhere at the golf course. We searched but didn't find anything. And just think, all this time, Biscuit was trying to give us the answer!" Elizabeth concluded.

Gerhardt nodded. "I've been trying to prove my father's innocence for nearly twenty years. I've searched high and low, but the jewels were just gone. Then, several months ago, I found out the thieves had hidden in that old house, and I had a feeling this was my big break. I searched the area, and the golf course seemed the most logical hiding place for the jewels. After all, who would think to look at a kids' camp?

"That's why I really didn't want you girls snooping around. I was afraid you'd find them first and not tell anyone about them. I didn't mean to scare you girls." His eyes fell on Bailey. "I'm sorry I frightened you so much. I hope you'll forgive me," he said.

Bailey's cold-creamed face shone in the moonlight, and she smiled her million-dollar smile. "You're forgiven. Besides, this has been the most exciting two weeks of my life!"

The man tousled her hair then looked at Biscuit. "And you, little dog, are a hero. Just think, I've been trying to get rid of you, and you ended up finding the jewels for me!" He patted the filthy dog on the head, and Biscuit let out a friendly bark.

Kate laughed. "He has a thing for smelly old socks. That explains why he was so drawn to this golf club! All this time we were trying to solve the mystery at Discovery Lake, and Biscuit had the answer the whole time!"

Mr. Anzer approached Kate, examining the dog in her arms. "So this is the little guy who caused such a stir around here. He is quite the mystery maker, leaving evidence of his presence all over camp. But we could never find him! Now we know why. You were hiding him!"

Kate smiled sheepishly.

"I spoke with your father on the phone this evening, Kate," he continued. "I called him to discuss an equestrian society I located in Philadelphia, and he wanted to talk about dogs!" The group laughed, and Mr. Anzer reached for Biscuit. "You can keep this little fellow, but tonight he needs to go with the Animal Control men. They'll make sure he is healthy and is caught up on his shots. They'll probably even give him a bath before they bring him back to you!"

"Good luck with that!" said Sydney, and all the girls laughed.

Miss Rebecca stepped forward. "This explains the strange smells from your room. I just thought you girls were really stinky," she said with a wink. "And the socks! He must be the one who kept your room in a mess!" She knelt down, and Biscuit licked her on the nose.

The Camp Club Girls told Biscuit goodbye, and Kate held him tightly before handing him to Mr. Anzer. "I'm so glad you're safe, Biscuit. You really had me worried! After tomorrow, we'll never have to be apart again!"

Biscuit wagged his tail and covered her face with sloppy kisses before being carried to the Animal Control men. The limping man took him gently and slid into Mr. Anzer's cart. "Would you mind giving us a lift?" he asked the old gentleman.

The group of girls and counselors followed the golf cart back to the dining hall, and the talent show was soon back underway.

•—•—•

The girls awakened early the next morning, listening to the annoying trumpet reveille for the last time. They stretched and groaned. Bailey clutched her oversized panda under one arm and her blue ribbon in the other hand. She had been thrilled to win first prize in the talent show and had fallen asleep with the ribbon under her pillow.

"Okay, girls. Today is the day we win or lose," said Sydney. "Even with Bailey's points, we're still behind. Biscuit made sure we didn't win the cleanest cabin award. We have to win almost all of the competitions today, or we won't walk away as champions."

"We'll win. We have to win. We're the Camp Club Girls," said McKenzie.

Alex bounced to the center of the room. "Remind me again who is doing which competition?"

Kate sat up in her bed. "I took the nature studies quiz yesterday, and we'll find out our scores today at breakfast."

"I'm competing in scripture memory," said Elizabeth. "Mac, aren't you doing the horse-riding competition?"

"Yes," McKenzie replied. "I signed up yesterday."

"Alex, will you compete with me in the canoe races?" Sydney asked. "I really want to do that, but I need a partner."

"That sounds like fun. I think we really have a chance to win!" Alex said.

A short time later, as the girls sat at their usual breakfast table, the camp director took the microphone. "Good morning, ladies. May I have your attention?"

Miss Barr continued. "I hope you're ready for an exciting, fun-filled last day of camp. As you know, the Camp Club Girls of cabin 12 took the winning points last night at our talent competition." She paused for applause. "But the Princess Pack from cabin 8 is still in the lead. They had the cleanest cabin almost every day!" She paused again, but not as many people clapped.

"I have just received the results from the nature studies quiz taken yesterday," the woman continued. "Believe it or not, we have a three-way tie! Equal points will be given to Grace Collins of the Princess Pack, Rachel Smith of the Shooting Starlets, and Kate Oliver of the Camp Club Girls. Congratulations to each of you and your teams!"

The room erupted into a combination of applause and disappointed groans. "The first competition this morning will be barrel racing. The races begin at nine a.m., so I suggest you all finish your breakfast and head that way." The woman replaced the microphone into the stand and stepped down from the stage.

The Camp Club Girls congratulated Kate, who seemed unaffected by her win. She simply smiled, thanked them, and continued devouring her bacon-filled biscuit.

The girls finished their breakfast and headed toward the stables. "Are you nervous?" Elizabeth asked McKenzie.

"Not really," Mac replied. "I love to ride. I just hope I get the horse I want."

"We'll cheer for you!" called Sydney as McKenzie headed for the corral.

She was relieved when she saw that Spirit didn't yet have a rider. She walked over to his stall and began saddling him.

"I've seen you ride. You're good," came a voice from the next stall. McKenzie was surprised to see it was Taylor, one of Amberlie's roommates.

"Thank you," she responded.

"Well, good luck out there," the girl called as she rode into the paddock.

McKenzie stared after the girl. She had assumed that all of Amberlie's friends were just as mean as Amberlie. But this girl had been. . . friendly. "I guess that will teach me to make snap judgments," she told Spirit.

The dozen girls that competed in barrel racing lined up their horses. Most of them did a good job, but few had McKenzie's expertise. The Camp Club Girls' cheers could be heard above all others as they watched their friend effortlessly guide Spirit around the barrels and to the finish line, taking nearly a minute less than anyone else.

Mac smiled proudly, and her blush was almost darker than her auburn hair as she accepted the blue ribbon.

•—•—•

Elizabeth held a little white index card, reading the verse over and over. The other girls were confident that Elizabeth would win, but she wasn't so sure. Philippians 2:3–4 always tripped her up: "Do nothing out of selfish ambition or vain conceit. Rather, in humility value others above yourselves, not looking to your own interests but each of you to the interests of the others."

She always messed up on the "selfish ambition or vain conceit" part. She could never get those phrases in the right order. Taking a deep breath, she offered a silent prayer.

Miss Rebecca took the stage. "Welcome to the scripture memory competition. Round one will begin with verses you all have learned here at camp. I will give the reference for the verse. Then contestants must recite the complete passage word for word and repeat the reference. Any questions?"

No one spoke, and the two dozen contestants formed two lines on the stage.

"This will take awhile," whispered Kate, settling in her chair. But the contestants dropped like flies, and by round four, only three girls were left. Elizabeth stood at one end of the line and Amberlie at the other, with a quiet girl named Caitlyn in the middle.

Miss Rebecca began the round with Elizabeth. "Philippians 2:3–4," she said.

Elizabeth took a deep breath and briefly closed her eyes in concentration. Her five roommates held their breath as their friend began to speak.

"Come on, Beth, you can do it," whispered Bailey.

Elizabeth spoke. "Do nothing. . .out of. . .selfish conceit or vain ambition, but in humility value others above. . ." She stopped and looked directly at Miss Rebecca. "That wasn't right, was it?" she asked.

The counselor shook her head but smiled. "No, I'm sorry, Elizabeth. But you aren't disqualified yet. Remain on stage until another contestant correctly says the verse."

Caitlyn began to recite the verse but messed up in the middle. The audience leaned forward as Amberlie took the microphone. She smiled the sweet smile that was reserved for public use and began the verse. Without missing a beat, she recited it perfectly, and her team cheered.

Miss Rebecca said, "Congratulations to each of our contestants. We are proud of all of you, and I hope you will continue to memorize God's Word. And a special congratulation goes to Amberlie and the Princess Pack for winning this competition."

The audience applauded politely and dispersed for the next competition.

•—•—•

Sydney and Alex stood on the bank of the pond, looking fiercely competitive. They had to win this race if they had any hope of winning the championship.

"When the whistle blows, you will climb into your boats, paddle to the marker in the center of the pond, then turn around and canoe back," the counselor instructed. "At no time during the race can you exit the boat. If you fall or jump out of the boat, you'll be disqualified. Please make sure your life jackets are securely fastened."

Sydney and Alex checked each other's life jackets. "I think we can win," whispered Alex.

"We have to win," Sydney responded.

"On your marks. . .get set," the counselor called, then blew the whistle.

The two Camp Club Girls launched their canoe with skill and speed, and easily floated into first place. "One—two, one—two," shouted Sydney. They had spent more than a half hour after breakfast, sitting on dry ground, practicing their timing and technique. Both girls were naturally athletic, and the strokes came easily. In no time, they reached the marker in the center of the lake and rowed around it.

Elizabeth, Kate, McKenzie, and Bailey stood on shore, cheering as loudly as they could. The two girls in the center of the pond paid no attention, however. They concentrated on paddling as fast as they could. When they were within yards of the finish line, Sydney turned around to give Alex a high five. "We did it!" she called out.

Alex, caught off guard, was thrown off balance. She leaned to one side, trying to regain control, but it was too late. The boat tipped.

Splash! Two girls fell ungracefully into the water only inches from the finish line.

Sydney stood and yelled, "No! No way! This cannot be happening!" just as two girls from another cabin sailed past them to win the race.

Alex sputtered and pushed hair out of her eyes. The four remaining Camp Club Girls stood in shock until McKenzie broke into laughter.

"That was the funniest thing I've ever seen!" she called out. "That moment made losing the race worth it!"

Sydney and Alex frowned at her. But then they looked at themselves and their overturned boat, mere inches from the finish line, and the humor of the situation began to sink in. They had to laugh.

"Here, let me give you a hand," said McKenzie, holding out her arm. Alex and Sydney both reached out, grabbed their auburn-haired friend, and pulled her into the water with them. "Hey!" McKenzie yelled.

"Now that," Sydney said with laughter, "was the funniest thing I have ever seen!"

•—•—•

Elizabeth watched out the window as buses lined up to transport girls to the airport. The Camp Club Girls sat near the back of the room, frantically jotting down phone numbers and email addresses. Kate cuddled Biscuit, who had been returned to her just moments before.

The camp director, Miss Barr, took the stage, and the noise died down.

"Saying goodbye is always the most difficult part of the camp experience. I know you all have developed some lasting friendships during the last two weeks. I hope each of you will return next year. And now, let's announce this year's Discovery Lake champions. As you know, teams have built points during the entire camp. But the greatest source of points comes from the counselors' award, which is given to the team that has shown loyalty, friendship, and humility throughout the camp. This year, one special group of ladies has exhibited these characteristics in an outstanding way. Camp Club Girls, would you join me on stage?"

The girls looked at each other in shock and rose from their chairs. When they arrived on stage, Mr. Anzer and Mr. Gerhardt joined them.

"These girls have been friendly, sweet, and supportive during the past two weeks. But they have also gone above and beyond what anyone could expect of our campers," said Mr. Anzer.

Mr. Gerhardt took the microphone. "Girls, you helped me solve the mystery at Discovery Lake, and because of it, my father's name will be cleared, and he'll be set free. I'm pleased to award the Camp Club Girls with the title Team Discovery Lake. You deserve it!"

The room erupted in cheers. Elizabeth looked at the audience, and even Amberlie was clapping. Biscuit wiggled in Kate's arms, and the girls gathered into a group hug.

"We did it!" they called out, whooping and hollering.

"I wonder what mystery we'll solve next," Elizabeth said with a smile. Just then, her cell phone rang. It was her father, and she stepped away from the cheering group so she could hear.

"How's my girl?" asked her dad, and she filled him in on their win. "That's great," he told her. "I have a surprise for you. When you get home, you won't even need to unpack your bags!"

"What do you mean?" she asked him.

"We're going to Washington, DC! We leave on Monday."

Elizabeth had always wanted to visit the capital, and now she had a friend there. After hanging up the phone, she went to find Sydney.

As the girls said their final goodbyes and promised to keep in touch, they had no idea that another mystery was already beckoning the Camp Club Girls. From their various corners of the United States, soon they'd be embroiled in *Sydney's DC Discovery*.

"It was great to find the jewels for Mr. Gerhardt," Elizabeth commented as the girls hugged each other. "But the real treasure I found. . ." Elizabeth paused as she looked, in turn, into the faces of Kate, Bailey, Sydney, McKenzie, and Alex. "The real treasure is finding friends like you!"

Camp Club Girls:
Elizabeth's Amarillo Adventure

The Mystery Marbles

"Elizabeth! Come quick! My grandmother has lost her marbles!"

Elizabeth held the phone out from her ear, trying to understand what her friend was saying. "Megan, what are you talking about? I thought your grandmother was dead!"

"She is! Listen, you've got to get down here right now." Megan hung up the phone, leaving Elizabeth baffled.

Elizabeth replaced the phone on its base and dashed out the door. As an afterthought, she stepped back inside and grabbed a letter off the entryway table. Cramming it in her back pocket, she called out, "Mom, I'm going to see Megan—I'll be back in a little while!" She slipped her helmet on, jumped on her bike, and headed down the driveway.

"Wait!" her mother cried, and Elizabeth slammed on her brakes. The screen door squeaked as Mrs. Anderson stepped onto the porch, drying a coffee mug with a white dish towel. "I thought Megan was at work."

"She is, but she gets her break at 2:30. That was her on the phone, and she wants me to come," Elizabeth said, adjusting her helmet.

Mrs. Anderson continued drying the mug, and looked at her daughter a moment. "Okay, but be careful crossing streets, and come straight back here after Megan's break is over."

"Yes, ma'am," Elizabeth called as she lunged her bike forward. She practically flew the four blocks to the restaurant. If it hadn't been for the pesky stops she had to make at the intersections, she could have made it in half the time. But safety first.

Within minutes, she parked her bicycle next to her friend's scooter, near the back entrance. Going to the front of the restaurant, she pushed open the heavy door. The restaurant seemed black, compared to the bright Texas sunlight. It took her a moment to adjust her vision, and she looked around.

Jean Louise, the head waitress, greeted her with a wink. "You're just in time, girly. Megan just sat down at her usual table," she drawled.

"Thanks," Elizabeth told her. She sidled through the mixture of cowboys and tourists who were the customers at the Big Texan Steak Ranch.

"What took you so long?" Megan asked as she stood to greet her friend.

Elizabeth slid into the booth and said, "I got here as fast as I could. What's up with your grandmother?"

"I have no idea. Jean Louise is telling me some crazy story about my grandmother and some marbles and us being rich or something. That's all I know. And since you're the mystery girl, I called you."

Elizabeth didn't know what to say. Sure, she had helped solve mysteries with the Camp Club Girls, but she was surprised Megan would even remember that.

Megan leaned her chin on her hands then. "I'm exhausted. We've been busier than usual today. I've washed more dishes today than I have in my entire life! I'm just too tired to try to solve a mystery."

Elizabeth grinned. "Yeah, but just think of all that cash you'll have when you collect your first paycheck!"

Megan put her head on the table and moaned. "All I can think about right now is my tired back." After a few seconds, she sat up and added, "But it will be nice to be able to buy my saxophone. I know Mom can't afford it, and I don't want to ask her. But I really want to be in the band."

Jean Louise set a tall glass of iced tea in front of Megan. "What'll ya have?" she asked Elizabeth.

"Oh, nothing. I just—"

"Nonsense. It's on the house. Just tell me what you want," the tall redheaded waitress said around her gum.

Elizabeth paused, realizing the woman wouldn't take no for an answer. "I'll have a root beer," she said politely.

Jean Louise winked and said, "One root beer, coming up!"

Megan sat up and smiled at her friend. "I'm sorry. I haven't even asked about your day."

Megan and Elizabeth had grown up more like sisters than next-door neighbors. Though Megan was a year and a half older, she and Elizabeth had played together, walked to school together, and gone to church together for as long as they could remember.

Elizabeth pulled the letter from her back pocket and slid it across the table. "It's from my friend McKenzie. I told you about her—from camp? She's the one from Montana, the one who has horses. She's wanted to visit Texas, and she's finally going to. Her family is coming here to Amarillo for their vacation! She's coming to visit!"

Megan opened the envelope and pulled out the pages. She skimmed the contents of the letter, and then handed it back to Elizabeth. "That's great, Beth, really. I'm excited for you."

Both girls sat silently for a moment.

"And I promise to act excited, as soon as I have slept about forty hours," Megan continued with a yawn.

Just then, Jean Louise appeared with the root beer and two oversize pieces of apple pie, topped with enormous scoops of ice cream. "Here ya' go," she said.

Both girls perked up at the sight of the pie. "Wow! Thanks, Jean Louise!" they told her.

"Awww, hush up now. No need to thank me. You've earned that and more. You just eat and enjoy your break," she told Megan. She turned to go, then changed her mind. "So, what are you going to do about that special tip?"

Megan, whose mouth was poised for her first juicy bite of pie, stopped. "Well, actually, that's why I called Elizabeth. She's good at solving these kinds of things."

The waitress turned to Elizabeth. "So, you'll help her solve this mystery, huh?"

"I'm not sure," said Elizabeth. "First, I need to know more about those marbles."

"Shhhhh!" Jean Louise looked around her, as if not wanting anyone to overhear. "Honey, we need to talk. But not here. These walls have ears. Why don't you two head over to my place after work today?"

Megan nodded, and the waitress moved to take an order from the next table. "So, can you come?" the girl asked.

Elizabeth thought a moment. "I'll have to ask my mom. I'm supposed to stay with James while Mom and Dad go to a meeting at church, but maybe he can go with them."

"Okay. Meet me at the back door if you can," Megan told her. The girls finished their pie and drinks without much further conversation. Elizabeth was still thinking about this new mystery, and Megan was just too tired to talk.

•—•—•

Mrs. Anderson stood in her kitchen, looking between Elizabeth and six-year-old James, who were both talking.

"Megan wants me to go with her to Jean Louise's house at six," Elizabeth told her mother.

"Elizabeth promised she would watch me tonight, Mom! I want her to stay with me," James interrupted his sister.

"I know I said I'd watch him, but I think this is really important to Megan," Elizabeth continued. "Something about a special tip and her grandmother."

"But I wanted Beth to help me finish my Lego airplane. It's more fun when she helps me," James urged. "Make her stay with me. . .please!"

Elizabeth held in an exasperated sigh. She loved James. She just didn't like being his full-time playmate. She needed her space, and he didn't want to give it to her.

Mrs. Anderson looked at Elizabeth, then at James. "I don't think Elizabeth promised you anything, James. I asked her to stay with you tonight, and she agreed. But Josh's mom called earlier and is bringing Josh with her tonight, so you'll have a playmate."

James's face brightened as he said, "Cool! I'll go pack my toys so we can play!"

"You may take two toys, and that's it!" Mrs. Anderson called after him. Then she looked at her daughter.

Elizabeth slowly released her breath. She was off the hook with James, but she still didn't have permission to go with Megan.

"Is this Jean Louise Wilson, the waitress at the Big Texan?" her mother asked.

"Yes, ma'am. She's the tall lady with red hair. She gave us free pie today."

"I know her. She's nice," her mother said. She stood, clearly trying to make up her mind. "Okay, but you need to leave her house by seven thirty. I want you home before dark. And you girls stay together. If we're not home by the time you get back, go to Megan's house with her. We should be back around eight."

Elizabeth gave her mother a tight hug. "Oh thank you, thank you, thank you! You're the best mom in the world!" She kissed her mother's cheek and ran to her room.

At 5:58 p.m., Elizabeth sat on the back stoop of the Big Texan Steak Ranch waiting for her friend. At 6:01 p.m., the back door opened, Megan stepped outside and collapsed next to her friend.

"I'm not sure what I've gotten myself into," Megan told her. "Washing dishes here is a lot harder than washing dishes at home. They just keep coming and coming, and I can never get caught up!"

"I'll bet you'll get faster, the more you do it," Elizabeth encouraged her. "Besides, just think of the free pie!"

"Speaking of free pie, the cook sent these home with me," Megan answered, nodding toward two pie-sized boxes. "We'll never eat all of this, so one of them is going to your house."

"I won't argue," Elizabeth told her. "Should we drop them off before we go to Jean Louise's?"

"That's a good idea," Megan answered, and Elizabeth took the boxes from her.

"I walked, so I'll carry them. Then we can ride our bikes from home."

Soon the girls were bicycling through town, toward a section of small but well-kept hundred-year-old homes. They found the address the waitress had given them and rang the doorbell.

Jean Louise answered the door wearing cutoff jeans and a trendy T-shirt. It was an outfit that Elizabeth expected to see on a much younger person, but it looked good on the red-haired lady. The woman smacked her gum and said, "Come on in, y'all. I just made some fresh, sweet tea. And if you're hungry, I have some leftover fried chicken. You'll have to eat it cold, but that's how I like it."

The girls would have preferred to skip the tea and jump straight to the mystery, but they didn't want to be rude.

"I'll have some tea, thanks," said Megan. Elizabeth nodded that she'd have the same.

The two girls sat in the tidy, old-fashioned living room. A collection of salt and pepper shakers lined the mantel, and a pink porcelain teapot shaped like a pig rested on a tray on the coffee table. They could hear Jean Louise singing along with a popular country western song that was playing on an antique radio in the corner.

The older woman handed them the tea and placed a couple of pig-shaped coasters on the coffee table. She turned the radio down and sat across from them in a green overstuffed chair. "Megan, were you serious when you said you didn't know anything about a special tip?" she asked.

Megan set her tea down and answered, "Jean Louise, I still don't know what you're talking about. My grandmother died when my mother was a little girl."

The woman looked at her, as if deciding what she should say. "I don't mean to be nosy, honey, but why are you working as a dishwasher? Is money tight for you all?"

Megan blushed, but held her head high. "We do okay. We're not rich, but we always have what we need."

Jean Louise shifted in her chair. "Well darlin', with that tip your grandmother got, you should have everything you need, everything you want, and then some."

Elizabeth sipped her tea and remained quiet.

"Jean Louise, you're not making any sense," Megan said to the woman.

The woman looked out the window, then back at Megan. "You're really not kidding, are you? You don't know anything about the marbles."

"Jean Louise, please tell me what in the world you're talking about," Megan responded.

"Oh honey. Some rich fella' was head over heels in love with Emily Marie—your grandma. I remember it like it was yesterday. I was just a young teenager myself, and the whole thing was so romantic. Your grandma and my mama were best friends, and I used to hang out at the restaurant after school, till my mama got off work. This fella came in once a week or so, and he'd always sit at the same table in your grandma's section. Then he started coming several times a week. Before long, he was visiting the restaurant every day, ordering nothing more than coffee or tea. But he always left her a twenty-dollar tip. He was smitten.

"Then one day, he gave her this bag of marbles. They were the prettiest things you ever saw! There was a red one and a blue one and a green one, just about every color of the rainbow. There must have been a dozen of them in that bag. But the prettiest one was crystal clear."

She paused and looked out the window, as if remembering.

Megan interrupted her silence and said, "So the special tip was a bag of marbles?"

Jean Louise slowly brought her gaze to Megan. "Honey, those weren't just any old marbles. But hold your horses. Let me finish the story."

The two girls leaned forward, their eyes glued on the sassy waitress.

"So, the fella gives Emily Marie this bag of marbles, and tells her to keep them in a safe place. He tells her he wants to take care of her, and he knows these marbles will give her and her children a comfortable future.

"Well, at first she didn't know what to say. After all, you can buy a bag of marbles at any old five and dime store. But she didn't want to offend him, so she just said, 'Thank you.'

"Then, she started to pour them out on the table, but he stopped her. He pulled her toward him and whispered something in her ear. I remember it plain as day. I was sitting at the table across from them. I was eavesdropping, even though I knew I wasn't supposed to. Your grandma was such a pretty lady, and I used to watch her all the time."

She shifted, and the sofa squeaked. Elizabeth had a pretty good guess what Megan was thinking. They both wanted the woman to get on with the story.

The squeaking seemed to draw Jean Louise back to the present. She laughed. "Oh, listen to me, chasin' rabbits. Anyway, when that man whispered in your grandma's ear, she turned white! She looked at the bag in her hands. Her hands started shaking and she tried to give it back to him, but he wouldn't take it. He kept saying, 'They're yours. I've already put them in your name. The paperwork is all there.' Then, she sat down in the booth with the man. That was against the rules, but she did it anyway. Just sat right down and started crying and telling him thank you over and over again.

"He kept telling her, 'Don't cry. I want to take care of you!' I thought he was going to ask her to marry him, right then and there. But a whole bunch of cowboys came in, and your grandma had to get back to work."

She looked at the girls as if she had finished her story.

Elizabeth and Megan looked at each other, then back at Jean Louise. In unison, they nearly yelled, "What was so special about the marbles?"

Jean Louise looked surprised. "Oh, I forgot that part, didn't I? Silly me. I'll tell you that right now. But first, would you like some more tea?"

Camp Club Girls on the Case

The girls responded in unison, "No thank you!"

But Jean Louise didn't take the hint. She leaned forward, picked up her own glass, and said, "I'll just get myself some then. I'll be right back." She went into the kitchen, while Megan and Elizabeth sat on the couch. They shared confused looks, but neither girl spoke a word. An old Oak Ridge Boys song played softly on the radio.

After a moment, Jean Louise sauntered back into the living room. "Sorry to keep you waiting. I know you're anxious to hear about those marbles. But to be perfectly honest, I'm having second thoughts about telling you all this. Maybe your mama is the one I should talk to, Megan."

Megan told her, "My mama and I tell each other everything anyway. But she's working overtime this week, so you probably won't be able to get in touch with her for a few days."

"Your mama was just a little girl when all this happened," said Jean Louise. She sipped her tea, as if considering her next words. Finally she said, "Okay, I'll tell you. But don't go spreading this around. Tell your mama, of course, but don't talk about it to all your little friends." She glanced at Elizabeth.

"I won't tell a soul, unless Megan wants me to," Elizabeth responded.

Megan said, "Our lips are sealed."

Finally, the woman said, "The marbles were formed out of priceless gemstones. The red one was a ruby, the blue one a sapphire, and the clear one. . .a diamond!"

The two girls looked at each other wide-eyed, and then stood to their feet and squealed. "We're rich! We're rich!" Megan sang as she hopped up and down.

The older woman let the girls have a moment before she interrupted them. "Not so fast, Megan. If you're so rich, why is your mama working so much overtime? Why are you working as a dishwasher so you can buy a band instrument?"

Surprised, Megan looked at the waitress. "How did you know that?" she asked.

"I already told you I'm an eavesdropper!" Jean Louise said with a laugh. Then she grew serious. "There's one more thing you need to know. The reason I thought about those marbles after all these years, is because a man came into the restaurant the other day asking questions."

"What kinds of questions?" asked Elizabeth, shifting into her detective mode.

"He asked to see the restaurant manager. He wanted to know if anybody knew anything about some marbles that were given to a waitress there, years ago. Of course the manager didn't know anything. We've had so many managers since that time. And your grandma never told anyone except my mama about them."

"I wonder who would be looking for them, after all this time?" asked Megan.

Jean Louise snorted. "Honey, plenty o' folks will be looking for them if they know they're missing!"

Soon the girls thanked their hostess and started home. "What should we do?" asked Megan.

"I don't know. This is your mystery, not mine. I promised Jean Louise I'd stay out of it, remember?"

"No, you didn't. You promised not to tell anybody about it. That doesn't mean you can't help me solve the mystery," her friend said.

"I don't know, Megan. This one seems over my head. I wouldn't know where to begin," Elizabeth told her.

"Come on, Beth, you've got to help me. You're the one with all the sleuthing experience," Megan urged.

Elizabeth remained quiet, as if thinking it over. "Well. . .okay! I'll do it! But first thing, we need to let your mom know what's going on."

"Okay. I'll tell her as soon as—oh, wait! She works late tonight, and I have to be at work early tomorrow. I won't even see her until tomorrow night. But I'll tell her as soon as I can, I promise."

"It's a deal," Elizabeth told her. "Meanwhile, I'll google gemstone marbles, and see what I can come up with."

The girls were almost home, and Elizabeth could see her parents' van parked in the driveway. She looked at her watch—7:25. *It must have been a short meeting.*

"I'll see you tomorrow, Beth," Megan called as she headed toward her front door. "Join me on my break again tomorrow. We can talk about what you find on the internet!"

"See you then," Elizabeth called back, and climbed the front steps.

•—•—•

Later that night, Elizabeth sat at the family computer searching for information on the marbles. Her mother put the finishing touches on the now gleaming kitchen, and laid a fresh dish towel on the counter.

"What are you looking at?" Mrs. Anderson asked, laying a gentle hand on Elizabeth's shoulder.

"Oh, I'm just helping Megan with a project. Do you need the computer?" Elizabeth asked her mother.

"No, I'm going to bed now. Don't stay up too late, okay?" She kissed her daughter on the cheek and headed toward the back of the house. Then, she called over her shoulder, "Your dad will be home in a little while, though, and you know he'll want to check his email."

Elizabeth laughed. Her father taught Bible classes at the local seminary. He often got emails from his students, asking about their assignments. He enjoyed his job, and he loved helping his students understand the Bible better. To him, that was as exciting as a carnival would have been for Elizabeth.

She typed into the search engine, *Precious gemstone marbles,* and waited to see what appeared. Before long, she had links to museums and fine jewelers all over the world. There was a link for birthstone marbles, precious gemstones, forever gemstones, tigereye marbles. . .but nothing related to Amarillo, Texas.

If only I could send an SOS to the Camp Club Girls. Elizabeth thought of her friends from summer camp. *But I promised Jean Louise I'd keep my mouth shut.* She was in the middle of another search when a flag popped up in the bottom corner of her screen. HORSEGIRL96 WANTS TO CHAT the message read.

Elizabeth recognized McKenzie's online name and clicked on the flag.

Did you get my letter? McKenzie typed.

Elizabeth: *Yes! I'm so excited!*
McKenzie: *Me too. I can't wait to see you.*
Elizabeth: *What day will you be here?*
McKenzie: *Next Tuesday.*

Elizabeth smiled. She couldn't wait to see her friend. Then, she had an idea.

Elizabeth: *Do you think your parents will let you stay at my house while you're here?*
McKenzie: *That sounds like fun! I'll ask and email you tomorrow. Maybe you can stay at the hotel with me some too.*
Elizabeth: *Okay, I'll ask. Talk to you later.*
McKenzie: *Bye.*

Elizabeth was smiling at the computer screen when her dad walked in. "Hey, Bethy-bug! What are you so happy about?"

She stood and hugged her father. "Hi, Daddy! Guess what? McKenzie's coming to visit. She and her family will be in Amarillo next Tuesday!"

"That's great news, Sparky," he said, using one of his many pet names for her. "Why don't you see if she can sleep over while she's in town?"

Elizabeth giggled. "I already asked her. She's supposed to let me know tomorrow."

Mr. Anderson walked over to the computer and sat down. "What's all this about gemstones you've pulled up?"

Elizabeth had to think quickly. She didn't want to break her promise, but she wasn't going to lie either. "Oh, just some research I'm doing for Megan."

"You're a good friend, Elizabeth, and an all-around great gal. Just like your mama. 'A wife of noble character who can find? She is worth far more than rubies,' Proverbs 31:10. Tell Megan the real gem is your mama," he said.

Elizabeth smiled. Her parents were kind of sappy sometimes, always holding hands and kissing. It was embarrassing at times, but it was cute.

"I'll tell her, Daddy," she said, and kissed him on top of his head. "Good night."

•—•—•

At 2:33 p.m. the next day, Elizabeth pushed open the saloon-style doors of the Big Texan Steak Ranch and looked around. Megan was already sitting at her table. Two tall iced drinks and two big slices of pie were there too.

Elizabeth tossed her blond hair over her shoulders as she slid into the booth. Megan looked worn-out.

"I don't know how long I can keep this up!" she moaned. "I'm not sure I was created for hard physical labor."

Elizabeth chuckled. She remembered how tired she had been at camp, after she and her friends had to do kitchen duty for a few days. "You can do it. Hang in there," she encouraged.

Megan leaned forward. "So, did you find out anything about the marbles?" she whispered.

"Not a thing. I did an internet search, but nothing linked any gemstone marbles to Amarillo. I didn't have time to look at much. I'll keep trying."

"Why don't you get all your Camp Detective Club Friends, or whatever y'all called yourselves, to help?" Megan asked.

"Camp Club Girls," Elizabeth corrected. "I thought about that, but we promised Jean Louise to keep it hush-hush."

"Well, we don't need to talk about it to people around here. But as long as you trust your friends, I trust them."

Elizabeth sighed with relief. This would be so much easier if her friends helped her. "Okay," she said. "I'll send out an email tonight, and we'll see what we can come up with. You're still going to talk to your mom tonight, aren't you?"

"I hope so. As much as she's been working lately, I hardly see her. And when I do see her, she can barely stand up, she's so tired. I'm not sure how to break it to her that her mother lost her marbles," she said.

Elizabeth giggled and thought about the situation. It sure would be nice if Megan's mom didn't have to work so hard. Her dad had been killed a few years ago in a car accident, and things had been tough for their family since then. "I don't know about you, but I'm about to die if I don't start eating this pie! What is it today? Chocolate?" she asked.

"I think so," said Megan without much enthusiasm. But then she took a bite, and perked up right away. "Oh, this is *so* good!"

"I wonder if they'd hire me and let me work for pie," Elizabeth said. Both girls giggled and finished their pie in no time.

Just then, Jean Louise stopped by the table and bent down to their level. "You girls had better get crackin' on that marble mystery. That man was snooping around here again this morning, asking more questions."

The two girls looked at each other in surprise. Yes, they definitely needed to get crackin'.

•—•—•

Elizabeth typed into the subject line of the email: NEW MYSTERY; NEED HELP! She then moved her cursor to the body of the email, and began typing the whole story. She ended it with, *I don't know where to begin. Please help!*

She paused and said a little prayer before hitting the SEND button. *Lord, You know Megan and her mother haven't had an easy life. These gemstones could really help them. Please help us find them.*

There. She sent the email and sat staring at the blank screen. She knew it would only be a matter of minutes before someone answered her.

Since summer camp had ended, the six Camp Club Girls had conspired to solve several mysteries. Elizabeth had traveled to DC and helped her friend Sydney uncover a plot to assassinate the president! The other girls had been busy as well, using the sleuthing skills they had honed at camp to solve their own hometown mysteries. They were becoming quite the team, and Elizabeth knew she could count on them to offer helpful suggestions in this new case. The miracles of email, text messaging, and internet research had allowed them to keep in close contact, from Alex in California to Sydney in Washington, DC. Sure enough, just minutes after she sent her message, the red flag popped up. It was Bailey.

Gemstones? How exciting! Your friend will be rich! Wow, I wish I were there. You should check the local jewelers and see if anyone in your area sells gemstone marbles.

Elizabeth smiled. She missed Bailey, the youngest of their gang. Bailey was always excited about everything. Period.

Elizabeth typed back, *Great idea. Thanks, Bales!*

Just then, another red flag showed that Alexis was online.

Why doesn't your friend snoop around the restaurant and see if there are any hiding places there? She can act like she's cleaning or something. Tell her to try tapping on the walls. Nancy Drew is always tapping on walls to see if they are hollow.

A third red flag popped up, and it was Sydney.

Sounds to me like you need to investigate Megan's

grandmother's death. It's suspicious to me that she died just days after receiving the jewels.

Elizabeth felt her heart beating faster. This was getting more and more exciting. She typed the words, *Thanks, y'all. This will really help me get started. I'll keep you posted.*

She signed off the computer and walked to the front porch. She would wait there until Megan got home.

•—•—•

An hour later, the two girls sat on Elizabeth's front steps sipping the fresh lemonade Mrs. Anderson had brought out to them. "How much do you know about your grandmother's death?" asked Elizabeth. She had already shared the suggestions she'd received from her friends.

"Only that it was an accident. She was hit by a car."

"Are you sure it was an accident?" Elizabeth prodded.

Megan gave her an exasperated look. "I don't know, Elizabeth. I wasn't there."

Elizabeth giggled. "Oh yeah. Sorry. But how can we find out more?"

"We can ask my mom. But she doesn't like to talk about it. She loves talking about her mother. But when it comes to talking about her death, she clams up."

"What about Jean Louise?" Elizabeth asked. "She knew your grandmother. Maybe she can tell us more."

Megan's face brightened. "That's a great idea! Why didn't I think of that?"

"Because you're not an experienced detective, like I am," Elizabeth teased.

They heard the phone ring, and a moment later Elizabeth's mother called out, "Elizabeth, it's for you! It's your friend McKenzie calling, so hurry!"

Elizabeth went into the house, but Megan kept her seat.

"Hello? McKenzie?" Elizabeth spoke excitedly into the phone.

"It's me! I've been working outside, and I just now checked my email. I asked my parents, and the answer is yes! I can stay with you some while we're there. But they said if it's okay with you and your parents, you can stay some with me at the motel. We're staying at the Big Texan, because of their horse hotel. Isn't that cool, a horse hotel?"

"McKenzie, that's perfect! Did you read my other email?"

"I just skimmed it. I was so excited about staying with you, I went straight to ask my parents, and then I called you. I figured you could fill me in on the phone."

"Well, Megan works at the Big Texan Steak Ranch! That is the same restaurant her grandmother worked at, when she got the marbles. We may want to stay at the Big Texan as much as possible, so we can snoop around."

"Oh, this will be awesome! I was already excited about seeing you, but now we'll get to solve a mystery while I'm there! I can't wait," she gushed into the phone.

The girls said their goodbyes with promises to email later in the evening. Then Elizabeth returned to the porch.

"Guess what?" she asked Megan.

"Uhmmm, let me guess. McKenzie and her family are staying at the Big Texan, and you'll stay with her while she's here."

Elizabeth grinned. "I guess I did talk kind of loud. But I'm excited! I still have to ask my parents, though."

Just then, Megan's mom pulled into the driveway. She cleaned houses in the wealthy part of town. She also cleaned rooms for several local hotels, including the Big Texan.

"Are you going to tell her what's going on?" Elizabeth asked.

"I guess it's now or never," said Megan. "Why don't you come with me? You can fix Mama some pie and iced tea while I break the news."

The Charming Stranger

The girls walked across the driveway, and Megan hugged her mother. The woman's hair was falling out of its pretty clasp, and she had tired circles under her eyes. Still, she was beautiful.

Before Megan's parents had met, Ruby Smith had been Miss Amarillo. As small children, Elizabeth and Megan had enjoyed hiding under her bed and watching her experiment with different hairstyles or shades of lipstick. Once, she had fixed her hair in crazy crooked braids, and put cold cream all over her face. Then, she had said in a loud voice, "I think I'm ready. I sure wish Megan and Elizabeth were here to tell me how I look!"

The girls had burst into a fit of giggles. Mrs. Smith had coaxed them from under the bed and given them makeovers. But now, things were different. She didn't even wear makeup any more.

"Hi, girls," she said, offering an exhausted smile. "How are y'all today?"

"We're great, Mama," Megan responded. "Here, let me carry your bag. Come on in and sit down. I need to talk to you."

Elizabeth followed them into the house and walked into the kitchen. She felt as comfortable here as she did in her own kitchen. Pulling three glasses out of the cabinet, she filled them with ice. She figured she'd let Megan and her mom have some privacy.

She poured sweet tea from a pitcher in the refrigerator and transferred three slices of chocolate pie from the box to small plates. She found forks and napkins. Then she listened to see if Megan had told her mother the news yet.

"Megan, what are you talking about?" Mrs. Smith asked her.

"Mom, I'm telling you, we're rich! We just don't know where our treasure is."

" 'For where your treasure is, there your heart will be also,' " Mrs.

Smith quoted Matthew 6:21.

Megan paused. "Mom, this is serious. Some man gave Grandma some priceless gemstone marbles. We have to find out what happened to them!"

Though Megan had never met her grandmother, she still referred to her as "Grandma." She told Elizabeth once that she liked imagining what the woman was like.

Mrs. Smith yawned. "Elizabeth, what's taking you so long, child? I thought you were fixin' us some tea!"

Elizabeth appeared with the tea tray.

"Look at you!" the woman smiled. "Before ya' know it, you'll be working at the restaurant with Megan. How did you girls grow up so fast?"

Megan looked frustrated. Her mother clearly didn't understand how important the gemstones were. "Mom, aren't you going to try to find out more about the marbles?"

Mrs. Smith took a bite of her pie and then leaned back. "Megan, honey, that sounds like a wonderful story. But if any lost jewels existed, we would have heard about them long before now. If this little story makes you happy, and you want to go hunting these marbles, go right ahead. I'm tired, and I don't have room in my life right now for fairy tales." Then, seeing Megan's disappointed look, she sighed. "I'll tell you what. I'll call your Uncle Jack and see if he knows anything. I was only nine, but he was fifteen. Maybe he remembers something I don't. But then I don't want to hear any more about it. I—I don't like to think about that time."

Megan leaned over her mother's chair, hugged her, and then sat back down. The three finished their pie and tea, and Elizabeth excused herself. "Thank you for the refreshments. I'd better get home now. I'll see you tomorrow, Megan."

Megan waved goodbye, and Elizabeth let herself out. She could tell her friend was disappointed. But Mrs. Smith's disinterest might not be a bad thing. The woman had experienced a lot of discouragement in her life. It might be better not to get her hopes up.

"Those who hope in the Lord will renew their strength." Elizabeth thought of the verse she had known for years. *Lord,* she prayed, *Mrs. Smith could use some hope and some strength. Please help us find those jewels.*

•—•—•

The next couple of days passed quickly as Elizabeth continued to research the gemstones. She found several more dealers, but nothing about stolen or missing marbles. She was glad when Tuesday rolled around, and sat waiting by the phone. McKenzie was supposed to call when she arrived at the Big Texan Motel.

Elizabeth jumped when the phone finally rang. "Hello?"

"Beth, it's Mac. We're here!"

Elizabeth squealed. "I'll be there in ten minutes!" she told her friend, and nearly hung up before she asked for the room number.

"I'm in room thirty-four, right in front of this big, funny shaped pool," McKenzie told her.

Elizabeth stopped in her tracks. "Mac, surely you know that pool is in the shape of Texas."

McKenzie giggled. "I know. I just wanted to hear what you'd say to me. I've heard you Texans are very proud of your state."

"It's only the best place on God's green earth!" Elizabeth said.

"Well, that may be true, but I haven't seen much green yet. You didn't tell me you live in the desert!" McKenzie teased.

Elizabeth laughed. "I'll see you in ten—no, in five minutes!"

She kissed her mother on the cheek. Mom had invited Mac and her family for dinner, and was planning to stop by the motel later to introduce herself.

Elizabeth was almost out the door when James called, "I want to come!"

"That's not a bad idea," Mrs. Anderson said. "Elizabeth, James has been cooped up in this house all day. Would you take him with you? I'll be there in less than thirty minutes to get him."

Elizabeth sighed. "Come on, little brother."

James lunged at her, squeezing her. "Thank you, Bettyboo! You are the best sister in the world."

Elizabeth hugged him back, and said, "You won't think that if you keep calling me Bettyboo!"

James giggled and ran out the door ahead of her. "Bettyboo, Bettyboo, Bettyboo!"

Elizabeth took off after him. Some days she didn't know whether to hug her little brother, or clobber him.

An hour later, she and McKenzie sat by the large, Texas-shaped pool sipping sodas, while Mrs. Anderson visited with Mr. and Mrs. Phillips. James and McKenzie's eight-year-old brother, Evan, sat on the edge of the pool splashing their feet in the water and using a paper cup as a boat.

"So, when do I get to meet Megan?" Mac asked. "Is there any more news on the marbles?"

"We'll walk down to the restaurant in a few minutes. Her break isn't for another half hour. We've hit a dead end with the marbles. Her mother just isn't interested in finding out about them. She thinks it's a fairy tale."

McKenzie thought about that. "I guess she doesn't remember anything about the man or the marbles. I wonder if there is anybody else we can ask."

"I guess we can talk to Jean Louise some more, but I think she's told us all she knows," said Elizabeth.

The two girls leaned back in their lounge chairs, sipped their drinks, and thought about the mystery.

•—•—•

A little while later, the girls pushed open the doors of the restaurant and adjusted their vision.

"Well, look who's here!" Jean Louise greeted them in her nasal twang. "You must be here to see Megs. I think her usual table is open, and she'll be out in a few."

"Megs?" McKenzie whispered as they walked through the restaurant.

"That's Jean Louise. Megs is a pet name for Megan. Watch out. She has a pet name for everyone, and I'm sure she'll come up with something for you too."

McKenzie smiled. "What does she call you?"

After a pause, Elizabeth giggled. "Liza Jane. She sings a song about 'Li'l Liza Jane' to me."

Just then, Megan slid into the booth next to Elizabeth. "Hi! You must be McKenzie." She reached out her hand.

McKenzie returned the handshake. "And you must be Megan."

They were interrupted by Jean Louise, smacking her gum. "I see you've added a new person to your club," she said. "How ya' doin', Red?"

McKenzie smiled at the reference to her hair.

"McKenzie and Elizabeth are experienced mystery-solvers. They're going to help me find out about the—" Megan started to say.

"Shhhh!" Jean Louise snapped. She leaned forward. "I thought I told you to keep this quiet."

McKenzie looked confused.

Megan told her, "It's okay, Jean Louise. McKenzie is Elizabeth's friend, and I trust her. Besides, she's not from around here. She'll be gone in a few days."

Jean Louise eyed Mac with suspicion, but then her gaze softened. "Well, what's done is done. But you need to hush up. The man who has been nosing around is sitting right over there."

The three girls turned, trying to get a look at the man in the cowboy boots. His long legs stuck awkwardly from under the table, and he looked a bit like a giant at a tea party.

"Turn around!" Jean Louise whispered. "I thought you girls were supposed to be detectives. You don't want him to know you're staring at him!"

The girls whipped back around in their seats. "Oh yeah, she's right," said Mac. "Elizabeth, you have the best angle. Tell us what you see."

"Well, uh, he looks about my dad's age, and he's having a cheeseburger and french fries," she said.

"Who cares what he's eating?" Megan whispered.

Jean Louise rolled her eyes. "Look, girls, why don't you wait until he gets up to leave. Then you can get a better look. For now, just hold your horses. I'll bring you some leftover pecan pie." She turned to leave.

"Jean Louise," called Elizabeth.

The woman turned back around, and Elizabeth continued. "Is there any more you can tell us, or anyone else we can talk to?"

Jean Louise cocked one hip and rested her notepad there. "I've told you girls all I know, and nobody else was around back then, except my—hey! Why don't I take you girls to meet my mama? She would love the company, and Megan, she would just love to meet you. She loved your grandma so much. It nearly broke her heart when she died."

The girls perked up at the idea. "That sounds great," Megan answered. "When can we go?"

"You're off tomorrow, aren't you? Why don't we go about ten o'clock in the morning. Meet me here, and I'll drive you over." She looked at the other two girls. "Since y'all are in on this too, you're welcome to come if your parents agree." With that, the woman moved to another table to refill some iced tea glasses.

Elizabeth continued to discreetly eye the cowboy. "That is one tall man," she said. "Did y'all see how long his legs are?"

Just then, the man looked directly at Elizabeth and smiled. Had he heard her? She quickly looked away, then back. He winked at her!

She could feel the heat rising to her cheeks. Then she giggled.

"What? What are you laughing at?" the other two asked her.

"He winked at me!" she whispered. They all leaned to look at the man, who was now walking toward the cash register. His head nearly brushed against the ceiling fans, and he had to duck around the longhorn chandeliers.

"Let's follow him," Mac whispered. She and Elizabeth stood to leave.

"Wait! I'm not through with my shift!" Megan called.

Just then, Jean Louise showed up with their pie. "You're not leaving before you have this, are you?"

Elizabeth and McKenzie looked at each other, then at the man. "Can you put it in a box for us? We'll be back for it later!" Elizabeth told her, and they followed the man. "Thanks, Jean Louise!" she called over her shoulder.

Megan and Jean Louise stared open-mouthed after the two girls. "Apparently, they're serious about this detective business," said Megan.

Out in the sunlight, the girls looked to the right and the left. They barely caught sight of the tall man in the cowboy hat as he turned the corner. They followed quickly, trying to act casual.

As they turned the corner, they crashed into James. Mrs. Anderson was a few steps behind him.

"Beth! McKenzie's daddy is going to let me ride a horse! Mama's taking me home now to get my boots and cowboy hat!"

Elizabeth and McKenzie peered over Mrs. Anderson's shoulder at the tall man. He was going, going. . .gone.

"I thought you two were going to sit with Megan during her break. That was a short break," the woman said.

"Well, we. . .uh," Elizabeth stammered.

James jumped up and down. "Do ya' want to ride horses with me, Beth?"

McKenzie jumped in. "That will be fun, James. We'll meet you at the stables in a little while."

Mrs. Anderson and James waved and continued toward the parking lot. The girls went in the opposite direction, trying to determine where the man had turned.

"He could have turned here, at the ice machines, or up there, or. . .it's no use. We lost him," Elizabeth said.

"Well, since he walked toward the rooms, he's probably a guest here. Maybe we should hang out here today and see if he turns up again," McKenzie replied.

"Sounds like a plan to me."

•—•—•

Later that afternoon, the two Camp Club Girls leaned on the railing of the Big Texan Horse Hotel. Evan waited patiently as Mr. Phillips led

James, dressed in red hat and boots, on a black-and-white spotted pony. "Giddy-up! Look, Beth! I'm a cowboy!"

McKenzie laughed. "Your brother sure is cute!"

Elizabeth smiled. "Yeah, I guess he's okay, as far as brothers go." She waved at James as he rode by.

Sue Anderson and Jen Phillips sat on a long bench in the shade, talking.

Elizabeth continued, "I can't wait for you to meet my dad."

"Aren't we all going to your house for dinner tonight?" McKenzie questioned.

"That's the plan. Dad's going to cook out. We'll have hamburgers and hot dogs. Mom even got a watermelon."

"Yummm! I love watermelon," McKenzie continued. They both waved at James again. Neither noticed the tall shadow that appeared beside them until Mr. Phillips looked up and smiled.

"You've got a couple of mighty fine lookin' cowboys there," said the man, gesturing to Evan and James.

"Yep. Cowboys in training, anyway," said Mr. Phillips, helping James down from the pony. When both boys were safely out of the paddock, McKenzie's dad held out his hand. "Dan Phillips," he said.

"I'm Mark Jacobs," said the man, and the two shook hands.

"Is one of these horses yours?" asked Mr. Phillips.

The man pointed to a gorgeous brown-and-white quarter horse. "That's Lucy. She's one of the best horses I've ever owned. I'm going to miss her."

"You're getting rid of her?" Phillips asked.

"Yep. I'm here for the rodeo this weekend. I'm riding in it. But this rodeo life is getting tiresome, and I'm looking to retire. I want to buy a little spread of land about ten miles from here, but I need to sell all my stock to do it. I'm also waiting for a few other things to fall into place."

Elizabeth and McKenzie looked at one another, wide-eyed.

Phillips looked at Lucy. "Would she be any good on a ranch?" he asked.

"Oh, definitely. She was bred for ranching. Like I said, she's one of the best horses I've worked with," the man said.

"I've been looking to buy another horse for my ranch. We live in Montana. I may be interested in buying her when you finally get ready to sell. Of course, I'd like to see her in action," Mr. Phillips told him.

"Why don't you come watch the rodeo tomorrow night? Bring your whole family. I have a box reserved, but nobody to fill it," the man said.

Elizabeth and McKenzie made frantic eye contact but remained quiet.

Mr. Phillips and Mr. Jacobs began walking toward where the two women sat in the shade. Mr. Phillips introduced the ladies, then told them, "Mark, here, has invited us to be his guests at the rodeo."

"All of you," Mr. Jacobs said, looking at Elizabeth's mom. "Bring your families. I've got about a dozen seats just waiting to be filled."

"That is very kind of you," Mrs. Anderson replied. "Why don't you join us at our house this evening? We're having a cookout. When Robert, my husband, starts grilling, he goes a little overboard, and we usually have enough food to feed an army!"

Jacobs laughed. "He sounds like my kind of man. I'd love to join you. I'm on the road most of the time, and I don't get many home-cooked meals."

Elizabeth didn't know if this was a good development or a bad one.

Mr. Phillips noticed the girls and motioned to them. "Girls, this is Mr. Jacobs. Mark, this is my daughter, McKenzie, and her friend Elizabeth."

"I. . .uh. . .it's a pleasure to meet you, sir." Elizabeth held out her hand. McKenzie followed suit.

"I believe I saw these young ladies at the restaurant." The man smiled.

The men turned toward the bench where the two women were seated and continued their conversation.

"What are we going to do?" McKenzie whispered.

"What do you mean?" Elizabeth whispered back.

"Well, this man clearly is a crook. I can't let my dad do business with him! And we certainly don't want him coming to your house!"

"What makes you think he's a crook?" Elizabeth asked, though she had the same idea about the man.

"Just look at him! He's way too handsome to be honest," McKenzie whispered frantically. "Look at that smile. He's just oozing with charm. That can't be real."

The girls stared at the tall, good-looking cowboy who looked like he had just ridden into town straight from a movie set. At that moment, the man turned and saw them looking at him. He winked!

A Peek into the Past

Elizabeth and McKenzie looked at one another in shock, but remained quiet. They weren't sure what to make of this development.

Mrs. Anderson smiled. "It's settled then. You can come over with the Phillips family. We'll see you all around seven?"

The adults agreed to the time, and Elizabeth's mother stood to leave. "I'd better get going, so I can prepare our feast! Elizabeth, are you coming home with me, or would you like to stay awhile longer?"

"Oh, I'll stay here if that's okay. McKenzie and I really need to talk to Megan."

Mrs. Anderson looked at her. "You're not distracting Megan from her work, are you? I wouldn't want her to get in trouble."

"No, ma'am. That's why we're waiting here until she gets off."

"Well, be sure to invite Megan and her mother for dinner," Mrs. Anderson said. She took James by the hand and bid the group goodbye.

The two girls walked casually around the stables, pretending to look at horses.

"What should we do?" asked McKenzie.

"I think we should stay close, and see what happens," said Elizabeth.

"But now he's coming to your house! He'll know where you live!" McKenzie continued.

"So?" Elizabeth said.

"So, I just don't like the idea of the man we're trying to investigate getting so close to you and your family," McKenzie told her.

"Look," Elizabeth said. "We don't have any reason to believe he's dangerous. We only think he knows something about the gemstones. I think we should just play dumb, and see if he brings up the marbles."

After a moment, McKenzie nodded. "Okay. But this feels strange to me."

The two girls stopped a few steps from the stall where the cowboy and McKenzie's dad were talking horse talk.

"McKenzie, here, is a horse expert in her own right," her dad said, inviting the girls into the conversation.

McKenzie blushed and smiled. "I try," she said modestly.

"She'll take over the ranch for me one day, if she wants," her dad smiled proudly at her. "She could probably do it right now."

The cowboy smiled. "It's always good to have someone around who knows their business," he said. Then, he reached out and shook Mr. Phillips's hand and tipped his hat to the girls. "I have some other business I need to tend to, but I'll look forward to seeing you all at dinner," he said. And with that, his long, lanky legs carried him across the stables, around the corner, and out of sight.

•—•—•

The girls spent the next couple of hours sitting by the pool and looking at the different horses. Elizabeth enjoyed seeing the Big Texan from a tourist's point of view. She had lived in Amarillo all her life and had never stayed at the motel. It was fun.

At 4:00 p.m., they went to the motel lobby. McKenzie had noticed a computer available to the motel guests. They wanted to check their email and see if there were any more tips from the other Camp Club Girls. After waiting for two other people, they signed on.

Sure enough, there was a message from Kate.

Biscuit was sniffing around in the car today, and he found my reader pen! I've been looking all over for that thing. But it got me thinking. . .I wonder if Emily Marie hid the marbles in her car somewhere. What happened to her car after she died?

"That's a good question. Let's go ask Megan. If she doesn't know, maybe Jean Louise will know something," suggested Elizabeth.

They headed to the restaurant. Megan wasn't scheduled to get off until 4:30, but they were hoping to eat their forgotten pie while they waited. Jean Louise met them at the door.

"Well, well. If it isn't Sherlock Holmes and Watson," she said with a smile. "Did you track down the cowboy?"

The girls laughed. "Actually, he found us," Elizabeth told her. "It's been an interesting afternoon."

Jean Louise seated them, then brought their pie, all nestled in white Styrofoam containers. "Here ya go," she said. The restaurant was busy, and she didn't stay to chat.

Twenty minutes later, Megan joined them at the booth. "Tell me everything," she said.

"We will. But first, do you have any idea what happened to your grandmother's car after she died?"

Megan thought for a moment. "No, but my Uncle Jack will know. He's a mechanic, and Mom says he's always been interested in cars."

"Let's go see him right now!" exclaimed McKenzie.

"That will be hard. He lives in Houston," Megan said. "But I can call him."

The girls leaned their heads together, whispering and planning for the next half hour.

•—•—•

That evening, Elizabeth's backyard was filled with laughter and the scent of grilling hamburgers. James and Evan ran around playing cowboys and Indians, and Mr. Jacobs pretended to get shot in the crossfire. The man seemed to enjoy children, and moved back and forth between playing with the boys and helping Mr. Anderson flip burgers.

Elizabeth was inside filling red plastic cups with iced tea. She had left McKenzie sitting near the men in case anything was said about the jewels. She looked out the window at her friend, who looked bored. The last bit of conversation Elizabeth had heard was about football.

"You did invite Megan and her mom, didn't you?" Mrs. Anderson asked Elizabeth.

"Yes, ma'am. Megan said her mom gets home tonight around seven thirty, so they'll be a little late."

Mrs. Anderson looked out the side window toward the Smiths' house. "I sure wish she didn't have to work so hard. I wish we could do something more for them," she said.

"We're actually working on that," said Elizabeth without thinking.

"What do you mean?" her mother asked.

Catching herself, Elizabeth thought quickly. "Oh, just that Megan is working now, earning some extra money. She also makes straight A's in school, and in a few years she'll probably get a full scholarship to some college."

Mrs. Anderson ran a gentle hand across Elizabeth's hair. "That's nice, dear." Then, the woman held open the screen door with her backside, and the two joined the party, delivering iced tea to their guests.

A short time later, Megan arrived with her mother. When Mrs. Smith was introduced to Mr. Jacobs, the cowboy stood and took her hand. "It's a pleasure to meet you, Ruby. You add a whole new loveliness to your name," he said.

Mrs. Smith smiled and blushed, and the three girls looked at one another in alarm. What did that cowboy think he was doing? Did he know about the jewels and Megan's mother?

They continued to watch the interaction between Ruby and Mr. Jacobs throughout the evening. Those two didn't talk much, but their eyes kept wandering to each other. Finally, Megan whispered, "We need to have an emergency meeting in your room. Now!"

The three girls excused themselves. As soon as Elizabeth's door was closed, Megan burst into a chain of broken sentences that showed her anxiety, but didn't really make much sense.

"What in the—who does he think—and my mother! I've never seen her—she used to flirt with my dad but—of all people! I've wanted her to start dating—but not like this! Not with that no good, sweet-talkin', connivin', manipulatin' cowboy!"

"Whoa, calm down, Megs." Elizabeth put her arm around her friend. "She's not dating anyone. Sure, there were some sparks out there. But let's face it. She'll probably never see him again after tonight. Unless. . ."

"Unless what?" Megan and McKenzie asked in unison.

Elizabeth paused. If the looks on their faces were any indication, her two friends were thinking exactly what she was thinking. "Unless he knows the jewels were given to your grandmother. Do you think he's traced them to your mother somehow?"

"How could he? My mother didn't know about them until the other day. And she doesn't even care about them."

"She may not care about them, but he doesn't know that," said McKenzie.

The three girls moved Elizabeth's pink ruffled curtains to the side and peered at the group in the backyard. Cowboy had moved his lawn chair closer to Megan's mother, and the two looked engrossed in conversation.

"We'd better get out there. Now!" exclaimed Megan.

"Not just yet," McKenzie interrupted. "First, tell us if you had a chance to call your uncle."

Megan kept peering out the window as she answered. "Oh yeah. I called him this afternoon. He doesn't know anything about any marbles. He said the car stayed impounded for a couple of years while they investigated the accident. After that, he took it apart and sold it piece by piece. They needed the money. But if there were any marbles hidden in the car, he would have found them."

McKenzie let out a disappointed sigh. "I was just sure that's where they were."

The sound of Mrs. Smith's laughter floated through the window, and Megan said, "That does it. I've gotta get that cowboy away from my mother."

"Yep. And we'd better get crackin' on this mystery, before your mother really gets hurt," said Elizabeth.

•—•—•

The cookout ended around 10:30, but had seemed much longer. The girls did all they could to interrupt the conversations between Megan's mom and the cowboy, but the man was not easily deterred. This gave the three sleuths even more reason to think he was up to something shady.

They spent the night in Elizabeth's room and were awakened early the next morning with the sounds of humming from Megan's driveway. Megan sat up in her sleeping bag and peered out the window to see her mother leaving for work.

"My mother hasn't sounded like that in a long time," she said.

Elizabeth rolled over and propped her head on her elbow. "She really misses your dad, doesn't she?"

"Yeah," Megan answered softly. "So do I."

They were interrupted by James. "Who wants breakfast?" he asked, opening the door without knocking.

Elizabeth squealed, "Shut the door! James, you know you're not allowed in here without permission!"

He backed out and shut the door. "Sorry, Beth. But Mama wants to know who wants breakfast."

"I do," called all three girls in unison.

"Little brothers. . . ," muttered Elizabeth, and her friends chuckled. The three girls dressed quickly and dashed to the kitchen, where Mrs. Anderson had left toaster pastries, fruit, orange juice, and milk. James had already eaten, so they had the kitchen to themselves.

"We're supposed to meet Jean Louise at the restaurant at nine forty-five so she can drive us to her mother's house. Did you check with your mom, Elizabeth?" asked Megan.

"Mom," called Elizabeth around a mouthful of toaster pastry.

Mrs. Anderson popped her head around the corner from the laundry room. "Don't talk with your mouth full, dear."

Elizabeth swallowed her food and wiped her mouth with her napkin. "Sorry. May I please go with Jean Louise this morning to meet her mother? Megan's coming too, and McKenzie is going to ask her parents."

Mrs. Anderson smiled. "I think that sounds lovely. I'm glad to hear you girls are doing something constructive with your time. It reminds me of James 1:27."

Megan and McKenzie looked at Elizabeth after Mrs. Anderson went back to her laundry. "James 1:27?" Megan asked.

" 'Religion that God our Father accepts as pure and faultless is this: to look after orphans and widows in their distress and to keep oneself from being polluted by the world,' " Elizabeth quoted.

The other two listened in stunned silence. "How do you do that?" asked McKenzie. "I know a lot of Bible verses, but you're like a walking encyclopedia!"

Elizabeth smiled. "I don't know. I've just heard them all my life."

"Well, we're not exactly going to see this woman because she's in distress," said Megan. "So I'm not sure this visit will count."

"Maybe not, but I'll bet she'll enjoy our visit anyway! Hopefully, we'll get some information we can use," replied Elizabeth. "We've got to find those jewels before the cowboy does."

A short time later, having gained permission from McKenzie's parents, the three girls slid into Jean Louise's red convertible sports car.

"This is a cool car!" McKenzie exclaimed.

"Thank you," said the waitress.

The girls enjoyed the ride, laughing as their hair—blond, brunette, and auburn—flapped in the wind.

They arrived at Shady Acres Retirement Community a short time later, and Jean Louise led them through the well-kept apartment complex. She knocked and then used her key to open the door. "Mama!" she called. "We're here. I brought the girls I told you about."

A small, white-haired woman appeared, using a walker. Her eyes were bright, and she wore a cheerful smile. "Come in, come in!" she said. "I've been looking forward to this."

They entered the small, well-kept apartment, and smelled something delicious. Jean Louise wasted no time in introducing the girls, one by one. "And this, ladies, is my mother, Mrs. Wilson."

"It's a pleasure to meet you, Mrs. Wilson," the girls said politely.

"Sit down," she gestured, and moved slowly to stand in front of Megan. "Except you. I want you to stand here and let me look at you."

Megan smiled a bit uncomfortably while the woman looked her over, head to toe. Then, she reached out a gentle hand and touched Megan's hair, then her face. "Such a beautiful girl. You're the spitting image of Emily Marie."

McKenzie looked questioningly at Elizabeth.

"Megan's grandmother," Elizabeth whispered, and the redhead nodded.

"Your grandmother would have been so proud of you," the woman continued. "She was my best friend, you know. A real jewel. Your mother and your uncle Jack were her world. She would have loved watching you grow up."

Then, she gestured for Megan to sit down before taking a seat herself. She turned to her daughter. "Jean Louise, I made some lemon bars for these girls, and there is lemonade in the refrigerator. Would you get them, please?"

"Yes, ma'am." The woman moved swiftly to obey her elderly mother.

"I hope you didn't go to any trouble, Mrs. Wilson," Elizabeth said.

The woman responded by waving her hand in the air, as if any such talk was nonsense. Elizabeth liked this woman.

"I understand you have some questions for me," she said, keeping her eyes on Megan.

"Yes, ma'am," Megan said. "Jean Louise told us about some marbles, but I don't know anything about them, and neither does my mother."

The woman smiled. "Oh, the marbles. I remember that day so well. Emily Marie came walking into the break room at the restaurant, white as a sheet. She closed the door, and it was just the two of us. Then, she pulled out a little white cloth sack, and poured out the contents on the table in front of me. They were marbles, and they were the prettiest things I had ever seen."

She paused, as if remembering, then continued. " 'They're real,' she told me.

" 'Real marbles?' I asked. I was confused. Of course they were real marbles.

" 'Real gemstones,' she said, and plopped down in front of me.

'Foster gave them to me.'

"Now, Foster was the tall, handsome cowboy who had taken a shine to Emily Marie. He wasn't from around here, but he came through town a lot on business. He began to have more and more business in Amarillo, but no one was fooled. He came to town to see your grandma. She was a beautiful woman." Mrs. Wilson pushed her hair back from her face.

"I was speechless. I had never seen anything like the marbles in front of me. I picked up the emerald and held it up to the light. Then, we both started giggling like school girls."

Elizabeth smiled at the image.

The woman paused as Jean Louise brought in the refreshments and placed them on the coffee table. "Keep going, Mama. Don't stop on my account," Jean Louise said.

The woman leaned back in her chair with a smile. "After our giggles were under control, I held up the ruby. 'Won't this make a nice gift for your little Ruby, one day?' I asked her.

"She looked at me like I'd gone crazy. 'I can't keep them!' she said.

" 'Why in the world not?' I asked her.

" 'It's too much. It would be different if Foster and I were engaged, but we're not.'

" 'Oh, you will be,' I told her. 'I've seen the way he looks at you. And I've seen the way you look at him. You'll be married before the year is out.'

"When I said that, Emily blushed four shades of red. But she was smiling. 'Maybe so,' she said.

" 'Besides,' I told her. 'You can't give them back. He'll think you're rejecting him.'

"She sat quietly, looking at those jewels long after my break was over. I covered for her for a while. I knew she needed some time to think. Finally, she joined me back on the floor, waiting tables like nothing had happened."

"What happened to Foster? Was he still there?" Elizabeth asked.

"No, I don't know where he had disappeared to. But he was back later that evening. And before the night was over, Emily Marie was the happiest woman alive."

The Journals

The girls leaned forward, drinking in every word the elderly woman spoke. It seemed more like the makings of a romance movie than a real story.

The woman paused, and looked directly at Megan. "At closing time, Foster showed up again, wanting to talk to Emily Marie. They sat in one of the booths while I cleaned up. I tried to give them privacy and turned on the jukebox to a slow country song. But even over the music, I could hear bits and pieces of the conversation.

" 'Emily Marie, you must know how I feel about you. You must see it my eyes,' he told her. The whole thing was quite romantic. 'I want to spend the rest of my life with you. I'm going to sell my ranch in Colorado, and move down here, and we can get married. That is, if you'll have me,' he said.

"There she was, tears streaming down her cheeks. 'But Foster, I have my two kids to think about,' she said.

" 'I know I haven't met Ruby and Jack yet, but I promise I'll love them like my very own. I know things have been hard on you since your husband died. Let me rescue you,' he begged.

"Well, at that point I left the room. I figured the cleanup could wait. Emily Marie and I were best friends, and I had watched her struggle to make ends meet since Paul died. It looked to be a fairy-tale ending for her," Mrs. Wilson said as she leaned back in her chair.

The room was silent, except for the tick-ticking of the old grandfather clock in the corner. Finally, Megan broke the silence. "It sounds like my mom and my grandma had a lot in common. . . ."

Elizabeth reached over and squeezed her friend's hand.

"So what happened next?" Elizabeth asked.

Mrs. Wilson frowned. "The next few days are hard to talk about. I prefer to remember my friend in that moment, her face shining with joy."

The three girls remained silent. They didn't want to push the woman or be disrespectful, but they needed more information.

Jean Louise rescued them. "Mama, Megan wants to find out what happened to the marbles. Is there any more you can tell her?"

The woman looked at Megan again and smiled, a sad kind of smile. Then, she pulled herself up with her walker and started toward her bedroom. Jean Louise helped her mother, leaving the three girls alone in the living room.

"Why did she leave like that?" McKenzie whispered.

"I don't know, but it looks like she's our only hope for more information. We've got to find out what happened next," whispered Elizabeth.

Megan remained quiet, and Elizabeth put her arm around her friend. "This is hard for you, isn't it?" she asked.

"Not really. I mean, I never knew my grandmother. It's just strange that she and my mother were both young widows."

The girls heard the walker approaching and ended their whispered conversation. Jean Louise followed her mother, carrying several old notebooks. She handed them to Megan.

Mrs. Wilson was seated once again and took a moment to get settled. "These are my journals from that time. The whole story should be there, from the time Foster began coming to the restaurant, until. . ."

Megan looked at the books. It seemed she had just been handed her own treasure.

"You take them home and read them," the woman told her. "I hope they'll help you find what you're looking for."

Megan placed the journals on the coffee table in front of her, then walked to Mrs. Wilson's chair. She leaned over and hugged the woman. "Thank you so much," she said.

The old woman patted her on the shoulder, then wiped a tear from her wrinkled cheek. "You're welcome, my dear. You are more than welcome."

•—•—•

Back at the Big Texan, Megan had to report for work. "Here," she told Elizabeth, handing her the journals. "We can't afford to waste any time. Y'all start reading through these and see what you can find."

Elizabeth and McKenzie spent the better part of the morning by the Texas-shaped pool, reading through the yellowed pages and looking for clues. Much of what they found was insignificant—Mrs. Wilson's thoughts about her husband, her children, her job, even the price of groceries. Finally, McKenzie sat up in her lounge chair and said, "I found it! Listen to this: 'A man has been visiting the restaurant regularly and is obviously smitten with Emily Marie. He seems like a kind man. I hope she gives him a chance; she's been so sad since Paul died.' "

Elizabeth read over her friend's shoulder. "Jackpot!" she cried. "Now we have our starting point. Let's keep reading."

McKenzie wiped the sweat from her brow. "Okay," she said, "but can we continue this in the restaurant? I'm burning up out here, and I'm starving!"

"Me too," agreed Elizabeth.

They gathered the journals and headed toward the restaurant. Passing the stables, they noticed a regal looking horse across the paddock. "Wow, what a beauty," said McKenzie. "Let's get a closer look."

They were about halfway there when they heard a man's voice. It was Mr. Jacobs, leaning against the stable and talking on his cell phone. The girls shrank into the shadows of one of the stalls and remained silent.

"Yes, that's right," he said. "There were twelve marbles in a variety of gemstones. I tracked them to Amarillo, but it's been thirty years since anyone has seen or heard of them. They just vanished."

Jacobs began pacing in agitation. "I don't know how a set of priceless gemstone marbles can simply disappear. Surely somebody has to know something about them."

The man paused again, and then said, "I've got to find those marbles. I'm tired of all this rodeo business, never spending more than a week in the same place. I'm ready to settle down and live the good life, and those marbles will help me do it."

More silence, and then he said, "Okay. Let me know what you find out. I'll keep asking questions here." The man shut his cell phone and strode out of the stables and toward the hotel rooms.

"Whoa," said McKenzie. "That proves he's a crook."

"Not necessarily. But it does sound suspicious," said Elizabeth. "One thing is for sure. We're running out of time. We've got to locate those marbles before he does."

•—•—•

The girls kept their noses buried in the journals for the rest of the afternoon. The entries about Emily Marie were sporadic, interspersed with entries about housework and life as a waitress. It was like a treasure hunt—wading through the boring stuff to find the jewels.

Elizabeth liked the way Mrs. Wilson ended each journal entry with a one-sentence prayer. She felt she knew the old woman's heart better from those sentence prayers than from the actual journal entries.

Finally, after hours of searching, she found the following entry:

It seems that Foster, humble as he is, is very wealthy.

Tonight he gave Emily Marie a bag of marbles. But these aren't just any marbles, they're priceless gemstones!

The paperwork is even there—they're in her name.

She wasn't sure if she should keep such a gift, and fretted all evening. But after the restaurant closed, he showed up again and asked her to marry him!

Of course she accepted. But they won't make their plans known until he gets to know her children. He is a wonderful man, and I know he will be a good father to Ruby and Jack.

He's leaving town tonight. He told her to keep the marbles in a safe place, and he'll help her set up a safe-deposit box for them when he returns. She'll worry herself to death, carrying around something so priceless.

We talked about hiding them in the restaurant, but for tonight, she took them home. I'll bet she looks at them all night long.

Dear Father, please bless Emily Marie and her children with Your goodness. Amen.

"That's it! They're hidden in the restaurant!" shouted McKenzie.

Elizabeth shut the book and stood to stretch. Her eyes were tired from reading. "Maybe. Just like Alex suggested. But she could have gone ahead and put them in the bank too. Why don't we head over and tell Megan what we've found. Maybe she can start snooping around."

"Yeah, and maybe we can get some more of that pie!" McKenzie added.

•—•—•

Later that night, the group sat in the stands at the Greater Amarillo Livestock Show and Rodeo. Mr. Jacobs had generously given them his entire section of box seats. "I'd love to have someone cheering for me," he'd said with a smile. His eyes had rested on Megan's mom.

James and Evan sat two rows in front of the girls, exclaiming over the horses, and making their own plans to be cowboys someday. Elizabeth was glad that, for now, her brother had a distraction.

Ruby Smith sat with the ladies making small talk, and the two dads seemed absorbed in a conversation about the Old Testament book of Isaiah. The three girls, satisfied they wouldn't be overheard, huddled together.

"So, did you find anything?" whispered McKenzie.

"No," answered Megan. "I need more information. I have no idea where to begin. I did examine the floor boards in the kitchen area, but I couldn't find any loose ones. I'm just not good at this detective business like the two of you are."

Elizabeth patted her friend on the knee. "You'll be fine. We just need to find more clues. We're not even sure they're at the restaurant. She might have put them in the bank or something. Do you think you can ask your mom if your grandma left any accounts open?"

"I've never heard her talk about any accounts. It seems that anything like that would have been closed out long ago. But I'll ask Mom tonight," Megan said.

"Ask Mom what?" Ruby Smith asked. The girls were surprised to find that she'd moved down and was now sitting directly behind them. Her hair was fixed in a new way, and she was wearing makeup.

"You look pretty tonight, Mom," Megan said. Mrs. Smith smiled.

"What did you want to ask me?" the woman persisted.

Megan smiled sheepishly. "You remember those jewels I talked to you about? We're still trying to find them."

Surprisingly, Mrs. Smith laughed. "Well, I'm afraid you're going on a wild-goose chase. But go ahead, ask me anything."

"Did Grandma leave any bank accounts open?" Megan asked. "We're wondering if she might not have stored the marbles in an account somewhere."

"Oh, you mean like in a safe-deposit box?" Mrs. Smith responded.

Elizabeth jumped in. "Exactly! Did your mother leave behind any kind of safe-deposit box?"

Mrs. Smith shook her head. "Not that I know of. But come to think of it, my grandmother did mention a small checking account. She never touched it. She said she wanted to leave it for me and Jack someday. It's still there."

"Bingo!" McKenzie shouted with excitement. "We've found the—"

Elizabeth clapped a hand over her friend's mouth. "Let's not announce it to the whole world," she said.

"Oh yeah, sorry!" McKenzie whispered. "I tend to get a little excited."

The others chuckled good-naturedly. "It's okay," said Megan. "It is pretty exciting."

Mrs. Smith continued, "I have some business at the bank tomorrow anyway. I'll ask about the checking account. And since this is official mystery business, would you girls like to come with me? I'll take you all for ice cream afterwards."

The girls nodded, and Mrs. Smith returned to sit with the ladies.

Megan looked a little stunned, and Elizabeth asked, "What's wrong?"

"Who was that woman?" she asked.

Elizabeth turned and looked at Megan's mom, not sure how to respond to the question.

"My mom is fixing her hair, wearing makeup, coming to the rodeo... she's *smiling*! What has gotten into her?"

Elizabeth's and McKenzie's eyes swung to the handsome cowboy, sitting tall on a horse and getting ready to enter the arena.

No one answered Megan's question, but the looks of concern stayed on their faces for the rest of the evening.

•—•—•

The next morning, Elizabeth and McKenzie stared gloomily out the window of the Phillips' motel room. Rain poured down outside.

"I guess we won't do much sightseeing today," said McKenzie.

Elizabeth leaned over and lifted the stack of journals from the bedside table. "Well, as long as we're stuck here, we might as well read some more. Megan has to be at work at ten a.m., but she was going to come early and do some more snooping," she said, looking at her watch.

"Not snooping—*investigating*," McKenzie corrected her friend.

Elizabeth chuckled. "Same thing," she said. "But *investigating* does sound more official, doesn't it?"

The girls settled in, sharing the same journal page, skimming for more clues. Before long, they found what they were looking for.

Emily Marie might go ahead and put the jewels in a safe-deposit box. She thought about doing it today, but it was late when she got off work, and the banks were already closed. Carrying around something so valuable is making her as nervous as a cat in a room full of rockers.

She's anxious to put them in a safe place.

She was headed to work a party at the Cadillac Ranch

this evening. She said the pay is good and the tips are even better. She tried to get me to go with her, but I was just too tired tonight. I told her I'd go with her next time.

McKenzie shut the book and hopped from the bed. "There you have it. She deposited the jewels. What time is Megan's mom taking us to the bank today?"

"I think at three thirty, when Megan gets off work. Why don't we walk to the restaurant and see if she's there yet?"

The two sleuths quickly headed toward the Big Texan Steak Ranch, staying close to the buildings to keep from getting wet. They rushed through the swinging saloon-style doors, straight into a plaid cowboy shirt. Leaning their necks back, they looked up, up, up to see the owner of the shirt. It was Mr. Jacobs.

"Good mornin', ladies," he said, and tipped his big white cowboy hat. True to form, he winked at them before he strode out the door.

The girls didn't know whether to be angry or giggle. "I wish he didn't look so much like a movie star," McKenzie said.

"Why?" Elizabeth asked.

"Because it would be a lot easier not to like him," she replied seriously.

Just then, Jean Louise appeared. "What is it with you early birds this morning?" she asked. "Megan's already been here for twenty minutes, cleaning every nook and cranny of the supply room. She's not even clocked in yet."

The two girls looked at each other and then at the red-haired waitress. "Um, could we, uh. . ." Elizabeth stammered.

"Go on back," she said, pointing the way. "But if the manager catches you, she may put you to work."

The girls dashed through the kitchen area to the dark storage room. They pushed open the door, and Megan gasped.

"You scared me!" she whispered, looking guilty. "Quick, close the door!"

The Costumes

The girls entered the small room and shut the door behind them. Megan was on her knees, surrounded by cans of tomato paste. She held a dustrag in her hand and appeared to be cleaning the bottom shelf.

"Look at this," she said.

The girls leaned forward, but the dim lighting made it difficult to see. "Isn't there a better light in here?" Elizabeth asked.

"One of the bulbs is burned out," Megan told her. "But you can still see if you look close enough."

McKenzie got down on her knees and examined the wall where Megan was cleaning. Elizabeth bent low and looked over her shoulder. Sure enough, there was a square break in the paneling, just large enough for a small teenage girl to crawl through.

"Do you think it's a secret passageway?" McKenzie asked.

"I don't know what it is. I haven't been able to get it open. There are a couple of screws, but I need a screwdriver. Do you think the marbles could be hidden here?"

"That's what we were coming to talk to you about," Elizabeth told Megan. "We read in the journal that Emily Marie was planning to put the marbles in a safe-deposit box at the bank. We may be wasting our time here."

Megan looked at Elizabeth, then McKenzie, her mouth hanging open. "You mean I've been breaking my back in here for nothing?" she said.

McKenzie chuckled. "Well, look on the bright side. Just think how impressed your boss will be that you spent your free time cleaning out the supply room."

The three girls returned the cans to the lower shelf and left the small room.

"It's time for me to clock in," said Megan, looking at her watch. "I'll see you both this afternoon. Maybe we'll actually find the marbles!"

Elizabeth and McKenzie left the kitchen and spotted the Phillips family at a corner table in the restaurant. "Come on," McKenzie said. "Let's join them. I'm starved!"

"Me too," agreed Elizabeth.

Before long they were each devouring a tall stack of pancakes, drenched in syrup and covered with whipped cream. Outside the window, the sun peeked through the clouds. The rain had stopped.

As they ate, Mr. and Mrs. Phillips asked, "So, what do you want to do today?"

The girls both shrugged their shoulders and kept eating. They were having fun, as long as they were together.

"I'd like to go shopping," said Mrs. Phillips. "I saw some little boutiques a few blocks over."

Evan groaned, and Mr. Phillips shifted in his seat. "Why don't you girls go shopping, and Evan and I will hang out here with the horses and the cowboys?" the man suggested.

The girls nodded, and before long, the three females headed toward Amarillo's shopping district.

•—•—•

In and out of shops they went, looking at Texas-shaped handbags encrusted with rhinestones, flashy cowgirl boots and hats, and western wear in all colors and sizes. Before they knew it, two hours had passed.

They were on their way back to the motel when McKenzie spotted a fun-looking thrift shop. "Oh, I want to see what they have in there, Mom," she said.

"I want to run across the street to the post office and get some stamps," Mrs. Phillips said, waving a handful of postcards. "Why don't you two go over there, and I'll meet you after I mail these."

The girls entered the old store and were thrilled at the endless racks of vintage clothing, hats, and scarves. McKenzie wasted no time trying on a dark pair of sunglasses, an oversize hat, and a feather boa.

Elizabeth laughed at her friend's outfit and then spotted a large cardboard box filled with wigs. Within moments, she was a brunette with long, messy curls.

The girls giggled as they tried on an array of wigs, scarves, and jewelry. They were completely unrecognizable when the bell over the door jangled. The two looked toward the entrance expecting to find Mrs.

Phillips. Instead, Mark Jacobs walked toward them, a serious look on his face.

They froze. What in the world could a cowboy like Mr. Jacobs want in a girlie thrift shop like this? The man nodded at the girls, but kept walking. He didn't recognize them!

He approached the counter and asked to speak to the shop's owner. The clerk went to the back of the store and returned with an elegant, gray-haired woman.

"How may I help you?" she asked.

The cowboy introduced himself, then asked, "How long have you owned this shop?"

"Oh, I inherited this business from my grandparents. This little shop has been in our family since it opened, over forty years ago," she told him.

"I'm trying to track down a rare set of marbles," he said. "The last record I can find of them is here in Amarillo, about thirty years ago. I heard they were given to a poor waitress. I'm wondering if she sold them."

Elizabeth and McKenzie moved a little closer to the counter. They pretended to be looking at some jewelry, and the two adults paid no attention to them.

"Marbles? I don't recall any unusual marbles. Every now and then we've bought little toys like that, but we sell them pretty quickly. Usually to a young mother who is in here shopping," she told him.

"Oh, these marbles weren't toys. I'm sure the woman wouldn't have sold them cheaply. They were very valuable," he told her.

The woman thought a moment, wrinkling her brow in concentration. "No, I'm sorry. I don't recall anything like that."

Mr. Jacobs looked disappointed. He tipped his hat to the woman, thanked her, and headed out the door.

The girls stared after him, mouths hanging open, when the clerk startled them. "Can I help you find something?"

Elizabeth and McKenzie began taking off their costumes and returning them to the proper places. "Oh, no thank you. We were just having a little fun. This is a great shop you have," Elizabeth told her.

The bell jangled again as Mrs. Phillips walked through the door.

"Are you ready, girls?" she asked.

"Yes, ma'am," they called, and left the store. They wanted to discuss the scene they'd just witnessed, but that conversation would have to wait.

•—•—•

Back at the motel, Elizabeth and McKenzie exchanged frustrated looks. They hadn't found a moment of privacy since they were at the shop. First they had stopped at Dairy Queen for hamburgers. Then Mrs. Phillips had asked the girls to entertain Evan for a while.

They were about to meet Megan when the phone rang. "It's for you, Elizabeth," said Mr. Phillips. It was her mom.

"Hi, baby. Are you having fun?" Mrs. Anderson asked.

"Yes, ma'am. We've been busy today."

"That's good. Listen, I know Ruby is taking you to the bank, and then for ice cream. After that, why don't you swing back by the hotel and pick up Evan? I've already talked to the Phillipses about this. You all can spend the evening over here so McKenzie's parents can have a date."

Elizabeth groaned inwardly, but said only, "Yes, ma'am." Evan was a nice kid, but two little boys could put a real wrench in their sleuthing plans. After hanging up, she shared the news with McKenzie, who did groan. Loudly.

Mr. and Mrs. Phillips looked at the girls and chuckled.

With a wave, the two girls finally escaped to the restaurant. When the door shut behind them, they began their frantic whispers.

"Can you believe that man? Calling Megan's grandmother a 'poor waitress,' like she was some charity case. And who does he think he is, anyway? It's none of his business!" McKenzie said.

"Well, technically, she was a poor waitress. But we know the rest of the story, and he doesn't. I wonder how he knows that much, though," Elizabeth responded. The sun had disappeared behind some more gray clouds, and the storm threatened to return.

Rounding the corner, they found Megan and her mom waiting for them. Mrs. Smith was dressed in her maid's uniform. Her hair was coming out of its clip, and she wore no makeup. Still, Elizabeth thought she looked more like a runway model than a maid.

"Hop in, everyone. The quicker we get to the bank, the quicker we can hit the Marble Slab," said the woman, referring to the popular ice cream shop.

All three girls climbed into the backseat of the old sedan, and Ruby Smith laughed. "I feel like a chauffeur," she told them.

On the way to the bank, McKenzie and Elizabeth whispered to Megan, telling her about the event in the thrift shop.

They were interrupted by Mrs. Smith. "Am I supposed to be hearing this?" she asked. "Because I can hear almost every word you are saying. Something about a tall cowboy in a girlie thrift store? That must have been a funny sight."

The girls laughed nervously but stopped talking. They didn't want Mrs. Smith to know about Mr. Jacobs. Not yet, anyway.

They pulled into the bank parking lot, slid out of the car, and went inside the old building. "You all wait here while I make my deposits," Mrs. Smith told them, gesturing to a long bench. "After that, I have an appointment with Mr. Sanders, the bank's vice president. Megan, you can come with me and tell him what you've heard."

The girls took a seat and waited as Mrs. Smith approached the teller. A few minutes later, she joined the girls on the bench.

Before long, a balding man approached. "Hello, Ruby," he said. "This is a lovely group you have with you."

Ruby smiled and introduced the girls, and then she and Megan entered the office to the left of the bench. The door was pushed shut, but it bounced open just a crack.

Elizabeth and McKenzie scooted closer to the door, hoping to hear the conversation. They heard bits and pieces and knew Megan would fill them in on the details later. Still, they strained to catch the words being spoken.

Mrs. Smith's voice was soft and sweet. They heard, ". . .my mother. . . bank account. . .curious. . ."

Then the banker's voice, "Yes. . .did leave. . .lovely woman. . .still open. . .interest. . ."

They heard Mrs. Smith's voice again, "Megan. . .rumors. . . safe-deposit box. . ."

Megan added something to the conversation, but the girls couldn't make out the words. Didn't she know to speak up when her friends were eavesdropping?

There was a shuffling of some papers, then a faint noise. Was he typing on a computer?

The banker's voice came back. "No. . .record. . .safe-deposit. . . nothing. . ."

There was a scooting of chairs, and the two girls on the bench slid to their original positions. The door opened, and Mr. Sanders shook Mrs. Smith's hand. "I'm sorry I couldn't help you more," he said. "Good day, ladies."

Megan looked disappointed, and Mrs. Smith patted her on the

back. "It would have been nice to have found those mysterious marbles. But we've done fine without them, haven't we? We don't need a hidden treasure. I have all the treasure I need in you, sweet girl."

Megan smiled at her mother and gave her a hug. But Elizabeth knew this wasn't the end of the search. The group headed out the door. The mystery would have to wait; it was time for ice cream.

•—•—•

Back at Elizabeth's house, the girls shut the door to her bedroom. The young detectives were ready to talk seriously.

"Tell me again what happened at the thrift shop," Megan said.

Elizabeth and McKenzie took turns telling the story, and Megan laughed out loud when she heard about the costumes. "I wish I had been there!" she said. "I can just see you two, all decked out in sunglasses and wigs. You must have looked ridiculous!"

"Actually, we looked pretty good," said Elizabeth.

McKenzie giggled. "Um, Elizabeth, I hate to tell you this, but that black wig did not look good on you! You definitely can't pull it off like Hannah Montana can. I think you need to stay a blond," she said.

Elizabeth laughed. "Come to think of it, your freckles did look rather out of place with that yellow wig. And those tiny little sunglasses!"

"Well you looked like a demented movie star with those huge things you were wearing!"

All three girls were on the floor now, laughing at the silliness of it all.

Before they could get any further in the story, they heard a thud on Elizabeth's door. Then another, and another. Elizabeth got up and opened her door, only to have a miniature car crash into her ankle. "Ouch!" she cried.

James and Evan sat on the floor at the end of the hallway, with Matchbox cars lined up in front of them. "Sorry, Beth. We're racing," said James.

Elizabeth sighed a heavy sigh. "Why can't you do that in your bedroom?" she asked her brother.

"Because there's not enough space," he told her matter-of-factly. She stepped to his doorway and saw what he meant. Toys were scattered across every inch of the floor.

"You'd better clean up that mess before Mom sees," she told him.

James looked crestfallen. "But that will take too long," he said. "I want to race with Evan."

Elizabeth felt a wave of compassion for her little brother. He really was a good kid, even if he was annoying at times. "I'll tell you what. You and Evan pick up your toys, and then we'll sit with you in the driveway so you can race out there."

James looked at his sister as if she were his hero. He wasn't allowed in the front yard without supervision, but he loved to race his cars up and down the long driveway.

Just then, a loud clap of thunder startled them all. James's face fell, and he said, "We can't. It's raining."

Sure enough, it looked like the heavens had opened up. Lightning flashed, rain poured in heavy sheets, and water gushed off the sidewalks and into the gutters.

Another loud crash of thunder was followed by a pop, and everything went black.

The girls squealed and huddled together.

James and Evan stayed seated at the end of the hallway. Through the dark, they heard Evan's voice saying, "This is so cool!"

Then James said, "Hey, let's race cars in the dark!"

A moment later, Elizabeth yelped in pain. Another flash of lightning revealed that a Hot Wheels car had crashed into her ankle. Again. "James, cut that out!"

"Sorry, Beth," he said. She shut her door, leaving the boys in the black hallway.

The three girls gathered at the window to watch the show. Thunder clapped. A fierce wind forced the trees to sway into unnatural positions. Somewhere in the distance a car alarm went off. The whole scene was scary and fascinating.

Suddenly, a pair of headlights pulled into Megan's driveway, behind her mom's car. They shut off, and all was black again.

"I wonder who that could be," Megan said.

They peered through the darkness, trying to catch a glimpse of the unknown guest. A flash of lightning revealed a tall dark figure in a cowboy hat, heading for Megan's porch.

Through the Hole in the Wall

The three girls gasped. They peered through the darkness, hoping to catch another glimpse of the man.

"What in the world is he doing here?" asked McKenzie.

"I don't know, but my mom is alone. We've got to do something!" said Megan.

"I'll grab my flashlight. Megan, you unlock my window. We'll crawl through and stay hidden until we can figure out what's going on." Elizabeth felt around in the dark, pulling open the drawer to her bedside table. Locating the flashlight, she clicked it on and returned to the window, which was now wide open. Wind and rain gushed through, getting her curtains all wet.

The three girls slipped through the window, and Elizabeth pulled it shut behind her. She would have a lot of explaining to do if her parents found the wet room, but this was important. Ruby was in danger.

The girls ran, staying low to the ground. *Pow!* Rain soaked their skin. *Crash!* A flash of lightning revealed an empty porch. Mr. Jacobs's truck was still parked in the driveway.

"Come on!" Megan called out. Through the window, Ruby appeared to be lighting candles. Soon their soft glow gave light for the girls to see what was going on.

Jacobs spoke, but they couldn't hear the words. Ruby laughed. Then Mr. Jacobs began moving around the house with the flashlight!

"He's looking for the marbles," McKenzie said.

"But why is she letting him?" asked Elizabeth. "That doesn't make sense."

"Somebody has to stop him," said Megan. She stood and pushed open her front door.

Ruby Smith was startled. "Megan? What are you doing out in this weather? I thought you were at Elizabeth's house!"

Elizabeth and McKenzie appeared in the doorway. The girls shivered like puppies fresh from a bath, dripping water all over the hardwood floor.

"Oh my goodness! Girls, get in here. Let me find you some towels." Ruby pulled the girls inside and shut the door behind them.

Mr. Jacobs appeared from the hallway. "What on earth? Girls, are you okay?"

Ruby picked up a candle and brushed past Mr. Jacobs into the hallway. She returned with an armload of thick, fluffy towels. Each girl took one and dried herself. Suddenly, there was a loud *Pop!* and the electricity returned.

The house lit up, and the television began broadcasting the Home and Garden network, Ruby's favorite. Weather updates scrolled across the bottom of the screen.

Ruby stood, hands on hips, looking at the girls. Finally, her eyes rested on Megan. "Explain yourself, young lady. Why would you go running around in a storm like this? You could have gotten struck by lightning!"

Elizabeth and McKenzie looked at their sopping shoes. Megan lifted her chin and said, "We were worried about you, Mama. We were in Elizabeth's room, and we saw a strange car pull into the driveway, and. . ." her eyes flashed to Mr. Jacobs. "And we saw a man coming onto our porch."

Mr. Jacobs stepped forward. "Well now, that would be scary. That was very brave of you to come and check on your mother. I'm sorry. I never meant to frighten anyone."

Megan held the man's eyes, as if waiting for an explanation. She was usually very respectful to her elders. But she was also very protective of her mother.

Jacobs continued. "I was driving a couple of blocks from here when the power went out. I thought of you and your mama here by yourselves. I thought I'd come check on you." The man shifted his cowboy hat from one hand to the other, then back again. He looked nervous.

Megan held his eyes but said nothing. Elizabeth and McKenzie watched the scene. The electric clock on the side table flashed on and off, on and off.

Mr. Jacobs said, "Well, it looks like everyone is okay, so I guess I'll head back to the motel. Sorry to have frightened you girls."

Ruby held out her arm in protest. "Oh, don't go before I can fix you a cup of coffee. You're soaking wet! Here, take a towel."

The man smiled gently at Ruby and said, "Aww, no ma'am. I'll be fine. But thank you." With that, he tipped his hat to her and left.

Ruby Smith's eyes swung to the girls standing in front of her, landing on her daughter. "Let's get you three warmed up. Then, you have some tall talkin' to do."

The girls followed the woman into the kitchen and sat around the oak table as Mrs. Smith made hot cocoa. While the water was boiling, she picked up the phone and dialed. "Sue? This is Ruby. The girls are at my house. I just wanted you to know they're safe. . . . No, they haven't explained themselves yet. We're getting to that. . . . Okay, I'll see one of you in a minute."

Elizabeth groaned inwardly. How would she explain sneaking out the window? It hadn't seemed like a bad idea at the time. But now, it was going to be hard to defend.

Moments later, there was a knock at the door, and Ruby rushed to let Robert Anderson in. He didn't look happy. "Elizabeth, what were you thinking? The boys said you sneaked out your window! And in a storm? That's not like you at all. Explain, young lady."

Elizabeth took a deep breath and sent a desperate plea to heaven. "We weren't trying to be bad. We just got scared, and the electricity was off, and then we saw Mr. Jacobs coming toward the porch, and we knew Megan's mom was here by herself, and—"

"Wait a minute," interrupted Ruby. "You knew it was Mr. Jacobs? It sounded to me like you thought he was a stranger!"

Megan answered. "Mom, we thought it might be Mr. Jacobs, but we didn't know for sure. And there's more. We don't trust him."

The two adults looked at each other and then at the girls. Elizabeth's dad sat down and leaned forward. "We've got all night. Start talking."

The girls remained silent, not knowing where to begin. Finally, Elizabeth and Megan began pouring out the story from beginning to end, one pausing as the other jumped in, back and forth like a tennis match. McKenzie added a detail here and there.

The two adults looked at the girls, stunned. "So you've been trying to solve a mystery?" asked Mr. Anderson.

The girls nodded. Elizabeth's dad leaned back in his chair, and a great belly laugh erupted that continued for several minutes. The girls weren't sure how to respond.

Mrs. Smith chuckled too, but she appeared to be laughing more at her neighbor than at the situation.

Finally, the man pulled himself together and gave Elizabeth a stern look. "I'm glad you wanted to help Megan's mom. But what you did was foolish. First of all, it is never okay to sneak out your window, unless something dangerous is inside the house, like a fire. Second, it is never okay to go running around in a storm. You all could have been seriously hurt. Third, it was foolish of you to think you could save Mrs. Smith from any man. You should have come to me immediately."

Elizabeth looked at her father. She hated disappointing him. "I'm sorry, Daddy."

"You're forgiven," he said. "But you still have to be punished. I'm not going to ground you while McKenzie is here. But when the Phillips's vacation is over, you're going to be seeing a lot of the inside of our house."

•—•—•

Later that night, McKenzie and Elizabeth lay awake whispering. Their room at the Big Texan had a small living area with a pullout bed, which gave the girls some privacy.

"Did you notice that my dad and Megan's mom weren't concerned about Mr. Jacobs?" Elizabeth asked.

"Yeah, I did," whispered McKenzie. "Your dad thought the whole thing was funny."

"My dad has a good sense about people. But the fact that Mr. Jacobs is looking for the marbles is strange," she said. "Maybe we should just come out and ask him about it."

McKenzie thought. "No. He clearly has plans for those marbles. But Megan and her mom could use the money. I'm still not sure I trust him."

"Me neither," replied Elizabeth. "We have to find those marbles before he does."

The girls were quiet for a few minutes. Then McKenzie rolled to face her friend. "Hey, Elizabeth. . .since the marbles never made it to the bank, I wonder if they really are hidden at the restaurant."

"I was thinking that too. We'll go there first thing in the morning," she said sleepily.

•—•—•

The two sleuths were awake and dressed before dawn the next morning. They walked to the restaurant, which was open early for breakfast. A waitress they'd not seen before seated them, and the girls studied the menu.

"We need to get into that supply closet," said Elizabeth, her eyes scanning the walls and floor planks. "That secret panel seems like the perfect hiding place."

"What time does Megan come in?" asked McKenzie.

Elizabeth's eyes focused on someone behind McKenzie, and a grin spread across her face. "Right now," she said.

McKenzie turned to find Megan walking toward them. "I see we all had the same idea," she said. "I think we need to check that supply closet again."

Elizabeth scooted over in the booth to make room for her friend. "Did you and your mom talk any more last night?" she asked.

"Yeah. I ended up sleeping in her bed and we talked for a long time. She does think it's weird that Mr. Jacobs is looking for the marbles. She promised to keep her distance from him," Megan told them.

The other two girls observed something in Megan's attitude that seemed. . .not quite right. "You don't seem happy," said McKenzie.

Megan let out a heavy sigh. "It's just that my mom's been through so much. I wasn't thrilled when Mr. Jacobs flirted with her. But he made her smile! She was singing, and humming. For the last few days, she's seemed happier. I just hate that he's a fake."

Elizabeth thought about that. "He might not be a fake. My dad doesn't have a problem with him, and you know my dad. He's pretty good about figuring people out," she said.

"Maybe so, Elizabeth, but he's definitely after those marbles. We can't let him find them before we do," McKenzie said.

"I have a feeling that when we find the marbles, we'll find out the answers to a lot of our questions about Mr. Jacobs," McKenzie told them.

After a moment, Megan stood and said, "Well, we won't find them sitting in this booth. Let's get started. Come with me."

The girls followed their friend through the restaurant, into the kitchen area, and to the supply room. The early morning manager, a friendly-looking woman in her early fifties, said, "You're here early, Megan!"

"Uh, yes, Mrs. Edgar. I really want to get that supply closet cleaned out. My friends have volunteered to help."

The woman gave them a strange look, but smiled. "Interesting. I suppose it's a better way to spend your time than sitting in front of the television. It's good to see young people with a sense of responsibility. Have fun!"

The girls entered the supply closet, and Megan flipped on the dim light. "I guess I'll have to fix that light myself," she said, grabbing a step-ladder. "McKenzie, could you hand me one of those bulbs behind you?"

McKenzie did as she was asked. Elizabeth got on her hands and knees. She moved the tomato cans away from the hidden panel.

"Megan, do you know where a Phillips screwdriver is?" she asked.

"Well, I know where a Phillips is," Megan responded, and she and McKenzie laughed. It took a moment for Elizabeth to catch on to the joke about McKenzie's last name, but when she did, she laughed too. After a few minutes, the lightbulb was changed. Elizabeth was on her stomach unscrewing the panel in the wall. When the last screw was loose, the panel was removed to reveal a small square.

Elizabeth reached inside and felt around but found nothing. "This hole goes pretty far back. One of us will have to go in with a flashlight."

The three girls stood looking at each other, trying to decide who was least likely to get stuck. All three were slim but had different shapes and builds. Finally, McKenzie and Megan said in unison, "Elizabeth is the skinniest."

"Hey!" Elizabeth said, then looked down at her long arms and legs. "Okay, I guess I'm skinny. But so are y'all."

"Slim, yes. String beans? No. You're the only string bean in the bunch," said Megan.

Elizabeth sighed good-naturedly. "I knew I should have gotten three scoops of ice cream yesterday. . . ," she muttered. "Where is Kate when we need her?"

McKenzie laughed at the memory of their tiny camp friend. Kate had made them all look like giants.

Megan got a flashlight from the office, and Elizabeth shimmied into the opening. The beam from the light revealed years of accumulated dust, a crack in the concrete floor, and a few dead bugs. There was even an old label from a green bean can, which looked as if it had been there for decades. "Cool!" Elizabeth called out, examining the label.

"What did you find?" asked Megan.

"This old green bean label must be older than our parents!" she called.

Megan and McKenzie shared exasperated looks. "The marbles, Elizabeth! Stay focused," Megan called out.

Mrs. Edgar pushed the door open and poked her head in. "Megan, dear, since you're here early, why don't you clock in? We're shorthanded this morning. I may let you try waitressing."

Megan and McKenzie jumped and turned to block the pair of legs that were sticking out of the wall.

"Yes, ma'am," Megan said.

"Pronto," the woman said, shooing the two girls out of the supply room. "I thought there were three of you," she questioned.

Suddenly, a loud crash came from the kitchen, followed by a yelp. "Jessie, how many times do I have to tell you to wear oven mitts?" Mrs. Edgar said to a young man across the room. She closed the door, leaving Megan and McKenzie wondering what to do next. The woman called over her shoulder, "Megan, show your friend out of the kitchen. Too many people are back here as it is. Then go sign in and report to the waitress's station."

Trapped!

Elizabeth heard the muffled voices. She tried to draw her feet up into the hole, but something caught on her blue jeans. She was trapped! She couldn't wiggle backward or forward.

The voices faded, and she heard a loud crash, followed by the click of a door. Somehow, she knew she'd been left alone. She tried to shine her flashlight to find what was catching her jeans, but she couldn't wiggle her body that way in the tight space. She finally gave up and decided to wait.

Lord, what have I gotten myself into? she prayed silently into the darkness. *What will my dad say? He'll tell me I should have known better than to go crawling around in holes in buildings. But Lord, we have to find those marbles! Please help us.*

Elizabeth made herself as comfortable as possible and waited. After a while, she shined her light on the green bean label. Not very interesting.

She heard a sound above her head like running water. Shining her light, she tilted her head backward to find pipes. Water pipes. *So that's the reason for the panel. To let the plumber work on the pipes.*

"I wish I had a book or something," she whispered. Then, it dawned on her. The journals! In their excitement to solve the mystery, she and McKenzie had abandoned Mrs. Wilson's journals. But what if there was more?

How could we have been so blind? Elizabeth mentally berated herself for jumping to conclusions and not reading the journals at least to the end of Emily Marie's story. Her mind raced with the possibilities of those journals when she heard another click. She felt two hands on her ankles.

"Hello?" she called in a soft voice. "Who's there?"

Through the darkness, she heard a familiar twang. "What have you gotten yourself into? Gracious sakes alive, girl! Here, your jeans are caught. Be still now. Okay, I'm gonna pull."

After a few tugs from behind, Elizabeth was able to back herself out of the hole. She sat up, looked into Jean Louise's face, and sighed with relief. "Oh Jean Louise! Am I glad to see you! I was scared I was going to—"

"You should be whipped, young lady! What kind of stunt do you think you're pulling? Why, there could be rats in those walls, or loose wires. . ."

Elizabeth shuddered. She hadn't considered those possibilities.

"And you could have been arrested for breaking and entering. You have no business being back here!" the woman continued.

Elizabeth blinked back tears. "I–I'm sorry, Jean Louise. We were only—"

The woman grabbed her and hugged her. "Now don't you start crying. I'm just glad you're okay. You better be thankful I was on duty! When the girls told me what y'all were up to, I just about died. I've got to get back. Come on now, dust yourself off. And no more crawling around in holes, ya' hear me?"

Elizabeth nodded and promised. Jean Louise pushed open the supply room door. When the coast was clear, the two headed out of the kitchen.

Out front, Megan was frantically taking orders. When she saw Elizabeth, she smiled, but continued her work. Mac was waiting on a bench near the entrance and stood when she saw her friend. Without a word, the two girls headed back to the motel room.

•—•—•

Several hours later, Elizabeth and McKenzie were stretched out by the Texas-shaped pool. Elizabeth read aloud from Mrs. Wilson's journal, while McKenzie listened. They were determined to read to the end of the story this time.

Dear God, I can't believe this is happening. Why Emily Marie? Why now? Lord, You knew her car was going to break down. You knew she would be out alone after dark. Why couldn't You have stopped this from happening?

Oh, I'm not blaming You, Lord. It just doesn't make any sense. She's got those two precious children, and now Foster. Why did that car have to hit her?

If only I had gone with her, like she asked. Maybe then, none of this would have happened. Oh God, please let her be okay. It doesn't look good.

I sat with her tonight, Lord. She talked a lot, but she didn't make much sense. She kept asking about her babies, and then saying something about the big blue fin. She's hallucinating, Lord. I tried to hold her hand and comfort her. But she just kept telling me to look under the fin.

The next few pages told of Emily Marie's death and funeral. After that, the journal entries ended until nearly a year later, but nothing more was said about Emily Marie.

The girls thumbed back through the pages, trying to find something more that would help them. But it was no use. They found no more hidden clues.

McKenzie sat up in her lounge chair. "The big blue fin," she said. "What a strange thing to say."

Then, as if reading one another's mind, they both started talking at once. "The fish! Isn't there a—"

"A big fish! In the restaurant!"

"Yeah, it's hanging on that back wall! It's a—a swordfish or something!"

"A blue marlin, I think the sign said!"

The girls looked at each other, excitement flashing in their eyes, and started for the restaurant. They were halfway there when they realized they were wearing their swimsuits.

They practically ran back to their room and changed, and were at the restaurant in no time.

Jean Louise greeted them at the door. "Well, well. If it isn't Bonnie and Clyde."

Elizabeth laughed at the comment, then leaned over and whispered, "We think we may have found the marbles."

Jean Louise's eyes grew wide, and Elizabeth continued. "Can you seat us at that table under the big fish? Your mom put something in her journal about a blue fin."

The waitress looked skeptical, but led them through the restaurant. "That fish has been hanging there since I can remember. Just don't go crawling through any more holes in the wall without telling me first. I don't want to be bailing you kids out of jail."

The girls laughed and took their seats. They were thrilled to be sitting right beneath the fish, and felt certain this would be the end of their search.

They examined the fish closely. McKenzie lightly tapped the wall under the fish, but stopped when the people next to them looked curiously.

Elizabeth picked up the crisp linen napkin from the table. She dropped it on the floor. Crawling under the table to retrieve it, she examined the wall and floor. Suddenly, she felt a tap on her shoulder. Turning to find Jean Louise's white work shoes, Elizabeth scrambled out from under the table. She banged her head.

"Ouch!" she cried.

Jean Louise showed little sympathy. "Elizabeth Anderson, I don't know what I'm going to do with you."

"But Jean Lou—"

"Don't 'but Jean Louise' me! You'll get in big trouble if you don't stop poking around." The woman sighed and placed her hands on her hips. "I'll tell you what. The restaurant closes at ten p.m. If you can be here then, I'll let you look to your heart's content. I'll even help you. But you have to leave well enough alone while the customers are here."

Elizabeth jumped from her seat and hugged the woman. "Oh thank you, Jean Louise! You're my hero! I just know we're going to find the—"

"Shhh! Not so loud. You never know who might be listening." She gestured toward the opposite corner of the restaurant, and they noticed Mr. Jacobs for the first time. He was looking at them strangely. When they made eye contact, he waved.

Elizabeth sat back in her seat. "Okay. We'll meet you here at closing time," she said. The woman left them, and McKenzie and Elizabeth leaned their heads together, trying to decide whether the marbles would end up being in the floor or the wall.

"Just think. We may be sitting on them right now," McKenzie said.

Elizabeth's eyes grew round. "They could be in the booth! What if she pulled the stuffing out of one of the benches and put them in there?"

"They've probably replaced the benches since then," McKenzie told her. Their eyes grew wide at the thought. They pushed it aside and decided to deal with that possibility when the time came.

•—•—•

Back at the motel room, Mr. and Mrs. Phillips were looking at travel brochures. "We only have a few days left in our vacation, and we want to make the most of them. There's a water park, a cowboy museum, and the famous Cadillac Ranch," said Mr. Phillips.

"There's also an outlet mall I'd like to visit, and a zoo," added Mrs. Phillips. "What are you all interested in?"

"Water park!" shouted McKenzie.

"Cadillac Ranch!" shouted Evan.

Elizabeth remained quiet.

Mrs. Phillips placed the brochures to the water park and the Cadillac Ranch to one side. "That nice man, Mr. Jacobs, offered to take us back to the rodeo grounds and let us see the livestock up close. There's also a fair with the rodeo," she said while reading over some of the brochures. "We'll probably go there this afternoon."

"Cool!" said Evan. "Do you think he'll let me ride a bull?"

"No, but you might be able to ride a real rodeo horse," his father told him.

"Dad, are you going to buy that horse from him?" McKenzie asked.

"I'm thinking about it. He seems pretty anxious to sell. Says he wants to buy a house near here. But he's not sure what will happen until some inheritance of his comes through."

"Inheritance?" McKenzie and Elizabeth asked at once.

"Yeah, apparently his uncle left behind some priceless. . .marbles or something. But they've disappeared. Jacobs is trying to track them down."

Elizabeth stood and grabbed McKenzie by the arm. "I just remembered something I wanted to look at down at the gift shop," she said.

"Okay, girls. Stay close," said Mrs. Phillips.

As soon as the door closed behind them, McKenzie looked at Elizabeth questioningly.

"I have an idea. We've been skirting around Mr. Jacobs, trying to go behind his back. But since he's so interested in those marbles, why don't we go straight to him?"

McKenzie's eyes grew wide. "You mean just come out and ask him?"

"No. I have a plan," Elizabeth told her friend. They headed to the gift shop, where they purchased sidewalk chalk and a bag of marbles.

A half hour later, the two young detectives sat on the sidewalk near Mr. Jacobs's room, casually playing a game of marbles. Elizabeth had drawn a large circle using the sidewalk chalk, and the two girls took turns thumping their shooter marbles, trying to knock the other's marbles out of the circle. They were absorbed in the game and didn't notice when the door behind them quietly opened and shut.

McKenzie noticed the embroidered cowboy boots first. They were behind Elizabeth, who was concentrating on which angle to shoot her marbles. McKenzie's eyes followed the long legs up, up, up, until she looked into the amused eyes of Mr. Jacobs.

"You know, if you shoot to the left, it will ricochet and knock out the marbles on the right," he said.

Elizabeth nearly jumped out of her skin, even though she'd expected him. "Oh, hi, Mr. Jacobs!" she told him after she regained her composure. "Are we in your way? We're sorry."

"Oh no, not at all," the man told her. "I love a good game of marbles." He eyed the colorful balls with interest.

The two shifted into sleuth mode. "Really? Are you a marble expert?" McKenzie asked the man.

He stepped off the curb and sat on the sidewalk next to them. "I guess you could say that. I've played marbles since I was a little boy."

"Really? Not too many people play the game anymore. Did someone special teach you how?" Elizabeth asked.

"Yep," said the cowboy. "My uncle. He was more like a father to me than anything. He never married or had children, but he loved me like I was his son."

"Really?" Elizabeth probed him. Her plan was working perfectly. "Do you still see him a lot?"

"Unfortunately, no," he said. "He passed away about a year ago. But he had a soft spot in his heart for Amarillo. Never told me why, though. I suspect he fell in love here. He never talked much about the time he spent here. But whenever he mentioned Amarillo, he got a distant look in his eyes."

The girls remained quiet and let the man talk.

"I really miss him. I've decided to settle here, since he seemed to love the place so much."

"What was your uncle's name?" Elizabeth asked. Just then, Evan rounded the corner.

"McKenzie, Mama says to come. We're going to the fair," the boy told his sister.

Mr. Jacobs stood up and said, "I need to be going too. Nice talking with you girls." And with that, he left.

The girls gathered up their marbles as Evan watched. "Those are cool," he said. "Where did you get them?"

Elizabeth replaced the colorful round balls into their drawstring pouch and handed them to Evan. "Here you go. I got them at the gift shop, but you can have them," she told him.

"Cool! Thanks, Elizabeth!" he said.

The three of them walked back to the Phillips's motel room, where McKenzie's parents were waiting. "Elizabeth, call your mom and ask if it's okay if we pick up James. He'd probably enjoy a day at the fair, don't you think?" Mrs. Phillips asked.

A short time later, the four Phillipses and the two younger Andersons were oohing and ahhing over the sights at the fair. Elizabeth and Evan held dripping ice cream cones, while McKenzie and James opted for cotton candy.

They rode the Ferris wheel and held their arms high during the roller coaster ride. While they walked along a row of games, James spotted the balloon darts. He wasn't looking at the balloons, however.

"Look, Beth! Look at those cool cars! I need one of those for my collection!" he tugged at his sister's arm as he pointed.

Elizabeth looked at the row of model cars lined up as prizes. "Do you think you can pop three balloons?" Elizabeth asked him.

"I don't know, but I'll sure try!" the boy said. Elizabeth gave her brother a ticket, and James handed it to the man behind the counter.

While he was trying to pop the balloons, McKenzie leaned over and whispered, "It's getting late. We need to get back to the motel before ten so we can find the marbles."

Elizabeth couldn't hear her friend over the noise of the fair. "What?" she asked.

McKenzie repeated herself a little louder, but Elizabeth still couldn't hear. Finally, McKenzie ended up nearly shouting, "We've got to get back to the restaurant so we can look for the marbles!"

At that moment, Elizabeth spotted a tall flash of cowboy hat disappearing around the corner. She pointed, but the person was gone. "Was that—" Her question died. She decided she must be seeing things.

James popped one balloon but missed the other two. He was disappointed, and Elizabeth draped her arm over his shoulder. "It's okay, lil' brother. Come on. I see the house of mirrors. You'll love that!"

The four young people offered their tickets and entered. "We'll meet you at the exit," Mr. Phillips told them.

Inside, they giggled at the distorted images of themselves, some tall and wavy, others short and bumpy. They decided to chase each other through the maze, and before long, they were laughing and hollering. Each time they thought they'd caught one of the others, it turned out to be an image in the mirror!

Elizabeth began to see flashes of that cowboy hat again. Each time she focused on the image, it was gone. But then, there it was again, in the corner of her eye.

She told herself not to panic, but concentrated on finding the others. What in the world would Mr. Jacobs be doing in the house of mirrors? Was he shadowing them?

The Man in the Mirrors

"Hey y'all, I think we need to go. Everyone head for the exit," she called.

The others laughed. "Aww, you're not giving up that easily, are you?" called Evan.

Stay calm. Figure out how to get everyone out of here, away from that creepy cowboy, Elizabeth told herself. *Please, God, help.*

Then she had an idea. "I'll race you! The last one to the exit is a rotten egg!" she called.

Within moments, she heard footsteps and hoots of laughter as the other three dashed to the exit. But then there was a thud, and the sound of something rolling on the floor. The marbles! Evan had kept them in his pocket!

"Oh no! My marbles!" Elizabeth heard Evan calling out. She could see the images of marbles rolling on the floor but couldn't find them. Before long, she saw Evan's reflection. But everywhere she turned were more reflections. Where was the real thing?

"Here, let me help you with that," came a deep voice. Elizabeth looked, and there was that cowboy hat, attached to Mr. Jacobs! And there he was again, and again, and again.

She had to find the real Evan and protect him from the real Mr. Jacobs!

She stood up, closed her eyes, and just listened to the voices, to the sounds of the marbles on the floor. Without opening her eyes, she turned toward the sound.

Holding her arms in front of her, she slowly began to walk, letting the sounds guide her. Before she knew it, she bumped into something. Opening her eyes, she looked directly down on a cowboy hat, sitting on top of Jacobs's head. The man was on his hands and knees, examining a handful of marbles. Evan was next to him, gathering more of the round balls.

"Here, let me help you," Elizabeth said, trying to keep her voice calm. Her heart was pounding, and she felt sure the others could hear its loud thud. Still, she kept her composure, knelt, and began searching.

"Hello, Elizabeth," said Mr. Jacobs.

Elizabeth forced herself not to look directly at the man. She tried to watch him in the mirrors as she looked for more marbles. "It's funny to see you here, Mr. Jacobs," Elizabeth said.

The man chuckled. "Aww, I'm just a big kid at heart. I love these fairs. I was supposed to meet Dan at the rodeo, to let him look at Lucy. But I thought I'd wander around the fair for a while first. Then I spotted you all over at the balloon darts. I've got something for your brother, by the way. I saw you kids come in here, and thought I'd try to catch up with you."

Elizabeth turned to look at the man. "If I didn't know better, I'd think you were following us," she said.

The cowboy chuckled. Was that a nervous laugh? "Well, I was starting to think you were following me," he said.

Elizabeth averted her eyes and called out to her friends again. "Meet everyone at the exit!" She stood, but found herself at a loss for which way to turn. *I really need to do something about my sense of direction, or lack of it,* she thought.

Mr. Jacobs stood and towered over her. Sensing her hesitancy, he said, "Follow me. I'll get you out of here."

Drats! She hated to depend on her prime suspect to get her unlost, but she didn't seem to have much choice. She kept her eyes fixed on the back of his plaid shirt, and before long, stepped into the bright lights of the fairground.

Mr. and Mrs. Phillips laughed when they saw Mr. Jacobs. "You're a brave man," Dan Phillips said.

Mr. Jacobs smiled but didn't make eye contact with anyone. Did he feel guilty about something? He reached into his pocket and pulled out a tiny model car. He handed it to James.

"I saw you trying to win a car, James. I thought you might like to have this," he said.

"Wow, thank you!" said James, a smile lighting his face. "And it's blue too! My favorite color!"

Elizabeth and McKenzie exchanged glances. As the adults began talking and moving toward the rodeo grounds, the two girls stayed a few steps behind.

"What is he doing here?" Elizabeth whispered.

"He's meeting my dad, and they're going to look at that horse, remember?" McKenzie reminded her.

"Yeah, but it's strange that he seems to be following us. It's like he knows we know something," Elizabeth continued.

"Maybe. But I think it's a good idea for us to stay close to him anyway. We might learn something," McKenzie said.

The girls followed the rest of their group at a safe distance, so they could talk freely without fear of being heard.

"I wish the other Camp Club Girls were here. I think we need to email them all tonight and see if we can get any more ideas," said McKenzie.

"That's it!" said Elizabeth. "Why didn't I think of that a long time ago? We can get them to help us investigate Mr. Jacobs!" She pulled her cell phone out of her pocket. Scrolling down in her address book, she hit Kate's number.

It was busy.

She moved to Sydney's number. After a couple of rings, Sydney's grandmother answered.

"Hello, Mrs. Washington. This is Elizabeth. How are you?" she asked politely.

"Oh Elizabeth! What a nice surprise. I'm doing well, and you?"

"I'm fine, thank you, ma'am. May I please speak with Sydney?"

"Oh, she's not here. She's at a Wilderness Club meeting. She'll back in about an hour or so. Would you like me to have her call you back?"

"Oh, no thank you. I'll just email her. Tell her I'm sorry I missed her."

"She will be so disappointed. I'll tell her you called. You take care now," said the woman.

Elizabeth hung up, and then sighed a frustrated sigh. McKenzie watched as she moved the arrow down to Alex's name and number, and pressed the button. It rang.

"Hello?" came Alex's voice from the other end of the line.

"Hi, Alex!" Elizabeth said.

"Elizabeth Anderson, is that you?" the girl exclaimed from the other end of the line.

"Yep, it is," replied Elizabeth.

"Is McKenzie with you? She better be. You emailed us all about your new mystery, and then it was like the two of you just dropped off the face of the earth. Haven't you been checking your emails?"

Elizabeth was surprised at Alex's scolding. She felt like a child who had gotten caught sneaking a cookie. The truth was, Elizabeth and McKenzie had been too busy to think about emailing. "Uh. . .sorry," she said.

"You're forgiven," said Alex. "Now tell me everything! Did you find the jewels? Are Megan and her mother wealthy heiresses? Oh, this is *so* Hollywood! I can see it now. 'Impoverished Woman Inherits Millions!' It will be made into a television movie, I just know it! You'll have your own mystery show. An *iCarly* on the go!"

Elizabeth held the phone away from her ear a bit. McKenzie could hear Alex's excited chatter from a couple of feet away. The two laughed. Same old Alex. She handed the phone to McKenzie, who said hello to her friend, then handed the phone back to Elizabeth.

"We haven't found the marbles yet. And Megan isn't exactly impoverished. But we need your help," she said.

"What can I do?" asked Alex.

"We couldn't find anything in our search for the marbles. But there is this cowboy named Mark Jacobs. He keeps snooping around. We know he's after the marbles too. He claims to have inherited them from a rich uncle, but I think he's a fraud.

"We know a man named Foster left them to Megan's grandmother before she died. We're still trying to find where she might have hidden them. But can you check out Jacobs for us? And get the others in on the search too. Mac and I are at the fair now, tailing the cowboy."

"Oh, how exciting! I wish I were there. I'll get right on it. I'll call you back if I find anything."

"Thanks, Alex." The two girls hurried to catch up with the rest of their group.

Mr. Jacobs and Mr. Phillips were talking, and the cowboy led them to a row of stalls where the horses waited to enter the rodeo arena. The announcer said something funny, and the crowd laughed.

"I ride again in about a half hour. Lucy has been a great horse. I hate to sell her, but at least I know she'll be in good hands."

"Tell me again why you're selling her," Mr. Phillips requested, and the girls scooted in closer, pretending to watch the rodeo. Evan and James were on the ground, driving the tiny car through tracks of loose hay.

"I'm ready to retire. The rodeo life is fun, but I want to put down roots somewhere. I don't have any family still living, but Amarillo was always special to my uncle, and I like it here too. I've found a piece of land with a creek and a nice little house, and I want to settle here. I thought I had a sizable inheritance coming my way, but that doesn't seem to be panning out. So my backup plan has always been to sell my stock and supplies for a down payment."

"So if your inheritance comes through, you may not want to sell her?" asked Mr. Phillips.

Mr. Jacobs paused. "I hope my inheritance comes through, but I'm trying not to count on it. It's a long story," the cowboy said. His voice sounded so sad that Elizabeth couldn't help but look at him. When she did, she was surprised to see him looking at her! She looked away, but it was too late.

McKenzie's dad studied the horse, and Mrs. Phillips was talking to the boys. Jacobs stepped to the railing where the girls were leaning, and whispered, "I heard you talking to that waitress at the restaurant about some marbles. What kind of marbles are you looking for?"

Elizabeth couldn't believe her ears. Was the man really questioning her about the marbles? How could she get out of this conversation? Panicked, she looked at McKenzie, but Mac appeared as flustered as she felt.

Suddenly, the announcer's voice boomed over the loudspeaker. "We invite all of our young people, ages eight to fourteen, to enter the arena for the pig chase. You might get a little muddy, but you're sure to have a barrel of fun! The first one to catch a baby pig wins $250 cash."

McKenzie grabbed Elizabeth and pulled her into the arena. A woman at the gate attached a number to each contestant's back and instructed them to stand along the railing. Elizabeth looked at her new pink tennis shoes and knew they would never be the same.

"That was a close call," whispered Mac, as they waited for the event to begin.

"Tell me about it! The nerve of that man, just coming out and asking me like that!"

"I feel sorry for him," said McKenzie. "He's all alone in the world, and now it looks like he'll have to sell his horse. I'd die if I had to sell mine."

Elizabeth looked at her friend in shock. "Don't tell me you're falling for his sob story! Don't let him fool you." Elizabeth tried to convince herself as much as she tried to convince her friend. Deep down, she shared

McKenzie's sympathy. But he had to be a bad guy. He just had to be.

"Yeah, you're probably right," whispered McKenzie.

The gate closed, and the dozens of contestants were instructed to scatter throughout the arena. The announcer's voice said, "In just a moment, six piglets will be released into the arena. Oh, and did I mention they are covered in baby oil? When you hear the starting gun, you do whatever you can to catch one of these pigs. Of course, there will be no hitting or shoving or foul play of any kind, or you'll be disqualified. The first one to successfully catch and hold a pig wins the cash. Are you ready? Get set!"

The sound of the gun set the arena into chaos. Piglets raced into the arena, and the contestants sprang into action. The crowd roared with laughter and cheers. For a moment, Elizabeth stood frozen to her spot. She had never done anything like this!

McKenzie, on the other hand, was quite at home. She'd singled out a tiny black-and-white spotted pig and was trying to corner him. "Elizabeth, don't just stand there! Get moving!" she called out. "I could use a little help!"

Just then, a small pink blur ran over her foot, leaving behind tiny mud prints on her shoes. Elizabeth reached for the creature, but it was too late. She sprang forward to chase the offending animal. She could hear McKenzie calling her name, but Elizabeth had no interest in any other pig. This one had muddied her shoes. He was going to pay.

The pig ran around the arena, Elizabeth close at his heels. He led her through the center of the ring, around the outer edge, and into a mud puddle. In the background, she could hear James calling, "Go, Bettyboo! Go, Bettyboo!"

Suddenly, all of Elizabeth's frustrations took the form of the tiny piglet in front of her. She leaped forward in a stunning show of determination, grabbed the oily little creature, and held him to her chest. She wasn't about to let him escape.

The crowd stood to their feet and roared, and the announcer's voice exclaimed over the loudspeaker. "We have a winner! The pretty little blond, now covered in mud, has caught herself a pig! Folks, did you see her jump? She was determined to win that cash! Congratulations, miss!"

Elizabeth stayed where she was, her jeans soaking in the mud beneath her. She looked up to find McKenzie standing over her, hands on hips and a huge smile on her face.

"Congratulations! I didn't know you had it in you!" Mac told her.

"I didn't either," Elizabeth replied, as she gripped the wiggling animal in her arms.

A rodeo official approached and asked her name. The woman then spoke into a cordless microphone, "Our winner is Miss Elizabeth Anderson. Miss Anderson, on behalf of the Amarillo Livestock Show and Rodeo, we would like to present you with this certificate, and a check for $250. Congratulations!" She held out a large manila envelope as the crowd cheered.

Elizabeth still didn't move. She was afraid to let go of the pig, afraid he would escape.

The woman leaned forward and whispered, "You can let go now. You've already won."

Elizabeth laughed, then gave her wiggling bundle a kiss on the head and set him free. The crowd applauded as she stood to her feet and accepted the envelope. The contestants exited the arena, and the two girls were greeted by their group.

"Congratulations, Beth! Did you hear me cheering for you?" asked James.

Elizabeth took a muddy finger and smeared the tip of his nose. "Yes, I did, little brother. And your cheers helped me win!"

"We'd better get you home and out of those muddy clothes, Elizabeth," said Mrs. Phillips.

For the first time, Elizabeth noticed that McKenzie was as clean as a whistle. Not a mark on her, except for a little mud on her shoes. "How did you stay so clean?" she asked her friend.

"I guess I've had a little more experience than you," Mac laughed.

Then Mr. Jacobs clapped her on the back. In the excitement, Elizabeth had forgotten all about him! "That was great, Elizabeth. I have a feeling you're the kind of girl who always does what she sets out to do!"

Elizabeth shifted nervously from one foot to the other and looked at the ground. She wished the man would leave her alone. "Uh, I guess so," she whispered.

The man leaned in and whispered, "Whether it's catching a pig or solving a mystery, huh?"

Elizabeth jerked her head up and looked at him. The man winked at her and tipped his hat to the group. "I'll see you folks later," he said, and walked away.

A Fishy Clue

As they left the fair, the Phillipses stopped at the Andersons' house to drop James off and give Elizabeth a chance to change clothes. Then they returned to the motel, where the girls headed to the restaurant.

It was 9:45 when Jean Louise greeted the girls. There were still a few scattered customers. "Take a seat, girls, and mind your manners till all the customers are gone," the woman told them.

They sat under the blue marlin. "I'm itching to take that thing off the wall and look behind it! I know we'll find the marbles there," said McKenzie.

Elizabeth's eyes lit with excitement. "I do too. Hey, what if they are actually inside the fish? Maybe it's hollow!"

The girls continued whispering until it looked like the last customer had left. Just as Jean Louise was about to lock the door, it pushed open, and Mr. Jacobs walked in! Had he been looking for them again?

He looked around, tipping his hat to the girls before greeting Jean Louise. "Pardon me, ma'am. I know it's closing time, but could I trouble you for a tall glass of that wonderful iced tea?"

"Why certainly. I'll get it for you right now," said the waitress.

While he waited, he looked at the girls. "Fancy meeting you here," he said. "What are you girls doing here so late?"

Elizabeth looked like a deer caught in the headlights. She had no idea how to respond.

McKenzie, thinking fast, eyed the grand piano sitting in the corner of the restaurant. "Uh, Elizabeth plays the piano. Since she's spent the week here with me, she's hardly gotten to practice. So she's going to practice after everyone leaves."

"That's right. Elizabeth's going to play the piano. Here's your tea, sir," said Jean Louise, handing the man a large Styrofoam cup. Megan had followed her out of the kitchen and had a towel draped over her shoulder.

"I see. I'd love to stay and listen. Would you mind?" the man said.

Elizabeth looked at Mac, then at the old piano. Taking a deep breath, she walked across the room and sat at the bench. Mr. Jacobs dropped into one of the booths and watched. *Why won't he just go away?* she thought. *I don't like to play in front of anybody, and especially not sneaky, low-down cowboys!*

She began to play Mozart's Sonata in C, and then transitioned into a praise song. Before long, she became absorbed in her music, and she played nearly flawlessly for the next several minutes. By the time she had finished, she had almost forgotten anyone else was in the room. She was startled by their applause and cheers, and began to blush.

"I'm impressed," said Jacobs. "Not very many people have a gift like that. 'I will sing and make music to the Lord,' Psalm 27:6."

"Thank you," she whispered, and turned back to the keyboard. *Now he's quoting scripture?* Elizabeth had no idea what to make of this man.

He stood to his feet and tipped his hat. "Thank you for the tea, and for the music. Good night, ladies," he told them, and walked out the door.

As soon as he was out of sight, the girls all sighed with relief. "What are we going to do?" Elizabeth asked. "He's following us. He knows we're on to something."

Jean Louise stopped smacking her gum and said, "You do the only thing you can do. You keep looking, and you beat him to the treasure. Come on, ladies. Let's tear this place apart!"

Megan climbed on the table and hefted the large fish off the wall. The four of them examined it, but didn't find any secret compartments or hollow spots. They looked at the wall behind the fish. They examined the floor beneath the fish. They even moved all the booths and benches to make sure there was nothing hidden beneath them.

"What if they're hidden in the stuffing of one of the benches?" Elizabeth asked. She was about ready to tear into a bench with a steak knife when Jean Louise stopped her.

"Whoa, there. This furniture gets replaced every ten years or so. If Emily Marie hid the marbles in one of the benches, they are long gone by now."

Frustrated, the girls sank into one of the booths. Megan looked close to tears as she said, "We might as well hang it up. We'll never find those marbles."

Elizabeth wanted to argue, but she was feeling the same way. Then she remembered her prize money.

"Megan, do you know what I did tonight before I came here?" Elizabeth asked.

"I don't know. What?"

"I caught a pig," Elizabeth said with a giggle.

Megan sat up, and said, "You did what?" She looked to McKenzie for confirmation.

"She did," Mac told her. "She caught a pig at the Livestock Show and Rodeo, in front of the entire stadium. And she was covered from head to toe in mud!"

"You're kidding!" Megan laughed at the thought. "You mean Miss Perfect, always-keeps-her-room-clean, never-a-hair-out-of-place Elizabeth was covered in mud?"

"Yep. And she won the prize too," Mac said.

"Really? What was the prize?" asked Megan.

"It's money. Not much, but I already know how I'm going to spend it," said Elizabeth. "I'm going to buy a saxophone."

"A saxophone?" the two girls asked in unison.

"I didn't know you wanted to play the saxophone," said Megan.

"I don't. But I would love to have someone accompany me on the saxophone. Me on the piano. . .you know. A duet," Elizabeth said.

Slowly, Megan realized that Elizabeth wanted to purchase her band instrument for her. "Elizabeth, I can't let you do that."

"Why not? It's my money. I'll spend it however I want," Elizabeth told her.

They were interrupted by Jean Louise. "Girls, I promised your parents I'd have you all home before midnight, and it's almost that time now. We'd better go."

They piled into the woman's car, and within minutes they were pulling up to Elizabeth's house where the girls were going to spend the night. They were surprised to see the lights still on. "Thanks, Jean Louise!" they called from the porch. The woman waved and drove away.

Inside, Elizabeth's mom, dad, and brother were in the living room. James was chattering a mile a minute about spooky houses and greasy pigs and somebody losing marbles. Between sentences, he zoomed the tiny blue car through the air.

"Why are y'all still awake?" Elizabeth asked.

"Someone had too much cotton candy," her mother nodded to James. "Besides, we wanted to make sure you girls made it home safely."

"Can anyone explain to us what the spooky house is?" asked Mr. Anderson. James was still zooming his car around the room.

"Probably the house of mirrors. Evan's marbles spilled out of his pocket while we were in there."

Mr. and Mrs. Anderson burst into laughter. "So that's what he was talking about when he said Evan lost his marbles! We thought Evan had gone crazy!"

The girls giggled, and the adults stood. "There are snacks in the kitchen, girls. Try not to stay up too late. James, it is way past your bed-time. Come on. Into bed you go."

James obeyed, still zooming his tiny blue Cadillac as he headed down the hallway toward his room. "This is the coolest car I've ever seen. Just look at those fins!"

The girls looked at one another in stunned excitement. "Fins!" they all three called out at once. "The Cadillac Ranch!"

•—•—•

Within the next half hour, emails were flying. Alexis had contacted the other Camp Club Girls, and they were expecting Elizabeth and McKen-zie to be online around midnight.

Elizabeth's fingers clicked away at the keyboard: *We searched the restaurant. No luck. We wonder if the marbles are hidden at the Cadillac Ranch. Did anyone find information on Mark Jacobs?*

Bailey: *The only thing I found on your Roy Rogers is that he's an award-winning rodeo rider. I found his picture too. You're right! He is handsome.*
Elizabeth: *We can't figure the guy out. One minute he's follow-ing us and asking questions. Then he quotes scripture. Either he's a really nice guy, or he's a great crook. I guess we'll see what happens at the Cadillac Ranch tomorrow.*
Kate: *Too bad u can't attach a secret spy camera or recorder to him to see what he's doing and saying when you aren't around. That might help.*
Sydney: *What are you going to do? Just go there and start dig-ging? You might get arrested.*

McKenzie took over the keyboard: *Well what else can we do? Any suggestions?*

Alexis: *What led you to the Cadillac Ranch? I thought we were looking for fins or something. I'm confused.*

Mac typed out the events of the evening, including James's exclamation over his car's fins.

McKenzie: *We plan to visit there tomorrow. I guess we'll look around and see what we can find. Maybe we'll have to go back after dark.*

The girls all signed off, promising to do further research and stay in close contact.

During this time, Megan sat quietly at the kitchen table, observing the exchange. "You need to take a shovel with you tomorrow. I'll be working—as usual."

"How can we take a shovel without everyone seeing it?" asked McKenzie.

Elizabeth eyed the pot of geraniums on the kitchen windowsill. "We can't take a full-sized shovel. But I know what we can take." She stood up and walked to the back door. Flipping on the porch light, she stepped outside.

McKenzie and Megan looked at each other and shrugged their shoulders. They could hear Elizabeth rummaging around on the porch. Finally, they heard their friend call out, "Got it!"

Elizabeth walked back into the kitchen holding a garden spade. "It may take us awhile, but this will definitely dig a hole. Trust me. I've dug plenty of holes with this for my mom's garden."

"That's a great idea, Beth, but Sydney is right. We can't just go out there in broad daylight and dig."

The three girls sat drumming their fingers on the table, trying to think of a solution. "We've got to get out there in the evening when there aren't so many tourists. But how?"

Megan sat up straight. "We could ride our bikes. It's only a couple of miles outside of town."

"Do you know how to get there?" Elizabeth asked her.

"Yeah," the older girl answered. "I even know a shortcut from the church."

"Mac can ride my bike, and I'll ride my mom's," said Elizabeth.

"We've just got to figure out a reason to go to the church tomorrow evening, since it's not a church night," said McKenzie.

"That'll be easy," Megan told her. "Elizabeth's family practically lives at the church anyway."

The girls talked a little longer, but their conversation was interrupted by yawns. Before long, the three young detectives scooted to bed.

•—•—•

The next morning, the girls slept in. The sun was high in the sky by the time Elizabeth woke to a paper airplane landing on her face. She fluttered her eyes and found James staring at her.

"Mama said to get up if you want to go to the Cadillac Ranch. McKenzie's parents will be here in a little while to pick us up."

Elizabeth rolled over and pulled the covers over her head, but James was persistent.

"Mama said if you get up now, she'll make homemade doughnuts. But if you wait too long, you'll only get cereal."

McKenzie popped up from her pallet on the floor.

"Homemade doughnuts? I love doughnuts," she said sleepily.

Megan stirred from her sleeping bag, and said, "Tell your mom we'll be there in a minute, James."

James jumped from his spot on Elizabeth's bed, and she heard him padding down the hallway. Groaning, she forced herself to sit up.

The girls looked at each other, each one wanting a hot doughnut, but none wanting to actually leave bed.

McKenzie finally spoke. "Tomorrow is our last full day here. We go home the next day."

Elizabeth groaned and flopped back down in her bed. "I don't want to think about it. I've gotten used to having you around twenty-four hours a day."

"Y'all, we've got to find those marbles," Megan said, rummaging around in her bag and pulling out her toothbrush.

"Let's review the plan. We'll ride our bikes to the church this evening. And you know a shortcut from there to the Cadillac Ranch?" Elizabeth asked.

Megan nodded.

"It sounds like the perfect plan," said McKenzie. "So why do I have a bad feeling about the whole thing?"

"Riding our bikes two miles out of town doesn't sound great to me either," said Elizabeth. "But sometimes you've just got to do what you've got to do. And we've got to find those marbles before Mr. Jacobs does."

James banged on the door, hollering, "Mama says come now while the doughnuts are hot!"

"We're coming!" Elizabeth called back. Then she said, "Let's just take this one step at a time. We're going out there today. Maybe we'll be able to dig some. Let's see what happens."

Nodding, the girls stood up and followed the smell of fresh, hot doughnuts.

•—•—•

Elizabeth and McKenzie stared at the row of Cadillacs, noses buried in the ground, tails sticking high in the air. "Cadillac Ranch my foot. This is a Cadillac graveyard!" McKenzie said.

Elizabeth giggled. "Who would think of doing such a thing?"

"Apparently, Chip Lord, Hudson Marquez, and Doug Michaels," Mac replied, referring to the brochure she held. "They are supposed to represent the birth and death of the early model Cadillacs, and an era in American culture. They are buried at the same angle as the Great Pyramid of Giza, in Egypt."

"Groovy," responded Elizabeth, and Mac giggled at the old-fashioned word.

The sun glistened off the shiny metal, and the girls shielded their eyes from the glare. Evan and James were already running in and out of the cars, exclaiming over the bright colors and shapes.

"Well, there's the blue one, third from the end," said Elizabeth. "We might as well take a look."

The girls smiled as they passed another group of tourists. "We'll never get to explore with all these people around taking pictures at every turn," whispered McKenzie.

Elizabeth fingered the garden spade in her purse as they approached the blue Cadillac. "I have an idea. Stand in front of me, and I'll kneel down like I'm inspecting the motor. Watch for people, and tell me when anyone is coming."

McKenzie did as she was told, exclaiming loudly over different features of the car every time a tourist walked by. At one point, she even posed for a picture one of them was snapping.

"What are you doing?" Elizabeth asked her.

"Hiding in plain sight," Mac answered.

"Huh?" Elizabeth grunted, confused.

"If it looks like we're trying to hide what we're doing, people will be suspicious. But if we just act like goofy tourists, no one will suspect a thing!" Mac explained.

"Mac, you don't have to act like a goofy tourist. You are one," Elizabeth said with a laugh.

"Just keep digging," ordered Mac, and Elizabeth obeyed.

All of a sudden, she hit something in the dirt. Something hard. "Mac! I think I've found it!" she whispered.

Mrs. Phillips chose that moment to call, "Girls! Come on. We have several more stops to make today."

Mac stiffened and told Elizabeth, "Quick! Cover it up! My mom's coming over here. We'll have to come back tonight."

Elizabeth frantically replaced the dirt in the hole she'd dug, and slipped the spade back into her purse as Mrs. Phillips approached. "You two sure are fascinated with this blue one. Hey look, Elizabeth, it matches your eyes. I'll tell your dad he needs to buy you a blue car one day."

Elizabeth laughed and replied, "A blue *Cadillac.*"

Mrs. Phillips chuckled and began moving toward the car. The two secret sleuths took deep breaths, gave one last look over their shoulders at the loose dirt beneath the motor of the car, and followed her.

Danger in the Dark!

That evening, the girls sat in the Andersons' kitchen acting bored. Mrs. Anderson was putting the last dish in the dishwasher.

"I need to get some exercise," said McKenzie. "All this vacationing and lounging around the pool is making me tired."

"Why don't we ride bikes?" Elizabeth asked.

"That sounds great. But I don't have my bicycle here."

"Why don't you ride mine? That is, if my dear mother will let me ride hers," Elizabeth said, smiling at her mom.

Mrs. Anderson smiled. "That sounds like a wonderful idea. It's a beautiful evening for a bike ride."

"I have an idea. Mom, I left my library book at church last Sunday. Can we ride up there to get it?"

"I suppose. Just stay on the back roads. Don't go in the busy streets," she said. "And why don't you ask Megan to go too. She needs to get out more."

Within minutes, the plan was underway. The three girls rode their bikes the short distance to the church. When Megan led them on a narrow trail behind the church, Elizabeth said, "What about my library book? We need to stop and get it."

"We'll stop on the way back," Megan called over her shoulder. "Let's get out there while we still have some light. The church doors will still be open till at least ten. I think the senior high teens are having a volleyball tournament or something there tonight."

"This is so exciting," said Mac. "I can't believe we're actually going to find the marbles."

"We *hope* we're going to find the marbles," Elizabeth corrected. "But I do have a good feeling about this. Something was down there this afternoon when I was digging. And that's the last place your grandmother was, Megan, before she got in the car wreck. Remember, she was serving at a party there so it would have been easy for her to step outside and hide them there. "

The bike trail grew bumpy, and tall ears of corn formed a wall on either side of them.

"Uh, Megs, are you sure you know where you're going?" asked Elizabeth.

"Trust me. It's just a little further," she called over her shoulder.

Sure enough, a few minutes later they pulled into a clearing. Ahead of them was the row of cars, half buried in the ground.

"I had no idea this was so close," said Elizabeth.

"Yeah," agreed McKenzie. "It seemed a lot farther in the car today."

"It is farther when you take the main road. That's why they call it a shortcut!"

The girls stowed their bikes in the tall stalks of corn and surveyed the field before them.

With whispers and giggles of excitement, they started digging through their backpacks, pulling out supplies.

"Where's the other flashlight?" whispered Megan.

"I have it," Mac answered, clicking on the beam.

"Turn it off. You'll run the battery down. We don't need it yet," Megan whispered, and McKenzie turned it off.

"I have the spade and another small shovel," whispered Elizabeth. Then, as an afterthought, she asked, "Why are we whispering? No one is around."

The girls giggled nervously. "I don't know. It just feels like we're supposed to be whispering," answered Mac. The three made their way across the country field to where the ten Cadillacs stood with their rear ends sticking in the air.

Stopping in front of the blue one, they found the place where Elizabeth had dug that afternoon.

"Here it is," Mac whispered. "Megan, you've been working all day. You keep watch while Elizabeth and I dig."

"Okay," the sixteen-year-old answered. Something in her face held a look of hope that made her look much younger than the other two. "Please, God, let the marbles be here."

"I'm surprised they don't have more security here," McKenzie said.

"Why? They're just a bunch of junk cars," Elizabeth pointed out.

"But they could still be vandalized," McKenzie said as she started to dig.

"Guess they're not too concerned," Elizabeth said.

Elizabeth and Mac moved the loose dirt to the side and found the hard object Elizabeth had felt earlier. With grunts and groans, they pulled the object out of its resting place.

"A rock," they all three sighed with disappointment.

"Let's keep digging," Elizabeth said, and she and Mac went back to work. They dug and dug, finding nothing. Finally, sweat dripping down her brow, Elizabeth realized she had a problem.

"Uh, y'all?"

"Yeah?" the other two answered.

"Remember that soda I drank earlier?"

"Yeah?" they answered again.

"Remember the refill?"

"Uh-huh," came the reply.

"I have to go to the bathroom."

Mac giggled, and Megan sighed.

"I really have to go. Now!"

"Well, go! Nobody can see you," Megan told her.

"I'm not going to the bathroom right here! That's disgusting!" Elizabeth said.

"You could go back to where we parked the bikes," Mac suggested. "But then again, that might be too corny!" She laughed at her own joke, and the other girls snickered.

Elizabeth crossed her legs. "It's getting dark," she whispered.

Mac and Megan kept working.

"Will somebody go with me?"

"No," they both responded.

"Here, take the big flashlight. Mac and I will stay here with the smaller one. Hurry back," Megan said, handing her the larger of the two lights.

Elizabeth dashed toward the direction of the bikes. Only she couldn't actually see the bikes, and there were several little trails that led off the field. She didn't know which one to take. Soon, she couldn't wait any longer, and just followed one of the trails a few feet from the opening. Turning around, she could still see her friends' flashlight beam, and knew she could find her way back to them. Shining her light, she found a place that seemed to offer enough privacy, and took care of her business.

Suddenly, a flash of headlights flooded the area, and she ducked behind the corn. Her breath caught in her throat as she watched the pickup truck pass on the road in front of the cars and saw the silhouette of the driver, wearing a cowboy hat.

Mr. Jacobs!

Had Megan and Mac seen? She had to warn them! But their flashlight beam had disappeared. Where had they gone? Had they seen the headlights too?

The truck pulled to the side of the road. Its headlights lit up the small gate before they died down. She heard the sound of the truck door opening. Closing. The beam of another flashlight clicked on.

The new flashlight steadily moved toward the row of upturned cars! She watched, not knowing where to go or what to do. Turning around, she realized she was lost. She had no idea where the bikes were. And the sun had disappeared from the horizon.

The night was black, except for her flashlight.

It can't be too far, she thought. *I think I need to go. . .this way.* Staying low behind the corn stalks, she cupped her hand around her flashlight beam. *Maybe this will keep Jacobs from spotting me.*

Dear God, she prayed, *this was a stupid idea. What were we thinking? Riding out here alone at night. . . God, I'm scared. Please be with Megan and Mac, and keep them safe. And please help me to find my way back to them!*

She looked toward the old cars. Only one beam of light. She knew by its brightness it belonged to Mr. Jacobs—the girls had kept the tiny light for themselves. "Where are they?" she whispered. Suddenly, the clouds shifted. The moon cast a soft glow on the area.

Then, a rustling sound! She put her fist in her mouth to keep from gasping.

"Elizabeth?" Megan's whisper came through the darkness.

"Meg? Where are you? I got turned around, and I can't find the bikes!" Elizabeth whispered back.

A tiny beam of light flickered on and off, and Elizabeth scooted toward it. She saw the shapes of her two friends, and she let out the breath she hadn't known she was holding. Sliding onto her bike, she commanded, "Let's get out of here!"

The girls pedaled faster and faster, away from the Cadillac Ranch, away from danger. Corn husks slapped their faces and ankles. Elizabeth nearly lost her balance on the bumpy trail, but she kept going.

No one said a word until they approached the lights of the church. The only sounds were the tires on the rough road, and the girls' heavy breathing.

Elizabeth spoke first. "What happened back there? I was so scared!"

Mac turned around on her seat. "A couple of minutes after you left, we saw the truck's headlights coming up the road. We thought it would just pass, but we turned off our flashlight just in case. Then, when it stopped, we knew we had to get out of there!"

"We hoped you'd be at the bikes when we got there, but I should have known better. How could you have gotten lost? It's a bare field. Nothing's there!" Megan teased her friend.

"You know how easily I get turned around. When I saw him stop the truck, and then I couldn't find y'all, I just about died. I was so scared!"

"So were we!" Megan and Mac replied.

"When we turned our flashlight off, we couldn't see a thing! Then the clouds shifted, and the moon gave us just enough light to find our way back to the bikes. But you weren't there," Megan continued.

Elizabeth felt a warm feeling and knew that God had sent that moonlight as an answer to her prayer. Then she remembered their reason for going out there in the first place. "Did you find the marbles?" she asked.

Megan kept her eyes on the road but said nothing. Mac silently shook her head.

As they turned onto the street that Elizabeth and Megan called home, they were surprised to see five adults standing in the driveway. None of them looked happy.

Elizabeth watched relief cover her mother's face, and she realized they had been out longer than they'd realized.

"Where have you girls been? It got dark half an hour ago! We've been worried sick!" exclaimed Ruby Smith, first hugging her daughter and then giving her a frustrated look.

The other two sets of parents reached for their own daughters. "You girls had better have a good explanation," McKenzie's father told them.

"Why don't we go inside? I have a feeling this is going to take awhile," said Mr. Anderson.

The three girls filed into the living room, followed by the adults. Evan was sound asleep on the sofa, and Elizabeth assumed James was down the hall, in his own bed.

"Let's go in the kitchen. I'll make some coffee," suggested Mrs. Anderson. The adults sat around the table, leaving the three girls to lean against the counter.

"We're ready when you are. Spill it," said Ruby Smith, looking at her daughter.

Megan took a deep breath, and said, "Mom, those marbles are real. And Mark Jacobs is after them. He's been looking for them this whole time, and I think he knows they belong to you and Uncle Jack. You work so hard all the time, and I just thought—"

"That's what this is about? Those silly marbles? Megan Rebecca Smith, I ought to tan your hide! That is the most ridiculous—"

"Excuse me, Ruby, but what's this about Mark Jacobs? He seems like a decent man to me," said Mr. Phillips. He looked to McKenzie. "Would you like to tell me what's going on?"

McKenzie looked at her father, and said, "I'm sorry, Daddy. But we think he's a con man. Megan's mother inherited some jewels, but she didn't know it. Now Jacobs is trying to get them before she does."

"Jewels?" he asked. "Megan said you were looking for marbles!"

"Hold on a minute," Elizabeth's father interrupted. "I think we'd better back up and start from the beginning. Elizabeth, why don't you start?"

It took a lot of starting and stopping, but eventually the adults were filled in on the entire account. It was late, and the adults decided to withhold judgment until the next day. McKenzie cast Elizabeth a worried look over her shoulder as she stepped onto the front porch.

Megan kept her head down as she followed her mother to their own front door. When everyone was gone, Elizabeth turned to face her parents. She hated the disappointment she read there.

"We'll talk about this in the morning. There is cold pizza in the refrigerator, if you're hungry. Get a snack, and go to bed," her father told her, and then joined her mother in their own bedroom. She could hear them talking but couldn't make out any words as she poured herself a glass of milk. She tried to drink it, but the knot in her throat made it difficult to swallow. She was about to place the glass back in the refrigerator when she noticed the email light flashing at the bottom of the computer screen.

Sitting at the desk, she opened her inbox. There was a message from Kate. It read:

Did some research. The Cadillac Ranch has moved. Is now in a different location than it was 30 years ago.

You're looking in the wrong place.

The next morning, Elizabeth sat at the kitchen table with her parents, listening to the lecture she knew she deserved. "I can't believe you girls rode out there at night, alone. Why didn't you come to us?"

Elizabeth tried to explain. "I know it was a dumb thing to do. I can't even begin to tell you how sorry I am. I know there's no excuse, but I was only thinking of Megan and her mom. They've had such a hard time since Mr. Smith died, and these marbles would help them so much. And I guess I was afraid you wouldn't take the whole thing seriously."

Her mom and dad looked at one another, then back at her. "Maybe you're right. We might not have taken this seriously," her mom said. "We still see you as our little girl, playing make-believe. But Elizabeth, you can always come to us about anything. There's no excuse for what you did last night."

Elizabeth looked at her hands. She was truly sorry for sneaking around behind their backs.

Her dad spoke up then. "First you sneaked out of your window, in a storm. Then, you go riding off without telling us where you are. At night! Anything could have happened. I know your intentions were good, but that's no excuse for acting foolish. You're grounded to the house for the next two weeks. But we won't start the punishment until after McKenzie goes home. We know you want to spend as much time with her as possible."

Elizabeth scooted her chair back and threw her arms around her parents' necks. "Thank you so much! I promise I'll never do anything like that ever again!" Then, remembering Kate's email, she said, "Uh, Mom and Dad? There's one more thing I need to talk to you about." She shared the latest discovery, only to be interrupted by her father.

"That's right. I had forgotten about them moving the Cadillac Ranch. I know exactly where it used to be."

"Really?" Elizabeth questioned. "Will you take us there?"

He smiled at his daughter and said, "Of course I will. But it's not that simple. The old location was in a huge wheat field. Trying to find your marbles there would be like looking for a needle in a haystack."

"Dad, you do the driving and leave the rest to me," she told him. Sitting down at the computer, she typed "*Cadillac Ranch—original location—pictures*" into the search engine.

Sure enough, dozens of pictures popped up. Elizabeth knew she was on the brink of discovery when she noticed something. In each of the pictures, the Cadillacs were painted differently. Some of the pictures even had graffiti covering each of the cars. How in the world was she supposed to figure out which one was the blue one?

She let out a groan just as the phone rang. "Hello?" she spoke into the receiver.

"Elizabeth? It's Mac. Are you in as much trouble as I am?"

"I'm grounded for two weeks. But Mom and Dad said it can wait until after you leave."

"That's good. We leave tomorrow, and I'd hate it if we couldn't spend my last day together. But I have bad news."

Elizabeth braced herself for whatever Mac had to say. But she never would have guessed just how bad that news was. . . .

The Best Vacation Ever

"This morning when I woke up, I heard voices outside our door. I peeked out the window, and my dad was out there talking to Mr. Jacobs. And he was showing him the journals."

Elizabeth nearly dropped the phone. "He what?" she croaked. Visions of the tall cowboy, riding off into the sunset holding the bag of marbles flashed through her mind. "Why would he do such a thing?"

McKenzie sighed. "He's convinced that Jacobs is a nice guy. Even after hearing the whole story."

Elizabeth took a deep breath. "Well, we can't do anything about it now. But Mac, listen. After y'all left last night, I had an email from Kate. The Cadillac Ranch has changed locations! We weren't even digging at the right site!"

"You're kidding," said McKenzie with a groan. "What will we do?"

"My dad said he'd take us out there today. I've got pictures of where the cars used to be, but they've been painted over the years. I'll do some more research. Do you think your parents will let you come?"

"I don't know. Let me call you back."

"Okay, but hurry. We've got to get there before Mr. Jacobs does," Elizabeth told her.

Within the hour, the Andersons, Phillipses, and Smiths were all squeezed into the Andersons' van. Heavy, dark clouds were moving in, giving a sense of urgency to the situation.

"The storm looks a ways away. I think we can beat it," Mr. Phillips said. Elizabeth's dad started the car, and they headed toward the old Cadillac Ranch.

Elizabeth, McKenzie, and Megan sat in the backseat of the van. Elizabeth had printed some pictures so they could get an idea of the location. She had even found a picture dated close to the time of Emily Marie's death.

"Why are the cars different colors in the pictures?" asked Megan.

"The cars are repainted every so often. Once, they were all painted pink, in support of breast cancer victims. Tourists are allowed—even encouraged, to paint graffiti on the cars, and every so often they are repainted to offer a fresh canvas," Elizabeth told them.

"So we have no way of knowing which car was blue at the time of my grandmother's death?" asked Megan.

"Not really. This picture is dated the same year, and the blue car is the fourth from the right. Look, it's lined up with this telephone pole, and there are two big oak trees in the background, one on either side of it. Hopefully, the telephone pole and the trees are still there," Elizabeth said.

Before long, Mr. Anderson stopped the car on the edge of an endless wheat field. "This will be tough," murmured McKenzie.

Everyone piled out of the car, and immediately James and Evan began chasing one another in and out of the rows of wheat.

Elizabeth looked at her father. "How will we ever do this?" she asked him.

"This is your job. Remember, you said all I had to do was drive." Patting her on the shoulder, he whispered, "I have faith in you."

Elizabeth stood a little taller and held the pictures to the horizon. "Okay, girls, it looks like it's up to us. First things first. Let's find these trees."

Before they knew it, everyone was hunting—even James and Evan. The pictures were passed from person to person, with cries of, "There's a tree!" and "Look! There's an electrical pole!"

They were all distracted with their scavenger hunt and didn't notice a beat-up truck pulling up behind them. An old farmer got out and asked, "Can I help you folks with somethin'?"

Mr. Anderson stepped forward and shook the man's hand. "Yes, sir, there is. We're looking for the original location of the Cadillac Ranch."

The man scratched his head and chuckled. "Well, there's not much to see. But I can take you to it if you'd like," he said.

Elizabeth and McKenzie started jumping up and down. "Really? You'll take us to the exact spot?"

The old farmer shook his head and muttered, "Crazy tourists." He got in his truck, rolled down his window, and said, "Follow me."

A crash of thunder sounded, and the group piled in the car just as the first drops of rain started falling from the sky. The man led them to a spot about a half mile up the road, and veered off to the left. Rolling the window down, he pointed to a sign, half covered with wheat. It read, "Original location of the Cadillac Ranch." Small posts stuck out of the ground, to show where each car had stood. The man waved and drove away.

"I don't believe it," Megan whispered.

Thank You, God, Elizabeth prayed silently. *Please let us find the jewels. Marbles. Whatever they are, Lord, please help us find them.*

The three girls climbed out of the van, but the adults didn't want to get wet. Mr. Phillips handed McKenzie a shovel through the open window. They were splattering through the mud when they realized Ruby Smith was on their heels.

"I'm going to help. If those marbles are real, I want to be there when they are found," the woman told them.

Elizabeth smiled, reached into her purse, and handed her the spade.

They located the fourth post from the right and started digging. The rain softened the earth, making the digging easier. And messier.

Thunder continued crashing, but the four females paid no attention. They were so focused on their task that they didn't notice a large pair of mud-covered cowboy boots approaching.

"May I give you a hand?" Mark Jacobs's voice spoke over the sound of the rain.

Startled, Ruby looked up at him and continued digging. The three girls weren't sure how to respond to his presence and stopped what they were doing.

Gently, the man took the large shovel from McKenzie and started digging on the opposite side of the post. His muscles took the shovel deeper into the ground than the girls had been able to dig, and after a couple of scoops, the shovel revealed an old, small tin cashbox. Ruby's mouth dropped open, and she looked up at the man.

"I bet this belongs to you," he said.

The woman reached down and took the box from the shovel. Her mud-covered hands shook as she opened it. Inside was a velvet bag. Inside that were some papers and a smaller cloth bag with a drawstring tie.

By this time, Elizabeth's and McKenzie's parents had joined them. No one spoke as Ruby Smith opened the bag her mother had buried so long ago. She emptied its contents into her hands, and twelve of the most beautiful, brightly colored marbles spilled out.

"Oh!" the woman cried. "Oh Mama!"

Megan knelt in the mud beside her mother and hugged her as they both wept.

The rest of the group decided to give them privacy and headed back to the van. Jacobs turned to go, but Ruby called out, "Wait! I have so many questions. Where are you going?"

The tall cowboy smiled and said, "We'll have plenty of time to talk later. Right now, you enjoy this moment with your daughter and her friends." He tipped his hat and left.

Without warning, the rain stopped, and the sun broke through the clouds. The marbles in Ruby's hands cast a brilliant glow on her face as she looked at her daughter. "We're going to be okay," she whispered.

The group sat around the table at the Big Texan Steak Ranch, drinking in the exchange between Ruby Smith and Mark Jacobs. Even Jean Louise, who was their waitress, had broken the rules and pulled a chair up to the table.

"I can't believe Foster Wilson was your uncle. I never met him, though I do remember Mama talking about a nice man she wanted me and Jack to meet," Ruby told the man sitting across from her.

"It's as much of a surprise to me as it is to you. I always knew Uncle Foster fell in love here in Amarillo. I just never knew the whole story," Mr. Jacobs responded. He looked around the table, and his eyes rested on Elizabeth. "I knew you were on to me, and I'm sorry I made you nervous. When I realized you were after the same thing I was, I just figured you were some detective wannabe. You were always one step ahead of me, though. When I figured out you really knew what you were doing, I began to follow you. Sorry if I scared you."

"That's okay. I'm sorry I thought you were a con m—"

"Elizabeth!" her mother stopped her.

Mr. Jacobs tilted his head back and roared. "It's okay, Sue. She had every right to believe I was a con man."

Everyone laughed this time. Then Ruby spoke again.

"I've given this a lot of thought, Mark, and my brother, Jack, and I have talked about it on the phone. He agrees with me, and I don't want to hear any arguments. There are twelve marbles, and we're going to split them. Jack and I will take six and the other six belong to you," Ruby said.

"Oh no, Ruby, I couldn't, now that I know the whole story. Those were a gift to your mother. I wouldn't dream of taking them," Jacobs replied.

"Now, Mark Jacobs, you listen. Your uncle would have wanted you to have them as much as he wanted me to have them. You can argue with me all you want, but I'll get my way. Each marble is worth close to one hundred thousand dollars. We can certainly afford to share them," Ruby argued.

Jacobs opened his mouth, but Ruby cut him off. "Not another word!" she said.

The handsome cowboy leaned back in his chair and grinned. "How do you know what I was going to say?" he asked.

"You were going to argue with me, I know that," the woman told him.

"No, ma'am. I know better than to argue with you; I have the feeling that once your mind is made up, there's no changing it."

"You're right about that," Ruby told him. The two bantered back and forth as if no one else were in the room.

McKenzie nudged Elizabeth under the table, then whispered, "I don't know why she's giving him the marbles. When they get married, they'll belong to both of them."

The two girls giggled. "Let's not rush things," Elizabeth whispered back. "But they do make a nice couple, don't they?"

They turned their attention back to Ruby and the cowboy. "So, what were you going to say?" Ruby asked coyly.

Jacobs looked her in the eye and said, "I was going to say that I came here looking for a treasure. I believe I may have found one, whose worth is far more than rubies. And her name. . .is Ruby."

The group applauded, then Jean Louise began taking their orders.

Elizabeth focused her attention on Megan, who was smiling and watching her mother. "You look happy," she told her friend.

Megan turned to Elizabeth and McKenzie. "It just feels so good to see Mom smile. It's been a long time since I've seen her so happy. And it's all thanks to the two of you and the Camp Club Girls."

Elizabeth glanced at Megan's mom, laughing at something Jacobs had said. "I'm not sure if we can take the credit for making your mom smile. I think that goes to a certain handsome cowboy," she told her friend.

Megan laughed. "He may have something to do with it, but the sadness is gone from her face. Now she won't have to work so hard all the time. Now she doesn't have to worry as much about paying the bills every month. And I owe it all to the two of you and your excellent sleuthing skills."

"I just wish we didn't have to leave as soon as we finish our lunch here," said McKenzie. Then, reaching into her backpack she said, "Oh! Before I forget. . .these belong to Jean Louise."

She pulled out the journals. Then she turned again to Megan. "Thank you for letting me help solve the marble mystery. This has been the best vacation ever!"

•—•—•

Elizabeth sat at the kitchen table, chin propped on her elbow, flipping through a library book. She loved to read, but reading was all she had done during the past week. One more week, and her grounding would be over.

"Hello, princess. What are you reading?" her father asked as he came into the kitchen.

"It's a book about an Amish girl named Rachel Yoder. I'm a little over halfway through," she told him.

He pulled out a chair and sat down across from her. "Did I ever tell you how proud I am of you?" he asked.

Elizabeth smiled but said nothing. He had told her many times.

"You are like those marbles you found—rare and precious. I'm proud of you for being so determined to help Megan and her mom," he told her.

"It was kind of fun, looking back on it. Maybe I'll be a detective someday," she said with a laugh.

He leaned forward and rested his arms on the table. "Ruby told me that you offered to use your prize money to buy Megan's band instrument. That was very generous of you."

Elizabeth blushed. She hadn't meant for others to find out. "I didn't need the money, and they did. It was no big deal."

"God loves a cheerful giver, you know," he told her, reaching out to pat her hand.

"I know—2 Corinthians 9:7," she said.

Mr. Anderson smiled at his daughter before standing up and mussing her hair. "Like I said, princess, I'm proud of you. By the way, your computer screen shows that you have email waiting."

Elizabeth wasted no time in moving to the computer and clicking on her email. It was from Alexis, addressed to all the Camp Club Girls.

I'm going to the London Bridge! Did you all know they moved it, and it's not in London anymore? It is at Lake Havasu, Arizona. Isn't that the craziest thing you've ever heard?

My grandmother is going to be a guest speaker at the London Bridge Festival there, at the end of October. And she's invited me to go along! I'm so excited!

Elizabeth read back through the email a couple of times. *Lake Havasu. Lake Havasu.* Why did that name sound familiar?

Suddenly, she remembered. "Uh, Dad?" she called over her shoulder. "You know that convention or whatever that you go to at the end of October every year? Isn't that at Lake Havasu, Arizona?"

"Yes, it is. It's during the London Bridge Festival there. Why do you ask?"

Elizabeth felt the excitement mounting inside her. She was almost afraid to ask her next question. "Any chance I could go with you this year?"

"Funny you should ask that. I've been thinking about taking the whole family. I think you'd enjoy it."

Elizabeth lunged from her chair and threw her arms around her father's neck. "Oh thank you, Daddy! Thank you, thank you, thank you!"

Surprised, he laughed and returned the hug. "Whoa! You're welcome! You want to tell me what this is about?"

"I will in a minute. First, I have to email Alexis!"

Camp Club Girls:
Elizabeth's San Antonio Sleuthing

Trouble on the River

Splash! Fourteen-year-old Elizabeth gasped as cold water covered her face and clothes. She stood and shook the liquid from her blond hair and tried to wipe it from her clothes before it soaked through.

"Please remain in your seat at all times," the riverboat captain reminded her.

Didn't he see what just happened? Elizabeth's mother took her hand and gently pulled her back into her seat, helping Elizabeth brush the water off.

"What happened?" Elizabeth whispered, not wanting to interrupt the captain's tour speech. No one else seemed to notice her.

"It looks like a water balloon. I didn't see where it came from. We'll deal with it when the boat stops," her mother said. Elizabeth spied the small red piece of broken balloon at her feet.

"But who? Where?" Elizabeth looked at the tourists on the sidewalks. Surely no one would be brazen enough to throw a water balloon right out in the open. *The bridge!*

She looked behind her at the bridge they'd just passed. Empty.

Puzzled, she took the tissue her mother held out to her. Elizabeth's dad and brother were seated in front of her, and never even turned around. Apparently, no one else knew what had just happened.

Once again, she looked back at the bridge. This time, she saw three teenagers leaning over the other side. One was wearing a red cap and a plaid shirt. They were pointing and laughing at another riverboat making its way toward them.

Suspicious. Well, Mr. Red-cap. You haven't seen the last of me.

Elizabeth kept her eyes behind her, on the group of two boys and one girl, until a curve in the river blocked her view. Finally, she leaned back and tried to enjoy the rest of the ride.

When the riverboat pulled to the edge and the passengers were instructed to get off the boat, Robert Anderson turned and smiled at his daughter and wife. "I never get tired of San Antonio. As many times as I've ridden this riverboat and heard the same historical facts and the same corny jokes, I love it every time. Hey, what happened to you?" he asked Elizabeth, noticing her soaked hair.

"Some prankster dropped a water balloon on her," Sue Anderson spoke for her daughter. "It seemed to come out of nowhere."

"I saw who did it," said Elizabeth. "Or at least, who I think did it. Some teenagers were leaning over one of the bridges right after it happened."

Robert Anderson placed his hand on his daughter's shoulder and grinned. "I'm sorry, baby. That was a mean thing for someone to do. But if they were aiming for a pretty girl, I have to give them credit. Their aim was right on target."

Elizabeth crossed her arms. She didn't see the humor.

"Let's not jump to conclusions," said her dad as he helped her off the boat. "We'll go right now and talk to the captain. But just because you saw some kids on the bridge doesn't necessarily mean they're guilty."

Elizabeth nodded, but she wasn't convinced. She was going to be on the watch for that red ball cap and plaid shirt. She was so caught up in her thoughts, she wasn't even aware that the captain was talking to her. Suddenly, she realized he was asking her a question.

"Your parents just told me what happened, young lady. Did you see anything strange or suspicious?" the man repeated his question.

"Well, not really. Not right away. But when we got down the river a piece, I looked back to where it happened, and a group of teenagers was standing on the bridge. One of them was wearing a—"

"Did you see them with a water balloon?" the man interrupted her.

"No, but—"

The man shook his head. "I'm sorry, miss. Truly, I am. I had no idea. Sometimes people pull pranks on the tourists. But unless someone actually catches them in the act, we can't do much."

"I understand," Elizabeth told him. But that wasn't exactly true. She didn't understand why the man didn't tell local authorities and the sheriff's department and the CIA and the FBI and go on an all-out manhunt until those hoodlums were found, handcuffed, and thrown in the slammer.

Okay, maybe that's a little extreme, she thought. *But only a little.*

"Come on. Let's head back to the hotel and get you into some dry clothes. Or better yet, put on your swimsuit and we'll spend some time at the pool," said Mrs. Anderson, sensing her daughter's mood. "This time tomorrow, your friend Kate will be here."

Elizabeth brightened. "I can't wait! Kate is so cool—you'll love her. And she's bringing Biscuit too. I'm glad Uncle Dan arranged for Biscuit to stay in the room with us."

She smiled at the thought of the scruffy little dog she and her sleuthing friends, the five other Camp Club Girls, had rescued at camp. "And I bet she'll bring tons of nifty little gadgets with her." *And maybe one of those gadgets will help me catch Mr. Red-cap and his friends.*

•—•—•

Later, Elizabeth lounged by the pool, sipping lemonade from a large cup. She didn't appear to have a care in the world. But her mind was racing with thoughts of water balloons and red ball caps. Her cell phone startled her, beeping to indicate she had a new text.

It was Kate: JUST ARRIVED @ LITTLE ROCK. WHERE ARE YOU?

Elizabeth tried to think of where Little Rock was. *Oh, Arkansas!* she realized. *Only two states away!*

The phone beeped again.

Kate: YOU THERE?

Elizabeth smiled. She carefully texted back: RELAXING BY POOL IN SAN ANTONIO.

After a moment, Kate's reply came: DON'T HAVE TOO MUCH FUN. WAIT FOR ME. WE'LL ARRIVE IN OUR VAN AT 3 TOMORROW.

Elizabeth smiled. *Less than twenty-four hours and she'll be here, in the flesh!* She typed in: CAN'T WAIT!

A shadow covered her, and she looked up to find her mother. Taking the lounge chair beside her, Mrs. Anderson shook her head and laughed. "I'll never understand you kids and those text things. You have free long distance on that phone. Why don't you just make a phone call?"

Elizabeth laughed too. "I guess that would make more sense. But texting is fun. Kind of like reading code."

Mrs. Anderson leaned back in her chair and flipped open a magazine. "To each her own," she said. "By the way, there's a puppet show this evening at the Fiesta Noche del Rio. Your father and I are taking James to it. You're welcome to come, but since Uncle Dan will be on duty, you can stay here if you want."

"Thanks, Mom. I'll think about it," Elizabeth said, reaching for her lemonade. She sipped the cool drink then leaned back and closed her eyes. She was almost asleep when she gasped, covered in cold water for the second time that day.

James giggled and continued splashing her from the pool. "Come in the water with me, Bettyboo!" he taunted.

"I told you to stop calling me that!" she demanded. A moment later, she was in the pool with her little brother, splashing and laughing at his antics.

"Cannonball!" Mr. Anderson yelled out just before hitting the water with a gigantic splash.

"Oh Robert! You got me all wet!" cried Mrs. Anderson. "I guess I'll have to climb in there too just to protect myself."

The Andersons spent the rest of the afternoon splashing in the pool. When they left the pool for dinner, they were famished.

•—•—•

Elizabeth pushed back from the table at the riverside café and eyed the pile of corn husks on her plate. "Those were the best tamales I've ever tasted," she said.

"You say that every time we eat here," Mr. Anderson reminded his daughter, his eyes twinkling.

"It's true. I'm glad we come to San Antonio often. Maybe someday we can convince the chef to give us the recipe," she replied.

Mrs. Anderson laughed. "Oh, I think it will take more than the recipe to duplicate those tamales. It takes years of practice to learn to cook like that."

"Well, I'm young. I can learn. I'll practice as much as it takes, if it means I can have these tamales anytime I want them," Elizabeth said.

"Here, Beth. You can have the rest of mine. I'm full," said James.

Elizabeth groaned. She was stuffed too. But she couldn't turn down more tamales.

Mrs. Anderson watched her daughter take another bite and laughed. "Well, at least I know how to make you eat. Normally, you don't eat enough to feed a bird."

Elizabeth put down her fork. "I can't do it. I love these things, but I just don't have room for another bite," she said. "If you don't mind, I think I'll skip the puppet show. I'm going back to the hotel to lie down. Maybe watch television."

"Okay," her father said. "Just be sure to check in with Uncle Dan. If you need anything, you know he'll be at the front desk. We'll be there in about an hour."

"Yes, sir," Elizabeth replied, and stood to her feet. "I'll see you in a little while."

Ambling back to the hotel, she watched for signs of that red ball cap. She saw tourists of all shapes, sizes, and ages, but no gangs of laughing teenagers.

Oh well, she thought. *There's always tomorrow. And tomorrow, Kate will be here to help me.*

"Howdy, Elizabeth," called Uncle Dan when she stepped into the lobby.

"Hi," she said, walking over and leaning against the desk.

"Where is the rest of the Anderson clan?" he asked, rolling his wheelchair so he could look directly at her.

"They're going to see a puppet show. I'm headed upstairs to chill out for a while."

"Okay. Have fun. You know where I am if you need me," he said.

With a wave, Elizabeth walked to the glass-walled elevator and pushed the button. One side of the elevator offered a view of the Riverwalk, and Elizabeth enjoyed looking out on her way to the fourth floor.

Maybe I'll just ride up and down the elevator for a while, she thought.

She pushed the button for the top floor, even though her room was on the fourth. She pressed her nose against the glass as she rode to the highest point of the hotel. The elevator stopped and opened its doors, waiting for her to exit.

Instead, she stood, still looking out the glass at the view of tourists and riverboats, restaurants and mariachi bands. To her left, she saw the Fiesta Noche del Rio, and after a few moments, identified her parents and brother. James was bouncing up and down, clapping for the puppets. Elizabeth smiled. He wasn't bad, as far as brothers were concerned.

Shifting her gaze to the right, she counted the little stone bridges up and down the Riverwalk. These bridges were located at different places along the Riverwalk so people could easily cross the narrow man-made river. Restaurants and souvenir shops lined both sides of the river. Elizabeth watched a family pose for a picture on the steps of one of the bridges.

She looked on to the next bridge, still counting. *Three, four, five. . . what's going on there?* She noticed a commotion on one of the bridges. *Why are those people ducking down on the bridge? Are they trying to hide from the people below? And was that*—It was! A plaid shirt! But no ball cap.

Wait! There it was. The boy in the middle, who was about the size of an ant from her vantage point, pulled something red out of his back pocket and placed it on his head.

The group of two boys and one girl stood up. Mr. Red-cap pointed at a riverboat in the distance, and the others appeared to be laughing.

That's them! she thought. *Those are the ones who dropped the water balloon on my head! Well, they're not going to get away with it.*

She whipped around and pressed the button for the ground floor. Keeping her eyes on the group of teenagers, she went down, down, down and waited for the doors to open.

When the elevator stopped on the ground floor, Elizabeth pressed against the doors, willing them to open. Funny, she hadn't noticed the doors being this slow before. When the doors opened, she took off running through the lobby.

"Whoa! Beth! Where's the fire?" asked Uncle Dan as she whizzed past the front desk.

"Can't talk now. I'll explain when I get back," she called, and continued through the ornate doors to the Riverwalk.

Outside, she looked around to get her bearings. The bridge where she saw the teenagers was. . .this way. She dodged tourists as she dashed to the bridge. She took the steps two at a time, but when she reached the top, no one was there.

Where did they go?

Looking this way and that, she only saw a sea of tourists. To one side, a mariachi band played an upbeat song, and people clapped in time to the music. Scanning the crowds, she looked for that red cap. If he wasn't wearing it, she had no hope of finding the group.

Finally, she saw them seated at a riverside café table, munching on tortilla chips.

The nerve! she thought. *They're just sitting there enjoying the Riverwalk, as innocent as lambs! Well, they won't get away with this.*

Elizabeth walked down the stone steps and in the direction of the little group. She smiled sweetly at the waiter and sat at a table a few feet from the threesome. She pretended to study her menu, while straining to hear their conversation.

"One of these days, you'll get caught, you know," said the girl.

Red-cap Boy, whose cap was now hanging out of his back pocket, stretched his legs out from under the table and smiled. "Aww, we're not hurting anybody. People should expect to get a little wet at the Riverwalk."

The girl shook her head. "Well, from now on, when you pull your little stunts, I'm leaving. I don't want to get grouped in with you and your shenanigans."

Red-cap Boy laughed and said something in Spanish.

The girl said, "What do you mean, you won't get caught? You don't know that."

Elizabeth peeked out from behind her menu and saw Red-cap smiling. His white teeth, framed by two deep dimples, stood out against his creamy brown skin. "Even if we do get caught, what will they do to us? We're not breaking any laws. Besides, who would convict this face?" He gave the girl a cocky smile.

Why, that conceited little criminal! thought Elizabeth. *You really think you're something special, don't you? Well Mr. Red-cap, you just wait. We'll see who's smiling when your gig is up. And trust me, your gig will be up very soon.*

The threesome pushed back from the table and began to leave just as Elizabeth's waiter returned to take her order. "What can I get for you, miss?" he asked.

Thinking quickly, she said, "You know, I don't think I'll eat right now after all. Sorry to have troubled you." She excused herself and followed the group at a distance.

Through the crowds she went, keeping her eyes glued to that red cap. She almost didn't see the rolling hot dog cart until it was too late. Scooting aside at the last moment, she said, "Oh, excuse me, sir."

The old man smiled. "No problem, miss. Would you care for a hot dog?"

"No thank you," she said politely and moved forward. But it was too late. The red cap was nowhere in sight.

Elizabeth turned and made her way back to the hotel. *You may have escaped me today, buddy, but just wait until tomorrow. . . .*

Breakdown!

Mr. Anderson woke up his family bright and early, and they spent the better part of the morning at the Tower of the Americas, a 750-foot-tall tower with a revolving restaurant at the top. As they left the tower, he said, "I love the view from the top! Too bad the restaurant wasn't open yet. Let's take another riverboat ride, then get some lunch. I never get tired of riding those little boats!"

Now, as Elizabeth sat in a River City Cruise boat watching the bridges and sidewalks for any signs of the boy with the red cap, she heard a strange noise.

Pu–pu–pu–put, puput, pu–pu. . .rrrrrr. . .rrrrrr. . .pu. . .put. . .pu. The engine of the small riverboat groaned and sputtered. Then it died, as concerned tourists looked at each other in confusion.

"That's nice. I fork out ten bucks to ride this heap of junk, and now we're stranded," called a tall, thin, middle-aged man from the back of the boat.

"I'm very sorry for the inconvenience, folks," replied the frustrated boat captain. "All of your money will be refunded, as soon as I push this boat to shore. Just report to the ticket office and tell them what happened."

Elizabeth felt sorry for the captain. The crowd gasped in surprise as he suddenly jumped overboard! Their surprise turned to laughter, however, as he stood up. The water of the famous San Antonio Riverwalk only came to the man's waist.

Another riverboat passed but didn't stop to help. Its captain looked long and hard at the stranded group. The man leaned forward, one foot propped on the boat's railing, and the sun glinted off his polished shoe.

Is he smiling? thought Elizabeth. *Why doesn't he offer to help us?* She noticed the competing company's logo on the side of the boat—SANTA ANNA TOURS. *Maybe they have rules about helping the competition or something. . . .*

"Here, let me give you a hand," said Elizabeth's father, leaping into the water. Together, the two men pushed the boat to the edge of the water and secured it to the cement siding with ropes.

The riverboat captain hefted himself onto the sidewalk then held out a hand to help Mr. Anderson. "Thank you, sir. I'll make sure your family gets free rides for the rest of your visit here in San Antonio."

"That won't be necessary," said Robert Anderson. "I was happy to help."

The captain helped his passengers disembark. The tall, grumbly man from the back row stepped off. In a loud voice, he said, "I'd rather have a refund than a free ride. From now on, I'll take my business to Santa Anna Tours. Now *that's* a boat you can count on."

The rude man walked away, continuing his tirade as he went. The riverboat captain kept a polite smile pasted on his face, but Elizabeth wasn't fooled. The man was concerned about his business.

"Hey, can I jump in before I get out?" asked James. Elizabeth's little brother loved an adventure. And he loved to get wet.

"No, you can't," replied Sue Anderson, helping the six-year-old off the boat. "One wet male in the family is enough for now."

Elizabeth helped her mother step across to the sidewalk. "I'll go swimming with you when we get back to the hotel," she told James. Moving close to her father, she listened to the conversation between him and the captain.

"I don't understand what could have happened," the man said. "We service the motors every week. But this is the third time this has happened in two weeks!"

"That is strange," replied Elizabeth's dad. "Who services your boats? Perhaps they've started doing something different. . .ordering parts from a new company or something."

"Maybe so. . . ," said the man. "Thank you again for your help."

"No problem," replied Elizabeth's dad. He was sopping wet from the waist down, and he looked pretty funny. "Let's go eat Mexican food!" he said to his family.

"Uh, Dad? Don't you think you should get into some dry clothes first?" Elizabeth asked.

"Nonsense. In this Texas heat, I'll be dry in no time. And besides, I'm starved!" He led his family the few steps to the closest outdoor café, the Rio Rio. The Riverwalk was lined with restaurants, and the Andersons had decided to eat at every one. The host seated them at a table bordering the water.

Elizabeth's family studied their menus, discussing which new dish to try, but Elizabeth wasn't interested in food. Looking at her watch, she said, "In two more hours I'm going to see Kate!"

•—•—•

A couple of hours later, Elizabeth sat in the ornate lobby of the plush hotel. The Andersons could never have afforded such luxury if Uncle Dan hadn't gotten them a discount. He had also helped Kate's youth group get a good rate for their San Antonio mission trip.

Pulling the letter—actually an email that Elizabeth had printed—from her pocket, she unfolded it. It was wrinkled and smudged from all the times Elizabeth had read it during the past few weeks.

Dear Elizabeth,

I'm coming to Texas! My church youth group is planning a mission trip to the San Antonio Riverwalk, and they're letting me come along. I have always wanted to see Texas.

How close are you to San Antonio? Do you think you could meet me there? I would love to see you again. Since it doesn't look like you'll come to Philadelphia any time soon, maybe this will work.

We are still in the planning stages of the mission trip. I'm not sure where we'll stay yet. Let me know if you think you can meet me there. You have to come. You just have to!

I'll talk to you soon. Biscuit sends kisses.

Love,
Kate

Elizabeth smiled as she refolded the letter. San Antonio was one of the Andersons' favorite getaway places! Within two weeks after Elizabeth received the letter, Uncle Dan had helped Kate's youth minister make all the arrangements. And now, the youth group from Kate's church would be here any minute! She watched out the front windows of the lobby, looking for a church van from Philadelphia.

"A watched pot never boils," said a voice from behind her.

"Hi, Uncle Dan. I can't help it! I can't wait to see Kate!" Elizabeth told him.

"I heard you had an exciting morning at the Riverwalk," he said.

"Yeah, it was the strangest thing! We were puttering along listening to the captain tell stories and point out the sights when the motor just died!"

Uncle Dan looked concerned. "The owner of that riverboat company is a friend of mine. That's been happening a lot lately, and it's not good for his business."

"I sure hope they fix the problem so— They're here!" Elizabeth jumped up as she saw the blue church van pull into the parking lot. Rushing through the ornate doors, she stopped herself before running into the flow of traffic.

"Maybe you should wait here for her," said Uncle Dan, following her.

Soon, the van doors opened, and teenaged boys and girls climbed out. One by one, Elizabeth watched each new person. *No Kate. No Kate. Where is Kate?* The group of teens approached the lobby, laughing and talking. Some of them smiled politely at Elizabeth.

Suddenly, like the parting of the Red Sea, they started moving to either side as a blond wisp of a girl with black-framed glasses pushed through. "Excuse me! Pardon me, coming through! I've got to find my friend. . .Elizabeth!"

Kate dropped her bags and dashed to Elizabeth. "Oh, am I ever glad to see you! That was one long trip. But I'm finally here! And you're here!"

Suddenly, Kate's backpack began barking.

"Biscuit!" shouted Elizabeth. "Wow, Kate, I can't believe you're both here at last! We are going to have so much fun!" She hugged her friend, then helped free the wiggling dog.

"Biscuit, did you ride the whole way in that backpack?" Elizabeth stroked the small dog's black-and-white fur while fighting off slobbery puppy kisses.

"He slept most of the way," said Kate. "I'm so glad your uncle said I could bring him. He's missed you, Elizabeth! And so have I."

A twentysomething man approached and said, "You must be Elizabeth. Kate has talked of nothing else for the entire trip. I'm Gary, Kate's youth minister."

Elizabeth shook the man's hand. He said, "Kate, we'll be on the fifth floor if you need us."

"Thanks, Gary," she said, and the two girls gathered Kate's backpack and suitcase and headed for the elevator.

Biscuit, on the other hand, gave a series of excited barks. "Maybe we'd better find a patch of grass first, so Biscuit can take care of business," said Kate.

Both girls laughed, and Kate clipped a leash onto the dog's collar. Uncle Dan pointed them toward the back door, which led to a small courtyard. Within minutes, they were on their way to the Andersons' room on the fourth floor.

"I can't wait to tell you what happened this morning," Elizabeth told her friend.

"I can't wait to see the Riverwalk! And the Alamo! And the Tower of the Americas! How soon can we get started?" asked Kate.

"Whoa, there! Slow down, tourist. We have plenty of time. We don't have to see everything today. Why don't we start by getting your things unpacked? Then we'll head to the Riverwalk. Are you hungry? The food here is great," Elizabeth said.

Kate gave her a comical look. "What do you mean, 'Am I hungry?' I'm always hungry!"

Elizabeth's parents were in the suite when the girls arrived. The room was set up with two bedrooms—one for Mr. and Mrs. Anderson, and one for Kate and Elizabeth. James slept on the pull-out sofa in the living room.

"Wow, this place sure is fancy. I've never stayed in a hotel this nice!" exclaimed Kate.

"Neither have we." Elizabeth laughed. "It's one of the perks of having an uncle who works here. Mom, Dad, I'd like you to meet Kate. Kate, this is my mom and dad, Robert and Sue Anderson."

"It's very nice to meet you both," said Kate, reaching to shake their hands.

Suddenly Biscuit growled. Something was moving under the kitchen table. The chairs shifted, and James crawled out. Biscuit decided the moving boy wasn't a threat, and began wagging his tail.

"This is my little brother, James," continued Elizabeth.

James waved, but kept his eyes on Biscuit. "Can I pet him?" he asked.

As if to answer the question, Biscuit jumped on James and began licking his face. James fell over, giggling, but Biscuit showed no signs of letting up.

"It looks like those two will be fast friends," Kate said.

Elizabeth picked up Kate's bags and said, "Come on. I'll show you our room."

The two headed into their bedroom, and Kate flopped on the

bed. "This will be so much fun. I'm so glad you and your family could come."

"San Antonio is one of our favorite places. We come here a lot, but we usually stay at a discount motel. Now that Uncle Dan's working at this hotel, we'll probably visit even more."

Kate unzipped her suitcase and pulled out her laptop. "I need to set up my computer. I haven't been able to update my blog or check the comments in two days! Oh hey, check out my new business card." She handed Elizabeth a small card that read:

Super Sleuths, Inc.
Kate Oliver, Super Sleuth
http://supersleuthsinc.blogspot.com/
For answers to all your sleuthing questions!

"Cool!" said Elizabeth. "Bring a handful of them with you to the Riverwalk. You can pass them out."

"Good idea," said Kate as she plugged in her small computer.

Elizabeth glanced into the open suitcase and had to laugh. Only a few clothes were in the suitcase. Most of it was packed with electronic gadgets and doodads.

Kate's fingers began to fly as she punched in her blog's address and logged in with her password. "Hooray! I have six comments!" she exclaimed.

Elizabeth looked over Kate's shoulder as she began responding to each one. "Your blog is really getting popular. Besides the comment from Bailey, the rest are from people I've never heard of."

Kate smiled. "Two of them are from my cousins. But the other three are from strangers. My blog is getting famous!"

"Well, hurry up. I want to hear about all these gadgets you brought. And I'm eager to show you the Riverwalk," Elizabeth told her.

"Most of these comments are just telling me they like my blog. It's more fun when I get actual questions to answer. But hey, I'm not complaining." She finished typing her last response, then turned her attention to her suitcase. "A lot of these are the same ones I had when we were at camp together. But here's a new one. It's a bug."

"A bug?" Elizabeth asked, crinkling her nose.

"Yeah, you know. Like the spies use. You can hide it and listen. It's better than the one we used on Biscuit's collar at camp. Instead of recording, we can actually listen as the conversation is taking place."

"Oh, kind of like a walkie-talkie?" asked Elizabeth.

"Well, sort of. Picture those police shows, where the police hide outside the house in a van, listening to the bad guys' conversation. This is what they use."

Elizabeth's eyes widened as she held the tiny tool. "Whoa," she whispered. "This is too cool."

Kate held out another small device. "This is a tracker. Why don't you put it on your phone while I'm here, to keep from losing it. During the trip, I had it on Biscuit's collar, in case we got separated."

"That's a good idea," said Elizabeth, slipping the device on her phone. "So, are you ready to go?"

"Yep," Kate said, and the girls headed to the living room.

"Mom, Dad, can we roam around the Riverwalk for a little while?" asked Elizabeth.

"Yes, but don't go past the Fiesta Noche. The time now is two forty-five. Take your cell phone and check in with us in an hour. Plan to meet us in the lobby at five o'clock for dinner," said Mrs. Anderson.

Kate slipped the leash around Biscuit's neck and attached the small tracker to his collar. With a wave, the two girls headed out the door.

In the lobby, the girls pushed open the heavy glass doors that led to the Riverwalk. Outside, Kate adjusted her glasses. "Whoa! This is so cool. It's even better than the pictures! Here, hold this," she said, handing Biscuit's leash to Elizabeth. She rummaged through her backpack and pulled out her camera phone. "Smile!" she said, and snapped a picture of Elizabeth kneeling next to Biscuit. A riverboat rumbled past in the background.

Kate then pulled out her cell phone and dialed a number.

"Who are you calling?" Elizabeth asked.

"My parents. They told me to call them as soon as I arrived, but I got so excited, I forgot."

There was an answer at the other end of the line, and Kate began talking to her mother. Elizabeth walked with Biscuit to the water's edge, taking in the scenery. Soon, she heard a familiar *pa–pa–pa–put. . .rrrr. . . rrrr. . .pa–pa–put.* Looking to her left, she could see that once again, a River City Cruise boat had died.

Kate hung up the phone and said, "What are we waiting for? Let's go!" Then, noticing Elizabeth's concerned look, she said, "What's wrong?"

"Oh, another riverboat just died. Let me tell you what happened to us this morning."

The two girls walked toward one of the stone bridges while Elizabeth relayed the story.

"Maybe we should use a different riverboat company, if we ride at all. I'm not sure I want to end up in a dead boat!" Kate responded.

"Maybe," Elizabeth said. "I just think it's strange. My family has been to this Riverwalk many times, and we ride the boats every time. This has never happened before. Now, all of a sudden, riverboats are dying all over the place!"

Another boat puttered by, this one from Santa Anna Tours. The girls watched as the new boat moved past the stalled boat without even offering help. This time, they could hear its captain make a joke about the stalled boat, and the passengers laughed.

"I guess you folks chose the right boat to ride," said the captain of the working boat.

Biscuit pulled away from Elizabeth and barked. A bird had landed just feet from him, and was pecking on a tortilla chip someone had dropped. With one last look at the boats, the girls tugged on Biscuit's leash and headed in the opposite direction.

"Come on," said Kate. "I'm starved."

"Okay! Let's go over this bridge. The restaurant on the other side serves the best tortilla chips and salsa you've ever tast—"

Elizabeth stopped short as they reached the top of the stone bridge. A group of teenagers stood there, pointing and laughing at the stalled boat, and shouting things in Spanish.

And right in the middle of them was the boy with the red cap.

Kate and Elizabeth on Duty!

"Come with me," Elizabeth said, grabbing Kate's arm and dragging the girl behind her.

"Whoa, what's the rush?" Kate asked, doing her best to keep up.

The group hushed as Elizabeth, Kate, and Biscuit appeared, but barely gave them room to pass. One of them smiled at Biscuit, who barked in return.

"Easy, little guy. I'm not going to hurt you," the boy said.

Elizabeth kept moving. She wanted to stay close, but she wasn't ready to talk to her suspects yet. As soon as the girls and Biscuit were descending the stairs on the other side, the group started talking again. Biscuit resisted Kate's lead and continued barking at the group.

"Biscuit, cut that out!" she scolded. Finally, the little dog obeyed.

Elizabeth led Kate to a nearby café and found an empty table. The waiter immediately placed a basket of tortilla chips and a bowl of salsa in front of them. "Cool!" said Kate. "Now that's what I call service! Now, do you want to tell me what that was about?"

Elizabeth leaned forward and motioned toward the group, which was still standing on the bridge. "I haven't told you about the water balloon." Over chips and salsa, she explained the whole story to her friend.

"Aha! A mystery to solve. Never fear, Elizabeth my dear. I have everything we could possibly need to catch those guys. And when they're caught, we'll throw the book at them!"

Elizabeth giggled at Kate's enthusiasm. *Yep. Those guys don't know what they're in for,* she thought.

They continued munching and chatting about their plans.

"Gary wants me to help with the Bible club every day. I told him you'd probably want to help too."

"That sounds like fun. What will you be doing?" Elizabeth asked, keeping an eye on the group, which had now moved to a café on the other side of the bridge. She had a clear view of them from her spot.

"It's supposed to be right here on the Riverwalk somewhere. Something about a little church in a plaza or something? We're going to do a Bible club for kids and hopefully draw in some of the locals. Apparently, a lot of kids hang out at the Riverwalk, and we're going to try to get them involved."

"Sounds like a good idea to me. It's probably at the Little Church at La Villita. It's a historic landmark, but also an active church."

Just then, Biscuit wagged his tail and pulled against his leash, which was attached to Kate's chair. A little girl in a pink dress walked by, holding her mother's hand. She looked about four years old. Large brown eyes peeked through brown curls that cascaded down her cheeks and covered most of her face. When she noticed Elizabeth and Kate looking at her, she buried her face in her mother's skirt. The two continued on their way.

Biscuit barked a friendly yap and settled back beneath Kate's chair. "Biscuit loves children," Kate said. "That's one of the reasons Gary let me bring him. He hopes Biscuit will attract kids to the Bible club. Oh look! There's Gary now!"

Kate's youth minister and several teenagers were headed toward the girls. "Hey there, Kate! Are you having fun yet?" Gary asked.

"You'd better believe it! And Biscuit is already drawing attention."

"Good," said the man. "Don't forget, our mime troupe is performing at seven p.m. at the Fiesta Noche del Rio—it's a little theater area right here on the Riverwalk. Elizabeth, I hope you'll help us out this week. Kate tells me you're a real firecracker when it comes to ministry work."

Elizabeth blushed. "I don't know about that. . . ," she replied.

"Don't let her fool you. She plays the piano, sings, and has over half of the Bible memorized," Kate said.

"I do not," Elizabeth said, laughing.

Gary smiled. "Well, you'll be a great addition to our team. You two have fun, and I'll see you both at seven o'clock." He followed the teenagers into a T-shirt shop.

Elizabeth waved goodbye then looked across the river to find the group of teens. They were gone.

•—•—•

Later that evening, Kate groaned. Mr. and Mrs. Anderson had treated the girls to a huge plate of the gooiest, cheesiest burritos Kate had ever eaten. "I'm stuffed," she said.

"Would you like some sopapillas?" asked the waitress, and the Andersons laughed. "Maybe later," Mr. Anderson said.

"It's six forty-five," Elizabeth said, looking at her watch. "Why don't we go on over to the Fiesta Noche and try to get good seats. I can't wait to see your youth group perform," she told Kate.

"We'll all go," said Mrs. Anderson. "But we'll meet you girls there. I want to walk around for a few minutes."

Kate and Elizabeth waved goodbye and headed toward the Fiesta Noche. When they arrived they were surprised to see the red-cap boy and his friends. They were sprawled out in the center of the seating area, talking and laughing loudly. In Spanish. Elizabeth caught a few of the words, but her Spanish was rusty.

When the teens saw the girls and Biscuit, they started talking about the *perro*. Elizabeth knew they were referring to Biscuit. The little dog strained his leash and barked. Red-cap Boy said something the group thought was hilarious.

Elizabeth and Kate looked at each other and took seats a few rows in front of the group. "Maybe we'll overhear them admit to something," whispered Kate. Biscuit watched the teenagers. He continued to softly growl.

"No, Biscuit. Stop that!" said Kate, and the dog calmed a bit. But his ears remained stiff.

The two girls tried to focus on the stage. "This is so cool!" said Kate. "I've never seen anything like this! The river runs between the stage and the audience. I guess they don't have to worry about anyone rushing the stage."

Elizabeth laughed. "I guess not. They're pretty safe over there, unless one of them falls in the water!"

A door at the back of the stage opened, and two girls from Kate's youth group stepped out. "Hi, Kate! Do you guys want to help us? You can cross at the bridge and come to the back if you want."

The two girls stood, Biscuit in tow, and retraced their path to the bridge. Just as they were about to cross they saw the Andersons.

"Where are you going? I thought the show was about to start," asked Sue Anderson.

"We've been asked to help," Elizabeth told her mother.

Mrs. Anderson smiled. "That sounds like fun. We'll be in the audience. We'll meet you at the seating area after the performance."

Elizabeth, Kate, and Biscuit hurried across the bridge and through the back door of the stage area. Gary greeted them with a smile. "Hi, girls! You're just in time. Most of our people are in costume, and we don't want them to go onto the stage until the show starts. Could you two wheel this box of props out there? Just put the box by the back wall and come right back."

"No problem," replied Elizabeth.

Kate wasn't sure what to do with Biscuit, so Elizabeth took the small dog and placed him inside the box.

The two girls pushed the heavy box on wheels to the stage area. The seats were filling up, and Elizabeth waved at her parents.

"Look! It's Beth!" shouted James.

Suddenly, Elizabeth lost her footing and fell on her backside. Center stage. Red-cap, having heard James call her name, started laughing. "Way to go, Beth!" he called.

Why, the nerve of that boy! she thought. *I'll show him!* Instead of being embarrassed, she decided to play up her public disaster. Standing to her feet, she faced the audience and took a grand bow.

Red-cap hooted with laughter, and the audience cheered. She kept bowing until Kate ran out and grabbed her, pulling her, smiling and waving, off the stage.

"What was that about?" asked Kate with a laugh. "What happened to the girl who doesn't like to be on stage?"

"I never said I don't like to be on stage," Elizabeth countered. "I said I don't like to play the piano or sing in front of others. Falling and looking like an idiot? I can handle that just fine."

Gary and the others in the youth group laughed and patted Elizabeth on the back. "Good job, girls. You can head back over and sit in the audience now, if you want."

"Okay," said Elizabeth, realizing they wouldn't be able to see much of the show from backstage.

They were halfway across the bridge when Kate stopped. "Biscuit!" she cried. "We left him in the box!"

The girls saw that the performers were already walking onto the stage. Wide-eyed, they looked at each other.

"What will we do?" asked Elizabeth.

"I don't know. I guess we can't do anything except watch and see what happens!"

The two girls quickly went to the seating area and sat down. The performers had white painted faces and began presenting a mime. Music played in the background as the main character mimed being lost. His facial expressions were comical, and the audience laughed at all the right times.

However, Elizabeth and Kate watched the box at the back of the stage. At any moment, they expected Biscuit to leap out and make his grand stage debut.

Pa–pa–pa–put! Rrrrr. . .rrrrrrr. . .pa–pa put. . .rrrrrrr. . .rrrr. . . rrrrr. . . The audience's attention turned to the riverboat coming around the bend. This time, however, the boat seemed out of control, and was headed straight for the stage, straight for the performers!

Boom! The boat banged into the platform. The passengers on the boat gasped and clung to the sides. Fortunately, it wasn't going fast enough for anyone to fall overboard.

It did, however, cause quite a stir on the stage. The performers backed away from the boat, and one of the mimes landed in the box where Biscuit was! They heard a loud yelp, and then saw Biscuit wiggling out of the box! He leaped onto the stage, causing even more excitement among the mimes.

Biscuit ran this way then that way on the stage, not knowing how to escape. Kate yelled, "Biscuit! It's okay, boy! Calm down!"

Hearing his beloved owner's voice, he searched the crowd for her. Spotting her across the river, he didn't even hesitate. He splashed right into the water and swam to the other side, while people cheered and clapped. The riverboat captain looked frustrated, his passengers looked confused, and the audience wondered if it was all part of the show!

Reaching the other side, Biscuit climbed out, shaking water onto the entire front row and leaving them squealing. The little dog lunged through the audience, leaving wet, muddy paw prints in his wake, and flew into Kate's arms.

"Hey, cut that out," Kate cried as he covered her with drippy kisses. He transferred his messy love to Elizabeth for a moment, then back to Kate. Before long, the audience began applauding, as if they had enjoyed the show.

Gary came onto the stage and announced, "Hello, folks! As you can see, we are having some technical difficulties. Just hold tight, and we'll start our performance again in a few minutes."

He then helped the riverboat captain onto the stage. Together, they helped the boat's occupants onto the stage and out the back door.

Elizabeth heard snickering behind her. She turned to see Red-cap pointing and laughing at the riverboat captain, just as he and his friends had done earlier in the day.

"I wonder what could be causing so many of the boats to break down," she said.

"It's a mystery to me," Kate replied. "Maybe we should investigate. This sounds like a job for the. . ." She paused, waiting for Elizabeth to chime in.

"Camp Club Girls!" they said together, then laughed.

"Why do we find mysteries everywhere we go?" asked Elizabeth.

"It's almost as if the mysteries find us," said Kate.

Elizabeth began speaking under her breath.

"What? I can't hear you," said Kate.

Elizabeth laughed. "I just thought of a mystery verse. 'God has chosen to make known among the Gentiles the glorious riches of this mystery, which is Christ in you, the hope of glory.' It's in Colossians 1:27."

Kate just stared at her friend. "How do you do that? You know a verse for everything."

"Well, I wish I were half as good at figuring out all those gadgets you carry around with you."

Kate laughed. "I guess we can't all be good at everything. But at least we're both good at solving mysteries. And I have a feeling this will be a tough one."

The girls leaned back as the mimes made their second entry onto the stage. Yep. This was going to be a tough one, all right.

•—•—•

Later that night, Elizabeth looked over Kate's shoulder as she typed onto her blog:

Hypothetical Mystery Challenge:

A taxi company that has always been reliable suddenly begins to experience difficulties. All over town, the taxi motors begin dying, even though the cars are serviced weekly. The company's reputation suffers.

Who or what might be responsible?

"That's a really good idea, Kate!" said Elizabeth, patting her friend on the shoulder.

Kate smiled with satisfaction. "From time to time, I write a pretend mystery for my readers to solve. Little do they know, the mysteries are real. I just change enough details so no one will figure it out."

"What a clever way to get some outside help. Now, let's send out an SOS to the other Camp Club Girls. They're sure to help us figure it out. I don't even know where to start."

Kate typed the whole story, including the riverboat mishap, Elizabeth's water balloon experience, and the teenaged troublemakers. In the subject line, she wrote: *New Mystery! Need Help!*

She continued on, typing what she and Elizabeth had seen so far. Just a couple of minutes after she pressed SEND, Elizabeth's cell phone rang. It was Sydney.

"Hey, Beth. I just read the email. Tell Kate she'd better learn to swim if she's going to solve a river mystery."

Kate, who was standing close enough to the phone to hear, responded, "Ha, ha. Very funny. I plan to stay on dry land for this mystery, thank you very much."

Elizabeth and Sydney laughed. Kate was brilliant. Nearly a genius. But an athlete, she was not.

"We don't even know where to start. Do you have any suggestions?" Elizabeth asked Sydney.

"Well, those teenagers sound suspicious to me. You said they were laughing and pointing at the boats? It doesn't seem funny. Maybe they had something to do with it."

"That's what I'm thinking," said Elizabeth.

"Well, keep me posted. And tell Kate not to fall in." With a quick goodbye, Sydney hung up.

Checking the computer screen, they saw two more emails had come in. One was from Bailey:

Nail the teenagers! Follow their every move. I'll bet they are the guilty parties.

The next was from McKenzie:

Are there any competing riverboat companies?

Elizabeth and Kate looked at each other.

"There is that other company that never stops to help. I wonder if they are trying to drum up more business for themselves," Elizabeth mused.

"That's a definite possibility. I wonder what Miss Hollywood is going to suggest." As if on cue, Alex's user name popped up on the live chat page.

Alex: *Oh, this is soooo Nancy Drew! I wish I were there with you all.*
Kate: *We wish you were here too. Any ideas about the first step we should take?*
Alex: *I think you should follow those teenagers, but don't rule out other possibilities yet.*
Kate: *We haven't.*
Alex: *Notice everything. Does anyone have anything to gain by forcing this riverboat company out of business? Who owns the company? Do any company leaders have any enemies?*

Kate moved to the side, and Elizabeth typed:

Those are good questions. I think we have enough to get us started now. Thanks.
Alex: *This will be tough. Send me the names of the riverboat companies, and I'll do some background research.*
Elizabeth: *Will do. We'll get started now. Talk to you soon!*

Just then, there was a knock on the door, and the two girls peeked out of their doorway into the living area. It was Uncle Dan. "I hope I didn't wake you all up," he said.

Robert Anderson invited his brother in. "No, we're still wide awake. Come on in."

Uncle Dan wheeled into the room. He looked worried. "My friend Lyndel needs me to go with him to the police station. He owns River City Cruises—the one with all the boats breaking down. Now, one of his boats has been spray-painted by vandals. Neon pink! Of all people for this to happen to. He's got enough to deal with already."

"I'm so sorry," said Sue Anderson. "What is this world coming to?"

Mr. Anderson rubbed his chin. "Lyndel. . .I believe that was the name of the captain I helped this morning. Can I do anything?"

Uncle Dan shook his head. "No. He just wants me to come for moral support. I wanted to let you know I'll be gone for a while, but you can reach me on my cell phone."

He said good night and left.

The two girls looked at each other, and retreated into their room. Vandals! Could the two events be related?

Teenagers Ahead!

The next morning, Kate, Elizabeth, and Biscuit stopped by the breakfast buffet at the hotel on their way to the Little Church at La Villita. Kate finished off a banana, an orange, a chocolate chip muffin, and was working on a cherry Danish.

"I don't know where you put it all," said Elizabeth, laughing. "You're like a hummingbird—so tiny, yet always eating."

Kate smiled and kept working on her last bites. "I can't help it. I'm always starving," she said. "But then, last month I went about two weeks when I wasn't hungry at all. I hardly ate a thing, and my mom thought I was sick. Go figure."

When the girls arrived at the church, Gary smiled and welcomed the girls. "I'm so glad you're here. Elizabeth, Kate told me you are musical. The girl who was planning to lead music for us lost her voice. Would you mind leading the children in a few songs, while we finish setting up?"

Elizabeth looked at the children gathering in front of the church. The Bible club wasn't supposed to start for another half hour, but these children looked eager to begin.

"No problem," Elizabeth told the man, and walked up the steps in front of the small church.

"Good morning, everyone! My name is Elizabeth. Welcome to Bible Camp!"

A dozen pairs of eyes looked at her in expectation. "How many of you like to sing?"

A few of the children raised their hands. "Great!" Elizabeth told them. "Why don't you, and you, and you come up here and help me lead everyone in some songs?"

She pointed out three of the children who'd raised their hands, and they scrambled up the steps to stand next to her.

Elizabeth tried to think of songs everyone would know. "Let's sing, 'This Little Light of Mine,' " she said, and started singing.

Only a few of them seemed to know the song, but they were quick learners. The group continued with "Jesus Loves Me," and Elizabeth taught them the motions to some silly songs. The crowd grew as more children joined the group. Before long, Gary signaled to Elizabeth that she could stop, and the man climbed the steps and addressed the group.

"Welcome to Bible Camp!" the man said. "We're glad you're here today. We're going to have a lot of fun."

As Gary continued telling the children about the upcoming games, snacks, and Bible stories, Elizabeth heard snickering. She turned to see the same group of teenagers from the day before. They were standing in the shadows of a small art museum, and they seemed to be making fun of Gary.

Why, the nerve! she thought. *Well, good. You're here, right under my nose. And I'll find a way to make you 'fess up!*

Gary didn't miss a beat, though. "Hey guys! Glad you're here. Come on up here with the rest of us. We'll put you to work!" Gary's smile was genuine, and the teenagers looked embarrassed.

"No thanks," said Red-cap Boy, and the group shuffled away.

"Come back if you change your minds," called Gary, and continued his speech.

The group of forty children was divided into three rotating groups: games, crafts, and Bible stories. Kate was helping with crafts, and moved to a long table set against the side of the old church. Elizabeth moved inside the church to help keep the children quiet during the Bible story time.

As she was about to enter the tall double doors, she noticed a movement to her right, in the shadows.

Those pesky teenagers again! Why won't they just leave us alone? Leaning over the railing, she peered further into the shadows, and saw a little girl. *Is that the little girl we saw with her mother on the Riverwalk yesterday?*

Biscuit, whose leash was attached to the railing, barked and wagged his tail.

"Hello?" Elizabeth called. "Would you like to join us? We're going to have a lot of fun!"

Silence.

Elizabeth moved down the steps, unhooked Biscuit's leash from the railing, and stepped into the shadows where the girl was hiding.

"What is your name?" she asked.

No response.

"Would you like to pet Biscuit? He seems to like you," she told the little girl.

Slowly, the girl lifted her eyes just enough to look at Biscuit. Her hair covered most of her face, and she reached out a tiny hand and rubbed Biscuit behind the ears. His tail wagged even more, but he remained calm. It was almost as if he knew he needed to be gentle with this girl.

"Why don't you come inside with me?" Elizabeth asked, and took the girl by the hand. The girl looked only at the ground, and her thick, dark curls cascaded around her face. But when Elizabeth led her up the steps and into the church, she didn't resist.

The two girls, with Biscuit, found seats behind the others. A brunette girl from Kate's church was just starting. "Hello, everyone. My name is Charis, and I'm going to tell you a story."

Elizabeth was thrilled when the girl began placing felt figures on a flannel board. Looking around the room, she saw every child's eyes glued to the board.

The little girl beside her kept her head down, with her hair covering her face. But those two large brown eyes peered upward, taking in every word of the story. Elizabeth started to gently push the girl's hair away from her eyes, but the girl moved out of reach.

"I'm sorry," Elizabeth whispered, and turned her attention back to the story of Jonah. *I wonder what makes her so afraid of people.*

Eventually, Charis finished the story and asked everyone to bow for prayer. During the prayer, Elizabeth heard rustling beside her, but figured it was just Biscuit. When she opened her eyes, the little girl was gone.

The rest of the morning passed quickly, and before long, Kate approached Elizabeth outside the church. Her hands were covered in marker and glue.

"I don't know why Gary asked me to help with crafts. It was fun, but I'm not very crafty. Give me some nuts and bolts and wires, and I'm good to go. But ask me to glue a circle onto a piece of paper, and I'm all thumbs. It was fun, though," said Kate, using the back of her hand to push her glasses up on her nose. She pulled her backpack onto her shoulders, getting ready to leave.

"Did you see a little girl leave the church? She had thick, dark curls, and she walked with her head down," Elizabeth asked her.

Charis approached them, hearing the last part of the conversation.

"I noticed she left early. What happened? She listened to every word I said, but after the prayer, she was gone!"

Kate nodded. "I did see her leave, but I was covered in glue at the moment."

Biscuit barked and wagged his tail. "I'll bet Biscuit can find her, if she's still around here," Elizabeth said.

Kate knelt down and stroked the little dog's fur. "Can you find the little girl, Biscuit? Take us to her!"

With a bark that told of understanding, the dog led the way. Kate held his leash, and Elizabeth waved to Charis before following Kate and Biscuit.

In and out of old stucco buildings Biscuit led them, stopping here and there, sniffing an area before moving forward. Suddenly, his ears perked up, his tail stuck straight out, and he growled.

Pulling the leash tight, he moved forward, practically dragging Kate. "Whoa, boy! Where are you taking us?"

Biscuit continued pursuing some unknown party, Kate and Elizabeth in his wake. They rounded the corner of an old building just in time to see a flash of red ball cap disappear behind another building.

Elizabeth and Kate looked at each other, but Biscuit gave no time for the girls to talk. Tugging fiercely on his leash, he pulled Kate, with Elizabeth following.

Before long, they had left the vicinity of the Riverwalk. "I sure hope Biscuit can lead us back, because I'm lost!" said Elizabeth. Then, she saw a sign that read THE ALAMO, with an arrow pointing to the right.

Biscuit barked and pulled even harder at his leash.

"Come on," said Kate, and they let Biscuit lead the way. They kept seeing glimpses of the red hat ahead and knew they were following the group of teenagers.

Before long, they arrived at the Alamo site. It was crowded with tourists, and the girls could no longer see the gang of teens.

"Whoa," breathed Kate. "So this is really the Alamo. I've always wanted to see the place where the Texans won their famous battle."

Elizabeth stopped in her tracks. "Kate," she said. "We lost the Alamo."

Kate stopped abruptly. "What? That can't be true. In all the old Westerns, the cowboys ride around saying, 'Remember the Alamo!' Why would they want to remember it if they lost?"

Elizabeth took Kate by the arm and led her toward the old structure, which was now a museum.

"Come on, Yank. You've got some thangs to larn," Elizabeth said in an exaggerated Texas accent.

"Yank? Who are you calling a Yank? Exactly what is a Yank, anyway?" Kate asked.

Elizabeth laughed. "A Yankee is just a person from up north who doesn't really understand the Southern way of life."

"Well, technically, Texas isn't in the South. It's in the West," Kate corrected her.

"The Southwest," Elizabeth answered playfully. "Actually, we're not Southern or Western. We're just plain Texan."

They stopped just outside the large wooden doors and read a small plaque on the wall. "Originally named Misión San Antonio de Valero, the Alamo served as home to missionaries and their Indian converts for nearly seventy years."

"Mission? The Alamo was a church?"

"Not exactly. It was a missionary home," Elizabeth clarified. "But it was probably used for church services too."

"And they blew it up?" Kate asked with disbelief. "Churches are supposed to be safe places!"

Elizabeth took her friend by the arm and led her inside, but not before picking up Biscuit and placing him in her friend's backpack. "Come on. I think it's time for a history lesson."

The girls entered the mission just in time to join a tour group. Kate looked in awe at cannons, rusty pistols, even weathered sticks of dynamite as the tour guide gave them an overview of Texas history.

They were about halfway through the tour when Elizabeth spotted the red cap in the group in front of them. "Look!" she whispered, but Kate ignored her. She was fascinated with the tour guide's words.

Kate raised her hand to ask a question. "So Santa Anna was trying to reclaim Texas to be a part of Mexico?"

"That's correct," the tour guide answered.

Elizabeth tried to get Kate's attention again, but couldn't. The red hat was moving toward the exit.

"And Santa Anna's men lost on the first and second tries, but came back a third time and climbed the walls?" Kate continued.

"Yes," the woman answered. "Many more of Santa Anna's men were killed than Texans. But there were more to start with so when all was said and done, Santa Anna and his men won the victory."

"It doesn't seem like a fair fight to me," Kate said.

"Many Texans felt that way. That's why the battle at the Alamo caused many to join Sam Houston's army, which resulted in Santa Anna's defeat," the woman said.

"Now I get it. That's why they wanted to remember the Alamo. They didn't want to let Santa Anna bully them anymore," Kate said.

The boy with the red hat, along with the rest of his gang, were leaving the building. Elizabeth grabbed Kate by the arm and said, "It's been a wonderful tour. Thank you so much. We're sorry we have to leave now."

"Hey! What are you—" For the first time, Kate caught a glimpse of the gang of teenagers just as the door was closing.

"Oh! Bye!" Kate waved at the group of tourists and followed Elizabeth.

The girls stepped into the bright Texas sunlight and looked around. Nothing. The group had vanished.

Elizabeth shook her head. "I'm glad you're so interested in Texas history, Kate. Really, I am. But your timing is a little. . .off!"

"Sorry," said Kate. "It's just that I had no idea! I can't believe I'm really standing at the Alamo! I could be standing in the exact spot where. . . where. . .where John Wayne stood!"

Elizabeth, who had begun moving forward, stopped in her tracks. "Now that sounds exactly like something Alexis would say. You do know John Wayne was an actor in a movie, don't you? He wasn't really at the battle of the Alamo."

Kate giggled. "I know. I just wanted to see what you'd say!"

Biscuit, whose face was poking out of Kate's backpack, became agitated. He began wiggling and barking. Elizabeth reached over, removed Biscuit, and placed him on the ground. She was about to snap his leash into place when the little dog took off running!

"Biscuit, wait!" called Elizabeth, but Biscuit kept running. The girls had no choice but to chase their four-legged sidekick. He didn't make it easy for them. He dodged in and out of tourists' legs, causing several to drop their bags. Kate and Elizabeth followed after him at high speed, calling out, "Excuse me!" and "So sorry!"

At last, Biscuit stopped. When they caught up with him, he was barking fiercely at the gang of teenagers, and had Mr. Red-cap backed into a corner.

"Whoa, boy! What is your problem? Why don't you like me, little dog?" the boy was saying. His back was flat against the brick wall of an art shop, and the customers and other tourists were gathering.

"Biscuit! Stop that!" said Kate, kneeling beside him and attaching his leash. "Sorry about that," she said to the boy. "I don't know what's gotten into him."

Biscuit continued growling, but submitted to Kate.

The boy, who looked to be fifteen or sixteen, said, "This has never happened before. Dogs usually love me. I have two dogs at home."

Elizabeth spoke up. "Maybe he smells your other dogs and doesn't like them."

The boy laughed. "I doubt it. My mom can't stand the smell of dogs. She bathes them in some kind of girly lavender wash twice a week."

Kate's jaw dropped. "Lavender? Your mom bathes your dogs in lavender? Biscuit hates lavender!"

The group took a moment to process that, then they all burst into laughter.

"Mystery solved!" the boy said.

"At least one of them, anyway," said Elizabeth.

Red-cap Boy looked at her strangely, then held out his hand. "I'm José. My friends call me Joe. This is Maria and Pedro." He indicated his friends.

Elizabeth shook each of their hands, and said, "Nice to meet you. I'm Elizabeth, and this is Kate. And the growling, four-legged fellow is Biscuit."

Joe knelt down and spoke softly to Biscuit in Spanish. Ever so slowly, he reached out his hand and gently touched the dog's coat.

Gradually, Biscuit relaxed. He never wagged his tail or licked the boy's hand as he usually did when someone was kind to him. His look seemed to say, "I guess I won't attack you. But I'm not going to be your friend either."

"Well, I guess that's a start. So what other mystery were you trying to solve, Elizabeth?" Joe asked, looking down at her with a crooked smile.

Elizabeth blushed. *Why am I blushing?* She stole a quick glance at Kate, who leveled her with a steely stare.

"Oh, she was just talking about the mysteries of life," Kate rescued her. "That's Elizabeth. The philosopher. She's always pondering the deep mysteries of the universe, and stuff like that."

Joe looked at Kate, then back at Elizabeth. "That's, uh. . .nice," he said.

Elizabeth blushed even more, then said, "Well, we'd better be going. We'll see you around!"

Chased!

The group waved goodbye, and the girls headed toward the Riverwalk, Biscuit on his leash. "What was that about?" Kate asked.

"What do you mean?" Elizabeth asked, trying to play dumb.

"I mean that little googly-eyed Romeo and Juliet scene back there. Don't forget, Miss Anderson, that Señor Charming is one of our prime suspects."

"I don't know what you're talking about," said Elizabeth.

Kate gave her a hard stare, but said nothing.

Finally Elizabeth said, "Okay. He has a nice smile. His teeth are so white, and those dimples. . .never mind. But I was *not* googly-eyed."

Kate rolled her eyes. "The lady doth protest too much, methinks," she said.

"Huh?" Elizabeth looked at her friend as if she were speaking a foreign language.

"It's from Shakespeare's *Hamlet*. It means that by denying so strongly that you were googly-eyed, it actually proves my point that you were googly-eyed."

Elizabeth laughed. "Kate, you are truly one of a kind."

Kate smiled.

"And I was *not* googly-eyed. Whatever that means," Elizabeth said.

"My point exactly." Kate gave a smug grin.

Elizabeth changed the subject. "Look, there's a riverboat getting ready to leave. Let's ride!"

"I don't know. After what's been happening with these boats, I'm not sure I want to take the chance."

"Aww, come on. It's part of the San Antonio experience. Besides, maybe we'll get some more clues," Elizabeth encouraged.

Kate adjusted her glasses. "Santa Anna Tours," she read the side of the boat. "The company that crashed into the stage last night was River City Cruises. I guess this one's safe."

"Santa Anna Tours. . . ," Elizabeth read. "That must be a new company. River City is the only one I've ever ridden." She started to get in line, but Kate grabbed her arm.

"Wait. I need to clean my glasses," she said, and Elizabeth followed her to a nearby water fountain. When they returned to the line, they were surprised to see Joe and his friends already sitting on the boat.

"Hola, chicas," he said with his dimpled grin. "Going for a ride?"

Elizabeth suddenly felt shy. She looked to Kate for a signal of what to do.

"You bet we're gonna ride," Kate told him, giving him her fiercest stare. Moving onto the platform, she held his gaze, and forgot to look where she was stepping.

"Watch out, miss!" cried the captain, but it was too late. Kate made a loud splash as she fell into the water.

Biscuit followed with a smaller splash. The little dog frantically paddled to the edge of the Riverwalk and climbed out, but Kate looked like she was drowning.

"Help!" she cried between sputters. "Help! I can't swim! Somebody help me!" She splashed and flailed. Elizabeth read the terror in her friend's face.

"Kate! Stand up! The water is only waist deep!" Elizabeth called out, but Kate was too terrified to understand.

Suddenly, there was another loud splash.

Joe!

The boy grabbed Kate and hoisted the tiny, dripping girl into his arms. "Calm down. I've got you," he said.

Kate clung to the boy for dear life. He walked her to the edge and set her on the concrete walkway.

Another tourist, a woman with two children, pulled a beach towel out of her tote bag and draped it around Kate's shoulders. "Here you go, honey. You'll be just fine."

Kate nodded her thanks as Joe fished around in the water for Kate's glasses. He handed them to her and grinned. Looking at Elizabeth, he said, "Good thing I was here to save your friend. I guess that makes me a hero."

Elizabeth busied herself, using the towel to dry Kate's hair and clothes. "Are you okay?" she asked her friend.

"Physically, I'm fine," Kate said. "My ego, on the other hand, is suffering."

Elizabeth laughed. "I suppose I'll have to give you swimming lessons when we get back to the hotel."

"No thanks. I'd prefer to stay inside with my computers and books and gadgets. It's safer that way," she said.

The captain, a short, bald man with a protruding belly, had been useless during this ordeal. Laughing nervously, he said, "Okay, folks. The excitement's over. Now who wants to go for a ride?"

Elizabeth was surprised when Kate walked to the small boarding platform. "You still want to ride?" she asked.

Kate leaned close and whispered, "Of course I want to ride. We have a mystery to solve, don't we?"

Elizabeth chuckled and followed her friend onto the boat. They sat on the opposite side of the boat from the three teenagers. Joe, now soaked, sat directly across from Elizabeth. He flashed her that grin, and she determined then and there to not look at him again.

As the boat purred to a start, the captain picked up his microphone. "Welcome, ladies and gentlemen, to Santa Anna Tours. We are thrilled to have you as passengers, and we believe you'll find our Riverwalk tour superior, in every way, to our competitor's tour. Please remain seated at all times, and keep your arms and legs inside."

"Eeeeeeeeeeeek!" screamed a middle-aged woman sitting in the middle section of the boat. "A snake! There's a snake in the boat!"

Her husband leaned over and picked up a deadly looking rubber snake. "Calm down, Rita. It isn't real."

Rita covered her mouth with her hand and took a deep breath. "Well, it certainly looked real," she said.

The captain leaned over and took the snake from the man.

"I'm so sorry. I don't know how this could have happened." He eyed Joe, but the boy just returned the captain's gaze with an angelic look.

"I'll bet you a chimichanga I know who put that snake there," Kate whispered as the boat continued on its way. The captain pointed out all the familiar sights, explaining how the Riverwalk had been built for the 1968 World's Fair. Elizabeth never grew tired of hearing how their hotel—the Palacio del Rio—had been assembled and furnished elsewhere, and put in place—room by room—by a huge crane, as builders scrambled to get things ready for the World's Fair. They were able to get the hotel put together just in time.

"Stay calm, folks. We're gonna get you out of this. Please stay in the boat," they heard a man's voice over a microphone up ahead of them. The Santa Anna passengers strained to see what the commotion was about.

Up ahead was a River City Cruise boat filled with passengers. And it seemed to be filling with water. The captain was trying to keep the passengers calm and steer the boat to the side of the river.

The Santa Anna captain said nothing. Did nothing. Just kept on with his tour script.

"Uh, excuse me, sir?" Elizabeth raised her hand.

"Yes, miss? Did you have a question?" the captain acknowledged her with an artificial smile.

"Don't you think we should stop and try to help those people?" she asked.

The man laughed and said, "Oh, they'll be fine. Things like that happen all the time to River City Cruises. You all made the right choice, choosing Santa Anna Tours! Of course, if you're in the mood for a swim, perhaps you should try River City next time. They'll be sure to deliver!" The captain laughed a little too loudly, and the crowd responded with a few chuckles. No one seemed to think his joke was very funny.

Once again, Elizabeth heard a loud splash—and another. Joe and Pedro had jumped in the water and were wading to the stranded boat. The Santa Anna boat continued, with the captain desperately trying to regain his audience's attention.

"Well, well, this has certainly been an exciting ride today, hasn't it, folks? Let me direct your attention to the bridge up ahead. That was the first bridge built here on the Riverwalk. . . ."

As the captain droned on, Elizabeth watched the two boys push the stranded boat to the edge. Then they helped the passengers onto the sidewalk.

"I can't figure them out," she whispered to Kate. "They are our main suspects in. . .several mysteries. But they seem to be pretty good guys."

Kate said, "Yep, this is a job for the Camp Club Girls."

Elizabeth's gaze left the boys for a moment and landed on Maria, sitting by herself. She too was watching the scene behind her. "You're right," she whispered. "But first, I think we need to interview someone."

When the boat ride was over, Kate handed the towel back to the kind lady. "Thank you," she said.

"No problem, honey. I'm just glad you're okay," the lady said.

The two girls waited for Maria to disembark, and the girl smiled at them. "That was some boat ride!" she told them.

"I'll say," answered Kate.

The girl smiled, and the three stood in awkward silence. "Well, I guess I'd better go look for my cousins," she said.

"Your cousins?" Elizabeth and Kate exclaimed.

"Yeah," she said. "Sometimes I'm not proud of that fact. Other times, like just now, I remember that they're pretty good guys."

"Do you mind if we walk with you?" asked Elizabeth.

"Sure!" the girl said. "I mean, no, I don't mind."

All around them, bright streamers of *papel picado*—hand-cut paper decorations—seemed to dance to the mariachi music playing in the distance, and the girls naturally walked in time with the rhythm.

"What makes you say that sometimes you're not proud to be related to them?" asked Kate.

"Oh, you know how boys can be," she said.

Elizabeth and Kate nodded

"And my cousins—Joe, especially—is all boy. He loves to get into mischief, play pranks. Sometimes I wonder why I hang out with them so much," she said. "But they are pretty fun, and it beats staying at home, watching television."

"So you live around here?" Elizabeth asked.

"Yeah, we live a couple of blocks from here. Our parents work near here, and it makes it nice. We don't need a car. We can walk or ride our scooters everywhere we need to go."

"What kinds of pranks do they pull?" pressed Elizabeth. She was determined to wrangle a confession out of someone.

"Oh, you know," the girl said. "This and that." She was beginning to look uncomfortable. Just then, they rounded a curve in the Riverwalk and saw the boys ahead. They were standing at attention, hands by their sides, as a police officer spoke with the captain of the River City Cruise boat—the boat they'd helped rescue.

As the girls drew closer, they could hear the agitated voice of the captain saying, "It's sabotage, I'm telling you. Someone has been meddling with my boats. And these boys seem to be hanging around the Riverwalk with too much time on their hands."

The police officer looked at the boys. "What have you been doing all morning?"

Joe spoke with respect. "We attended some kind of Bible club this morning, down at the church at La Villita. Then we went to the Alamo. After that, we came back here to ride on that other riverboat. We just jumped in to help him because he was stranded. No one else helped him, so we did."

The captain spoke up. "These boys are always hanging around whenever something bad happens. I can't prove it, but I think they're behind the problems I'm having with my boats."

The officer wrote on a notepad, and then questioned the boys further. "You say you were at a Bible club, then the Alamo before you rode on the other boat?"

"Yes, sir," Joe answered.

"Can you prove that?" the officer asked him. "Did anyone else see you at those places?"

Elizabeth stepped forward then. "Excuse me, sir, but these boys are telling the truth. I saw them at those places."

"And your name is. . . ?" questioned the police officer.

"Elizabeth Anderson," she replied.

"And I'm Kate Oliver," Kate spoke up. "I saw them too. Elizabeth and I are helping with the Bible club. I can take you to my youth minister, if you'd like, and he'll verify that."

The police officer eyed the girls, then shut his notepad. "That won't be necessary." He looked at the boat's captain. "I know you're frustrated. And it does appear that someone is trying to sabotage your business. But without proof, I can't hold these boys. It looks to me like they were just doing a good deed."

The captain looked sheepish. He took off his hat and nervously twisted it in his hands. "I'm sorry, boys. I guess I jumped to conclusions. I'm just anxious to get to the bottom of all these mishaps. I do appreciate your help today."

Joe smiled. "That's okay, sir. I hope everything works out for you, and you catch the real bad guys."

The police officer dismissed the boys and continued talking to the captain. Joe and Pedro sighed with relief and turned to Elizabeth and Kate.

"Thanks," the boys told them.

"I don't know what would have happened if you two hadn't shown up," said Pedro.

"Yeah. I was afraid we were going to end up in handcuffs or

something, all for trying to help the guy," Joe added.

Marie looked smugly at her cousins. "I told you all to quit playing all those tricks. People can tell when you're up to no good, and then you get blamed for worse things. It's your own fault."

Elizabeth couldn't resist cutting into the conversation. "And exactly what tricks are you talking about, Maria?"

Joe laughed nervously. "Oh, Maria is *loco*. Crazy. She doesn't know what she's talking about. Just ignore her."

"Would any of those tricks happen to involve a water balloon?" Elizabeth pressed. It didn't matter to her whether or not these boys were criminals or just pranksters. She knew they were guilty of something, and she was going to get to the bottom of this.

Joe smiled a cat-ate-the-canary smile and said nothing. Pedro laughed, and Maria just shook her head before launching into a tirade of rapidly spoken Spanish words. Elizabeth caught a word here and there, but she didn't know very much Spanish.

Something in the shadows caught her eye. Was that the captain of the Santa Anna? And the man he was talking to looked familiar. . . .

It's the rude man from the boat yesterday! The one who was complaining about the River City boats right after the boat died! And. . .what was that on his hands?

She nudged Kate and pointed. Maria continued on with her tirade as the boys tried to ignore their cousin. Joe, noticing that Elizabeth's and Kate's attention was elsewhere, followed their gaze.

The captain of the Santa Anna boat pulled a wad of money out of his pocket and handed it to the man, who stuffed it in his own pocket with fingers stained with neon pink paint. Too late, the men noticed they had an audience.

"Hey! What are you kids doing?" the captain yelled.

Each member of the group seemed to know, without being told, that they had just witnessed something sinister. They took off running. Biscuit, who'd been comfortably napping in Kate's backpack after his morning swim, suddenly came to life. Barking and growling, the little dog wiggled his way out of the backpack, scattering a stack of Kate's business cards in the process.

"Biscuit!" Kate yelled, and scooped her dog into her arms before the men reached him.

"This way!" called Joe, and motioned for them to enter a doorway to. . .Elizabeth had no idea where the doorway led. But she and Kate followed. Joe slammed the door behind them, and Elizabeth peered out the small window.

The two men had stopped running. The captain bent and retrieved one of Kate's cards. He read it, looked toward the doorway, and slipped the card into his pocket.

As the pink-handed man walked toward the doorway, Joe called out, "Get down!" The boy clicked the dead bolt on the door just before they heard the door being pulled. The man on the other side of the door began rattling it, and then his shadow blocked the light coming through the window as he peered inside.

Elizabeth's heart pounded. Who were those men? And what were they doing? Why was the captain paying the other man?

Deep voices came from the other side of the door. "It's locked. Do you want me to go after them?" Elizabeth recognized the voice of the taller man with painted hands.

"Leave 'em alone for now. I have an idea that will shut them up, once and for all."

The Quiet Child

The five young people looked at each other and sighed in unison.

"What was that about?" asked Maria.

"Those guys aren't up to any good, that's for sure," said Joe.

Elizabeth stood on her tiptoes and peered out the tiny window. The men were gone. "Kate. . .we need to get back to the hotel," she said.

"I know! My clothes are still wet, and my sneakers are sloshing," Kate complained.

"And you need to check your blog," Elizabeth added.

"Check my blog? That's right. I need to update my blog," she replied.

"Kate, those men have your card," Elizabeth told her.

Kate's eyes grew wide and round. "My business cards! That's right, they scattered when Biscuit tried to escape. . . ."

"Well, as long as we are careful, it could be a good thing. Maybe we can figure out a way to mislead them or something," Elizabeth told her.

Joe spoke up then. "A blog? What kind of blog? And you have a business card? How old are you, anyway?"

Kate adjusted her glasses then addressed the group. "I know this may come as a surprise to you, but Elizabeth and I are detectives."

The group burst into laughter, including Elizabeth. Kate sounded so serious.

"Laugh if you want to, but it's the truth. And I have a blog you can access online. I discuss different mysteries and ways to solve them."

"Whoa," said Pedro. "We don't know anything about the internet."

"Yes we do!" said Maria. "Remember, we had to take that class in school?"

"Oh yeah. A lot of the kids at school have computers at home, but none of us do. So we're pretty clueless when it comes to that type of stuff," said Joe.

"A lot of people don't have computers at home. But I'm sure your library has a computer you can use for free," Elizabeth said.

Joe smiled at her again, and she looked away.

Stop looking at him. Look at Maria when you talk, Elizabeth told herself.

"And if I went to the library, who would teach me how to use the computer?" he asked.

"The librarian," said Kate. "By the way, can somebody please tell me where we are?"

"We're in a secret passageway. I thought you detectives would know all about that," Joe teased.

"Well, you obviously knew it was here. I'm hoping you also know where it leads!" Kate retorted.

"Follow me," Maria chimed in. She began walking down the long hallway, and the others followed her. They turned to the right, and then pushed open some swinging doors that led into a kitchen. Immediately, people called out greetings in Spanish. Elizabeth recognized the logo on the red aprons.

This is the kitchen of Rio Rio!

One woman began speaking in rapid-fire Spanish to Joe. She was standing over a dish of the most delicious-looking tamales Elizabeth had ever seen.

Those tamales! Those are the tamales I love so much!

Joe turned to Elizabeth and Kate. "I'd like you to meet my mama, Elena Garcia. Mama, this is Kate," he gestured, and the woman smiled.

"And *this,*" he said with emphasis, "is *Elizabeth.*"

The woman lifted her eyebrows at her son, then smiled at Elizabeth, who could feel herself turning every shade of red. *Why did he say it like that?*

"It's very nice to meet both of you," the woman said. Then she looked at Elizabeth. "Don't you let José give you a hard time. He is. . . how you say? . . . All bark and no bite."

Now it was Joe's turn to blush, and the group laughed.

Biscuit chose that moment to bark, and several people in the kitchen turned to look at the little dog. Joe's mother began speaking in rapid Spanish once again, finishing with, "*Andale! Andale!*"

Elizabeth knew she was telling them to hurry and get out. Dogs weren't allowed in restaurant kitchens.

Kate scooped Biscuit into her arms and said, "We need to be going. Thanks for everything," and looked for an exit sign.

"It was very nice to meet you, Mrs. Garcia," Elizabeth told the woman, and followed Kate through a door.

Once inside the door, they realized they were in a supply closet.

"Well, this is a little embarrassing," said Kate, turning to go back through the door.

As the girls re-entered the kitchen, the staff clapped and laughed. Joe stepped forward and said, "Allow me to accompany you," in a gallant tone.

Red-faced, the two girls followed their guide through another door, down a short hallway, and finally stepped into the sunlight of the Riverwalk.

"Thanks, Joe. We'll. . .see ya around," Kate told him, and began moving toward the hotel.

"Yeah, thanks," called Elizabeth with a slight wave. Joe watched them until they were out of sight.

•—•—•

An hour later, the girls lay across their beds in the hotel room talking on their cell phones and munching on french fries. Kate had set her phone for a conference call, and amazingly, had gotten in touch with each of the other Camp Club Girls.

"Okay," said Sydney. "Let me get this straight. Elizabeth got hit by a water balloon while riding in a River City Cruise boat, and another lady found a rubber snake at her feet while riding a Santa Anna boat. River City keeps having mechanical problems, but you don't think the mechanical problems are related to the pranks."

"We did to begin with," said Kate. "But we're pretty sure we know who the pranksters are, and they seem pretty harmless. I told you about the two men who chased us. And the tall, skinny guy had pink hands—the color one of the River City boats was painted. I think those men are responsible for the vandalism. At least, Elizabeth *hopes* it's those men."

"What is that supposed to mean?" asked Elizabeth.

"You know exactly what it means," said Kate in a teasing voice. "Elizabeth is swooning over one of the pranksters."

"I am not!" said Elizabeth, and the other girls began asking questions, all at once.

"Tell us more, Kate! Who is this guy? What is his name?" they asked.

Elizabeth pulled the pillow over her head, but continued listening to the conversation.

"His name is José Garcia," Kate said with a dramatic accent.

"Ooh! Is he from Mexico? I could be related to him!" said Alex. "If you marry him, Elizabeth, we could end up being cousins!"

"Y'all, stop it! I'm not marrying anybody. Kate is just making stuff up," Elizabeth defended herself, throwing a pillow at her roommate. "And he likes to be called Joe."

"Hmmmmm. . .Elizabeth Garcia," teased Bailey. "It has a ring to it."

The other girls laughed, until finally McKenzie said, "You guys, leave Elizabeth alone."

"Thank you, Mac," said Elizabeth.

"I'm sure she'll invite us all to the wedding, when the time comes," McKenzie continued.

"Mac!" Elizabeth yelled into the phone, and everyone laughed again.

"All right already," Kate said. "Sorry I brought it up, Elizabeth. I just couldn't resist. Now, can we please get back to the matter at hand? What should be our next step in solving this mystery?"

"Tell us more about the two men," Sydney said.

"Well, the captain is shorter, bald, pudgy. . .and he wears a captain's hat," Elizabeth responded.

"Like the hat the captain wore on *Gilligan's Island*?" Alex asked.

"Oh, I've seen that show! That's an old one. And yes, the hat is exactly like that," Elizabeth said. "And the other guy is tall and skinny, and seems to take orders from the captain."

"It sounds to me like you need to focus your investigation on Gilligan and the Skipper," said Bailey. Once again, she had come up with the perfect nicknames for their suspects.

Alex spoke up again. "Kate, you took your bag of gadgets along, didn't you?"

"Do you even have to ask?" Kate responded.

"Did you bring along one of those little listening thing-a-ma-jiggers?" Alex continued.

"You mean a bug?" Kate asked.

"Yeah," Alex laughed. "A bug. But 'thing-a-ma-jigger' is so much more fun to say."

Everyone laughed, and Bailey spoke up. "How far away can you be, and still hear a conversation through the bug?"

"That shouldn't be a problem," said Kate. "There are plenty of hiding places."

"But where will you plant the bug?" asked McKenzie. "Those men sound scary. I don't want you to do anything dangerous."

"We'll be careful," Elizabeth assured her. "There are several boarding areas for the boats, and they're often left unmanned when the boat is on a tour. We can probably put a bug on the fence railing at one of those areas."

"Yeah, and then we can hang out at one of the nearby restaurants eating chips and salsa until something happens," Kate said.

The other girls laughed. "Always thinking about food," said Sydney.

"Hey, if we're going to sit and wait, we might as well do something constructive," Kate retorted.

The girls laughed, and Elizabeth spoke up again. "Our biggest problem is that the two men know who we are. Kate dropped a business card, and one of them picked it up. Now they know we're sleuths."

Alex said, "Hey, maybe you could use that to your advantage. They know you are just kids, and they probably won't expect much of you. I remember an episode of *Hawaii Five-O* where McGarrett went undercover as a convict, and made it look like the police were after him. Maybe you can pretend to focus in on someone else as the guilty party, and the men will leave you alone."

"Hey, that might work," said Kate. "We could ask Joe to be our undercover guy, and act guilty. . . ."

Alex laughed. "Joe, huh? Well, that would be appropriate."

"What do you mean?" asked Elizabeth.

"The episode I'm thinking of was titled, 'The Ways of Love.' "

Everyone laughed, and Elizabeth said, "I'm never speaking to any of you again. For five whole minutes, anyway. Goodbye." She clicked her phone shut and pulled the pillow over her head again. The other girls recognized the teasing in Elizabeth's voice and laughed.

Kate finally hung up. "Hey, you're not really mad, are you?" she asked.

"No," Elizabeth said. "But I'm not googly-eyed, and I didn't swoon."

Kate ignored her friend's last comment, and instead opened up her laptop. "Now, to update my blog," she said.

Elizabeth watched her log into her stats page. Sure enough, comments waited. Clicking on the first of two, she read, *"Back off. You're in over your head!"*

The next read, *"You leave us alone, and we'll leave your little dog alone."*

The two girls stared at the screen.

"Elizabeth, those guys are serious. They threatened Biscuit! What are we going to do?"

Elizabeth stared at the screen, forming a silent prayer. Water balloons and rubber snakes were one thing. Threatening Biscuit was an entirely different matter. *What should we do, Lord?*

A Bible verse popped into her head, one of the first verses she had learned as a small child. She had actually learned it as a song. Elizabeth took a deep breath and began singing the words to Psalm 56:3. "When I am afraid, I will trust in You, I will trust in You, I will trust in You. When I am afraid I will trust in You, when I am afraid."

Kate leaned back on the bed and looked at the ceiling. "I know we're supposed to trust God in all things. But I also think we're supposed to use wisdom. I don't want to do anything to put Biscuit in danger and just assume God will rescue him."

Elizabeth reread the words on the screen. After a moment, she said, "You're right. We need to be careful, and use wisdom. But we won't let those men ruin our good time. We'll just be extra careful, keep Biscuit close, and trust God to show us what to do."

"Do you think we should let an adult know what's going on?" Kate asked.

Elizabeth leaned back on her elbows. "Probably. And I think I know exactly who to tell. . . ."

•—•—•

Later that evening, Elizabeth and Kate leaned on the counter in the hotel lobby, waiting for Uncle Dan to finish with a customer. He handed the woman a key and said, "Enjoy your stay."

As soon as the woman was out of earshot, he wheeled his chair back to the girls, and said, "Okay, I'm all ears. Tell me again how you got mixed up in all of this."

Elizabeth and Kate took turns filling him in on the details. "At first, I thought Joe and his friends were probably behind the problems with the boats, but I don't think that anymore," Elizabeth told her uncle.

Uncle Dan looked out the glass doors toward the Riverwalk. A Santa Anna boat was puttering by. "Ever since Santa Anna Tours opened for business, River City Cruises has had problems. They've been in business here for decades, and have a spotless record for safety and customer satisfaction. I've wondered about Santa Anna all along."

The girls waited and listened. During Uncle Dan's time in the military, he had worked for military intelligence. If anyone knew how to find clues and solve a mystery, it was him.

Uncle Dan leaned back in his chair and looked at them. "I want you girls to lay low until I've had a chance to think about this. Stay close to the hotel tonight, and keep a close watch on Biscuit. Let's all sleep on it, and we'll talk more tomorrow. I think we may be able to catch these guys, once and for all."

The girls agreed, and left Uncle Dan to his work. Holding Biscuit tightly, Kate said, "Let's go find something to eat."

Just as they turned to leave, Mr. and Mrs. Anderson walked into the lobby, James tagging behind them. "There you are!" said Mrs. Anderson. "We've hardly seen you girls today. Are you hungry?"

The girls nodded. Biscuit jumped out of Kate's arms and began playing with James.

"Why don't you all go ahead and reserve us a table at the café next door. I just need to do something to my hair, and freshen my lipstick," Mrs. Anderson told them.

"You look beautiful, sweetheart," Mr. Anderson told her, and the woman smiled sweetly at her husband.

"Thank you, darling," she said, "but I don't *feel* beautiful. I'll be right behind you." The woman headed for the elevators, and Mr. Anderson shook his head. "Women. I'll never understand them."

The group headed out the lobby doors and found a table at the nearby café. The waitress smiled at Biscuit as she placed their chips and salsa on the table. Suddenly, the little dog barked and leaped from Kate's lap.

"Biscuit!" the girls called out, but it was too late. Biscuit was in hot pursuit of. . .someone.

The girls and James chased the little dog through the outdoor restaurant, dodging tables and customers, working hard to keep the little dog in sight. Finally, they spotted Biscuit ahead, sitting sweetly and licking a little girl's hand.

Elizabeth gasped when she saw who it was. *The little girl from Bible Camp this morning!*

"Hi!" Elizabeth said, kneeling next to the girl. "Do you remember me? We met this morning."

The girl buried her face in her mother's skirt.

"I'm sorry," Elizabeth said to the woman. "I didn't mean to frighten her."

"It's okay," the woman told her. "Annie is very shy. She loves animals, but people make her nervous. You must be from the Bible camp she attended this morning."

"Yes, ma'am. I'm Elizabeth, and this is Kate and James. And this"—she gestured to the dog still looking up at Annie and wagging his tail—"is Biscuit."

"We hope she'll come back tomorrow," said Kate with a smile. "Same time, same place."

The woman looked sadly at her daughter. "I don't know," she said. "Some children can be so cruel."

Elizabeth and Kate looked at each other, confused. *Why would anyone be cruel to such a sweet little girl?*

The Bible Camp Band

Mr. Anderson approached the group. "Everything okay, Elizabeth?" he asked.

"Oh. Hi, Dad. Yes. This little girl was in our Bible camp this morning, and I guess Biscuit recognized her. He seems to like her!" Elizabeth smiled at the little girl, who was peering through her curls.

"Dan Anderson." Elizabeth's dad held his hand out to the woman.

"Teresa Lopez," the woman replied, returning his handshake. "And this is Annie." She gestured to her daughter, who was now squatting, rubbing Biscuit behind the ears. James knelt too and spoke softly to the dog and the girl.

Annie turned her head to the side, and for just a moment, her thick curls fell away from her face to reveal a large red birthmark. It covered the entire left side of her face. James didn't seem to notice, but smiled and looked directly into the girl's eyes. "Biscuit really likes you. He likes me too. He'll be at Bible Camp tomorrow. Are you coming?"

In that moment, Elizabeth wanted to pick her little brother up and hug him.

He is such a great kid! she thought. *Lord, I take back every bad thought I've ever had about my little brother. He is the best little guy in the world!*

Annie's mother noticed too and looked at Mr. Anderson. "What a nice boy you have," she whispered. "Annie's birthmark is called a strawberry hemangioma, and many of the children make fun of her. At home, she's outgoing and playful. Unfortunately, she has learned to be afraid of people she doesn't know."

Mr. Anderson nodded. "She's a beautiful little girl, even with the birthmark. Is it possible to have it removed?"

The woman looked close to tears. "Yes, it is possible, but not probable. It's an expensive operation, and I don't have medical insurance. I'm afraid Annie will have to live with her birthmark. At least until she's older."

Mr. Anderson smiled compassionately. Looking at the girls and James, he said, "We'd better head back to the café. Your mother will wonder where we are."

Elizabeth knelt and whispered to Annie, "I hope you'll come back tomorrow. I was lonely after you left today."

Annie looked into Elizabeth's eyes for just a moment. A smile crossed her face, but was gone in an instant.

"I'll bring her," said Mrs. Lopez, "but I can't promise she'll stay."

Elizabeth, her brother and father, and Kate went back to their table, where they found Mrs. Anderson munching tortilla chips.

"There you are!" she said. "I knew this was your table, because I saw Kate's backpack, so I sat down and started eating. I knew you'd be back. But then, I started wondering what would happen if someone else had a backpack like Kate's, and I was sitting here eating some stranger's chips."

"I see it didn't stop you." Her husband laughed.

"Well, I thought about leaving the chips alone until I knew for sure, but I was too hungry. Where did y'all go?" she asked.

They took turns telling about Biscuit and the little girl, and Mrs. Anderson listened intently. Finally, she said, "I have a cousin who had something like that. Her mother told her it was where an angel kissed her, and she seemed to accept that when she was very young. But as she got older, she became more self-conscious. Some children made fun of her, and made her life miserable."

"Did she ever get it fixed?" Elizabeth asked her mother.

"Yes. There was some organization. . . . I can't think of the name right now. But a charitable group helped finance surgeries like that for children. Perhaps you could do research on it, girls. I know how you like to chase down mysteries and such," she said.

The girls looked at each other, but said nothing. This was just one of the mysteries they were facing. And quite frankly, the other mystery had them a little nervous.

•—•—•

Morning came a little too early for the girls. They had stayed up late talking and doing online research. They'd wanted to update Kate's blog, but decided against it. "It's probably better if they think we haven't checked the blog in a few days. Let them think we don't know anything about their threats," Elizabeth had suggested, and Kate grudgingly agreed.

But in spite of their tiredness, the girls and Biscuit were at the appointed place at a quarter to eight, ready to help with Bible Camp. Mrs. Anderson agreed to drop James off at eight o'clock.

"Elizabeth! Glad you're here. Could you lead the kids in songs again?" Gary asked her.

Elizabeth eyed the keyboard set up to one side of the steps. "May I use the keyboard?" she asked.

Gary looked hesitant. "It's borrowed, and I promised the owner I'd take good care of it. . . ."

Kate stepped forward. "Gary, you don't have anything to worry about. When it comes to keyboards, Elizabeth knows her stuff."

Gary lifted his eyebrows then grinned. Moving his arm in a grand, sweeping gesture, he said, "In that case, be my guest."

Elizabeth smiled and moved to the keyboard. She hadn't played one for several days, and she missed the feeling of her fingers on the piano keys. She adjusted the volume then played through a few scales. Finally, she began playing the tune of one of the songs she'd taught the children the day before.

For a few moments, she became absorbed in the keyboard. She pressed a few buttons, and before long, she had added drum rhythms, bells, and even a comical whistling sound. People stopped what they were doing and gathered to listen to her music.

Elizabeth was surprised when she looked up and realized she had an audience. Normally she was self-conscious when she played in front of people. But this was such a relaxed atmosphere, it didn't feel like a recital or a concert. She smiled and spoke into the microphone Gary had placed in front of her.

"Good morning everyone, and welcome to Bible Camp! Do you remember the song I taught you yesterday? Sing it with me now!"

The children gathered at the church steps began singing loudly, and the teenagers and adults joined in. This continued for several songs until Elizabeth looked up and saw Joe smiling at her from the back of the crowd. She immediately missed a note and forgot the words. She finished the song as gracefully as possible, then handed the microphone to Gary and moved to the side of the crowd.

"Thank you, Elizabeth," Gary said. "Isn't she great? Let's all give her a hand!"

The crowd erupted in applause, and Elizabeth turned beet red. Then, she felt someone crowding against her leg. She looked down to see a mop of familiar curls. Forgetting herself, she hugged the little girl. "Annie! You came!"

The girl smiled shyly and took hold of her hand. Biscuit appeared at the girl's feet, wagging his tail. Annie reached down and petted him gently.

When Gary dismissed the crowd to go to their sessions, Elizabeth took Annie into the church and sat down. The children were still getting settled in their seats when Elizabeth heard a voice behind her.

"Are you some teen prodigy or something?"

Elizabeth turned to look at Joe, trying not to blush. "No, I just like music. I'm usually nervous in front of people, but this was just a bunch of little kids. I didn't feel as nervous as I usually do."

"I play the guitar a little, but not as well as you play the piano. Still, we should get together and jam sometime," he said.

The Bible story teacher called the group to attention, and Elizabeth faced the front. *He wants to jam with me? Oh Lord, what do I tell him? I wish he would leave me alone. Actually, I don't want him to leave me alone. What in the world is going on here, Lord?*

Her thoughts swirled, and she didn't catch a word of the Bible story. *Oh my goodness, Kate is right. I am swooning. I've never swooned over a boy. What is getting into me?* She was painfully aware of Joe's presence right behind her. *Lord, help me to know how to act. I don't even know if he's a Christian! And I'm only fourteen.*

The rest of the morning flew by. Joe, Maria, and Pedro jumped in to help where they could, and they seemed to really listen to the Bible stories and verses. Annie relaxed some and even talked to James as they worked together on a craft.

When it was time to clean up, Gary called Elizabeth to the front. "Why don't you play the keyboard for us while we work. I'll put this sign advertising our camp next to you, and as people walk by, maybe they'll notice and send their kids tomorrow. Here, I'll put up this sign for our mime show this evening too."

Elizabeth agreed, and for the first time noticed the symbol at the bottom of the sign. "Gary, what is that?" she pointed.

"Oh, that's the symbol for the Kiwanis Club. They own the Fiesta Noche del Rio, the outdoor theater where we are performing each night. They like for their symbol to be on everything that advertises the theater. It helps with donations."

"Donations?" she asked.

"Yeah, they're a charity," Gary said, then called out some instructions to a couple of teenagers who were cleaning up.

Elizabeth turned and began playing the keyboard. She noticed Joe and Pedro talking to Gary and pointing to a guitar case. Gary smiled, nodded, and then knelt to open the case. The two of them approached the soundboard behind Elizabeth, and she tried to ignore them. People passing stopped and read the signs. Many of them stood for a few minutes, enjoying her upbeat music. The teenagers and some of the children sang along as they worked.

After a few moments, Elizabeth heard a bass guitar coming from behind her. Turning her head just a little, she saw it was Joe. A rhythmic clicking noise from the other side of her was Pedro. A drummer? He had two pencils, and was clicking away on the stair railing. It sounded good.

The three of them continued playing for a half hour. Surprisingly, Elizabeth didn't feel self-conscious. She got caught up in the music and just enjoyed herself.

Finally, they wrapped up their little concert and received light applause from the people gathered around. Unplugging the keyboard, she heard Pedro say, "That was so cool! We need a keyboardist for our band, Elizabeth. Too bad you don't live here."

"You have a band?" she asked, and Joe laughed.

"We want to have a band. So far it's just me with my borrowed guitar and Pedro with his pencils. We're both in the band at school, but we use the school's instruments. During the summer, we have trouble finding good instruments to play."

"What kind of music do you like to play?" Elizabeth asked.

"All kinds," said Joe. "Mostly rock 'n' roll. But I really like what you're playing. I never knew Christian music could be so cool."

Elizabeth smiled. "Being a Christian is pretty cool," she told him.

Joe looked at his feet. "Yeah, my mom's always trying to get me to go to church. Maybe I'll have to try it."

Kate approached, Biscuit at her heels. "So, did you talk to them about. . .you know?" she asked Elizabeth.

Her question immediately got his attention. Maria and Pedro approached and joined the conversation.

"Talk to us about what?" asked Joe.

Elizabeth shot Kate a frustrated look, but Kate simply adjusted her glasses and smiled.

What is she up to? Elizabeth wondered. *We're supposed to check with Uncle Dan before we make any more plans.*

Just then, Elizabeth's mother waved to her. James was seated on the ground beside her, dangling his feet into the river. "Elizabeth, what are you girls planning to do for lunch? Your father and I want to go to the mall, if you're interested."

"Well, we told Uncle Dan we'd meet him after Bible Camp. If it's okay, we'd like to hang around here for a while," she told her mother.

"Okay," Mrs. Anderson said. She made sure Elizabeth had money for lunch, and waved goodbye. "We'll meet you back at the hotel at two o'clock," she called over her shoulder.

When she was gone, Joe asked her once again. "Talk to us about what?"

Kate spoke up. "We may need your help with a little project we're working on. But right now, Elizabeth and I have to meet someone. Why don't we meet you in an hour at the Rio Rio. You can order us some of those great tamales your mom was making yesterday."

The threesome agreed, and Elizabeth and Kate headed toward the hotel. "What was that about?" Elizabeth questioned. "I thought we were supposed to keep our mouths shut until we talked to Uncle Dan again!"

"My mistake," Kate apologized. "I saw you all deep in conversation and assumed that's what you were talking about. What were you talking about, by the way?"

Elizabeth smiled. "We were talking about music. Did you hear Joe playing the guitar? He's good."

"It's a match made in heaven," Kate teased, and Elizabeth reached over and pulled Kate's pink ball cap over her eyes. "Hey, stop that!" Kate called, straightening her cap.

Uncle Dan was waiting for them when they entered the lobby, and wasted no time in small talk. "I've been thinking about how we can catch these guys," he said. "Kate, didn't you say you brought a bag full of spy gizmos and gadgets?"

Kate nodded. "I have a bug we can plant to listen in on conversations. We thought we'd start with that."

"Perfect," said Uncle Dan. "I talked to Lyndel this morning—he's the owner of River City Cruises. He said the problems started a couple of weeks before Santa Anna Tours opened for business. I also found out that the owner of Santa Anna Tours has a history of illegal behavior. I'm not sure what he's capable of, so you girls need to stay safe. Don't go wandering off into any lonely alleys or tunnels. Stay on the Riverwalk, stay together, and stay where there is a crowd."

Elizabeth felt chills go up her spine. "This guy sounds dangerous."

"He's never been accused of anything violent—mostly petty theft and vandalism—but the bottom line is, he can't be trusted. We don't know what he's capable of. Can I trust you girls to act responsibly?"

The girls nodded, wide-eyed.

"Okay then. Here's the plan," he said, and the three spent the next half hour plotting and planning.

•—•—•

At 1:15 p.m., Kate and Elizabeth spotted their friends seated at the Rio Rio.

Joe smiled at Elizabeth. "We were about to give up on you," he said. "Mom made this huge plate of tamales just for you, and I thought I would have to eat them myself."

"Don't you dare!" Elizabeth told him, and the group laughed. They made room for the two girls to sit down and politely joined Kate and Elizabeth as they prayed over their food.

Then, Maria leaned her elbows on the table, resting her chin on her hands. "Joe said you wanted to talk to us about something," she said.

Elizabeth took a bite of the delicious tamales, and closed her eyes. "I have dreamed about these tamales. These are the best things I have ever tasted. Joe, do you think your mom would give me the recipe?"

He smiled. "We might be able to work something out. But first, you need to tell us what Kate was talking about earlier. What's the big secret?"

Kate swallowed her bite of tamale then leaned back in her chair. "Well, you remember those guys who chased us yesterday? We think they're the ones who are sabotaging the River City Cruise boats. But we may need your help to catch them."

The Plan

The three cousins leaned forward. "Sounds exciting. What do you need us to do?" asked Joe.

Elizabeth began filling them in on the plan. "We'd like to use all of you, or at least a couple of you, as scapegoats. We want to blame you, very loudly and in public, for the problems with the River City boats. Then, the real bad guys will think we're off their tails, when we'll actually be watching their every move."

Joe and Pedro looked at each other.

"What makes you think anyone would believe we had anything to do with it?" Joe asked. "We're innocent."

Maria burst into laughter. "Innocent? You? That's the funniest thing I've heard in a long time!" The girl looked at Elizabeth and Kate. "Trust me. Joe and Pedro have a reputation around here. Everyone would believe they did it."

Pedro's eyes grew large. "What do you mean, Joe and Pedro? What about you? You're right there, whenever we do anything!"

"Hey, all I do is watch! The water balloons, the rubber snakes. . ."

"Shhhhh! Stop talking. You'll make us look bad," he told his friends, glancing at Elizabeth. Maria laughed.

"If you're so innocent, why are you worried about looking bad? Your actions will speak for you," Elizabeth said. She finally had him cornered. He had practically admitted dropping the water balloon on her.

Joe leaned back in his chair and looked down at his hands. Finally, he looked up at Elizabeth, and she could see the hurt in his eyes. "So you think we're a bunch of hoodlums. Obviously, we'd be the best ones to take the rap for the vandalism."

Elizabeth felt terrible. Yes, she had thought they were hoodlums—in the beginning. But now she knew better, and she wouldn't want to hurt her new friends for anything.

The table grew quiet. She didn't know what to say.

After an awkward silence, Kate saved the day. "Look, nobody is accusing anybody of being hoodlums. If we thought you were hoodlums, we wouldn't ask you to help us. But don't even try to play innocent with us, Joe. We know all about your little games. Innocent fun? Perhaps. But you dropped that water balloon on Elizabeth, and everyone knows it. So why don't you just apologize and get it over with?"

Joe turned four shades of red, starting at his collar, then creeping up his chin, past his ears, and all the way to his head. After a moment, a smile crept onto his embarrassed face.

Elizabeth was taken off guard when he left his chair and knelt in front of her. The others snickered as they witnessed what was sure to be a great show.

"Señorita Anderson, it has been brought to my attention that, in my carelessness, I may have accidentally dropped a water balloon on your head," Joe told her. "I am so clumsy, and that balloon just slipped right out of my hands. I would never, ever intentionally drop a water balloon on someone as sweet and lovely as you. Will you please forgive me?"

Now, it was Elizabeth's turn to blush. Why couldn't she think of something clever to say? "Wait a minute," she said, rewinding his words in her mind. "Did you say it was an accident?"

The snickers got louder, and Joe just smiled.

"You expect me to believe that your dropping that water balloon on my head was an accident?" she continued. "I don't think so. Try your little apology again."

The group of witnesses laughed and waited to see what would happen next.

Joe laughed too but didn't back down. "Of course it was an accident, Elizabeth. I was aiming for the person in front of you!"

There. He had admitted it. He had dropped that water balloon on purpose, and Elizabeth wasn't sure she wanted to forgive him. She crossed her arms and tried to look angry, but it didn't work. The whole thing was too funny.

Finally, in a dramatic show of mercy, Elizabeth stood to her feet, took the long-handled teaspoon that rested on the table, and looked at Joe like a queen looking down on a peasant.

"Although you don't deserve my forgiveness, Señor Garcia, I shall grant it anyway. You"—she placed the teaspoon on one of his shoulders, like a scepter—"are pardoned." Lifting the teaspoon over his head, she touched his other shoulder.

The boy pretended to be overtaken with relief and gratitude, and the others at the table shook with laughter. Kate and Maria even had tears rolling down their cheeks, they were laughing so hard.

When they finally got under control, Pedro pulled the conversation back to its original topic. "So, tell us again what we can do to help you."

For the next half hour, they plotted and schemed over tortilla chips and tamales. When Kate and Elizabeth stood to leave, they felt both nervous and excited about the plan that would take place later that day.

•—•—•

Elizabeth sat in the overstuffed chair in the living area of their hotel room. Her feet were draped over the arm of the chair, and she casually twirled her long hair with her fingers.

"Mom and Dad, Kate and I were wondering if we could hang out with Uncle Dan this afternoon. He invited us to run some errands with him. Would that be okay?"

"Well, I just don't want you girls getting in his way," Mr. Anderson said. "But if he invited you, I suppose it's okay," he said.

Elizabeth rewarded him with a huge smile.

"I know how much you love your Uncle Dan, but he is coming to visit us in a couple of weeks. Not only that, but today we're going to the science museum, and we don't have anything like San Antonio's Science Museum in Amarillo. Are you sure you don't want to come with us?" said Mrs. Anderson.

Elizabeth nodded. "I know. The Science Museum is really fun, and I hate to miss it. But I'm excited about spending time with Uncle Dan. I think I'll enjoy that more."

"Okay. But stay with Uncle Dan, and stay out of trouble," her mother told her with a wink. "We'll probably go out to eat too, so I'm not sure what time we'll be back. Keep your cell phone with you, and call us if you need anything."

"Yes, ma'am," Elizabeth called as her parents and James walked out the door.

"Whew, that was close," said Kate. "For a minute, I thought they were going to insist we go with them!"

"Well, they're gone now, and we don't have much time. Let's get the other Camp Club Girls on the phone, and see what they've come up with," Elizabeth told her.

Soon they had Bailey, Alex, and McKenzie on the phone. Sydney was at her gymnastics class, so they'd have to fill her in later.

"Okay, everyone, it's crunch time. Since we talked to you last night, we've come up with a plan. In about forty-five minutes, we're going to stage a big scene, and my uncle Dan and his friend, who owns the River City Cruises, are going to blame Joe and Pedro for all the vandalism that's been happening. Before that, we need to plant a listening device at the Santa Anna dock, but we're not sure how we'll do that. The Skipper knows who we are. They know we're onto them, so they'll be watching us. Any ideas?"

"What about having one of your new friends plant the device, before the whole scene plays out?" suggested Alex.

"That won't work," said Kate. "We were all together when those men chased us. They'll recognize them too."

"Well then, what about Uncle Dan? They probably don't know who he is, do they?" asked McKenzie.

Elizabeth and Kate looked at each other. That could work.

"That's a good idea, McKenzie. Later, he'll go down there, strike up a conversation with the captain, and somehow hide the bug on the dock," Kate said.

"Then, Joe and Pedro can walk by," Elizabeth added. "Uncle Dan will call out, 'Hey, there they are!' and start accusing them of vandalizing the riverboats. They'll defend themselves for a few minutes, then leave. Then, Uncle Dan will change his mind about riding the boat, and leave too."

"This is where the listening device comes in," Kate added. "After the whole scene plays out, we're hoping the captain and his sidekick will start talking and say something that will incriminate them."

"In-what-anate them?" asked Bailey.

"Incriminate," Kate said. "It means we hope they'll say something that will prove to us, and the police, that they are guilty of something."

"Well. . .it could work. Let's just hope Gilligan and the Skipper don't figure out that Uncle Dan is related to you," said Alex.

"Yep," said Elizabeth. "We've already talked about that. Kate and I will sit at a nearby café. Lots of people just sit and talk. We'll act oblivious to the whole thing."

"Well, be careful. You don't know what those men might do," said McKenzie.

Kate promised that yes, they would be careful.

Elizabeth looked at her watch. "We've got to get going. Uncle Dan's probably waiting for us. Oh! Did anyone research surgeries for a strawberry hemangioma birthmark?"

"I did, and I found out some interesting things," said McKenzie. "But we'll talk later. You go on, and call us as soon as the plan is executed. We want to hear every detail!"

The girls hung up, and after taking some deep breaths, Kate and Elizabeth headed downstairs to the lobby.

Uncle Dan was waiting for them, as expected. "Are you ready to go?" he asked, a gleam of excitement in his eyes.

Elizabeth nodded. "We talked to our friends, and everything is set up. But we're hoping you can be the one to plant the listening device. The boat captain will be suspicious if he sees us hanging around his dock."

"That shouldn't be a problem for you. Just wait until the boat is on a tour, and the captain's not around. But I'll do it if you want."

"You'd better. There were two men, and even if the Skipper isn't around, I don't know where Gilligan might be," Elizabeth told him.

Uncle Dan nodded, and Kate handed him the device. He held it up to the light and examined it. "Wow. This is tiny. How far does the sound broadcast?"

Kate smiled proudly. "Elizabeth and I can be all the way at the other end of the Riverwalk, and we'll still hear the conversation."

"That's cool," he said.

Elizabeth looked out the glass lobby doors and saw Joe and Pedro standing near the Riverwalk. The lobby doors opened, and Maria walked in.

"The guys are ready to look guilty. They'll follow your cue," Maria told them, then returned to her cousins.

Uncle Dan eyed the group. "So they're the ones, huh? Let's hope they're good actors. I suppose it's good that they've never met me. It will seem more natural."

Something in the pit of Elizabeth's stomach told her this wasn't going to go as planned. But she kept quiet. They had gone to all this trouble; she couldn't see the point in backing out now.

"You girls go find a place to sit and wait. I suggest you go to that little ice cream parlor with the balcony. If you sit up high, you'll be able to see us better," he suggested.

"Ice cream parlor?" asked Kate. "Sounds good to me. I'm starved!"

Elizabeth laughed. "Let's go," she said. "Uncle Dan, we're turning the listening device on now. Give us five minutes, and then tell us when you're leaving the lobby. You won't be able to hear us, but we'll hear you."

Uncle Dan nodded, and Kate and Elizabeth exited the lobby, trying to ignore their four friends standing outside. The last thing they needed was for the captain or his friend to see them together again.

For a split second, Elizabeth glanced at Joe. She couldn't seem to stop herself. He was watching her! She looked away, and led Kate to the ice cream parlor. Together, they climbed the steep stairs. "You go in and order, and I'll stay here on the balcony. This table is perfect. Look! We have a clear shot of the boat dock. We'll be able to see everything."

"Okay," agreed Kate. "I'll go get our ice cream. What do you want?"

"Anything chocolate," Elizabeth replied as she sat down.

Kate soon returned, and the girls were taking their first bites of ice cream when Elizabeth spotted something. "Kate, look!" She pointed to a small shoe-shine booth. There, enjoying a shoe shine, was the Skipper. He was only a few yards from his boat dock, but his back was to it.

Uncle Dan's voice came over the tiny speaker. "Leaving the lobby, heading for the boat dock." The girls watched as Uncle Dan rolled his wheelchair to the railing as if to wait in the ticket line. He grabbed onto the railing as if he needed it for support, and Elizabeth smiled. She knew he was actually planting the listening device. The magnetic back clung securely to the underside of the metal railing—they had tested it earlier.

The Skipper approached with his newly shined shoes. He reached out to help Uncle Dan, and smiled.

"Welcome to Santa Anna Tours! How can I help you?" he asked.

So far, so good, thought Elizabeth.

"I'm thinking about taking one of your tours. But I'm a little hesitant," Uncle Dan told the man.

The captain lifted his eyebrows. "Oh? Why is that?"

"I've noticed a lot of the boats are breaking down. As you can see, since I'm in a wheelchair, it isn't easy for me to get on and off the boats. I certainly don't want to take the chance of getting myself or my chair wet."

"Oh, no need to worry. Santa Anna Tours has a perfect record. It's the other boat company that has had all the problems," the man said.

"I've heard that vandalism is suspected," Uncle Dan said. The other man suddenly looked uncomfortable.

"I think I may know who is behind the vandalism too," Uncle Dan continued.

The captain looked surprised. "Oh really? Who might that be?"

Uncle Dan leaned closer to the man.

He is such a great actor! thought Elizabeth. *He should be on stage!*

"Some teenagers have been wandering around here, and they look like they're up to no good. There are two boys and a girl, and I don't trust them. If I were you, I'd watch out for—hey! There they are now!" Uncle Dan pointed, and the captain turned to see Joe, Pedro, and Maria walking past.

Dog-napped!

Elizabeth and Kate licked their ice cream cones and watched the scene below, still listening on their tiny speaker. It was almost like watching a movie.

"Hey, you there!" Uncle Dan called out. "Didn't I see you at the other boat dock? You looked like you were up to no good. I think you've been messing with all the boats!"

The teenagers stopped, looking like they'd been caught.

Perfect, thought Elizabeth.

"I don't know anything about any boats," said Joe defensively, and the other two agreed.

Uncle Dan wheeled his chair forward. "You'd better stay away from here. I'm onto you, and if I see you hanging around, making trouble, I'll call the police!"

So far, so good, thought Elizabeth. Some ice cream dripped from her cone, and Biscuit quickly cleaned it up.

Uncle Dan and the teens exchanged a few more angry words before the threesome moved on. Uncle Dan looked at the Skipper and said, "I think I'll pass on that ride. I'm going to call the police and report my suspicions right now."

The captain shook Uncle Dan's hand. "Thank you, sir. You're a good citizen. If more people would report hoodlums instead of just letting them wander around getting into trouble, we'd all be better off."

Elizabeth caught a glimpse of someone in the shadows, beneath the bridge. *It was Gilligan!* He seemed to listen to the conversation between Uncle Dan and the captain.

The hairs on Biscuit's back stood up, and he gave a low, throaty growl. Kate grabbed his collar. "Easy, boy," she whispered.

Uncle Dan began to wheel away. When his back was turned, the girls saw the captain motion for his sidekick to come closer.

"It looks like the heat is off, for a while. That guy thinks those teenagers have caused River City's problems. He's going to call the police," the Skipper told his partner.

Gilligan laughed. "That's perfect. And while everyone is focused on them, we can make another move."

Kate and Elizabeth looked at each other, wide-eyed. This was going exactly as planned! Now, if the recorder had worked correctly, all they'd have to do was take the recording to the police.

They were startled when a voice below them yelled, "Kate, Elizabeth! What are y'all doing up there? Come down and join us!"

It was Gary, and his loud voice echoed on the buildings around them. To the left and the right, tourists turned to see who Elizabeth and Kate were. The Skipper and Gilligan turned too. Elizabeth locked eyes with the Skipper and realized he recognized her.

Just then, Gary spotted Uncle Dan, who was trying to wheel back into the hotel lobby. "Dan! Over here! I just spotted your niece and her friend. We're going to rent a riverboat. Do all of you want to come?"

Oh no. Did Gary just point out to the whole world. . .and to those men. . .that I'm Uncle Dan's niece? That can't be good.

All of a sudden, the Skipper's face went white. His jaw clenched, and he seemed to realize he'd been duped. "Hey you!" he called out to Uncle Dan.

Without warning, Biscuit leaped from the low balcony and dashed straight for the Skipper! The little dog bared his teeth and growled.

"Why, you little mutt. . .," the man said, kicking at Biscuit. The little dog backed up, but continued to growl.

"Hey!" Uncle Dan yelled, wheeling his chair around. "Cut it out!"

The Skipper looked around at all the witnesses and took a deep breath. Rage flooded his eyes. But he pasted on a smile and said, "Sorry about that, folks. I get a little nervous when a dog bares his teeth at me."

By this time Kate and Elizabeth were on the ground, and Uncle Dan wheeled up beside Elizabeth. He didn't say a word, just gave the Skipper a steely-eyed stare. Even in a wheelchair, Uncle Dan offered a powerful presence. He was a war veteran. A war hero. He'd faced things far more dangerous than a crooked riverboat owner.

The Skipper held eye contact with Uncle Dan, then turned. "Well folks, the show's over. Now, who wants to go for a ride?"

The line that had been forming dispersed, causing the captain more frustration. But he continued to stand there, smiling and nodding. "Come back another time," he said weakly.

About that time, Kate looked around. "Where's Biscuit?" she asked.

Elizabeth looked to the spot where Biscuit had stood moments earlier, but the little dog was nowhere in sight.

"Biscuit?" Kate called. "Biscuit, where are you?" Her voice came out in a squeak.

Elizabeth put her hand on Kate's shoulder and said, "He was just here a minute ago. I'm sure he's around here somewhere. The captain doesn't have him, and—" She looked around for Gilligan. He was gone too.

Oh no! It can't be! God, please don't let that man have Biscuit! God, please keep Biscuit safe!

Soon, everyone around was calling for the little dog. Even strangers were looking beneath restaurant tables and in shadowy corners, hoping for a sign of Biscuit.

Elizabeth looked at Uncle Dan, who had his eye on the captain and his empty boat. "Are you thinking what I'm thinking?" she whispered.

"If you're thinking we need to keep an eye on that man and his sidekick, then yes," he said. "Do you have the recorder? Let's go see if we got a good recording of the whole thing. Then we'll come up with a plan to find Biscuit."

The recorder! In the excitement, had they left it on the table at the ice cream shop?

"Kate!" she called, scanning the crowd.

She spotted Kate next to Gary, who was trying to calm her. "We'll find him. There were too many people around for him to have just disappeared. Surely someone saw something!"

Kate continued to look through the crowds. "That man took him. I know he did," she told her youth minister.

Gary looked confused. "That man? What man? What are you talking about?"

Elizabeth interrupted their conversation. "Excuse me, Kate. I think that little recorder might lead us to Biscuit. Do you have it?"

For a moment, Kate looked dazed, as if she didn't comprehend. Then understanding dawned, and she began feeling in her pockets. "The recorder! Oh no! When Biscuit jumped off the balcony, I just went after him. I think I left it on the table!"

The girls ran to the ice cream shop. They took the low, curved steps two at a time, and found a mother with two small boys sitting at their table.

"Excuse me," Elizabeth approached the woman politely. "My friend and I left something at this table. Did you see a small, round, black device by any chance?"

The woman shook her head. "No, I'm sorry. I didn't see anything," she said.

"Is this what you're looking for?" asked one of the boys. He held up the recorder. "I found it in the chair. It's really cool! I've been pushing the buttons."

Pushing the buttons? Oh no!

Elizabeth took the recorder from the boy and smiled. "Thank you," she told him.

The girls went down the stairs and found Gary waiting for them at the bottom. "Kate? What man? I think you need to tell me what you're talking about."

Kate sighed, but said nothing. Elizabeth knew her friend was too distraught to think clearly.

"Gary, why don't you come with us? We're going to talk to my Uncle Dan. We'll explain everything." Elizabeth led Kate through the maze of tourists.

They pushed open one of the sparkly, double glass doors of the hotel and found Uncle Dan waiting for them. "Did you find it?" he asked.

"Yes," she answered. "But there's no telling what kind of shape it's in. A little boy had it. He was about James's age. And he was pushing all the buttons."

Uncle Dan pushed the PLAY button, and heard a child's laughter. Then he heard a woman's voice saying, "Be careful, Joshua. You don't want your ice cream cone to fall on the floor." Then, more laughter.

Great, thought Elizabeth. "What are we going to do now?" she asked.

Kate spoke up, seeming to have gained control of her emotions. "We're going to find Biscuit! That's what we're going to do."

Gary put his arm on Kate's shoulder. "We'll do all we can to find Biscuit. But first, I think you need to tell me what's going on."

•—•—•

An hour later, a massive search party had been formed. Gary organized the teens from Kate's youth group into teams, and they were instructed to search the east side of the Riverwalk. Joe, Pedro, and Maria were to search the west side leading to the Alamo. Uncle Dan, Kate, and Elizabeth decided to go through the underground tunnel that led to the mall.

Before they left, however, Uncle Dan turned to Kate. "I need you to bring all of your spy gadgets. You never know what we might need. I have a couple of gadgets of my own. You go get your equipment, and I'll meet you back here in five minutes."

The girls wasted no time. While Kate was piling the gadgets into her backpack, Elizabeth sent a text to the other Camp Club Girls: BISCUIT MISSING. SEARCHING NOW. PRAY.

She pressed the SEND button, then did a little praying of her own—out loud, so Kate could hear. "Dear Father, we don't know where Biscuit is, but You do. Please keep him safe. If those men have him, please don't let them hurt him. And please help us to find him. Soon."

Kate wiped a tear from her cheek and whispered, "Amen." She zipped up her backpack, and they headed to the lobby. In the elevator, she said, "Elizabeth, I'm scared. I'm really scared. This is even worse than at camp, when Biscuit was missing. Then, he just ran away. This time, I really think he was kidnapped. What if. . ."

Elizabeth put her arm around her friend's shoulders. "We're not going to think about 'what if.' We've asked God to help us find Biscuit, and to keep him safe. Now, we just have to trust God to do that. Remember Mark 11:24, 'Therefore I tell you, whatever you ask for in prayer, believe that you have received it, and it will be yours.' "

Kate nodded. "I know. I want to believe. But in this case, that's easier said than done."

"I know what you mean," said Elizabeth. "I guess if faith in God were easy, more people would believe."

"I wish I'd left that tracking device on his collar!" Kate said. "If only I hadn't taken it off when I got here!"

The elevator doors opened into the lobby, where Uncle Dan was waiting. After a quick show-and-tell of the gadgets, they headed toward the mall. Instead of the usual way, however, Uncle Dan led them through a tiny door in the side of one of the buildings.

"Where are we going?" asked Elizabeth.

"We're still going to the mall," Uncle Dan answered. "But if Biscuit was truly taken, the kidnappers wouldn't have him right out in the open. There are dozens of these passageways between the mall and the Riverwalk, and few people even know about them. They were built so store owners would have a back way in and out of their stores, but they are hardly used." He pointed to a series of doors along the side of the passageway. "These rooms are mostly used for storage, and each one has a door on the other side leading to one of the stores. Most of the store owners prefer to go through the mall, and get to their storage rooms from there."

"I don't blame them," said Elizabeth. "There's something creepy about this. . .I wouldn't want to walk through here every day either."

"I think we need to search these passageways," said Uncle Dan. "I think it's the only way that guy could have escaped unseen. I don't know where all the entrances are; most were built to blend in with the landscape of the Riverwalk. They're difficult to see, if you don't already know where they are."

"Wow," whispered Kate. "It's like we've just walked into a spy movie. Only it's real."

Uncle Dan stopped his wheelchair, turning to face them. "Elizabeth, you have your cell phone, right?"

Elizabeth nodded.

"You two go on into the mall, and see what you can find. Remember, you're not looking for Biscuit, though if you find him, that's great. You're looking for doors to these tunnels. Look around, ask around, see what you can find out. Call me as soon as you know something."

"What then?" asked Elizabeth.

Uncle Dan pulled out a long telescope-looking device. "This is a peephole reverser. It allows you to look the other way through a peephole in a door, so you can see what's going on inside the room. We have to use these sometimes in the hotel rooms, if we think someone is in danger. If you can find the doors, even if they are locked, we can look inside. As long as there is a peephole, that is."

The girls' eyes grew round. "Cool!" Elizabeth said.

"Why don't you do the honors?" Uncle Dan handed Elizabeth the device and gestured to the doors. Kate was too short to reach the peephole, and Uncle Dan was out of reach as well.

Elizabeth went from door to door, looking inside the rooms. Most of the rooms were dark, but a couple of them revealed only stacks of cardboard boxes. One had toys and stuffed animals on shelves, and she knew that was the toy store. Before long, she had looked through all the doors. No Biscuit in sight.

"Do you want me to keep this?" Elizabeth asked her uncle.

"No. If you're caught with it, you'll have a hard time explaining.

Thieves use these to check out the places they want to rob." Uncle Dan returned the device to his duffel bag and said, "Remember, you've got to think like the bad guys. Where would they go? What would they do? Go and see what you can find out, and meet me back here in half an hour. I'm going to find some of the shop owners and ask some questions. Maybe somebody saw something."

Kate and Elizabeth headed into the mall. After a few steps, Kate stopped. "Wait. Take this," she said, holding out a small pack of gum.

"Oh, no thanks," said Elizabeth. "I'm not in the mood for gum right now."

Kate continued holding the gum out. "Take it," she said. Then, moving a little closer, she whispered, "It's a walkie-talkie. See the button? I have one too." She held up another pack of gum. "This way, if we accidentally get separated, we can still communicate."

Elizabeth's eyes grew wide, and she examined the small rectangular device. It looked exactly like a pack of gum. But sure enough, there was a tiny button on the back.

"Kate, you are full of surprises," she told her friend, tucking the "gum" into her pocket.

The two girls had only passed a couple of stores when they spotted another passageway. Kate tested it, and sure enough, it was unlocked. "Should we go in?"

"Uncle Dan has the peephole reverser. He said to call when we found something." Elizabeth pulled out her cell phone, ready to call Uncle Dan, when she heard someone calling her name. She looked up to find Joe, Pedro, and Maria coming toward her.

"There you are!" Joe said, looking out of breath. "We've been looking all over for you! Come with us. We think we may have found something."

Maria grabbed Kate's arm, and said, "Come on! You've got to listen to this."

"Have you found Biscuit? Do you know where my dog is?" Kate asked, hope filling her face.

"Just come on!" said Pedro, pulling Elizabeth along behind him. They took off, jogging when possible, slowing to a walk when they were in crowds. They had gone almost the length of the mall when Joe gestured to a hidden doorway. "This way!" he said.

The six young people entered the doorway, and Joe led them to a small round hole in the wall. The rim of some PVC pipe was barely visible. Joe leaned and placed his ear against the pipe, then stepped back.

"Listen," he said to Kate.

She stepped forward and placed her ear against the pipe. Relief flooded her face. "It's Biscuit! He's okay! Listen, Beth! It's Biscuit!"

Elizabeth stepped forward and placed her ear to the pipe. Sure enough, she heard Biscuit's familiar howling.

"This is great!" Elizabeth cried. "So. . .where is he? Where can we find him?"

Their new friends looked at each other. "Well. . .um. . .we don't exactly know. These pipes run all through the mall, and even to other places on the Riverwalk. He could be anywhere."

Searching for Biscuit

Elizabeth pulled out her cell phone. "Let me call Uncle Dan. He was in charge of search-and-rescue missions in Iraq. He'll know what to do." She dialed the number and held the phone to her ear.

Nothing.

She dialed again, with the same results. "I can't get a signal. I guess these tunnels are too closed in. Come on, Kate. Let's go find Uncle Dan."

Kate stood her ground. "I'm not going anywhere until I know how to find Biscuit. I'm staying right here where I can hear him. Hey! I wonder if he can hear me?"

She cupped her hands around the pipe and called into the hole, "Biscuit! Biscuit, it's me. Calm down, boy. We're going to find you."

She placed her ear to the hole and reported, "He heard me! He's whimpering, but he's not howling anymore. He knows we're on our way."

Elizabeth placed her phone back in her pocket. They had no choice. They would have to split up. Someone had to go figure out where the other end of that pipe was, and Kate wasn't moving. "Okay. You stay here. I'll try to find Uncle Dan. If I can't find him, I'll at least find out what's on the other side of this wall. Whatever you do, don't go anywhere. The last thing we need is to lose you too."

Elizabeth left the group behind, but she wasn't surprised when she heard footsteps behind her. She turned to find Joe.

"I'm coming too. Maria and Pedro can stay with Kate. There's safety in numbers, you know," Joe told her.

She nodded and kept walking. She wasn't sure if she was glad for the company or not. *I don't have time to be distracted by you, Mr. Charm. I have a dog to find and a mystery to solve.*

As if reading her mind, Joe spoke up again. "I won't get in your way.

I'm here to help."

They turned the corner to see what was on the other side of that wall. A shoe store. Elizabeth entered the store and headed straight to the back wall.

"May I help you?" asked a young sales clerk.

Elizabeth didn't respond, just kept studying the wall behind the shoes.

"Uh, no thank you. We're just looking," Joe answered the woman, and she moved to another customer.

"What are you thinking, Elizabeth?" he asked her.

"I wonder if there's a way we can get into those storage rooms. Legally, I mean. If we had access to the back entrances, it would be easier to explore the tunnels. As it is, we don't even know where all the entrances are," she told him.

A slow smile spread across his face, lighting up his green eyes.

Those are the nicest eyes I've ever seen, thought Elizabeth. *Stop it! Do not get distracted!*

She forced herself to look back at the shoes.

"I have an idea. Follow me," Joe told her, and led the way out of the store. Elizabeth followed him two stores down, to a music store. In the window hung a sign that read HELP WANTED.

He approached the counter and asked the clerk for a job application form. While he waited, he looked at Elizabeth and smiled. "I've been wanting a job here, anyway. Now maybe we can kill two birds with one stone."

Elizabeth smiled. She had to hand it to him. It was a brilliant idea. Noticing a shiny grand piano in a corner of the store, she approached it. Almost reverently, she sat at the bench.

Wow, she thought. *I'd love to have a piano like this.*

Gingerly, she pressed one of the keys, and it let out a sweet, pure tone that only a true musician could appreciate.

"Go ahead. Give it a try," said the clerk.

"Really?" she asked in disbelief. "You don't mind if I play it?"

The clerk smiled, and Elizabeth settled in front of the keys. Within moments, she was lost in Mozart's Sonata in C. Then, without warning, she transitioned into a blues scale and began playing an old Elvis Presley hit. Her music was beginning to draw a crowd when she heard a beeping sound. *Where is that coming from?*

She continued to play, but the beeping persisted. Suddenly, she realized it was coming from her pocket. *The gum!*

She abruptly stopped playing. A few people in the crowd groaned, then left. Elizabeth smiled, stood, and walked behind a large set of drums. Pulling the walkie-talkie gum gadget from her pocket, she pressed the tiny button and whispered, "Hello?"

"Elizabeth! Where have you been? I've been beeping you for five minutes!" Kate's voice came over the tiny speaker.

"Uh, sorry. I, uh, didn't hear you. What's going on?"

"There were voices. Human ones. I couldn't make out everything they said, but one of them sounded like the Skipper," Kate told her. "They're gone now. I can still hear Biscuit, so I know he's okay—for now. But we don't know what those men are capable of. We've got to find him. Soon."

Elizabeth stood behind the drums, peering into the mall beyond the store entrance. "I know. We'll find him. We just have to believe that."

As she waited for Kate's reply, she spotted something in the crowd—or rather, someone. A tall, awkward-looking man, pressing his way through the shoppers. *Was that. . .it was Gilligan!*

"Kate! Gotta go. Stay put!" Elizabeth said, and took off through the maze of people, after the man.

"Elizabeth! Wait up!" Joe called, but Elizabeth didn't slow down. Joe caught up with her and asked, "Did I just see you talking to a pack of gum?"

Elizabeth pointed. "That's the man! We have to follow him. He may lead us to Biscuit!"

A crowd was forming ahead, and the man pressed through it. Elizabeth walked as fast as her long legs would carry her, trying to keep an eye on him. But by the time she approached the crowd, she'd lost him. A teenage girl was in the center of the crowd passing out free ice cream samples. But suddenly she had no appetite.

"Did you see where he went?" asked Joe, and Elizabeth turned. She had almost forgotten he was with her.

"No," she replied.

"Well, he didn't seem to be carrying anything. Wherever he is, I don't think Biscuit is with him. Maybe we should go back and find the others," Joe suggested.

"I agree. But first, I need to make a phone call."

•—•—•

Back at the hotel, Kate, Elizabeth, Maria, and Pedro entered Uncle Dan's suite. Joe had been hired at the music store, and had been asked to rearrange some boxes in the storage area. With a discreet nod, the boy had assured his friends he would find out what he could with his new access.

This suite was Uncle Dan's home for as long as he worked for the Palacio del Rio. It had everything he needed: kitchen, living room, bedroom, bathroom, even a guest room, though most of his guests ended up staying in another hotel room.

Kate paced back and forth. "I can't believe I just left Biscuit there. I should go back. He needs to hear my voice. It calms him."

Uncle Dan looked at her compassionately. "I know you didn't want to leave him. But we still don't know where he is. I think we need to pull an all-out spy mission on the Skipper. But he'll suspect us, so we have to look like we're going about business as usual.

"Kate, let's get a look at all of your gadgets. We'll compare yours to mine, and together, I'm sure we'll be able to find Biscuit and put those men in jail before you know it."

Kate emptied her backpack onto Uncle Dan's coffee table while he wheeled into his bedroom. A moment later, he reappeared with a hard black suitcase. Scooting Kate's gadgets to the side, he set the suitcase down and opened it. Inside, the suitcase looked like something from a spy movie.

Together, Kate and Uncle Dan had miniature cameras and recorders, trackers, voice distortion tools, telescopes of various shapes and sizes, and more.

Elizabeth picked up one of the tiny devices and looked at it. "I wish we could figure out a way to track the Skipper. But to do that, we'd have to attach a tracking device to him. And I don't know how we can do that."

Pedro spoke up. "I have an idea," he said. "I know a place the Skipper visits several times a day."

•—•—•

Elizabeth and Kate had a perfect view from their private balcony, and they watched breathlessly as Pedro pulled the cap low over his head and sat in the shoe-shine booth. His friend had been happy to take a break and let Pedro take over the business for a few minutes.

Sure enough, right on schedule, the Skipper showed up. He didn't even look at Pedro! He just dropped a few coins in the jar and placed his right foot on the stand. Pedro worked diligently at shining first the right shoe, then the left one.

Though the girls couldn't see the details, they noticed Pedro took a bit longer with the left shoe. Finally, they saw him give his rag a final pop, and the Skipper walked away without so much as a nod.

Kate held up her tiny tracking screen, and sure enough, it sprang to life. The tiny red dot was moving—barely—as the Skipper marched to the boat.

Elizabeth texted the other Camp Club Girls, who had been briefly informed of the situation: MISSION ACCOMPLISHED. Or at least, Phase One had been accomplished. Within moments, her cell phone rang, and she knew it was them, standing by on a conference call.

"It went off without a flaw," Elizabeth spoke without even saying hello.

Kate picked up her cell phone, which was also ringing, and joined the conversation.

"I can't believe Elizabeth's uncle wants us to lie low," complained Kate. "Biscuit is out there. I need to go rescue him."

"You have a better chance of rescuing him if Gilligan and the Skipper think you're backing off. You know he's okay—for now. But if they feel like you're putting pressure on them, you don't know what they'll do," said McKenzie.

"McKenzie's right," said Alex. "The reason they kidnapped Biscuit in the first place was to warn you to back off. You want them to think you've taken their warning."

"You know, guys, I remembered something I learned in nature study, and I've pulled up some sound travel research on my computer," Sydney said. "Sometimes, when traveling through a tunnel—or a pipe—the sound can become distorted. It can sound like Biscuit is close, when actually, he could be very far away."

"And your point is?" Kate asked, frustrated.

"Just that you may not want to limit your search to the mall. He could be on the other side of the river," Sydney continued.

"Yes, but I saw Gilligan in the mall, just after Kate heard voices," Elizabeth said.

"Did he know you were looking for him?" asked Bailey.

"Of course he knew we were looking for him. He took my dog!" Kate cried.

Everyone was silent for a few moments. Finally, Elizabeth said, "So you think he was purposely trying to lead us in the wrong direction?"

"I don't know," said Sydney. "I just don't want you to zero in on one area, while Biscuit may be in an entirely different location."

Kate groaned. "Poor Biscuit! My poor baby. He's all alone and scared. What if we never find him?"

"We'll find him," Elizabeth said with a confidence she didn't feel.

"How can you be so sure?" Kate voiced the question on everyone's mind.

"Because God is good," said Elizabeth.

"Well, it sure doesn't feel like He's good right now," said Kate.

Elizabeth did not have an answer for her. Then, a verse popped into her mind.

" 'For I am the Lord, your God, who takes hold of your right hand and says to you, Do not fear; I will help you,' " she said. "Isaiah 41:13. We'll find him, because God will help us."

There was a knock at the door. Elizabeth set her phone on the bed and cracked the door to find Gary. Behind him was Charis, the girl who taught the Bible stories.

"We've looked everywhere," Gary said. "We've got to stop and get ready for tonight's performance."

"Tell Kate we're sorry," said Charis.

With a nod, Elizabeth softly closed the door. She turned to find Kate behind her. Kate had heard every word.

Elizabeth picked up her phone and called the Camp Club Girls on a conference call. She told the others about Biscuit, and they were silent for a few moments.

Finally, Bailey changed the subject. "Hey, who was it that had news on the strawberry?"

"Oh yeah. The strawberry birthmark," said Sydney. "The strawberry nevus is quite common, and as many as one in ten babies have them. They usually disappear in early childhood."

"That's great news!" said Elizabeth. "Maybe Annie's birthmark will just go away, all by itself!"

"Probably not," continued Sydney. "The strawberry hemangioma is a little different. If the birthmark continues to grow, it's probably a hemangioma, and it won't go away on its own. Didn't her mother mention that it was growing?"

"Yes," Elizabeth replied, disappointed.

"This is terrible," said McKenzie. "That poor little girl!"

"There's more," Sydney told them. "If it's not taken care of, it has the potential, down the road, to become cancerous."

Elizabeth thought of sweet little Annie. *God, no. Please don't let her get cancer.*

"I don't know how much more bad news I can take," said Kate, flopping on her bed.

"Well, there is some good news," said Sydney. "There is an organization called the Kiwanis Club. They have chapters all over the US, so I'm sure San Antonio has one."

"Hey, I saw something about them on *Walker, Texas Ranger*! Don't they do things to help little children?" exclaimed Alex.

"Yes," Sydney replied. "They help improve the quality of children's lives, especially young children. Each chapter tries to sponsor at least one service project per year. Maybe you can hook Annie up with a local Kiwanis Club. Maybe they'll help."

Elizabeth couldn't believe what she was hearing. "Kate!" she said, causing Kate to jump from her spot on the bed.

"What?" answered the startled girl.

"Do you remember seeing that sign on the stage where the teens perform each night?"

Kate looked thoughtful. "I remember seeing a sign, but I didn't pay much attention."

"It's a Kiwanis sign!" exclaimed Elizabeth. "They must own the Fiesta Noche!"

"Come to think of it, Gary did say we were renting it from some organization. Hey, wouldn't that be cool if that money ended up helping Annie?"

"Thanks, Sydney. You're the best!" Elizabeth said. "All of you are the best! Kate, what time is it?"

"It's dinnertime," said Kate. "But for once, I'm not really hungry."

Elizabeth patted her friend's shoulder. "Let's go watch the show. Afterward, we'll talk to Gary, and maybe he can put us in touch with the Kiwanis director. Then we'll search for Biscuit some more."

Kate nodded slowly. Elizabeth wished she could take this burden from her friend.

McKenzie spoke up then. "Kate, it will be okay. I have this feeling it will all work out, and you'll find Biscuit. Just like at camp, remember?"

Bailey chimed in. "Yeah, and remember the verse Elizabeth told us, about God helping us!"

"And we'll all be praying," Alex said. "I'll bet you'll find Biscuit by tomorrow."

With a few more encouraging words, the girls said goodbye and promised to be in touch soon.

Elizabeth started to leave, but Kate stopped her. "Wait," she said. "Let me check my blog first."

Once again, there was a comment waiting. Kate nearly lost her balance when she read what it said: *"Back off. If you want to see your dog alive again, you'll keep your mouths shut."*

Elizabeth reached an arm out to steady her friend. "Don't worry, Kate. They won't hurt him. He's their bargaining chip," she said with more confidence than she felt.

Kate took a deep breath. She grabbed the tracking device, and the girls left the room without looking at it. But in the elevator, they couldn't help but notice. The device was lighting up like a Christmas tree.

The Skipper was on the move.

The Girls Confess!

Kate pressed the ground floor button on the elevator again and again, as if that would make the elevator move faster. "Hurry up! Stop being so slow!"

Elizabeth looked through the window, scanning the area, looking for signs of the navy blue captain's hat. Finally, she saw it.

"Calm down, Kate. He's getting a hot dog," she said. She watched the man pay for his snack, then turn back toward his boat.

Kate held up the tracker again, and sure enough, the tiny red dot was returning to its original location.

"Whew," she said. "I guess we need to keep a closer watch. He could have been from here to Timbuktu by now!"

The elevator doors opened, and the girls saw Uncle Dan talking to a gray-haired couple, obviously hotel guests. When they left, the girls approached. Kate held up the tracker so he could see.

"This is perfect," she told him.

Uncle Dan looked at the device. "Pedro and Maria stopped by after the tracker was in place. They were headed to the mall to see if Joe'd learned anything. They said they'd check back later."

"We're going to watch the kids' performance tonight. We need a change of pace, and we have another project we're working on. We have the tracker, and we can leave if the Skipper does anything out of the ordinary," Elizabeth told him.

Uncle Dan nodded. "I wish I could help you more, girls, but I'm back on duty. I think you're safe for another couple of hours. The Skipper will continue to give tours until after dark. And I have another surprise for you," he said with a smirk.

The girls looked at each other, then back at Uncle Dan.

"While Pedro was shoe-shining, I was doing a little detective work. There is now a mini-transmitter on the back of the Skipper's steering wheel." He handed the girls a tiny speaker. "You can now listen to him give tours. . .or anything else he may talk about when he's on or near the boat. This little baby will pick up any conversation for about twenty feet."

Kate looked at the device, eyebrows lifted. "Wow. This is the latest model, isn't it? I've been wanting this one."

Uncle Dan smiled, then turned to greet a new set of customers. The girls waved, then headed out the glass doors.

"I guess this means we can relax for a little while. The Skipper will give tours, and we'll be able to see when he moves, and hear what he says," Elizabeth said.

Kate held the tiny device to her ear. "Sounds like he's giving a tour now." Looking at the tracker, she watched the red dot move slowly across the screen. "His movement will be slow and steady as long as he's on the boat. I guess we can watch it, and if the pattern changes, we'll know something's up."

The girls were almost to the Fiesta Noche when they ran into Elizabeth's parents. James was wearing a hat shaped like a Tyrannosaurus rex.

"Roar!" he said, and Elizabeth pretended to be afraid.

"There you girls are," said Mr. Anderson. "We were just about to call you. You missed a lot of excitement this afternoon! They had a special dinosaur exhibit at the museum. Did you have a nice time with Uncle Dan?"

Elizabeth glanced at Kate, who was looking at her shoes. "Well, um. . .we had some excitement of our own," she said. "Biscuit's missing."

"What?" exclaimed Mr. and Mrs. Anderson in unison. "How did that happen? When?"

"It happened a few hours ago. We've been looking for him ever since," said Elizabeth.

"Why didn't you call us?" asked Elizabeth's mother.

"Uncle Dan has been helping us look for him, and I didn't want to bother you," said Elizabeth.

Mr. Anderson looked from Elizabeth to Kate, then back to Elizabeth. Was that suspicion on his face?

Elizabeth's mother put her arm around Kate, pulling her into a hug. "You know we'll do all we can to find him, sweetie," she said. Kate nodded.

"Are you two girls involved in another mystery of some sort?" asked Mr. Anderson.

Just then, Elizabeth spotted Gary talking to an older gentleman. He was handing him an envelope. "Excuse me, Dad. I really need to speak to Gary. Do you mind?"

Mr. Anderson excused his daughter, and Elizabeth politely approached the two adults. Kate followed behind, her eyes on the tracker.

When there was an appropriate break in the conversation, Elizabeth said, "Hi, Gary. I need to ask you a question. Are you renting this stage from the Kiwanis Club?"

Gary looked surprised. "Yes, we are. This is the Kiwanis representative, right here, Mr. Adams." He looked at the gentleman and said, "Let me introduce you to a couple of my biggest helpers, Elizabeth and Kate."

"Nice to meet you," said the girls, each shaking the man's hand.

"Are you interested in joining the Kiwanis Club?" he asked them.

"Possibly," Elizabeth replied. "But I'm also interested in letting you know about a possible service project," she said.

"Wonderful!" the man told her. "We're always looking for chances to help kids. Tell me about your idea."

Elizabeth began pouring out Annie's story, and the man gestured to a small bench. They sat down and kept talking. Soon, Elizabeth's parents joined them. Before long, the man was nodding and smiling.

"Yes," he said. "This sounds like exactly the kind of project we've been looking for. When can I meet Annie?"

"She's been coming to the Bible club every morning at the church at La Villita. Can you come tomorrow morning?"

"I'll be there. It may be late morning, but I will be there before your Bible club is over." He shook her hand, then Kate's, and said, "Thank you, girls. I love to see young people who care about others, and who want to help. You're exactly the kind of girls we need in the Kiwanis organization."

Elizabeth's parents smiled at the girls. "This will make such a difference in Annie's life. I'm proud of you girls," said Mrs. Anderson.

"I am too," said Elizabeth's dad. "But I still feel like you're not telling me something. Unfortunately, I'm starved. Are you girls hungry?"

"No, sir," Kate and Elizabeth responded.

Mr. Anderson reached over and tousled Kate's hair. "Try not to worry about Biscuit," he said. "He has to be around here somewhere. You know we'll do all we can to find him."

Kate nodded.

"We're going to get something to eat, and we'll meet you back here in time for the show. How does that sound?" he continued.

Elizabeth nodded, then watched her parents and James head toward a cluster of hamburger and hot dog stands.

"I'm not sure how much we should tell them," she said to Kate.

"Tell them everything," she said. "At this point, we can use all the help we can get."

The girls went to the Fiesta Noche stage and found Gary.

"Can we do anything to help set up?" Elizabeth asked.

Gary looked at Kate compassionately, then answered Elizabeth. "Why don't you do the usual—play for the crowd? And Kate, you come with me. I have the perfect job for you." He led Kate to a box of black microphone cords. "These have gotten all tangled. Could you please straighten them out for me, and coil each one neatly?"

Elizabeth smiled. *Perfect. Busywork is exactly what Kate needs right now to keep her mind occupied.*

Elizabeth sat down at the bench, feeling almost guilty. Everyone else was working, and here she was, getting to do the thing she loved most in the world. She didn't feel guilty enough to question it, though. She played a couple of scales to warm up. Then, she began playing a 1950s rock 'n' roll rhythm that was sure to draw attention. Sure enough, within a few minutes, the seats began to fill with people.

She was surprised when the sound of a bass guitar joined her. Turning, she saw Joe engrossed in the music. *When did he get here?* she thought, but continued to play.

Joe continued playing, but discreetly moved directly behind her. "I'm on a break, and I need to get back to the music store. I think I may have found something," he whispered. "Can you and Kate meet me at the store at eight o'clock?"

Keeping her eyes on the crowd, she whispered, "We'll do our best."

After playing a few more measures, Joe set the guitar down and left the stage. Elizabeth continued playing until Gary nodded to her, signaling it was time to begin the mime show. Kate waited for her at the stage door, and together they crossed behind the stage and over the small bridge. They found seats near Elizabeth's parents.

James laughed at the mime clowns. The girls, on the other hand, couldn't concentrate on the show. Kate once again held the tracker in her hand, watching the red dot move slowly in the center of the screen.

Something out of the corner of Elizabeth's eye caught her attention. There, coming around the curve, was the Skipper and his boat of tourists. She elbowed Kate. "Look," Elizabeth whispered.

Kate looked up, and Elizabeth watched the girl's hands clench into tight fists. "What did you do with my dog?" Kate whispered.

The Skipper floated by, his fake smile pasted in place, giving witty, memorized discourse about San Antonio and the history of the Riverwalk. At one point his eyes scanned the crowd, and he seemed to pause on Elizabeth and Kate. His smile faded for just an instant, with something akin to rage—or was that fear?—momentarily taking over his features. The man recovered quickly, pasting on that smile again, and the girls watched him and his boat float out of sight.

The show ended, and the crowd applauded and began to leave. Kate and Elizabeth didn't move. Neither did Elizabeth's parents. What should have been a fun, carefree vacation had turned into a nightmare.

"Okay, girls. Tell us everything," Mr. Anderson said. "Start from the beginning. I have all the time in the world."

Elizabeth took a deep breath, then began pouring out the story. She told him about Joe and the water balloon. She told him about Gilligan and the Skipper, and watching them in some sort of payoff. She told him about the men chasing them, the failed sting operation, about Biscuit's disappearance, the blog threats, and finally, about hearing Biscuit through the pipes.

During Elizabeth's speech, Kate sat watching the tracker. Fat tears splashed on the ground beside her shoes, but she said nothing.

Mr. Anderson sighed. "How in the world, Elizabeth, do you manage to get yourself caught up in these messes? All those years of taking music lessons of every kind. You're supposed to be sitting sweetly in a parlor somewhere, playing your piano. You're not supposed to be out chasing criminals and solving mysteries!"

Elizabeth wasn't sure how to respond, so she said nothing.

Mr. Anderson looked at the tracker in Kate's hand. "What is that?" he asked.

"It's a tracker. This light shows where the Skipper is. We're hoping he will lead us to Biscuit," Kate told him.

He noticed Elizabeth's earpiece and asked, "And what do you have in your ear?"

"Uncle Dan put a bug on the Skipper's steering wheel, so we can hear his conversations."

Mr. Anderson stood to his feet and began pacing.

Elizabeth's mom remained quiet. James was hopping down the stairs, one at a time. He reminded Elizabeth of Tigger.

Finally, Mr. Anderson said, "We're going to call the police, and I'm not letting you girls out of my sight until this thing is taken care of. We're going to have a nice, relaxing evening—perhaps we'll take a carriage ride around the city. And we'll let the police handle it from here." He looked at his daughter, waiting for her response.

"Yes, sir," she said.

He pulled out his cell phone and began dialing.

"Dan, what were you thinking?" he said after a moment. "Helping these girls get mixed up in something like this. What in the world were you thinking?"

He listened for a few moments, then said, "Could you please give me the number to the local police?"

Elizabeth watched her father hang up the phone, and he immediately began dialing another number.

"Uh, Dad?" she interrupted him. "If we go to the police, they may hurt Biscuit."

He stopped dialing and looked at his daughter. "Elizabeth, you'll have to trust me. Sometimes it's best just to let the authorities handle these things."

"Yes, sir," she replied. Then, as an afterthought, she said, "Kate and I were supposed to meet our friend Joe at his job in ten minutes. He works at the music store in the mall. Can we just go tell him we're busy this evening, so he and his friends won't be waiting for us?"

Mr. Anderson thought for a moment and said, "Is this the boy who was playing the guitar with you?"

"Yes, sir."

He looked at Kate, then back at Elizabeth. "Okay, but don't dawdle. Do you know where the horse and buggy depot is?"

Elizabeth nodded.

"Meet us there in twenty minutes. Don't be a minute late, you understand? And stay together!"

"Yes, sir!" the girls said in unison. They dashed for the Riverwalk entrance to the mall. It would have been quicker to use one of the secret passageways Uncle Dan had shown them, but with Elizabeth's father watching, they didn't want to take any chances.

As soon as they were inside the mall, they began to jog. Within minutes, they were in the music shop, but there was no sign of Joe.

Elizabeth approached a young clerk and said, "Excuse me, we're looking for Joe Garcia. Is he still working?"

The clerk gestured to a door that led to the back of the store. "He's back there unloading some boxes. Go on back."

The girls entered through the door and called out, "Hello! Joe, are you back here?"

"Over here," came a voice from the far left corner, and the girls headed that way. They found Joe behind a large drum set.

"You won't believe this," he said. "Remember how we thought Biscuit was on the other end of some maze of pipes?"

The girls nodded.

"Well, we were wrong. Biscuit is on the other side of this wall! Look!" He pointed to a locked door with a tiny window near the top. Elizabeth stretched to see through, and sure enough, there was Biscuit! He was locked in a kennel. He looked like he was sleeping. Poor little thing.

"Kate, I can see him," she said. Then, looking her friend in the eyes, she smiled and said, "God is good."

Joe found a wooden crate and moved it below the window, so Kate could see. "It's Biscuit! I see him! Biscuit, wake up! Here, boy!"

"Shhhh!" Joe told her. "That Gilligan man has been in and out all day. He comes in every time Biscuit starts howling. You don't want to wake him up again!"

"Why didn't you tell me you had found him, when you were at the Fiesta Noche?"

"Because I hadn't found him until about ten minutes ago. I could hear him all day, though, and Gilligan too, and I knew they were close. But these boxes were piled in front of this door. I didn't even know there was a door here," Joe told them.

Suddenly, Biscuit's howling cut through the air like a knife. Apparently, he had heard Kate's voice.

Standing on the box again, Kate called out, "Hey, boy! It's okay. I'm here. We're gonna figure out a way to—" She stopped in mid-sentence. Her eyes grew wide, and her face grew pale. Finally, she whispered. "It's—it's him! And he saw me!"

Within moments, the door in front of them was shaking, and they heard the man's voice yelling, "Hey! Get out of here! You kids will be sorry!" Then the lock in the door began to turn.

The three of them looked at each other, but it was Elizabeth who spoke. "We'd better get out of here!"

Captured!

The three of them took off through the storeroom, into the store, barely missing keyboards and drum sets, and into the mall.

"This way," Joe called, and the girls followed. "I'll explain to my boss later."

They ran into a bath store and hid behind a large shelf filled with towels and large bottles of bubble bath. Out of breath, they stood panting and peeking through the cracks in the shelving.

"There he is," whispered Elizabeth, spotting the man. He was looking this way and that, trying to figure out where they had gone. Finally, he moved out of sight, to the left of the bath store.

"I have to go back and get Biscuit," whispered Kate.

"But what if he catches us?" Elizabeth asked.

"It doesn't matter," Kate responded. "If we don't go back and get him now, there's no telling what will happen to him."

"She's right," whispered Joe. "The door is probably still unlocked. If we're going to do it, we need to do it now."

The three of them carefully stepped from behind the shelf and looked around. There was no sign of Gilligan. They dashed back to the music store, where the clerk gave them a frustrated look. "Joe, what do you think you're doing? And who was that old guy who came crashing through here?"

"Sorry, Harry," Joe called. "I'll explain later, and I'll clean up the mess, I promise!"

Kate led the way back through the storeroom. Biscuit's howls were getting louder. The girl pushed her way through the instruments, squeezing between boxes, until she got to the door. Sure enough, it opened easily. "Biscuit!" she called out.

Elizabeth tried to help her open the kennel door, but it was stuck. In the process, she bumped the tiny speaker, which had been muted. Suddenly, they heard the Skipper's voice. It sounded like he was talking on his cell phone.

"What do you mean, they've found the hideout? How could a bunch of kids—never mind. I'm on my way. You keep looking for them. Where are you now?"

There was static, and Elizabeth looked at the tracker clipped to Kate's belt loop. The Skipper's dot was getting closer. . . .

The Skipper's voice came over the tiny speaker again as the three of them continued to struggle with the kennel door. "You're what? Get back to the hideout, you big dope! Those kids want the dog. That's where they'll go! I'll be right there."

"We've got to get out of here," said Elizabeth.

"Here, let me have the kennel," said Joe. He grabbed the bulky metal cage with both arms and said, "Go! I have Biscuit!"

Just as they were about to move back through the door into the music storeroom, their passage was blocked.

"Going somewhere?" asked Gilligan. The three kids stopped, frozen in their tracks.

God, help us out of here! prayed Elizabeth.

"This way!" shouted Joe as he motioned to a door at the back of the room. It obviously led to the Riverwalk.

Suddenly, that door banged open, and the Skipper loomed in the doorway.

"Well now," he snarled, "what do we have here?"

The two men began pressing in. Biscuit growled from his kennel, and the Skipper yelled at Kate, "Make your dog be quiet!"

Oh God, please help us!

Harry appeared in the doorway to the storeroom. "Hey, what's going on here?" the young man asked.

The two men turned to look, and Joe took advantage of the moment by barreling into Gilligan with Biscuit's kennel.

"Run!" Joe yelled.

The crash forced the kennel door open, and Biscuit leapt from the cage, biting Gilligan on the ankle.

"Ow! Get off me, you little mutt!" the man cried.

Elizabeth and Kate sprang through the door.

"Come on, boy!" Kate yelled.

Biscuit followed his beloved owner. Crashing and banging all the way, the girls ran past Harry, through the storeroom, and into the mall.

"This way!" Elizabeth called, remembering the horse depot. She didn't know if the men were following, but she knew where to find safety, and she ran for her father.

"Stop those kids!" the Skipper yelled.

Mall shoppers turned to watch as the two girls and the dog ran with the Skipper wheezing behind them, and Gilligan limping behind him.

Out the mall doors they went, onto the sidewalk. The Texas heat was a startling contrast to the air-conditioned mall. It was difficult for the girls to see in the dusky gray of the evening. Making sure Kate was still close, Elizabeth yelled, "Follow me!"

She could see her father ahead, right in front of the horse depot, paying the carriage driver. A police officer stood behind him, notepad in hand.

"Dad!" Elizabeth yelled, and he looked up.

They were almost home free when Kate tripped. The Skipper, unaware of his audience, caught up with her and grabbed her by the arm. "I've got you now, you little—"

Biscuit lunged at the man, attacking him, growling, biting, barking. . . . The man did all he could to free himself of the ferocious dog. Then, seeing Mr. Anderson and the police officer running toward him, he grabbed Biscuit and ran down a narrow alley leading back to the Riverwalk.

By this time, Gilligan had caught up with them. Confused, he followed his leader.

There they went, the Skipper with Biscuit clamped tightly to his arm, the injured Gilligan, Elizabeth, Kate, Mr. Anderson, the police officer, and bringing up the rear, Joe. As they reached the other end of the alley, the crowds parted. The Skipper, who was still struggling with Biscuit, was running faster than his out-of-shape body could handle. He failed to slow down in time to gain his balance, and plunged right into the river.

"Don't worry, boss! I'll save you!" called Gilligan, and jumped in after his leader. Then, realizing he was being pursued by the police, he tried to swim to the other side.

Biscuit, finally loose of his kidnapper, swam to the edge and climbed out. Kate scooped the sopping dog into her arms.

"Biscuit! You're safe! I thought I'd never see you again!"

Biscuit rewarded her with slobbery kisses all over her face, knocking her glasses askew.

By this time, the officer had called for backup, and more police officers were starting to arrive. The girls watched as one of them pulled the Skipper out of the water and handcuffed him. Another officer waited for Gilligan on the other side.

Mr. Anderson placed his hands on either side of his daughter's face, examining her, making sure she was really okay.

"Do I even want to know what just happened here?" he asked.

Elizabeth threw her arms around her father's neck and said, "I love you, Daddy!"

•—•—•

An hour later, the horse trotted along at a slow pace, pulling the eight-passenger carriage through the streets of San Antonio. Mr. and Mrs. Anderson sat facing the front, along with James, Kate, and Biscuit. Elizabeth, Joe, Maria, and Pedro faced the back.

"This is cool," said Maria. "Thank you, Mr. Anderson, for letting us come along."

"My pleasure," said Mr. Anderson. "Any friend of Elizabeth's is a friend of mine."

"I can't believe there was actually a reward for those guys," Joe said. "Did you hear the officer say they were wanted for fraud, theft, and vandalism in three states?"

"Yes," Mr. Anderson answered. "Apparently, they've tried before to start a business and destroy the competition. You'd think by now they'd realize they can't destroy competition by force. You all helped to solve a federal case."

"Man, Joe." Pedro shook his head. "I guess you'd better think twice next time, before you try to get a girl's attention by dropping a water balloon on her head!"

Elizabeth gasped. "You said that was an accident, that you weren't aiming for me!"

Joe looked embarrassed, and suddenly, so did Elizabeth. Everyone laughed. Kate took pity on her friend and changed the subject. "When we divide the reward money five ways, we each get four hundred dollars. That's a lot of money! What will you guys do with your money?"

"Drums!" called Pedro.

"Bass guitar!" said Joe.

Maria looked thoughtful. "I may open a savings account. I've always wanted to go to college, and that will be a nice start," she said.

Elizabeth looked thoughtful. "I'm not sure what I'll do with the money yet. I may use it to go to a piano competition in Nashville. I've always wanted to see Music City."

"I won't have any problem spending my money on gadgets," said Kate.

"Well, whatever you spend your money on," said Mrs. Anderson, "you've earned it. I'm glad those men are finally behind bars."

Everyone agreed, and the carriage fell silent for a time as they listened to the clip-clopping of the horse and enjoyed the San Antonio city lights.

•—•—•

The next morning, Elizabeth was putting the finishing touches on her french braid when the phone rang. It was Uncle Dan.

"Congratulations, detective," he told her.

"Thanks, Uncle Dan. We couldn't have found Biscuit without your help," she answered. "You really should let us give you part of the money."

"Oh, I don't know about that. You've got some pretty good sleuthing skills, and I had nothing to do with that. Are you and Kate about ready to come downstairs?" he asked.

"Yes, sir. Why? Did you need me to bring you something?"

"Yes. Bring Biscuit," he answered, and hung up the phone.

Elizabeth wondered about his cryptic instructions. "Kate, Uncle Dan wants us to bring Biscuit with us."

"That's strange. We always bring him. Why would he call to tell us that?" Kate questioned.

Elizabeth shrugged. "I don't know, but we need to get going anyway."

Kate clipped Biscuit's leash to his collar, and he snorted.

"I know you don't like this leash, boy, but I'm not taking any chances." She gave her dog a hug, scooped him into her arms, and followed Elizabeth out the door.

When the elevator doors opened to the lobby, Uncle Dan was waiting for them. Next to him was Captain Lyndel, holding a huge bone in his hand. Tied around the bone was a big red bow.

"Good morning," the man greeted. "I wanted to stop by and say thanks for all your help. Because of you, my business will be back on track in no time. I'm sorry Biscuit was kidnapped in the process."

Kate set Biscuit on the floor, and the man placed the bone in front of him. They laughed as Biscuit tried, unsuccessfully, to get his tiny jaws around the bone.

"Here are some other treats for him," the man said, holding out a large gift bag. "There might be a few things in there for you girls too. Go ahead. Open it."

The girls thanked the man, and peeked into the bag. Sure enough, along with the squeaky toys and bacon-flavored treats, were a couple of furry pink journals and glittery ink pens. There was also a certificate for each of them, offering free River City Cruise rides for life.

"Cool! Thank you so much!" the girls told the man, and Uncle Dan smiled proudly.

"It's my pleasure, girls. I only wish I could do more for you. You saved my business—you and those friends of yours. Would you give them these for me?" He held out three more certificates.

"Certainly," Elizabeth said. "I know they'll be excited to have these. Thank you."

The man tipped his hat and bid them goodbye. Biscuit wagged his tail and barked after the man, then went back to his oversized bone.

"Have I told you I'm proud of you?" Uncle Dan asked Elizabeth.

"The feeling is mutual," she replied, hugging her favorite uncle.

•—•—•

Elizabeth sat across from little Annie at Bible Camp, helping the kids with their craft projects. She was so glad that James had befriended the lonely girl. While some of the other children seemed alarmed about Annie's large birthmark, James didn't seem to notice. He shared his crayons and complimented Annie's picture. Without warning, Elizabeth hugged her brother from behind, placing a kiss on top of his head.

"Hey, cut that out!" he fussed, wiping the place where she had kissed him. She laughed, then looked up to see Mr. Adams walking toward them. His timing was perfect. Annie's mother would be here any minute to pick up her daughter.

"Hello, Elizabeth! I believe you had someone for me to meet," he said with a smile.

"Yes, sir. I'll introduce you to everyone." Quickly she named each child sitting at the table, ending with, "And this is Annie."

The man knelt in front of Annie, who hid her face with her curls. "Hello, Annie. It's very nice to meet you."

Annie's mother appeared, and Elizabeth waved to her. "Hello, Mrs. Lopez. I'd like you to meet Mr. Adams. He represents the local Kiwanis

Club, and I think he wants to talk to you about something."

The man stood and smiled at the woman.

"That's quite a little girl you have," he told the woman. "I understand she needs surgery. Our organization would like to help. It may take us awhile to raise the money we need, but we'd like to take care of the surgery, if that's all right with you."

The woman looked confused, then relieved, and then joyful as she listened to Mr. Adams. Elizabeth went to find Kate, who was packing sound equipment.

"It's going to happen. Annie's really going to get the surgery she needs!" Elizabeth told her.

"Yeah, I saw them talking. That's great. And, you know, I've been thinking. . ." Kate paused.

"Yes?" Elizabeth probed, wondering if Kate was thinking the same thing she'd been thinking.

"I just. . ."

"Yeah?" Elizabeth leaned forward in anticipation.

Kate pushed her glasses up on her nose. "Instead of buying gadgets, I think I want to give my reward money to Annie, for her surgery."

Elizabeth threw her arms around her friend, nearly knocking Kate over.

"Whoa, there. Easy, girl." Kate laughed. "You're almost as bad as Biscuit!"

"I wanted to do the same thing, but I didn't want you to feel bad, or feel like you had to give your money!" Elizabeth told her.

Kate nodded. "It would be fun to go a little gadget crazy. But I don't *need* any more gadgets. I have more than I can play with now. And Dad will keep giving me what his students invent. Annie *needs* that surgery. I think that's what I'm going to do with my money."

"And I don't *need* to go to that piano competition," said Elizabeth.

"Hey, where's the music?" called a voice from the shadows. It was Joe, followed by Pedro and Maria. Joe was holding a brand-new guitar case.

"Yeah, I came to hear a concert!" Maria added.

Elizabeth smiled. It looked like her new musician friend had gotten his wish. "Wow, look at you! Is that a new guitar?"

Joe grinned with pride. "It's used, but it's top of the line." He set the case down, opened it, and pulled out a beautiful guitar. Elizabeth fingered the notches, admiring the workmanship.

"I told my new boss about the reward money. He was impressed that I helped solve a crime and offered to let me take this now. He said I can pay him whenever the reward check comes in."

"So play something!" Elizabeth urged him, and the boy began to strum the strings.

Pausing, he looked at Elizabeth, then Kate, then back at Elizabeth. "You know, I've really enjoyed the last few days. And it's more than just making new friends and getting to buy a guitar. I think it's. . .it's. . ." He struggled for the right words.

"I think it's God," Elizabeth whispered.

"Yeah, that's it. I've never known people who were so excited about God. I think I want to know more about Him. I'm going to start going to church, and start reading the Bible my mom gave me."

"Me too," Maria and Pedro chimed.

Elizabeth noticed Gary working on the soundboard nearby. He winked at her.

"Why don't you give us another concert," Gary said. "Pedro, why don't you play the drums? Then, after the concert, I'd like to spend some time with you guys."

Elizabeth smiled, and her heart seemed to dance as she and her new friends began playing. She looked at Kate, who gave her a thumbs-up. She knew exactly what her friend was thinking: *God is good.*

Camp Club Girls:
Elizabeth and the
Music City Mayhem

Angels in the Snow

Dear God, please don't let me die today. I'm too young to die!

Elizabeth's knuckles were white where she clutched the armrests. The plane hit another bump, and Elizabeth held her breath.

Please God, please God, please God. . .please get me to the ground safely. . . . Lightning flashed and rain pelted against her window, and she felt certain that today, she would meet her Maker.

The man in the seat next to her turned the page of his wrinkled newspaper as if nothing at all were happening. As if today were any other day. As if the plane wasn't threatening to plummet them to a certain death at any moment.

The flight attendant smiled as she faced the crowd and pressed the button on her little microphone. "Ladies and gentlemen, we apologize for the mild turbulence we've encountered. We think we've seen the worst of it, and we should be landing at Nashville International Airport in approximately fifteen minutes."

Gradually, the plane ride smoothed out, and Elizabeth allowed herself to breathe. Her neighbor turned another page of his newspaper, seeming unaware of anything other than the stock reports listed on the page. Elizabeth leaned her head on the windowpane and looked through the clouds at the city below.

"Is this your first time to fly?" the man asked, folding his newspaper and placing it in the pocket of the seat in front of him.

Elizabeth looked at him, surprised. "No, sir. But I've never flown through anything like that before."

"I fly several times a month with my job. I've learned to trust the pilots. They know what they're doing, and they won't fly the plane if it's too dangerous."

Elizabeth nodded.

"Praying helps too." The man smiled at her and shifted in his seat.

Elizabeth didn't know how to respond. Had she been praying out loud? She hadn't meant to. . .

"So what brings you to Music City?" he asked.

"Um. . .a music conference. I'm attending the Young Musician's Conference just outside Nashville. This is my first time to attend."

The man looked interested. "Really? Do you play an instrument? Sing? Write music?"

Elizabeth smiled. She loved talking about music. "All of the above."

"So, you want to be famous. . ." the man said.

"Oh, not really," Elizabeth told him. "I just love music, and I want to be the best I can be. I'd love to be able to really help people with my music, but I'm not sure exactly how I can do that. So for now, I'm just trying to become a better musician. This conference has some of the greatest talent from Nashville and around the country teaching classes. There are classes on songwriting, performing, and even classes about the business end of the music industry. There's a talent competition as well, but I'm not sure I'll be in it. I just love music. I'm a Christian, and I want to use my music in whatever way God wants me to," Elizabeth spoke with passion, then smiled weakly. She thought she probably sounded corny to him.

"Interesting," said the man. He seemed impressed by her answer.

"My friend Bailey, on the other hand, wants to be famous. She's meeting me at the airport."

The man chuckled. "Well, I hope you have fun. And I hope all your dreams come true." He pulled a small planner out of his pocket and began flipping through calendar pages. Elizabeth realized she hadn't asked him anything about why he was coming to Nashville, but didn't want to interrupt him now.

Soon the captain's voice came over the loudspeaker. "Ladies and gentlemen, we are now approaching Nashville International Airport. Please remain seated until we come to a complete stop on the ground. We hope you enjoy your stay in Music City, and thank you for flying with us today."

Elizabeth gripped the armrests once again. Flying usually didn't make her nervous. But the rain, the lightning, and the midflight bumps had caused her to be a little jittery. She closed her eyes and tried to remember to breathe.

Before long, she felt the wheels touch ground, and the plane coasted to a stop. Letting out a deep breath, she opened her eyes. The man was smiling at her.

"Here we are, all safe and sound," he reassured her.

She smiled back, but didn't say anything.

The man stood and took his bags from the overhead compartment. "Let me guess. I'll bet this is yours." He handed her the pink-and-green polka-dotted duffel bag with ELIZABETH embroidered on the side. Around her name were tiny music notes. Her mother had ordered it especially for this trip.

"Yes, thank you," she told the man. She remained seated while the passengers in front of them filed out. Finally, the man stepped back and let her into the aisle in front of him. As soon as they entered the long tunnel leading from the plane to the airport, the man disappeared into the crowd.

Suddenly, Elizabeth heard a familiar voice and smiled.

"Elizabeth!" Bailey called out. Elizabeth looked in the direction of Bailey's voice and saw a big sign with WELCOME BETTYBOO printed on it. She started to walk toward the sign and voice. As the crowd cleared, she saw the tiny, dark-haired girl jumping up and down, attracting all sorts of attention. But Bailey didn't even notice Elizabeth approaching from the side.

"Elizabeth!" She called out again.

Elizabeth leaned forward and whispered in Bailey's ear, "I'm right here."

Startled, nine-year-old Bailey jumped and nearly dropped her poster. "Oh! You scared me. You shouldn't sneak up on people like that!"

Laughing, Elizabeth apologized to her friend. "How long have you been here?" she asked.

"About an hour. I had some time to kill, so I bought this poster and some markers in the gift shop. Do you like it?"

Elizabeth smiled at the poster with her name decorated with hearts and smiley faces.

"I love it," she said. "Now, where do we need to go from here?"

"I have to check in with Kimberly, that flight attendant over there. She's been assigned to me, sort of like a babysitter," Bailey giggled. "She's really nice. She told me the shuttle that will take us to the conference center will be here in half an hour. We need to get the rest of your luggage and head to the waiting area," Bailey told her.

Kimberly, a twentysomething flight attendant with dark hair and a bright smile, gave Bailey a friendly hug. "I see you found your friend," she said, and Bailey introduced the two. Kimberly directed them to the luggage area, then pointed the way to the shuttle. Elizabeth looked around the huge airport and was glad to have some help with directions.

Together, Bailey and Elizabeth approached the round luggage carousel that dumped suitcases from the plane. Weary travelers watched, bleary-eyed, while the endless line of red, black, and brown suitcases traveled the circle.

"You'll never guess who I saw while I was waiting for you," Bailey told Elizabeth. "Dolly Parton!"

Elizabeth was impressed. She knew that Dolly Parton was one of the most famous women in country music. Dolly Parton had been important in country music since Elizabeth's mom was a little girl.

"Wow! Did you get her autograph?"

"No. I don't think it was really her. I think it was just someone dressed up like her."

"Why do you think that?" Elizabeth asked.

"Because she was carrying a monkey in a cage."

Elizabeth asked. "Yeah, you're probably right. Something tells me the real Dolly Parton would have someone to carry her monkey for her."

Soon, Elizabeth spotted her pink-and-green hang-up bag, and the girls followed the signs to the shuttle waiting area.

"I can't believe we're actually in Nashville. I just want to sing something. Hey, do you think anyone has ever been discovered in an airport?" Bailey asked.

Elizabeth chuckled. Same old Bailey.

"I suppose it's possible," she told her friend.

"That girl over there looks just like Carrie Underwood," Bailey pointed. But then the woman turned, and it clearly wasn't the country star.

"I'll bet there are a lot of people here impersonating famous country stars," Elizabeth told her as she pulled out her cell phone to check for messages.

"Yeah, like that man over there. He's trying so hard to look like Willie Nelson. It's so obvious it's not really him," Bailey said.

Elizabeth looked around. She didn't know much about Willie Nelson, but knew that he was a long-time country music legend—over decades, like Dolly Parton was. Elizabeth spied the man Bailey was talking about. She looked at him, and then did a double take.

Bailey continued. "I mean, really. He's my grandpa's age. Look at that long hair, and that bandanna. Who wears a bandanna like that?"

"Uh, Bailey. . ." Elizabeth said.

"And look at him, carrying that beat-up guitar case. Why would a famous man like Willie Nelson have an old guitar case like that?"

The man was standing only a few feet from them, and Elizabeth tried to quiet her friend. "Uh, Bales, I think that really is Willie Nelson," she whispered.

"Don't be ridiculous," Bailey said, making no effort to lower her voice. "That couldn't possibly be Willie Nelson."

The man turned, then smiled at the girls. Was he coming over to talk to them?

He was!

"Pardon me, miss, but I couldn't help but overhear. Did you say there is someone around here impersonating me? Where is he?"

Bailey stared, her mouth open, but didn't say a word.

Elizabeth stood and held her hand out to the man. "Mr. Nelson, it's a pleasure to meet you. I'm Elizabeth, and this is my friend, Bailey, and we're here for the Young Musician's Conference."

"It's a pleasure to meet you ladies. I hope you enjoy your conference. And Bailey," he said. "If you see that impersonator again, please tell him to stop pretending to be me."

Bailey could only nod. The man laughed, and with a friendly wave, he was gone.

"I—can't—believe—" For perhaps the first time since Elizabeth had known her, Bailey was speechless.

Elizabeth good-naturedly patted her young friend on the back. "Well, believe it. You actually met Willie Nelson!"

Bailey snapped to attention and said, "Oh no! I didn't even get his autograph! Or a picture!"

Elizabeth grinned and held her phone out to her friend. "Look at this."

Bailey's eyes grew wide, and she grabbed the phone. "You took a picture of him talking to me! How did you do that without me knowing?"

"I know a good photo opportunity when I see one," said Elizabeth smugly.

Soon, the shuttle pulled up outside the glass doors, and the girls gathered their luggage. Several other young people, some carrying guitars, joined them in the small van. The driver introduced himself, and served as a tour guide on the short drive to the conference center, pointing out various points of interest along the way. Elizabeth heard little of what he said, though. She was distracted by the white, fluffy snow all around her.

"Wow," she told Bailey. "We hardly ever get snow in Amarillo! That, all by itself, will make this trip wonderful!"

"When we get there, we'll have to find a place to make snow angels," Bailey told her.

The van pulled up in front of a large glass building. "You can register just inside those doors. You'll receive your room assignments, and then you're free to do whatever you wish for a few hours. The first session will be held in this building, and will begin at 7 p.m.," the driver told them.

Elizabeth and Bailey gathered their things and followed the others into the building.

"I can't believe I'm actually here," Bailey said. "I'm so glad you could come, Elizabeth. When I read about this Young Musician's Conference, and all the people who have been discovered here, I knew I had to come! But my parents didn't want to send me here alone. When you decided to go, they felt better about it."

"I'm just glad you emailed me the information. I've wanted to go to something like this for a while, but until now, I haven't been able to," Elizabeth replied, taking in the upscale facilities. "This place really is beautiful."

The girls registered, got their room key, and followed the map to their room. The hotel-like building housed boys on the first floor, girls on the second. They found room 208 and tossed their things on each of the two twin beds. Elizabeth started to look in the closets and in the bathroom, but Bailey was eager to explore the grounds.

"Come on! We have all week to look at this room. Let's go survey the lay of the land. I saw some beautiful gardens with mounds of fresh snow!" Bailey told her, one foot already in the hallway.

Elizabeth grabbed her room key and followed her friend back outside. She pulled her furry parka up over her head—she seldom got to wear the coat in warm Amarillo. She breathed in the cool, crisp air. This was going to be one winter break she would never forget.

"This way," called Bailey.

The girls turned down a well-kept, winding path. Elizabeth was in awe of the snow-covered branches and the crystal-covered ground.

Bailey seemed impressed as well, for the girls walked in silence for a few moments. Then they heard humming.

"What's that?" asked Bailey, and Elizabeth shrugged her shoulders in response. The humming continued—a beautiful sound, almost as if an angel had come down to offer musical accompaniment to this winter wonderland.

The girls followed the sound around a curve in the trail. There was a girl, a little older than Elizabeth, humming and scrawling away with a pencil on a wrinkled napkin.

"Hello," said Bailey, but the girl just held up her left hand and kept humming and scrawling.

Fascinated, Elizabeth and Bailey watched her. The girl continued for another minute or two, and then looked at them with an apologetic smile.

"I'm sorry. I didn't mean to be rude, but I had that melody in my head, and I had to get it down on paper before I forgot it! I'm Kristi." She held out a gloved hand to them.

Elizabeth stepped forward and shook Kristi's hand. "I'm Elizabeth, and this is Bailey. No apologies necessary. You have a beautiful voice! We thought an angel was hiding in the woods."

The girl laughed and said, "Not quite an angel. I just got here. I haven't even registered yet. My car is parked right over there." She gestured to a parking lot on the other side of some trees, "But as I said, I had to stop and get that song on paper. I always have songs in my head, and if I don't write them down right away, they get lost forever."

"Come with us," Elizabeth told her. "We'll show you where to register, and then we'll help you with your luggage."

The girl gave them a warm smile. "Wow, thanks!"

Together, the three girls tromped through the snow-covered garden and to the main conference building. Kristi quickly registered and got her room key, and the three headed back to her car.

"Is this your first time to come to the Young Musician's Conference?" Elizabeth asked the older girl.

"Yes, but I already know a lot of the people here. My dad is a musician, though he hasn't been able to do much in the last few years. I'm here for the competition, but also to sell my dad's guitar. That's my ticket to college."

"Your ticket to college?" asked Bailey.

"Yes," Kristi answered. "I want to go to Julliard. Unfortunately, we don't have that kind of money. But my dad used this guitar to play for some of the greatest country music legends of all time. Johnny Cash, Conway Twitty, Loretta Lynn, Dolly Parton. . .and others. Because of the history attached to Dad's guitar, and because it's a handmade Gibson, it's worth a pretty penny. Dad got in touch with some of his old cronies, and I'm supposed to show it to some of them this week. He wants me to sell it to the highest bidder."

"Wow," breathed Elizabeth. "You have the guitar here with you?"

"Yep. It's all safe and sound in my trunk. Here, I'll show it to you!" Kristi offered.

The girls approached an old, blue Honda, and Kristi used her key to unlock the trunk. She pulled out a couple of black duffel bags and set them on the ground, then reached for a battered guitar case. It was covered with stickers from all over the world. Elizabeth took a deep breath, knowing she was about to view something very valuable.

Kristi pulled the case from the trunk, and it nearly flew out of her hand. "What? What in the world?" the girl sounded alarmed.

She set the case back in the trunk, opened it, and gasped.

The case was empty.

Gone!

"What? How? My dad's guitar!" Kristi cried out.

Elizabeth and Bailey peered into the empty case, as confused as their new friend.

"I don't understand! How could it be missing?" Kristi's face was white as a sheet, and she grasped the edge of the open trunk.

"Take a deep breath," Elizabeth told her, resting her arm around Kristi's shoulder. "We'll find it. I'll bet it's back at your house, lying on your bed or something. You probably forgot to put it in the case."

"No, I didn't," said Kristi. "I was so careful, and I remember putting it in myself."

"Did anyone help you load the car?" Bailey asked.

"My mom and my little brother, but they didn't open any of my things," the girl said, her voice shaking. "It's not at home. It's been stolen!"

Elizabeth spotted a security guard at the other end of the parking lot.

"Bailey, go get that guard!" she suggested.

Bailey was off like a bullet, as Elizabeth tried to console the girl. "Is anything else missing?" she asked.

Kristi glanced at her other bags. "It doesn't look like it. The only thing I had of any value was in that guitar case!"

Within moments Bailey reappeared, the security guard at her heels.

"What seems to be the problem?" the man asked.

"My guitar! It's been stolen!" Kristi told him.

The man pulled out a walkie-talkie and pushed a button. "Headquarters, this is Officer Wilson over at parking area four. We have what looks like a burglary. Would you send the sheriff's department right away?"

The person on the other end of the device agreed, and Officer

Wilson pulled out a notepad and began asking questions.

As Kristi told the man her name, age, and what time she arrived at the parking lot, Elizabeth and Bailey looked at the guitar case.

"Why would someone take the guitar and leave the case?" Bailey asked.

"I don't know. Maybe they thought it would take her longer to notice it was missing," Elizabeth answered.

The officer looked over his shoulder at them, frowned, and then turned back to Kristi.

"I think he wants us to keep quiet," Elizabeth whispered. In silence, the girls leaned over the trunk to examine the case more closely.

Soon, a brown-and-white sheriff's car pulled up beside them. "We were told there was a burglary here?" said a man in a sheriff's uniform.

His partner was a younger woman with dark hair and eyes. She immediately got out of the car and put her arm around Kristi, who was in tears.

"It's okay, honey. My name is Deputy Kate Collins. We'll get this all sorted out," she told the girl. Then, looking at Elizabeth and Bailey, she asked, "Is this your friend?"

"We just met her today," Elizabeth told her. "We were going to help her unload her trunk, and when she pulled out her guitar case, it was empty."

The woman opened the back door to the sheriff's car and told Kristi, "Here. Sit down and tell us exactly what happened."

Kristi wiped her eyes with the tissue the woman held out, and then sat sideways in the car, her feet on the graveled parking lot.

Elizabeth and Bailey listened as Kristi answered their questions. "That guitar was my future. I drove here from Georgia for this conference, and I was supposed to meet with some people who wanted to buy that guitar!"

"What made the guitar so valuable?" asked Officer Wilson.

"It was a handmade Gibson Les Paul model. But my dad made it even more special. He used to play for some of the greatest country legends of all time! Since he's had multiple sclerosis, people have made him some pretty generous offers. But he's never been willing to part with it until now. He wanted to use the money to send me to Julliard!" her tears started pouring again.

The officers looked at each other over Kristi's head and shook their heads. Elizabeth had a feeling she knew what they were thinking. This was Nashville. There were guitars everywhere.

The woman knelt in front of Kristi. "Why don't you describe the guitar to us. We'll file a report and see what happens."

Something about her tone made Kristi look up. "You don't think you'll find it, do you?"

The woman looked grim. "We'll do our best. But I have to be honest. Finding a missing guitar in Music City can be like finding a needle in a haystack."

Kristi took a deep breath and looked at Deputy Collins in the eyes. "You have to find it. Please," she pleaded.

The woman looked at her partner, then back at Kristi. "We'll do our best."

Elizabeth and Bailey looked at each other. "It doesn't sound like they think they'll find it," Bailey whispered.

"I know," Elizabeth whispered back. "I'm sure they'll try. But a missing guitar probably isn't a very high priority to them, with all the other crimes that probably happen in this city."

They looked at each other, each knowing what the other was thinking. If this crime was to be solved, it was up to them. It sounded like another job for the Camp Club Girls!

They began looking at the guitar case again, this time as closely as they could without removing it from the trunk. "Look," Bailey whispered, pulling a hair from the blue velvet liner. "It's red. Kristi's hair is brown, almost black."

Elizabeth examined the hair.

"Hold on to it. Maybe someone in Kristi's family has red hair," she whispered. Then, leaning farther into the trunk, she saw something white caught in one of the folds of velvet.

"What's this?" she whispered.

Before they could look more closely, the speaker in the sheriff's car began blaring, "Disturbance at the city park. All units to the city park."

The tall officer shut his notebook, and Deputy Collins said, "Thank you for the information, miss. I'm sorry about your guitar. We'll do our best."

Kristi stood, dazed, and allowed the door to be shut behind her. The two sheriffs climbed back into their car, turned on the siren, and sped off.

Officer Wilson shook his head compassionately.

"A Gibson Les Paul model. That's too bad," he said, and then walked away.

Kristi stared into the empty guitar case, looking forlorn.

"Come on," Elizabeth told her, shutting the case. "Let's get your stuff to your room."

Bailey grabbed one of Kristi's bags, and Elizabeth grabbed the other. Kristi started to shut the trunk lid, leaving her empty case, but Elizabeth stopped her. "No, bring it," she said.

Kristi thought about it a moment, then nodded. She grabbed the bulky case, slammed the trunk, and followed the girls to the building that housed the conference participants.

The three said little, each lost in her own thoughts. Finally, in the elevator, Kristi sighed heavily.

"What am I going to tell my dad? How am I supposed to tell him I lost his guitar?" she asked.

"You didn't lose it," Bailey reassured her. "It was stolen. And we'll do all we can to find it."

Kristi shook her head. "You're sweet, but you heard the officers. They don't think there's a chance in this world they will find it."

Bailey grinned. "I didn't say *they* would find it!"

Kristi looked confused, and the elevator doors opened to the second floor. Elizabeth held a finger to her lips, because people were milling about the hallway.

"This way," she guided the other two girls, checking Kristi's key for the room number. They arrived at room 214; it was empty.

The three girls filed into Kristi's room, and Elizabeth shut the door behind them. Kristi laid the empty guitar case on the bed and sat beside it, wiping unbidden tears from her cheeks.

"Do you want to talk about it?" asked Elizabeth.

Kristi stared off into the distance.

"My dad is a country music legend. You've probably never heard of him, but I guarantee you, nearly every established musician in Nashville knows my dad. He is one of the best guitarists in the history of country music. No one can do what he did with a guitar." Kristi brushed unwanted tears away with the back of her hand.

"I don't understand," said Bailey. "You talk like he's no longer playing. What made him quit?"

Kristi fingered the old guitar case. "Three years ago, my dad started having some problems. His arm was tingling, and it felt numb. His vision became blurred. He started losing his balance. He even fell down once on stage. The audience laughed, thinking he was drunk, but my dad doesn't drink any alcohol."

Elizabeth and Bailey listened quietly.

"After the falling incident, Mom convinced him to see a doctor. They found out that my dad has multiple sclerosis. It has progressed pretty quickly. He can barely hold a guitar anymore, much less play one." She ran her hand along the top of the case. "All his dreams, all his accomplishments in life were symbolized by this guitar. And he was willing to sell it—for me. And now it's gone."

Elizabeth didn't know what to say. Finally she asked, "What is your dad's name?"

"Joshua Conrad," she whispered.

Elizabeth's eyebrows lifted. "Your dad is Joshua Conrad?"

Kristi looked up. "Yeah. Have you heard of him?"

Elizabeth nodded, amazed she was sitting in the room with Joshua Conrad's daughter. "I have one of his albums!"

Kristi's face lit up. "You must have his only album," she said. "He only did one solo album, but he played backup for hundreds of others."

Elizabeth smiled. "My parents used to play that album for us at bedtime, kind of like a lullaby. It's some of the most beautiful music I've ever heard."

"Thanks," Kristi whispered, and Elizabeth fought back her own tears. To have such a gift taken away by such an awful disease was beyond her imagination.

No one seemed to know what to say next. Finally, Elizabeth spoke up. "Kristi, Bailey and I can help you find your guitar."

Kristi gave them a half-hearted smile. "Thanks, but I don't think there's much any of us can do, except look for someone carrying it around here at the conference. I doubt the thief will be dumb enough to flaunt it right in front of me."

Elizabeth bent down on one knee in front of her new friend, and looked into her eyes. "Kristi, Bailey and I have dealt with this kind of thing before. We'll tell you all about that later, but first, we need you to answer some questions." She looked at Bailey, who reached into her pocket, then held out the strand of red hair.

"Does anyone in your family have red hair?" Bailey asked her.

Squinting, Kristi took the hair and held it up to the light. "No, we're all brunettes. Except for my dad—his hair is gray. Where did you get this?" she asked.

"From inside your guitar case!" Bailey told her.

While Kristi examined the hair, Elizabeth reached for the case. "I saw something else too. May I open this?"

Kristi nodded, her curiosity obvious.

Elizabeth snapped open the case and ran her hand along the edge of the blue velvet, moving the crushed folds to the side. "Here it is!" she said, and pulled out a ticket stub. The other two girls moved close, and Elizabeth read the words aloud. "Country Music Ha–" The ticket was torn down the middle.

"What could that be a ticket to?" Bailey asked. "A country music happening? Hat museum?"

Elizabeth added to the suggestions. "Hair stylist? Hail and farewell?"

Kristi took the ticket and looked at it. "It's the Country Music Hall of Fame," said Kristi. "My dad has some ticket stubs like this in his scrapbook. And this isn't just any ticket." She pointed to the red stripe running across the end of the stub. "The tickets you buy at the door are plain white with red and blue writing. But the VIP tickets have a red band running across the ends. Whoever owns this ticket didn't just visit the Country Music Hall of Fame. He or she is a member."

"You think a superstar stole your dad's guitar?" Bailey's eyes grew wide.

Kristi shook her head. "People who work for some of the major studios are given a membership. They don't necessarily belong to a big star. . . but possibly to a musician."

The girls stared at the ticket stub, their minds processing the information. "So maybe the thief is a red-haired musician," Kristi said.

"Well, it appears that way. It gives us a starting place, anyway. But before we go any further, Kristi, we need to know something. Who knew you were bringing the guitar here?" Elizabeth asked.

Kristi laughed. "Everybody who is anybody in country music knew I was bringing the guitar here to sell. Dad has been talking to some bigwigs for weeks now. Some of them are teachers at this conference and others are stopping by to look at the guitar. I even had appointments to meet a couple of them at their recording studios."

Bailey and Elizabeth looked at each other. "And all of these people are probably members of The Country Music Hall of Fame," Bailey said.

Kristi nodded.

"Well, at least that narrows it down some. Do you know if any of them have red hair?" Elizabeth asked.

Kristi shook her head. "I know a couple of them, but not many. I have no idea what they look like."

Elizabeth looked at her watch. "We have about an hour. Let's go to the room Bailey and I are staying in. I brought my new laptop with me, and it has wireless internet access. Maybe we can do a search for the people who were interested in the guitar. If they are such country music bigwigs, surely their pictures will be on the internet."

"Good idea," said Bailey. "And let's bring the case. I don't want to take any chances!"

Kristi grabbed the guitar case, and the three girls headed for the door. Just as Elizabeth reached for the doorknob, she had to jump back. The door slammed open. There in front of them was a young woman dressed in a Western hat, boots, and a sequined Western shirt with fringe and tassels hanging from every possible place.

"Hi there! Which one of you is my roommate?" she asked.

The three girls just stared, openmouthed.

The girl's hair was flaming red.

Another Redhead!

An hour later, Elizabeth, Bailey, and Kristi sat down in a large conference room. Mary-Lynn, Kristi's roommate, had followed them into their room, chattering the hour away. She had finally left them to track down some of the agents.

"I can't believe we're actually here," whispered Bailey. "I have a feeling we're all gonna be famous by the end of the conference."

Elizabeth laughed. "I don't want to be famous. I just want to learn more about music. I'd love to be able to use my music to help people somehow. But I suppose being famous wouldn't be all bad. . .what about you, Kristi? What are your goals?"

Kristi looked thoughtful. "I know this probably sounds funny, but I couldn't care less if anybody ever knows my name. I just—I just have music in me, and I have to let it out. I have to write. I have to sing. And the more I learn about all kinds of music, the better I'll be able to express what's in my heart. That's why I want to go to Julliard. It's the best music school in the country, possibly the world. But, it looks like I may have to settle for community college. . ."

Elizabeth patted her friend on the leg. "Don't give up hope. We'll do all we can to find your—"

"There you are!" Mary-Lynn interrupted them. "I've been looking all over for you! Do I look okay? Do you think I'll be noticed?"

The three girls looked at Mary-Lynn's sparkly, glittery skirt and satin shirt. Yes, she would be noticed. No one commented, but the red-haired diva didn't seem to notice.

She sat down next to Bailey, her eyes scanning the room. "Have you spotted any of the agents yet? I hope I'll be picked up by an agent this weekend."

Bailey pounced on the opportunity to question the girl. "Mary-Lynn, um. . .tell me your last name again?"

Mary-Lynn leaned forward as if sharing a secret. "Shhhhhh. My real last name is Smith. But I registered for this conference under my stage name. Mary-Lynn Monroe."

Elizabeth stared at the girl, trying not to laugh. *Mary-Lynn Monroe? Like Marilyn Monroe? Is this girl for real?*

Then, Elizabeth saw a flicker of. . .something. Something in the girl's eyes showed insecurity. *She just wants to be loved,* Elizabeth realized.

"Well, no one is likely to forget that name, Mary-Lynn. And you look lovely in your outfit too."

Bailey flashed her a shocked look, but Elizabeth ignored it. She didn't know if Mary-Lynn was involved in the guitar theft or not. But one thing was certain: This was going to be an interesting week.

The girls' attention turned to the front of the room, where a twenty-something man adjusted the microphone. There was a guitar hanging from a strap around his neck, and soon he began strumming. The crowd was delighted when he began to sing a hilarious welcome song in an exaggerated country twang:

"Welcome young musicians
To our conference.
We hope when you are done here,
You'll be glad you went.
We'll teach you about music
And being in the spotlight.
By the time we're through with you,
You won't have stage fright."

A young woman joined him in harmony for the second verse, and then an older man added his voice for the third. By the time they were finished, the room was filled with laughter and applause.

When those three exited the stage, a familiar-looking man took the microphone. Elizabeth tilted her head, trying to place him.

Is that. . . ? No, it couldn't be. He would have said something. But when the man spoke, Elizabeth knew his voice. *The man from the plane!*

"Welcome to the Music City Young Musician's Conference! My name is Rick Forrest, and I'm the conference director. I know you all are excited to be here, and we're excited to have you. It's my hope and prayer that you'll leave here with the tools to become better musicians and performers."

The man went on to introduce the staff, more than a dozen experts in different aspects of the music business. There was a songwriter, a pianist, a guitarist, a fiddle player, and several other instrumentalists. There was a computer expert, who would teach about running soundboards and setting up recording studios. There was a choreographer, a lighting expert, a costume designer, and others.

"I'll have a hard time deciding which classes to go to," whispered Bailey.

"Me too," whispered Elizabeth. "Maybe we should divide and conquer. We'll take different classes, and then teach each other what we learn."

"Good idea," Bailey agreed.

"Shhhhh!" Mary-Lynn gave them a pointed look, and the girls straightened in their seats.

Finally Mr. Forrest said, "Now, it's time for the highlight of our conference. . ." A soft drumroll played in the background as the man paused for effect. The audience leaned forward in anticipation.

"Dinner!" he said, and everyone laughed.

The man led them in a dinner prayer. The audience dispersed, and Elizabeth went to the front of the room. She waited politely for Mr. Forrest to finish speaking to the drummer. When he turned to face her, a smile lit his face. "Elizabeth!"

She smiled back at him. "Why didn't you tell me you were the conference director?"

"Ahhhh, I wanted it to be a surprise. I hope you got all settled into your room. Are you making some nice friends?"

"Yes, sir. My roommate and I met Kristi Conrad and her roommate, Mary-Lynn."

"Kristi Conrad. . ." Mr. Forrest wrinkled his brow. "Is that the young lady who had her father's guitar stolen?"

"Yes," Elizabeth told him. She knew the security officer must have told him all about it.

"That's too bad," he said. "We'll do all we can to help recover it." Then a staff member needed his attention, so Elizabeth told him goodbye and went to find her friends.

•—•—•

Elizabeth, Bailey, and Kristi held their red plastic lunch trays and waited in line. "Have you decided which class you'll go to first?" asked Bailey.

"I'm still trying to decide between songwriting and stage performance. I could use some work in both areas," Elizabeth said.

"I'm thinking about taking the choreography class, but the costume design seems fun too. What about you, Kristi?"

The girl jumped when she heard her name. "What? I'm sorry. I didn't hear the question."

Elizabeth's heart went out to the girl. "That's okay. Bailey was just wondering what class you're going to take tonight."

"Um, I don't know. I was supposed to meet with a man who wanted to look at Dad's guitar. It's too late to call and cancel the appointment. I guess I'll just have to tell him about the theft when he gets here. And I'm supposed to meet with three others tomorrow." Kristi seemed to be talking more to herself than to Elizabeth and Bailey. "I guess I need to call home. This is going to break Dad's heart."

Elizabeth and Bailey didn't respond since they didn't know what to say.

"Beef or chicken?" the lady behind the counter asked them.

"Beef," replied Bailey.

"Chicken," said Elizabeth.

Kristi looked lost in her thoughts again, so Elizabeth nudged her. "Beef or chicken?" she asked.

"Oh, sorry. Chicken," she responded. The girls filled their trays and found a table near a window.

"I'm starved!" said Bailey. "All I had on the plane was a tiny little bag of peanuts!"

As Bailey dug into her food, Elizabeth noticed Kristi hadn't even picked up her fork. She just stared out the window.

Lord, I wish there was something I could do for her. Help me know what to say to her.

"You know, Kristi, we actually have some pretty good leads. And once Bailey and I get the other Camp Club Girls on this case, I feel certain we'll find your guitar," Elizabeth told her.

Kristi offered a weak smile. "Tell me some more about these. . . Campfire Girls?"

Elizabeth and Bailey laughed.

"Camp Club Girls," said Bailey. "And we're only the best kid detectives in the country! We've got Sydney in Washington, DC; Alex in California; Kate in Philadelphia; McKenzie in Montana; Elizabeth in Texas; and yours truly in Illinois. Since we met we've solved. . .how many mysteries have we solved, Elizabeth?"

"A lot," said Elizabeth with a laugh. "Around twenty now. You should never underestimate the Camp Club Girls."

"Yeah," continued Bailey. "Trust us. We're going to find your guitar. Once we get started on a mystery, there's no stopping us."

Kristi pushed the broccoli around on her plate. "Thanks, you guys. But I don't think—"

They were interrupted by a loud, "Oh, there you are!"

The girls turned to find Mary-Lynn headed their way. "I've been looking all over for you!"

The way she spoke, a little too loudly, caused everyone's heads to turn toward her.

The girl looked frustrated. She plopped down next to Kristi and said, "I've been trying to speak with an agent."

Elizabeth's eyebrows lifted. "Really? Who?"

"Rick Forrest! You know, the conference director. He represents the Olive Branch Talent Agency, and I've been trying to get an appointment with him." The girl tossed her hair. "Elizabeth, didn't I see you talking to him?"

"Uh. . .yeah. But I was just saying hello. I didn't even know he's an agent."

"You mean you know Rick Forrest personally?" Mary-Lynn gushed. "You are so lucky!"

Elizabeth shook her head. "No, I didn't mean—"

"Oh, that lady over there looks like she might be a talent scout. I think I'll go meet her," Mary-Lynn said, and then she was gone.

Bailey, Kristi, and Elizabeth looked at each other in stunned silence, and then started laughing.

"She certainly knows what she wants," said Kristi. "And she's not afraid to go after it!"

Elizabeth looked at the red-haired girl across the room. The woman she was speaking to seemed uncomfortable, but Mary-Lynn didn't seem to notice.

"Well, she can't be trusted," said Bailey. "She has red hair. And for now, she is our prime suspect."

The three girls studied the redhead silently for a few moments, each lost in her own thoughts.

•—•—•

Elizabeth followed Kristi to the third floor of the building, through the doorway labeled, THE ART OF SONGWRITING. The room was already filling up, and they found seats near the back.

Bailey had decided on the choreography class. "I even brought my tap shoes, in case I need to practice!" she had said.

Elizabeth smiled as she thought about it, remembering the talent show at Camp Discovery Lake, and Bailey's crazy costume. With pink sponge curlers in her hair and cold cream on her face, Bailey had tap-danced her way into first place.

Kristi pulled out a notepad and pencil and, humming, jotted down notes. Elizabeth was amazed. In the few short hours since their meeting, Kristi had penned three-and-a-half songs. And they were good too. Elizabeth found herself humming one of Kristi's melodies as she walked from the dining hall to this class. Kristi was truly gifted.

"Have you had any of your songs published?" Elizabeth asked the girl.

Kristi smiled. "Before my dad was diagnosed with MS, I used to help him write songs. He always gave me credit too. There are seven or eight published pieces that say, 'By Joshua and Kristi Conrad.' "

"Wow. It sounds like you should be teaching this class, not taking it!" Elizabeth said.

"No. I still have so much to learn," Kristi said humbly.

The mumbling in the class faded as a young man in faded jeans and a T-shirt walked to the front of the room. He had a guitar strapped around his shoulders, and he was wearing a faded ball cap backward. His hair was shaved close to his head.

"Good evening, songwriters!" he said with a grin, showing two deep dimples in his cheeks. When he smiled, he looked like he was about twelve years old.

Around a dozen or so people were in the room, and the teacher said, "When we write music, we really bare our souls to the world. It would be nice if we got to know each other a little better before we are asked to do that. Why don't you move your chairs into a circle, and we'll spend a little time introducing ourselves to each other."

After the chairs were moved, the young man instructed the students to share their names, where they were from, and what kinds of music they wanted to write.

"Tommy, from Alabama. I want to write country music."

"Ashley, from New York, and I want to write jazz."

"Jeff. I'm from Wisconsin, and I'm not sure what kind of music I want to write. I'm here to learn."

When Kristi's turn came, she said simply, "Kristi Conrad. Tennessee. All kinds of music."

The instructor leaned forward and asked, "What do you mean, 'all kinds'?"

Kristi smiled. "I listen to all kinds of music, and when I write, I hear different things. The kind of music depends on the message and mood of the song. I can't really say a certain type of music I like to write. I like all music, if it's uplifting. If it's done well."

The instructor studied Kristi for a moment, and Elizabeth almost felt sorry for her new friend. Finally, the young man nodded to Elizabeth.

"I'm Elizabeth. I'm from Texas, and I'll probably write mostly Christian music."

The introductions continued, but Elizabeth sensed the instructor's eyes on Kristi. Did he know who she was? Did he know how great her dad was?

Probably so. Everyone in the music business knew who Joshua Conrad was. He was a legend.

Finally, the songwriting instruction began. The teacher, who introduced himself as Robert Kranfield, was full of information. She remembered reading in the brochure that he was a staff writer for one of the local recording studios.

"Tonight, we'll work on a little group project," he told them. "We're going to write a song together. Most songs follow a pattern of verse, chorus, verse, chorus, bridge, chorus. That is the easiest pattern for most people to remember. So let's choose an idea, or theme, for our song."

Silence. No one wanted to be the first to suggest something.

Finally, Kristi said, "I lost something very valuable to me. Had it stolen from me, as a matter of fact. Could we write a song about that?"

Robert looked at Kristi as if he didn't know how to respond. His face was an emotionless mask.

Funny. He told us to bare our souls, yet he's like a brick wall. Maybe he doesn't want to influence our own creativity, so he's staying neutral. . .

"What are some other words that come to mind when you think of the loss Kristi described?" Robert asked.

A few people tossed out some words like grief, anger, sadness, and betrayal.

"Good," he continued. "You understand the mood of the song. How will that mood affect the actual music?"

The girl named Ashley said, "You don't want to write a sweet, happy melody with sad, hurting lyrics."

"Exactly," Robert agreed. "How would you write the music?"

"Slow," said one person.

"Sad," said another.

Kristi spoke up. "I'd write it in a minor key. But I'd write the bridge in a major key, to offer some hope. I don't like to write hopeless music."

Every head in the room looked at Kristi. She clearly knew more about music and songwriting than any other student in the class.

Robert studied her a long time before answering. Finally, he said, "You sound like one of the greatest songwriters I know, Miss Conrad. He also writes songs filled with hope. Maybe you know him."

Kristi looked at her teacher, not sure how to respond.

"His name is Joshua Conrad."

Kristi's face lit with joy. "You know my father?" she asked. The other students looked to Robert for more explanation.

"I don't know him personally," said Robert. "But I know his music. He is truly one of the greatest songwriters of our time."

Kristi beamed with pride, but Robert turned away. Before long, the class had composed a wordless song, with everyone contributing ideas.

"We're out of time," Robert said. "Our next songwriting session will be tomorrow morning, after breakfast. See what kinds of lyrics and melodies you can come up with to share with the class. You're dismissed."

Everyone shuffled chairs and gathered their things. Some of the students wanted to talk to Robert privately, but he didn't give them a chance. He tossed his things in a briefcase, straightened his ball cap, and strode out of the room.

Elizabeth caught just a glimpse of a tuft of red curls as he straightened that cap.

The Camp Club Girls in Action!

Back in the room, Bailey demonstrated the new dance moves she had learned in her choreography class while Elizabeth tried to send a conference call invitation to the other Camp Club Girls.

Kristi plopped on the bed and looked at the laptop Elizabeth was holding. "So that thing has speakers, and you can use it like a phone? And all of you can talk at once?" she asked.

"Yes. If I had my video hookup, we could all see each other as we were talking, but I left that at home."

Bailey stopped midspin and said, "Yeah, the cameras are really cool when they're working. Mine is in the shop right now."

"I'd be a little nervous to have a camera in my room," Kristi said. "What if I forgot to turn it off? That could be awful!"

"Yeah, you have to be careful with those," Elizabeth said. "My parents finally let me get one, but I can only use it at the kitchen desk, and I always have to turn it off and cover it with a towel when I'm done. That way, we're pretty safe."

"I have to do that too," said Bailey. "Once, I left the camera running after I'd been talking to Sydney. I was practicing a new song, and then I heard applause! Sydney had been there the whole time. I didn't even know I had an audience. But I bowed and blew her kisses anyway."

The other two laughed at Bailey's story. Then Elizabeth sat up. "Speaking of Sydney, I just got a confirmation email from her. She will call in fifteen minutes. And there's one from McKenzie. . .she's in."

"So how did you all get together and start solving these mysteries?" Kristi asked.

"All six of us attended the same summer camp, Camp Discovery Lake. While we were there, one of the camp employees was acting strangely. So we did a little investigating, and we ended up finding a stash of stolen jewels. The employee's father was in prison for stealing them and selling them. But when we found the jewels, it proved he couldn't have sold them. So he got out of prison!" Elizabeth told her.

"That is so cool," said Kristi. "I can't believe you all found stolen jewels."

"Well, we didn't actually find them. Biscuit did," Bailey said.

"Biscuit? Who is Biscuit?" asked Kristi.

"Kate's dog," said Elizabeth and Bailey in unison.

"We found Biscuit at camp, and he got to go home with Kate, who lives in Philadelphia," Elizabeth explained. "Speaking of Kate, she just emailed. She's in. Now we're only missing Alex."

Kristi rolled over and propped her head on her hands. "Do you really think you can find my guitar?" she asked.

"Of course we'll find it!" Bailey exclaimed, doing a pirouette and knocking over the trash can in the process.

Elizabeth looked at Kristi. "We'll give it our best shot."

After watching Bailey perform a while longer, Elizabeth started punching her keyboard. "Our conference call time starts in two minutes. I'm going to log in." Soon, they were connected with Kate, McKenzie, and Sydney.

"Are you having fun at your music camp?" McKenzie asked.

"Yes!" Bailey answered sashaying across the room.

"I sure wish I had my webcam so you all could watch the show," Elizabeth told them.

"What is Bailey doing now?" Sydney asked with a laugh.

"She's demonstrating everything she learned in her choreography class," Elizabeth replied.

The other girls laughed.

"That should be entertaining," said Kate.

"Everyone, I want you to meet Kristi. She's here with us, and she needs our help," said Elizabeth.

"What kind of help? Another mystery? Tell us everything!" said Sydney.

Just then, Alex beeped into the conference call. She sounded out of breath. "Sorry, you guys! I just got home from my gymnastics class. I'm beat! I saw your email, Elizabeth, and called right away. What have I missed?"

McKenzie chimed in. "Elizabeth's friend, Kristi is with her. They were just about to fill us in on a new mystery."

"I'll let Kristi tell you what she knows," said Elizabeth.

Kristi seemed hesitant. "Uh. . .well. . .I brought my dad's guitar with me. It's worth a lot of money because of the type of guitar it is—a handmade Gibson, and also because of who my dad is. He's sort of a country music legend. I made appointments with several important music people here in Nashville—I was going to sell the guitar and use the money to go to Julliard, if they accept me. I locked the guitar in my trunk and went to register. But when I returned to the car, my guitar case was empty."

The girls were silent for a moment as they took in the information.

"Do you have any clues at all?" Alex asked.

"Yes," Bailey chimed in. "We found a single strand of red hair in the guitar case. No one in Kristi's family has red hair. We also found a ticket stub to the Country Music Hall of Fame."

"Not just any ticket stub, though," said Elizabeth. "It's a VIP ticket. Those are only given to important people who are on the inside of the country music world."

"Interesting," said Sydney. "It's still not much to go on. Did you see anyone around your car?"

"No," said Kristi. "I took my time registering. I stopped and wrote a song between my car and the registration room. . ."

"You stopped and wrote a song. . .wow. How long were you away from your car?" asked McKenzie.

Kristi let out a heavy sigh. "Probably an hour."

"A lot can happen in an hour," said Alex. "But the thief probably didn't expect you to be gone that long. He or she probably worked quickly."

"I think first we need to figure out who all knew you had the guitar with you. Kristi, do you think you can make a list?" Kate asked.

"Sure," Kristi replied.

"Then we can do a cross search and find out if any of those people have red hair, and have VIP tickets to the Country Music Hall of Fame," Kate continued.

"How many red-haired people are at your conference?" asked Alex.

"Just one that we've seen. It's Kristi's roommate, Mary-Lynn Monroe," Bailey said in an exaggerated Southern accent.

"Mary-Lynn. . .Monroe?" asked Sydney. "You've got to be kidding me."

"Yeah, but I think she's too much of a space brain to have stolen the guitar. All she cares about is whether or not the agents notice her," Bailey added.

"I wouldn't write her off too quickly," said McKenzie. "It could be an act. Besides, she's your only suspect at this point."

"Uh. . .no she's not," said Elizabeth.

"What do you mean?" asked Bailey and Kristi together.

"Our teacher. Robert. I saw his hair when he adjusted his cap," she told them.

Kristi's face went pale. "You mean. . ."

"Red," Elizabeth confirmed. "But that doesn't mean he's guilty, just like it doesn't mean Mary-Lynn's guilty. Lots of people have red hair."

"Maybe not, but at least we have a couple of suspects," said Kate. "Kristi, get us that list as soon as possible, and we'll get to work."

"I thought of something else," said Sydney. "You said your dad is some kind of country music legend. Does he have a fan club?"

"Yes, he does. I'll email you the website. Why?"

"If a fan knew you were selling his guitar, he or she might have decided to take it," Sydney answered.

"Yes, but his old record company maintains the website. I wouldn't have any idea of how to find out who his fans are," Kristi said.

"Not a problem," Kate said with a chuckle. "Give me the web address. I'll do the rest. I can do a deep web search, and cross-reference the referring data, and use that to determine the email addresses of the site's visitors."

"You can. . .what?" asked Kristi.

"Don't question it," said McKenzie with a laugh. "None of us knows how Kate does it, but she can find anything on the internet. Nothing is safe from her!"

"Oh. . .okay," said Kristi.

The girls heard a knock on the door.

"Who is it?" Bailey called out.

"It's Mary-Lynn. Is Kristi in there?"

The three girls in the room looked at each other, wide-eyed.

"Uh, girls, one of our suspects is here. We've gotta go!" Elizabeth said quietly.

"Okay. Work on that list, Kristi!" said Kate. The girls said goodbye, and Elizabeth shut her laptop and slid it under her bed. Bailey opened the door.

"Hi, Mary-Lynn. Come in," Bailey told her. "Yes, Kristi is here."

Kristi gave a half smile and waved at her roommate.

"There you are! I've been looking all over for you. What are y'all doing?" the girl asked.

"Oh, not much. What have you been up to?" Elizabeth asked. She had a feeling that with one question about herself, Mary-Lynn would talk for hours.

"I went to the costume design class, and ended up staying and talking to the teacher. She liked my skirt, and asked where I got it!" Mary-Lynn giggled, fingering the sequined fabric.

"Where did you get it?" Bailey asked.

"I made it!" Mary-Lynn exclaimed.

"You made that?" the other three girls said in unison.

"Yes. I make all my clothes. Have you seen the prices of those fancy costumes all the big names wear? One day, when I'm famous, I'll have my own designer. But until then, if I want to look the part, I have to make my own stuff." Then, as an afterthought, she said, "My mom is a seamstress, and I've been sewing since I was a little bitty girl."

Elizabeth stood up and examined Mary-Lynn's outfit, turning the girl as if she were a mannequin. "Mary-Lynn, I would have never guessed. You are very talented."

Mary-Lynn laughed. "Oh, anybody can sew, if they just take the time to learn. It's fun, though. I like taking a plain piece of fabric and turning it into something fabulous. I do hair and make-up. I'd be glad to give you all makeovers if you'd like. Especially you, Elizabeth! Why, if we put some lipstick and blush on you, and teased your hair out a little, I'll bet—"

"Uh, no thanks. I'm good with how I look. But maybe you should think about being a costume designer or a make-up artist instead of a performer," Elizabeth suggested.

"Bite your tongue!" said the girl. "And please don't tell anyone that I make my own clothes. Well, except. . .I did tell the costume design teacher. Still, I want the agents and talent scouts to think I've already made it big, which is why I'm trying to dress the part. No one needs to know I'm too poor to buy my own costumes."

"None of the participants here have 'made it big,' Mary-Lynn. That's why we're here," said Bailey.

"Well, not all of us have famous fathers to pave the way for us," Mary-Lynn flashed a look at Kristi.

The room fell silent. Kristi's face held a mixture of shock and anger.

Finally, she said, "What is that supposed to mean?"

Mary-Lynn looked uncomfortable. "Oh, nothing. I don't know why I said that."

"What do you know about my father?" Kristi pressed her.

"What makes you think I was talking about your father? I could have been talking about anyone," the girl said as she played with her skirt.

"Mary-Lynn, Kristi is the only one in this room with a famous father. If she didn't tell you about him, we'd like to know who did," Bailey demanded.

Mary-Lynn sighed and flopped down on the bed. "I looked him up on the internet, okay? When I received the letter telling me who my roommate was going to be, I wanted to know more about you, and I googled your name. I wanted to see if you were already famous. Sure enough, your road to fame has already been paved by your dear old dad!"

Kristi's face turned pale, and she ran from the room. Bailey went after her.

Elizabeth didn't know what to do. "Mary-Lynn, that was a horrible thing to say."

"Why? It's the truth, isn't it? As soon as I googled her name, all sorts of links came up. 'Kristi Conrad, daughter of legendary songwriter and guitarist, Joshua Conrad'."

"Mary-Lynn, did you take the time to follow any of those links and read about him?"

"I read enough. He's famous, and she's got it made. That's all I needed to know," said the girl.

"Then surely you read that Joshua Conrad was diagnosed with multiple sclerosis several years ago. He's lost his ability to play. He hasn't performed in three years," Elizabeth told her.

It was Mary-Lynn's turn to look shocked.

"I had no idea," she said. "Gosh. I feel terrible."

Elizabeth wanted to tell Mary-Lynn that she *should* feel terrible. She wondered if the girl was really sincere, but decided to give her the benefit of the doubt. Besides, she didn't want to alienate one of their prime suspects by making her angry.

"Perhaps you could apologize," Elizabeth suggested.

"Yeah, I suppose I should. I don't know what's wrong with me. I just want my big break so badly that I guess I don't think about how I must sound to other people. She'll probably never speak to me again," Mary-Lynn said.

"Oh, I don't know about that," Elizabeth told her. "Let's go find her."

Hesitantly, Mary-Lynn followed Elizabeth out the door, down the hall, and to her own room. Elizabeth knocked lightly on the door. "Kristi? Are you in there?"

Bailey cracked the door open and peered out.

"I think Mary-Lynn wants to apologize," Elizabeth told her.

Bailey stood back and held the door open. Inside, Kristi was sitting on her bed, pencil and notepad in hand, scrawling away at another song.

Mary-Lynn stepped hesitantly into the room. "Um, . . .Kristi?"

Kristi held her hand up the same way she had when Elizabeth and Bailey had first met her on the outdoor pathway.

Mary-Lynn stood awkwardly, not knowing what to do or say. After a moment, Kristi raised her head to look at her roommate, but said nothing.

"I. . .uh. . .I'm sorry. I didn't know your dad was sick. I just googled your name and saw all sorts of links pop up, and I got a little jealous. I don't know a soul in this business, and I just wished I had your connections. I'm sorry."

Kristi gave a tentative smile. "You know, just because a person is successful or famous doesn't mean they have it made," she said. "People are just people. We all have our problems, and getting famous doesn't make those problems go away."

Mary-Lynn sat down on her bed, her skirt flaring around her. "Since I was a little girl, I've wanted to be onstage. I've wanted to be noticed, to be the center of attention. I guess I just figured if I were famous, my life would be perfect."

Elizabeth sat down next to Mary-Lynn. "No one's life is perfect, Mary-Lynn. We all just have to learn to be content with where we are right now, don't you think?"

Mary-Lynn looked at her blankly. "All I know is I'm going to be famous someday," she said.

The other three fell silent. Finally, Elizabeth said, "I hope all your dreams come true. In the meantime, we need to get some sleep. Bailey, are you ready to go?"

"Yep," Bailey answered. "I guess we'll see you both in the morning."

Kristi cast them a wistful glance, and Elizabeth knew she wasn't thrilled that she had to stay there with Mary-Lynn.

"Good night," Elizabeth called as she shut the door.

As soon as they were in their own room, Bailey said, "Miss Priss down there is so guilty I can smell it."

"What makes you so sure?" Elizabeth asked.

"Isn't it obvious? She is so shallow. All she thinks about is being famous. All she talks about is wanting to be discovered. She almost reminds me of—"

Elizabeth giggled.

"What?" Bailey asked.

"Oh, nothing. It's just that I know someone else who really wants to be famous. . . . A really good friend of mine, as a matter of fact."

Bailey grew quiet. Finally she said, "I'm not like her, am I?"

Elizabeth smiled. "No, of course you're not. Not really."

Bailey flopped down on her bed. "Yes I am! I'm just like Miss Priss over there, wanting to be famous. Oh my word! This is terrible!"

Elizabeth couldn't help but laugh. "Well yes, you are, at times, preoccupied with becoming famous. But you're also kind and thoughtful and a good friend. I didn't mean to imply that you're like Mary-Lynn."

"I sure hope not. Because that girl is guilty."

Suddenly, there was a loud knocking at the door.

"Who could that be?" asked Elizabeth. "At this rate, we're never going to get any sleep!"

Flying Hairs

"Who is it?" Bailey called through the locked door.

"It's Kristi. Let me in," came a hushed voice.

Bailey unlocked the door, and Kristi pushed her way in, closing the door behind her. She was carrying her duffel bag.

"I can't sleep in the same room as the person who stole my dad's guitar," she said.

Elizabeth motioned for Kristi to sit on her bed. "We were just about to put our pajamas on. You're welcome to spend the night here," she offered.

"Thanks," replied Kristi. "I was hoping you'd say that."

Elizabeth was glad to share her room, but something was unsettling about this whole situation. She wasn't that fond of Mary-Lynn either, but she wasn't sure the girl was a thief. "You know, Kristi, I'm not sure Mary-Lynn stole your guitar."

Kristi's eyes widened. "You've got to be kidding! She has red hair. And she admitted she was jealous of me. She sees me as her competition."

"Maybe so. But how would she have known you had the guitar in your trunk?" Elizabeth asked her. "Mary-Lynn may be annoying and self-centered, but she seems pretty clueless."

"I don't know. . ." said Kristi.

"And why would Mary-Lynn have a VIP ticket to the Country Music Hall of Fame? She said herself she doesn't have any connections," Elizabeth said.

Bailey was looking down as she listened. Suddenly she began pulling something off her dark sweater. "Elizabeth, remind me next time I room with you not to wear dark colors."

"What do you mean?" asked Elizabeth, confused at the odd statement.

"I've got your long blond hairs all over my sweater," Bailey said, holding up a strand. "They must just fly through the room."

"Oh, sorry," Elizabeth laughed. "Yeah, my dad is always complaining about my hair getting on his shirts. I guess I just have too much of it!"

The girls chuckled at Bailey's comical face as she searched her sweater for more blond hair.

But then, Kristi and Elizabeth looked at each other. Were they thinking the same thing?

"Bailey," Elizabeth asked. "What if my hair were on your sweater, and you brushed against someone else. Do you suppose my hair could end up on someone else's sweater? Someone I've never even had contact with?"

"I guess so. Why do you—" Bailey stopped midsentence. "Oh! I get it! The thief may not have had red hair at all. The thief might have just come in contact with a redhead. Then, when the guitar case was open, the hair could have fallen into the case!"

The three girls let the thought soak in.

Finally, Kristi stood. "You're right. Mary-Lynn may not be guilty at all. It's unfair of us to decide she's guilty when we don't have real proof." She grabbed her duffel bag. "I guess I should go back to my room."

Bailey let out a frustrated sigh. "Well, this theory puts us back to square one. If we aren't sure the villain has red hair, where do we start?"

"We start with this," Kristi said, digging through her bag and holding out a list. "These are the names of the people I contacted about buying Dad's guitar."

•—•—•

Early the next morning, Bailey read off the names and phone numbers of the people on the list as Elizabeth typed them into an email. A dozen or so names were on the list, so it would be plenty to keep the Camp Club Girls busy with research. After the last name was typed in, Elizabeth pressed SEND and leaned back to look at Bailey.

"How soon do you think we'll hear something?" asked Bailey.

"Knowing Kate, probably within the next few minutes. Unless she's still asleep."

"Tell me more about this songwriting teacher. Was there anything suspicious about him?" asked Bailey.

Elizabeth thought about the young teacher with the ball cap. "It's hard to say. He did know exactly who Kristi's dad was, and he seemed to kind of study her. But that doesn't mean he's a thief."

"It doesn't mean he's *not* a thief either," said Bailey. "Right now, everyone is a suspect. I say we tail the guy, see what he's up to."

"That's not a bad idea," said Elizabeth. "I want to take another of his classes, anyway. What do you say we see what Kristi is up to, and then get some breakfast?"

"Sounds good," said Bailey. She ran a brush through her hair, and then tossed the brush on the counter. "Let's go."

Kristi and Mary-Lynn were just locking their door behind them when Bailey and Elizabeth stepped into the hallway.

"Perfect timing!" Mary-Lynn said.

"How did you sleep?" Elizabeth asked, looking at Kristi.

Kristi looked at Mary-Lynn, who laughed. "We didn't sleep much at all. After Kristi came back from your room, we talked until after midnight!"

Kristi smiled. "Yeah. She's a great roommate!"

Elizabeth was thrilled to see a friendship developing between the two older girls. Bailey, on the other hand, seemed suspicious.

"What did you talk about?" Bailey asked.

"Oh, everything under the sun. And guess what? Mary-Lynn's uncle is a detective. She said she's learned a few tips from him over the years," Kristi told them.

Mary-Lynn laughed. "Oh, I don't know anything that can help you catch your thief. But if I'm ever kidnapped, I think I'll be able to escape. He taught me a few self-defense moves."

Elizabeth laughed. "Well, hopefully we won't need that information!"

"I don't know," said Bailey. "It's always good to know how to protect yourself! Show us some moves, Mary-Lynn."

And so, on the way to breakfast, Mary-Lynn moved herself off the suspect list and onto the friend list. She showed them a few kicks and jabs, but also told them the importance of drawing attention to yourself.

"It doesn't matter if they tell you to keep quiet. You yell, kick, and scream. In a restaurant, write a note on a napkin and give to the waitress. In a bathroom, leave a message scratched onto the wall. If you're in a car, bang on the window. And if you're ever locked in a car trunk, kick out the taillights and stick your hand through, so the driver behind you will see you."

"Wow, Mary-Lynn! Your uncle taught you some great stuff. But as I said, hopefully we'll never have to use that information," said Elizabeth.

"Better to know it and not need it than the other way around," said

Kristi, and the others agreed.

The girls arrived at a busy dining hall. After filling their trays, they scanned the room for a place to sit. They saw an empty table near the far corner, next to a window, and they headed that way.

Elizabeth nodded at her teacher, Robert, who sat alone in the corner. This time, he wasn't wearing his hat. After saying a prayer, Bailey kicked Elizabeth under the table.

"Is that your teacher?" she whispered.

Kristi and Elizabeth nodded.

"He doesn't look very old," Bailey continued. "I would have thought he was one of the students here," she said.

"He's a songwriter for one of the big record companies," Elizabeth said.

"Yeah," Kristi said. "I'll bet he doesn't get paid much either. My dad started as a staff songwriter, and he said he barely made enough money to live on."

"That's strange. I would think a famous songwriter would make tons of money," Bailey remarked, looking over her shoulder at the young man. He seemed absorbed in the newspaper that was lying across the table, next to his plate.

Kristi laughed. "If you write a hit song, then yeah, you'd make some good money. But do you have any idea how many people come to Nashville to record? And they all want original songs. And 99 percent of them never achieve any real success. Still, the record companies like to keep a steady supply of original songs for new artists, in hopes one of them will be a hit."

"Well, with his hair color, he's definitely a suspect," whispered Bailey.

"Hey!" said Mary-Lynn defensively. "Just because a person has red hair doesn't make him or her a thief!"

Robert shifted in his chair, but didn't look up.

"Shhhhh!" said Bailey, not sure how much to say to Mary-Lynn.

"It's okay," said Kristi. "I told her everything. She rode to the conference center on the airport shuttle and didn't even arrive until after the... incident. She has an alibi."

"A what?" asked Mary-Lynn. "I don't have anything of the sort!"

"An alibi is simply proof that you couldn't have committed a crime. You weren't even here yet when Kristi's guitar was stolen, and you have witnesses—the other people on the shuttle. That's your alibi," whispered Elizabeth.

"Oh," said Mary-Lynn, settling back in her seat. "In that case, then yes. I have an alibi."

Suddenly, they heard a phone ring, and Robert reached into his pocket. Flipping open the tiny device, he said, "Yeah?"

The girls concentrated on their food, trying to listen over the crowd to his conversation.

"Yeah. . .yeah. . .yeah," he said.

Elizabeth watched him out of the corner of her eye, and noticed him glance at their table. Then he said, "I can't talk here. Too crowded. I'll have to call you back." He clicked the phone shut, picked up his tray, and walked past them, leaving his newspaper on the table.

When he was out of earshot, Bailey said, "Whoa. That was strange. Why couldn't he talk in front of us?"

"Probably because it's crowded and noisy, and he couldn't hear," Kristi said.

"Or maybe because he didn't want us to hear what he had to say," Bailey retorted. "Let's follow him." She pushed back her chair and began loading her tray.

"No, wait. We can't all go. That would be too obvious," said Elizabeth. "I'll tell you what. Kate's supposed to call in a few minutes and let us know if she got the list. I'll go. It won't look as suspicious if it's just one of us, and I'm talking on the phone."

Hesitantly, Bailey sat back in her chair. "Okay. But tell us every detail."

Elizabeth started to load her tray, but Kristi said, "We'll take care of that. You go."

Nodding, Elizabeth followed Robert, who was already leaving the dining hall. She walked quickly, moving around tables and chairs. But when she pushed open the double doors, she didn't see Robert.

She scanned the area. She saw a couple of people talking on a bench and a teenage girl leaning against a tree, studying some sheet music.

But no Robert. Where had he disappeared to so quickly?

Then she thought she heard his voice coming from around the corner of the building. She couldn't make out the words, so she followed the sound, staying close to the brick wall. As she approached the corner, she leaned flat against the wall and listened.

"Yeah, the Conrad girl is here. And she's in my class. Can you believe that?"

Silence.

"Yeah, the whole staff is talking about that stolen guitar."

Silence.

"Yeah. Trust me. I know how much it's worth."

More silence.

"Okay. . .okay. I'll do what I can."

The sudden click of the cell phone caught Elizabeth off guard, and Robert came barreling around the corner, nearly bumping into her.

"Oh, excuse me," Elizabeth said. "I'm so sorry, Mr. . . .uh. . .Mr. . . . Robert."

"You should be careful, lurking around corners like that. Someone might think you were eavesdropping," the young man told her.

"Oh, no sir! I. . .um. . .I just couldn't hear very well in the dining hall, and I'm expecting a phone call. See?" She held up her cell phone. As if on cue, it started to ring.

Elizabeth flipped it open and answered, "Hello?"

Robert glared at her and walked away.

"Hi. It's Kate. I got the list this morning, and I'm working on it. Tell Kristi thanks for getting it to me so fast."

"Kate! Perfect timing. You'll never believe what just happened," Elizabeth told her.

"Really? Tell me," Kate said.

Elizabeth decided to hold off the conversation until she was in her room. No sense taking a chance on someone overhearing her.

"I–I'll have to tell you later. Can't talk now. But I'm glad you got the list. I need you to add someone to it, by the way. A fellow named—" she looked around, making sure no one could hear. Then she whispered, "Robert Kranfield."

"Say that again. I couldn't hear you," Kate told her.

In a slightly louder whisper, she said, "Robert Kranfield. K-r-a-n-f-i-e-l-d."

"Okay, got it," Kate replied. "Why are we adding him? Oh, never mind. You already said you can't talk. I'll see what I can find. When can we have another group call?"

Elizabeth dug in her pocket and pulled out the conference schedule. "How about one thirty this afternoon? We have a break after lunch. Can you get in touch with the others?"

"You bet. Talk to you then," Kate said, and the two girls hung up.

Bailey, Kristi, and Mary-Lynn were just exiting the building when Elizabeth approached the doors.

"So? What happened? Did you hear anything?" Bailey asked.

Glancing at her watch, Elizabeth told them, "Let's talk while we're walking. We don't want to be late to our classes."

"There's nothing suspicious about a group of girls being late to anything," Mary-Lynn said with a laugh.

"Maybe under normal circumstances," said Elizabeth. "But I don't want to give Mr. Robert Kranfield any reason to suspect a thing." She eyed Mary-Lynn, still not sure if she should trust the girl completely. She seemed to have loose lips.

One of the agents walked by, and Mary-Lynn's attention was drawn away from the conversation. "Oh, there is Roxanne Hargrove! I want to meet her. I'll catch you all later!" And the girl was gone.

Elizabeth chuckled. Mary-Lynn seemed harmless. And shallow. But she was sweet, in her own way.

"Well, what are you waiting for? Tell us what's going on!" Bailey insisted.

Elizabeth looked at Kristi. "I was able to hear part of his phone conversation," she said in a low voice. "And your name came up."

Kristi frowned. "Go on," she said.

"He was talking about your guitar and how much it is worth."

The girls walked in silence for a moment, trying to process the information.

Finally, Bailey said, "Well, it's no big secret her guitar was stolen. The security people probably told the conference staff what happened, don't you think?"

"Probably so. But why would Robert talk about it? And who was he talking to?" Elizabeth asked.

"Maybe we should add his name to the research list," Bailey said.

"Done. I already spoke with Kate," Elizabeth replied.

Kristi remained quiet. Finally, she said, "Now I feel weird about going to his class. What if he stole my guitar?"

Elizabeth and Bailey looked at each other, then at Kristi. "No matter what happens, act normal. Don't act strange around him. Don't give him any reason to believe he is a suspect. That could ruin the whole investigation," Bailey told her.

Kristi let out a heavy sigh. "I'm a musician, not an actress. But I'll do my best."

The girls entered the building where the classes were held. "I'm on the third floor. Meet me right here as soon as class is over," Bailey told the other two, and she was off.

"Do you think you can do this?" Elizabeth asked Kristi.

Kristi took a deep breath. "I don't really have a choice, do I? If I don't show up for class, Robert will wonder why. I'll just—I'll just keep my eyes on my notepad, and take notes like crazy."

Elizabeth smiled. "Just write a song like you always do, and he won't suspect a thing."

Elizabeth nearly walked past the door to their classroom, and had to backtrack when Kristi stopped.

"Where were you going?" Kristi asked her.

"Nowhere," Elizabeth said with a laugh. "All these doors look alike to me, and I'm always getting lost or going in the wrong doors." They entered and found seats. A few other students were waiting, but there was no sign of Robert.

After a few more students were seated, a well-dressed young woman walked to the front of the room.

"Hi. I'm Lori. Robert will be a few minutes late. I'm a friend of his, and he asked me to get you started."

The Plan

Kristi threw Elizabeth a confused glance. She pulled out her notepad and began scrawling as the woman spoke of chord progressions.

Elizabeth unfolded her conference brochure and scanned the faculty pictures. This woman wasn't there.

"What do you think this means?" Kristi wrote on her notepad.

Elizabeth shrugged her shoulders.

"Where could he be?" Kristi wrote again.

Again Elizabeth shrugged. She had no idea.

Kristi thought a moment and then wrote, *"What should we do?"*

Finally, Elizabeth took out her own notepad and pencil, keeping her eyes on the teacher as if she were fascinated by the woman's words. *"I guess we just stay here and try to act normal. We'll investigate later. At least we'll know how late he is."*

Kristi nodded, and they both tried to concentrate on Lori's words. The woman demonstrated several chord progressions for them, and explained how each one reflected a different mood. But Elizabeth was distracted by her long, bloodred fingernails, which clicked as she played the keyboard.

If she were a serious keyboard player, she'd cut her nails, Elizabeth thought.

After nearly twenty minutes, the classroom door opened, and Robert entered. Lori acknowledged him, and he took over the lecture.

"Thank you, Lori," he told the woman as she left the room. He slipped her a small piece of paper as she passed him.

"I see you were discussing chord progressions. Do we have any keyboard players in the room?" he asked.

He's acting like nothing has happened! But I'm not fooled. I want to know why he was talking about Kristi's guitar. Who was he talking to? Elizabeth tried not to glare at the man as she lifted her hand, along with a few others who played the keyboard.

"Great. There are several of you. How about you—Elizabeth, isn't it? Would you like to come up and play some chord progressions for us?"

The nerve of that man! Elizabeth thought. Still, she painted on a tentative smile and nodded. "Certainly, Mr. Kranfield."

"Please, call me Robert," he said as Elizabeth took her seat at the bench. He began calling out chord progressions to her, as if to test her skill. Fortunately, chords were easy for her, and she played with ease.

"Very nice," he said, but she thought she heard a slight edge in his voice. She heard little of what he said during the remainder of the class, and when he dismissed them, she breathed a sigh of relief.

"That was strange," whispered Kristi as they headed for the classroom door. As they exited, they heard a phone ring, and looked back to see Robert answer his cell. Elizabeth led Kristi into the hall, where they waited while the other students exited. Then, pressing her back against the wall, she leaned toward the open door, straining to hear Robert's words.

"Yeah. . .yeah, I got it. . . . No, can't talk now. Too many people around. Meet me in my classroom in one hour. No, there's not another class in here until late this afternoon, so we should be safe. . . . Okay, see you then."

The girls heard Robert click his phone shut, and they hurried toward the exit. When they were outside the building, Kristi said, "This is getting too weird. Surely you don't really think he's the one, do you? He's on staff here, at a music conference for a bunch of kids. They must have thought he was trustworthy."

Elizabeth shook her head. "You never know. If he doesn't have a previous record of theft, the conference directors probably wouldn't suspect him of anything. He's a songwriter. They were probably just looking to find qualified musicians to fill their teaching needs."

"And what about this Lori person? Do you think she's in on it?"

Elizabeth shrugged. "No telling. I did see Robert slip her a paper as she was leaving."

"Yeah, I saw that too."

In the middle of their conversation, Bailey arrived. "You guys are really missing out. My choreography class is so much fun! Would you like me to show you what—" she stopped when she saw the expression on Kristi's face. "What did I miss? Tell me everything."

"Robert was late to class. The woman who covered for him isn't listed on staff here. Then, after class, we overheard another of his phone conversations. He didn't say much, but he's meeting someone in his classroom in an hour," Elizabeth filled her in.

"Wow. We've got to figure out a way to listen in on that conversation," said Bailey.

"What do you think we should do?" asked Kristi. "Sneak in and hide?"

"There really aren't any hiding places in that room. The desks are too small, and the podium at the front is too skinny. Hiding is out of the question," said Elizabeth.

"I think there might have been a large desk in the back corner. . ." said Kristi. "But I'm not sure."

"What about a window?" asked Bailey. "We could go in ahead of time and open a window, and then we could stand outside and listen."

"Good idea, if the classroom were on the ground floor," said Kristi, looking at the building behind them. "I doubt we'll be able to hear a conversation three stories up, though."

The girls studied the building, trying to figure out a solution.

"Bales, remember at camp when we left the cell phone in Mr. Anzer's office?" asked Elizabeth.

"Oh yeah! Kate called your cell phone and then planted her cell phone under Mr. Anzer's desk. We could hear every word!" Bailey exclaimed.

Kristi looked at them, wide-eyed. "That's pretty sneaky. Did it work?"

Elizabeth and Bailey looked at each other.

"It worked perfectly," said Elizabeth. "Unfortunately, we ended up hearing the wrong conversation."

"Beth, I think it will work for us. After all, you have a class in there, so if Robert happens to find your phone, you can just say you left it," Bailey said.

Elizabeth pulled out her cell phone. "Bailey, where is your phone?" she asked.

"I left it in the room, but I can go back and get it," Bailey answered.

"No, I have my phone. Here, Elizabeth, let me see yours. I'll program my number into it," Kristi said.

About that time, Robert exited the building. "Shouldn't you ladies be getting to your next classes or something?" he asked.

Elizabeth glanced at her watch. *We've got fifteen more minutes. What's his hurry? Is he trying to get rid of us?*

"Uh, yes. . .sir. We're on our way," said Kristi.

The man watched them until they disappeared around the curve.

"Whoa. What was that about?" asked Bailey. "Why was he in such a hurry for us to leave?"

"I don't know," said Elizabeth. "But we're going to find out. Bailey, what is your next class?"

"I was thinking of attending the stage performance class. They're supposed to teach us how to play to a crowd," she said.

Elizabeth laughed. "I don't think you need much help there, Bailey. Where is that class?"

"It's in the main conference room, where we had the welcome last night. That room has the biggest stage."

"Do you think you can sneak out of it, maybe go to the bathroom or something, at ten forty-five?" Elizabeth asked.

"Sure. I think we're supposed to take turns on the stage, so I'll see if I can go first. Then I'll probably be done by ten forty-five," Bailey said.

"Okay, you take Kristi's phone since we don't have time to go back to the room. Kristi, where are you headed?"

Kristi looked at her schedule. "Let's see. . . . I think I'll go to the keyboarding class. I'm great on the guitar, but my piano skills lack a bit."

Elizabeth nodded. "I know what you mean. Only I'm the opposite. I can play the keyboard, but my guitar skills need work. But can you slip out at around. . .ten thirtyish?"

"Sure. What do you need me to do?" Kristi asked.

"I need you to meet me right here," Elizabeth said.

•—•—•

"Who would like to perform first?" the instructor, Mrs. Crenshaw, asked. Bailey was the first to lift her hand.

"You there," the woman called on her. "What is your name?"

Bailey stood and smiled her million-dollar smile. "My name is Bailey Chang," she said.

"Well Bailey, why don't you come on up here. Did you bring a song to perform for us today?"

"You bet," said Bailey, pulling the accompaniment CD from her backpack. She handed it to Mrs. Crenshaw and walked onto the stage with confidence.

"Hold on," Mrs. Crenshaw told her. "That was a pretty good entrance, but the audience wasn't ready for you yet. I'm going to teach you how to enter like a rock star! You want to wait until the audience is leaning forward, looking for you. Then, you make a grand entrance at the last possible second! Why don't you come back down here and try that again."

Bailey did as she was told, waiting while her teacher placed the CD in the player. "Bailey, I want you to wait until after the music has started. The audience will hear the music, but they will see an empty stage. They'll start looking for you, and that's when you need to begin your entrance. You should arrive at the microphone just as you are to begin singing."

The music began, and Bailey walked onto the stage. She arrived at the microphone a good four measures before she started singing.

Mrs. Crenshaw stopped the CD. "That was better, Bailey. But you were still too early. Figure out how much time it will take you to get to the microphone, and give yourself just that much time. You want to arrive center stage just as you open your mouth to sing."

And so Bailey started again, and began the performance four different times before she made it to the end of the song. She was so caught up in the thrill of it, she forgot to keep an eye on her watch.

•—•—•

Elizabeth slipped out of her seat on the back row of her guitar class and out the door. If anyone asked, she'd say she needed to use the ladies' room. It was the truth.

Kristi was waiting for her in front of the building. "Are you ready to do this?" she asked.

"I think so," Elizabeth answered. "I need you to stay here and stand guard. If Robert shows up, stall him until I get back. The last thing I need is for him to catch me planting the phone!"

"How do you know he's not already in there?" Kristi asked.

Elizabeth pulled out her conference brochure. "I'm pretty sure this says. . ." she scanned the paper. "Here it is. Robert Kranfield is one of the panelists in the Question and Answer Session. That's in the other building. Since he told the person to meet him here in an hour, I'm guessing he'll slip out around eleven o'clock."

Kristi looked unsure.

"Look, if he shows up, just act like you have a question about songwriting. I'll probably be back long before he shows up, anyway," Elizabeth reassured her.

Biting her bottom lip, Kristi sat on a nearby bench. "I'll do my best."

Elizabeth went into the building and found the elevator, then punched the button for the fourth floor. *Or was it the third floor? No, I'm pretty sure it was the fourth.*

She got off the elevator and looked to her right, then to her left. *Which way was the classroom? Man! Why did I have to inherit my mother's sense of direction? . . . I think it's this way.*

Elizabeth turned to the left. She remembered there was a sign on the door—something about songwriting? She walked to the end of the hall, checking every door. No songwriting classes. She turned and walked to the opposite end, but she still couldn't find the room. Why did they all have to look alike? Why couldn't they paint each of the doors a different color or something? She could remember colors, just not numbers.

She walked back to the center of the hall, in front of the elevator, and just stood looking from her right to her left. *I can't find it. What do I do now?*

Then she remembered. Maybe it was on the third floor after all. She got back into the elevator and went down one floor. Stepping into the hall, she heard the elevator doors close behind her. Looking from side to side, she thought, *It looks exactly the same as the fourth floor. I'll never find it.*

She was still standing there, trying to decide which way to go first, when the elevator doors opened behind her again and someone nearly crashed into her. It was Lori!

"Oh! I'm sorry. I didn't see you there. You're. . ." the woman looked at Elizabeth's name tag, "Elizabeth. I remember you from this morning. Aren't you supposed to be in class?"

"Uh, yes. But I, uh. . .was just looking for the bathroom," Elizabeth told her.

"Oh, I can help you. It's this way," Lori eyed her suspiciously, and then led her down the hallway to the left.

On the way, Elizabeth noticed the sign she was looking for. *Bingo!* she thought. "Thanks," she called, and entered the door. She hovered just inside the ladies' room, holding the door open a crack, watching where Lori was headed.

Another woman, a faculty member, was headed toward her. She

stopped to talk to Lori, of all places, right in front of the door to the songwriting classroom.

They talked.

And talked.

•—•—•

Kristi passed the minutes by looking over an old copy of *Musician's Digest* she kept in her backpack. She was in the middle of an article about her dad—she loved reading it over and over—when she heard someone approach. It was Robert Kranfield.

The young man nearly walked right past her into the building before she found her voice. "Uh. . .excuse me," she called.

He kept walking. Was he ignoring her?

"Uh, Mr. Kranfield?" she called, louder this time. Finally, as he was opening the glass door, she called, "Robert!"

The man paused, turned, and looked at her.

"Did you need something?" he asked. She couldn't quite read the expression in his eyes.

Leaving her things on the bench, she approached him, talking as she walked. "I. . .uh. . .yes, sir. I had some questions about. . .um. . .chord progressions."

He looked her square in the eyes, as if in disbelief. "*You* have a question about chord progressions?"

"Yes, sir," she nodded.

Robert laughed. "Well now, that *is* a surprise. I would think that *you* of all people. . ." He stopped midsentence. "I'm busy now. It'll have to wait," and he turned to go.

"Oh no!" She reached out, desperate to stop him. "This is very important!" She accidentally bumped his arm, causing him to drop his briefcase. Sheet music and staff paper scattered everywhere, along with magazines, article clippings, photographs, and a key.

"Oh, I'm so sorry!" Kristi knelt to gather his things for him.

The man tried to stop her, but it was too late. Kristi picked up an article about her dad. And another. And on the floor to her left was a picture of him. And the sheet music? Half of it was written by her dad. She wasn't sure what to think.

•—•—•

Elizabeth watched through the crack in the door as the two women finished talking. The stranger turned and went in the opposite direction.

Lori dug through her purse, and then went back to the elevator. She must have forgotten something. The coast clear, Elizabeth darted down the hall to the songwriting classroom. So far, so good.

Inside, she looked around for a good hiding place for her phone. Shoved in a back corner was a large teacher's desk. Kristi had been right. The rest of the room was pretty bare bones, with chairs and a podium. No good hiding places, even for a small phone. She'd put it under a corner of the desk.

Leaning against the desk, she dialed Kristi's number. Finally, the plan was underway. The phone rang. . .and rang. *Why isn't Bailey answering?*

•—•—•

Bailey had finally gotten to perform her song all the way through, and the room rang with applause. She took a grand bow, and Mrs. Crenshaw beamed.

"Excellent performance, Bailey! You are a natural. Now, who would like to be next?"

A couple of students lifted their hands, and as the noise in the room faded, sounds of a cell phone rose. Mrs. Crenshaw looked annoyed. "Students, please remember to turn your phones off before class."

The ringing continued.

"Would someone please answer that?" the woman directed. No one moved.

The ringing continued.

Bailey descended the stage, remembering for the first time that she was supposed to listen for her cell phone. But that ring wasn't her cell phone. Hers played "Oh, When the Saints Go Marching In," and this ring was just a standard cell phone ring.

Then she remembered. She didn't have *her* phone. She was supposed to be listening for Kristi's phone!`

Confession!

Kristi looked up at Robert, speechless. He snatched the papers out of her hands and jammed them back in his briefcase, then began stuffing the other things on the floor in there as well.

"I don't have time for this," he muttered, visibly shaken.

"Why. . ." she whispered.

He reached around her to retrieve an autographed picture of Joshua Conrad, but Kristi beat him to it. She stepped on the corner of the picture, pinning it to the ground.

"Watch out!" he said. "That picture is worth some money. You're going to damage it!"

"That picture is of my dad," she said. "But of course, you know that already."

Robert clenched his jaw and spoke through gritted teeth.

"Yeah, I know who you are. So I'm a fan of your father's. Big deal. Now give me the picture."

Slowly, Kristi moved her foot, and Robert bent and picked up the photograph. Dusting it off, he placed it in a manila folder and slid it into a side pocket of his case. Then, his features softened a bit.

"Look, I'm sorry. I must seem like a real fanatic. Truth is, I didn't know how it would look if one of my students knew how crazy I was about her dad. He's the best. I've followed his career for years, and I was devastated when. . .well, you know."

Kristi was surprised and touched by his sudden confession.

"I know. A lot of people were devastated. And you don't have to worry that I'll think you're strange. I know how great my dad is. I love it when I meet people who appreciate his talent."

Robert looked at her with. . .what was that look? She couldn't quite read him.

Finally, he said, "Did you really have a question about chord progressions?"

Kristi had forgotten all about her reason for stopping him! "Uh. . . yes. But now I can't remember what it was."

Robert chuckled. "Well, when you remember it, let me know. I'll be glad to help you any way I can."

Kristi nodded, and the man turned and walked through the door. She sure hoped Elizabeth was ready for him.

•—•—•

Elizabeth heard voices in the hall. *Where is Bailey? Why isn't she answering?*

The voices were coming closer. *Oh no! Is that Robert? And. . .Lori!*

She snapped the phone shut and scooted into the narrow space behind the desk. Sucking her stomach in, she squeezed down and folded her long legs into the cubby beneath. *Good thing this desk has a solid front.* She heard the door open, and tried not to breathe. *Please God. Don't let them catch me. How in the world do I end up in these messes?*

The door clicked, and footsteps crossed the room.

"Finally. We can talk," Robert Kranfield said.

"What took you so long?" Lori asked. "I was getting worried."

"You wouldn't believe it. That Conrad girl stopped me on the way into the building. I ended up dropping my briefcase, and. . .well, let's just say it was awkward."

Lori chuckled. "So now she knows you're a fan of her father's."

"To say the least. She saw all the articles, the autographed picture, everything."

"Well. . .not *everything,*" Lori said.

Silence. Elizabeth could hear her heart pounding in her chest, and felt certain they could hear it too.

Finally, Robert said, "Yeah, not everything. But now she has every reason to suspect me."

"Don't be silly," said Lori. "Just because you admire her father doesn't mean you're a thief."

"Oh, doesn't it?" Robert asked, and Elizabeth detected sarcasm in his voice.

Lori gave a heavy sigh. "Look. You did what you felt you had to do. If that little brat doesn't appreciate her own father's greatness. If she's just going to sell his guitar off to the highest bidder, then why shouldn't we have it? We'll obviously appreciate it more than she does."

Elizabeth fought to keep from gasping. Did she just hear what she thought she heard?

"I don't know," said Robert. "I'm starting to have second thoughts. Maybe I should just return the guitar. I could slip it back into her trunk tonight. . ."

"You've got to be kidding!" Lori's sweet voice turned harsh. "There's no way I'm going to let you give it back! They can still trace it to you, you know. Just because you return it doesn't make you any less guilty of stealing it."

"Why do you care?" Robert said loudly. "I thought you just wanted to hang it on the wall with your collection. The only reason I let you talk me into this is because you promised to let me play it whenever I wanted. It doesn't mean anything to you. This whole thing was your idea, and I'm the one who's going to get caught!"

She heard someone stand and take a few steps, and knew by the clicking of heels on the tile that it was Lori. "Calm down," she said. "Nobody's going to get caught, and nobody's going to return anything. Of course, if you're not sure you want to keep the guitar, we could always sell it. That thing is worth a fortune, you know."

Lori heard the sound of a chair scraping on the floor, then Robert's heavy footsteps.

"Don't be ridiculous. I knew I shouldn't have trusted you. You have no appreciation for the value of that guitar. It is worth more than just the money. Some of the most beautiful music of our time—of any time—was written and played on that guitar. It needs to be appreciated for its artistic value, not its monetary value."

"If you don't sell it, it will haunt you for the rest of your life. You'll always be wondering when they're going to find you out."

"Exactly. This whole thing was a bad idea. That's why I think we should return it. I think she already suspects me, anyway. She and that nosy little friend of hers."

The room grew quiet. Elizabeth drew in her breath and bit her knuckles. *Please, God, don't let them find me.*

"What little friend?" asked Lori in a low voice.

"Tall, skinny, pretty blond girl. I think her name is. . .Elizabeth."

Oh God, what will I say to them if they find me? Please get me out of this mess!

"She was up here," Lori said.

"Who was up here? Elizabeth? Why would she be up here—there aren't any classes scheduled on this floor until after lunch," Robert told her.

"I don't know why she was here. She said she was looking for the bathroom, and I showed her where it was. That's the last I saw of her."

Elizabeth heard footsteps, then the door opening. "There's no one in the hallway. You check the bathroom, and I'll look around the other classrooms. I've already caught the little snoop eavesdropping on me once today."

Snoop? Well, at least I'm not a thief, mister.

It sounded like they left the room. Then, things grew quiet. Elizabeth knew she was better off staying where she was. If she tried to leave now, they'd surely catch her. *Please help me out of here, Lord!*

She heard voices outside the door. "There's no one in the bathroom," said Lori.

"She's probably already gone. Let's get out of here. We'll talk about this more later."

Elizabeth heard their retreating footsteps. Then she faintly heard the ding of the elevator doors opening. After what seemed to be a sufficient amount of time, she scooted the desk forward and squeezed out of her hiding place. She had to find Kristi and Bailey.

•—•—•

Out of breath, Bailey slowed down when she saw Kristi outside the building. She had run all the way from the main building. It wasn't far, but the combination of speed and panic caused her heart to thump loudly.

"Where is she? Where's Elizabeth?" she asked between breaths.

"I don't know. She never came out."

"What! What do you mean, she never came out?"

"She went in about twenty minutes ago, and she—" Kristi stopped talking when Lori and Robert pushed open the door to the building. The two adults slowed down when they saw the girls, but said nothing. Kristi and Bailey remained quiet until the other two were out of sight.

"Did you get the phone call? Did you hear what they said?" asked Kristi.

"No! I forgot that I was listening for your ringtone instead of mine. I was on stage performing. By the time I realized what was happening and got to the phone, it stopped ringing. I didn't want to call the number back and risk Elizabeth getting caught."

"Yeah, that wouldn't have been good to have her cell phone ringing if she was trying to hide. Let's go look for her," said Kristi.

They entered the building and took the elevator to the third floor, which seemed deserted. In urgent whispers, they began calling, "Elizabeth! Elizabeth, where are you?"

Kristi led them to their classroom. "Look! This desk was flat against the wall. Now it's at an angle—she must have been hiding here."

Bailey's eyes grew wide. "Elizabeth!" she called out, this time in a loud voice. "Elizabeth, are you here?"

They looked under the desk, and when they were convinced their friend was nowhere in the room, they went back into the hall.

"Elizabeth!" they called over and over.

A door behind them opened. "I'm right here," came a familiar voice.

"Elizabeth," both girls cried, running toward their friend. "What happened? Where were you?"

Elizabeth laughed. "Just now, I was in the bathroom. But before that, I was in here. Hiding." She looked at Bailey, then at Kristi. "You're never going to believe what I heard."

"Tell us!" Bailey insisted.

Looking around, Elizabeth said, "Not here. You never know who might be listening. Let's go back to the room."

•—•—•

By the time Elizabeth reported what she'd heard, it was lunchtime. The girls tried calling the police, but they only got put on hold. Then, when they finally spoke to a real person, that person seemed unsympathetic.

"You want to give a follow-up report?" asked the man who seemed to have a mouthful of something.

"Yes. We know who stole the guitar."

"How old are you?" asked the man.

"I'm fourteen."

"Where are your parents?"

"In another state. Look, could I please just give the report?"

"Miss, are you a runaway?"

"No, sir! I'm at a music camp, and I just want to give a follow-up report about my friend's stolen guitar."

Kristi held out her hand. "Let me try," she whispered.

Elizabeth handed her the phone.

"Hello," Kristi said. "I'm the person whose guitar was stolen."

"And how old are you?"

"I'm seventeen."

"Look, the penalty for playing pranks on police officers is pretty stiff. I suggest you girls run along and find something constructive to do with your time."

"But sir—"

"We've got real crimes to solve here. Kidnappings and murders and such. If you have a petty theft report, you'll have to come down to the station. Or you can do it online."

"It's not petty theft! That guitar is worth—"

Kristi held the phone out and looked at it. "I don't believe it. He hung up on me!"

"Hmmmm. . .must have been his lunchtime." Bailey looked at her watch. "I think we should just skip lunch. We need to find out where Robert is staying, and snoop around his room."

Elizabeth wrinkled her brow. "I'm not sure that's a good idea, Bales. If Robert and Lori suspect us, they'll be watching for us to do something out of the ordinary. I think we need to just slow down a bit. We'll go to lunch, and then come back here for our conference call. Kate said she'd call at one o'clock, and she was going to get in touch with the others."

"I'm with Bailey. I want to get to the bottom of this. I can't believe that creep admitted to stealing my dad's guitar! But you're right, Elizabeth. We don't want to do anything to jeopardize our investigation," said Kristi.

Elizabeth placed a hand Kristi's shoulder. "Let's all take a few deep breaths and calm down. My grandpa always reminds me that God knew about our troubles long before we did. And He already knows the way out of them."

Just then, there was a knock at the door. Standing on her tiptoes, Elizabeth peered out the peephole. It was Mary-Lynn. She opened the door.

Mary-Lynn rushed into the room and announced, "I just had the best morning! I met two different agents, and they each spent more than five minutes talking to me! One of them even gave me his card!"

"Wow, Mary-Lynn! That's great," the other three congratulated her.

"So, what have you all been up to?"

The three girls looked at each other, then back at the redhead.

"Oh, nothing much," they told her.

•—•—•

Bailey picked at her food and listened to Mary-Lynn chatter about her connections with various talent agents, and how she had an appointment with another one right after lunch.

Elizabeth knew what she was thinking without asking. *Bailey wants to be discovered too. But she's gotten too involved in finding this guitar to pay much attention to her reason for coming to the conference.*

"I'll be right back," Elizabeth said abruptly. She scooted her chair back, stood tall, and marched right over to Rick Forrest's table. The man smiled when he saw her.

"Why Elizabeth! Hello. Are you having a nice time?"

"Yes, sir," she answered, smiling at the others at the table. One by one, he introduced Elizabeth to them.

"What can I do for you?" he asked.

She squatted down next to him and said, "I hate to ask you this, Mr. Forrest, but my friend Bailey has been busy. . .helping a friend, and she hasn't gotten to meet with any of the agents. Do you know if any of them still have appointments available?"

Mr. Forrest pushed back his chair. "Helping a friend, huh? Well, that shows she has character. I was just about to leave anyway. Why don't you introduce me to her."

Elizabeth stood with him. "Really? Oh, she'll be thrilled. Thank you so much."

She led the way through the maze of tables to her friend and tried to ignore Mary-Lynn's jaw, which was hanging open.

"Everyone, I'd like you to meet Mr. Rick Forrest. He sat next to me on the plane. Mr. Forrest, this is Bailey, Kristi, and Mary-Lynn."

Kristi and Bailey offered short greetings, but Mary-Lynn stood to her feet.

"Oh Mr. Forrest! It is so nice to finally meet you. I have wanted to meet you for so long. I actually have some things I'd like to give you. Here, let me get them—it'll only take a minute."

Digging through her bag, she pulled out a demo CD and a black-and-white glossy photo of herself.

Mr. Forrest smiled. "Why don't you mail those to my secretary?" Then, focusing on Bailey, he said, "Are you enjoying the conference?"

Surprised, Bailey smiled her million-dollar smile and nodded. "Yes, sir!"

"That's good. Are you performing in the talent show?"

"Yes, sir."

"Good. I'll be watching for you. I have to run now, but ladies, it was a pleasure meeting you." With a wink at Elizabeth, he turned and walked away.

As the four girls turned to watch him leave, they didn't notice Lori approach from the opposite direction.

The CCGs Check In

Elizabeth jumped as she heard her name.

"Oh, I didn't mean to startle you." Lori placed a well-manicured hand on Elizabeth's shoulder. "I was just wondering if you found your way back from the ladies' room without any mishaps. I know you mentioned how easily you get lost."

"Oh, um. . .yes, ma'am. I found my way out just fine." Elizabeth eyed the woman's red-tipped fingers on her sleeve. They reminded her of claws.

"That's nice. I was wondering. . .what were you doing there in the first place? There weren't any classes on that floor last hour."

Elizabeth watched Lori's perfectly lipsticked smile and nearly choked. "Oh, I—I—"

Bailey piped up. "You found your notebook, didn't you Elizabeth?"

"What? Oh, um. . .yes. I. . .found what I was looking for. Then I left," Elizabeth said honestly.

Lori studied her for a moment, and then smiled a catlike smile. "That's good. You wouldn't want to be caught somewhere you shouldn't be. I'd hate to see you get in trouble. They've been known to send troublemakers home from this conference. But of course, that would never happen to someone like you, Elizabeth. See you later!"

The girls stared, open-mouthed, after Lori, the click-clicking sound of her heels echoing in the dining hall.

"That was kind of weird," said Mary-Lynn.

"Yeah," added Bailey.

"That will be something else to tell the other girls," Elizabeth said. She looked at her watch. "And it looks like about time that we need to go back to the room for our conference call."

A little later the other Camp Club Girls listened in rapt attention as Elizabeth relayed all that had happened.

"Talk about a close call!" McKenzie exclaimed.

Alex giggled.

"What's so funny?" asked Sydney.

"I was just thinking of poor Elizabeth, trapped there under that desk with her long legs! What if she'd gotten stuck?"

Soon, they were all laughing at Elizabeth's expense. Elizabeth chuckled too. "I hate to think what would have happened if they had caught me!"

The girls laughed even harder, until Kate brought them back to the issue at hand. "Let me tell you what I found out. From the list Kristi compiled, I discovered that three of them are also members of Joshua Conrad's official fan club. I also googled Robert Kranfield, and I did find his name in the list of Star Records' songwriters. And here's the interesting thing. The president of Star, a Mr. Edward Miller, is on Kristi's list, and a member of the fan club."

"You think Mr. Miller is behind this? He's known my dad for years!" Kristi exclaimed.

"Maybe. I don't know. But there is one more thing I want to check." The other girls could hear Kate clicking away at the keys on her computer. "It seems like I remember. . . . You said that woman's name was Lori, right? Let's see. . . . Bingo! Mr. Miller has a daughter named Lori. She's sort of a celebrity in her own right. She's tried to break into the music world, but she's not that great of a performer. Most of her fame comes from the trouble she's gotten into. She always seems to be involved in one scheme or another. But her dad keeps bailing her out of trouble. Here. I'm sending you a link to a picture of her. See if it's the same person."

Elizabeth, Bailey, and Kristi watched for the email to come in, then clicked on the link. Sure enough, there was a picture of Lori, hanging on the arm of some young athlete.

"Yep. It's her, all right," Elizabeth said.

"It seems to me, based on what Elizabeth heard, that Lori is the one who wanted to steal the guitar. She just got Robert to do her dirty work for her," said McKenzie.

"At first I thought she was pretty. But now, I don't know," said Bailey. "She sort of reminds me of a cat."

"Just like the catwoman in the Batman shows. She uses her beauty to get people to do what she wants," said Alex.

Kristi leaned over Elizabeth's shoulder, studying the picture. "According to what Elizabeth heard, Lori wants to sell my guitar, though why she'd need the money, I don't know. Her dad is one of the wealthiest men in the business."

"Most thieves don't steal because they need something. They do it because they're selfish, or because they like getting away with something bad," Sydney said.

"Well, whatever her reason, we've got to get that guitar back before she sells it. We need to come up with a plan," Elizabeth stated.

Later that day, Bailey, Kristi, and Elizabeth sat in the main conference room waiting for the general session to begin. Announcements flashed on the large screen in front of the room, and Bailey read one of them out loud. "Deadline to register for the talent show is tonight! Don't miss your opportunity to perform on the stage of the Grand Ol' Opry!"

"Isn't it cool that they're letting us use the Grand Ol' Opry for our talent show?" asked Bailey. "I'd be in the show even if I had no talent, just for the opportunity to perform on that stage."

Elizabeth thought about that. It would be kind of cool to perform on that legendary stage, where so many great musicians had performed. But she still wasn't sure that she wanted to be part of it. . . .

"Are you going to be in the talent show, Kristi?" Elizabeth asked.

"No. I'd rather just enjoy it," she said. "How about you?"

"Oh, I don't know. I'll probably just help Bailey out."

Bailey stood and put her hands on her hips, leaning over Elizabeth like she was talking to a little child. "Now, you listen here, Elizabeth Anderson! You are one of the most talented people I know, and you need to be in that talent show. Who knows? You might even win and become famous, and I could be one of your backup singers!"

"But Bailey, I don't want to be famous."

"How can you say that? How can you not want to be famous?"

Kristi leaned forward. "Bailey, why do you think being famous is so great?"

"Because," Bailey replied. "When you're famous, you have a lot of money!"

Kristi lifted her eyebrows.

"Okay, so just because you're famous doesn't mean you have money. But when you're famous, everyone treats you better," Bailey continued.

"Maybe so, but you have to be careful. People who treat you better just because you're famous usually just want something for themselves. You always have to be asking yourself, 'Is this person really my friend? Or does he or she just want something from me?' "

Bailey sat down in her seat, frustrated. "Well, if there's nothing good about being famous, why do so many people want to be famous?"

"For the reasons you mentioned. They think they'll have lots of money, and sometimes they do. They think people will treat them better, and that's true too, though it's not always genuine," Kristi told her.

"But there are some good reasons to want to be famous," Elizabeth said, putting her arm around Bailey.

Bailey lifted an eyebrow. "Really?"

"Sure," said Elizabeth. "When you're famous, people listen to you. You can influence them in a good way."

"Oh. Like, how?" Bailey asked.

Elizabeth smiled. "All sorts of ways. You can tell them to stay off drugs, and to do well in school. You can convince them to be kind and compassionate. You can tell them God loves them, and He wants to have a relationship with them. The list goes on and on."

Bailey grinned. "So what you're saying is, being famous is a good thing?"

"It can be, yes," Elizabeth answered.

"Then it's settled." Bailey flashed a cat-ate-the-canary smile. "You're entering the talent show."

Elizabeth laughed and shook her head. "That's not what I—"

"I agree with Bailey. You should enter. What are you afraid of?" asked Kristi.

"I never said I was afraid!"

"Then why won't you enter?" Kristi pressed her.

"I don't know. I just. . .I'm here to work on my songwriting skills."

"Then why don't you perform one of your original songs?" Bailey asked.

"Because they're not good enough!" Elizabeth exclaimed.

"Why don't you let us be the judge of that?" Kristi asked her. "Come on. Sign up for the talent show, and I'll help you polish a song for it. It will be good for you."

"Yeah. Besides, just think how many people you'll encourage. Your songs can't help anybody if no one ever hears them!" Bailey exclaimed.

Elizabeth let out a heavy sigh and leaned back in her chair. Her heart was pounding in her chest as she thought about actually performing one of her originals. Finally, she looked at Kristi, then at Bailey. "Okay."

The other two cheered. "Yes! This is going to be great!"

•—•—•

Before Elizabeth even knew what was happening, Bailey and Kristi had her signed up, and she stood before a voice instructor who was working with talent show students.

Elizabeth looked at the voice instructor, took a deep breath, and opened her mouth to sing. Mrs. Crenshaw had given them each a number, and it was Elizabeth's turn. Each participant was to sing a song of his or her choice, and Elizabeth had made up her mind. She would sing one of her originals. She might as well get it over with.

"Help me help somebody
To see Your loving ways.
Help me help somebody,
Guide me through each day,
And help me help somebody."

She sang through one verse and the chorus before the woman stopped her.

"That's lovely. Who wrote it?"

Elizabeth felt the heat creeping up her neck and into her face. "I did."

Mrs. Crenshaw lifted an eyebrow. "Really? I like it. What a great message."

The others in the room nodded encouragement. Elizabeth could hardly believe it. They liked her song!

"You have a lovely voice as well," continued Mrs. Crenshaw. "But you sound like a scared little mouse. Believe it or not, stage fright comes from focusing too much attention on yourself. You're worried about whether you will mess up, or what the audience will think of you. Quit worrying about that, and just let yourself go."

Elizabeth nodded, and tried not to laugh when the woman put her hands around Elizabeth's waist. It tickled!

"Breathe deeply for me."

Elizabeth breathed. Why did she feel like she was in the doctor's office?

"No, no. You breathed into your chest. When you sing, you must breathe into your belly. Now breathe, and I want that skinny little middle of yours to get as fat as you can make it."

The class laughed as Elizabeth tried to do as she was told. It was hard not to laugh.

Mrs. Crenshaw smiled. "Now, I want you to sing it again, but this time, pretend you are singing opera."

Everyone laughed some more. Elizabeth wasn't sure she could do that.

"I know it sounds strange, but trust me. You'll sound great. Just try it."

Elizabeth breathed deeply, expanding her belly, and envisioned herself as an opera singer in full costume. She giggled, and the class laughed.

"Come on now. You can do it!"

She tried once more. Deep breath. Big belly. She opened her mouth and belted out the words. Amazingly, nobody laughed.

She continued through the second verse before Mrs. Crenshaw stopped her. "That was amazing! Could you hear how much stronger and better you sounded? And you didn't sound like an opera singer at all. You just sounded stronger."

Elizabeth nodded, and the class applauded as she took her seat. *They liked my song. I sang one of my originals, and nobody thought it was weird.*

She sat in a daze for the remainder of the class. After Mrs. Crenshaw dismissed the group, she said, "Elizabeth, may I speak with you for a moment?"

Elizabeth gathered her things and waited for the other students to leave, then approached the woman.

"Have a seat."

Elizabeth took a seat in the front row. *What could she want with me?*

She didn't have to wait long to answer that question. Mrs. Crenshaw sat down, leaving one empty chair between them.

"Elizabeth, you're very talented."

"Thank you," Elizabeth answered.

"I meant what I said about stage fright. You have much to offer. It's a rare gift to be able to sing well and write music. And you play the piano too?"

Elizabeth nodded.

"Do you play any other instruments?"

"Yes, ma'am. I play the guitar a little, but not as well as I play the piano."

Mrs. Crenshaw nodded. "Why do I get the feeling you don't like to perform?"

Elizabeth took a deep breath. "I'm okay with it, sometimes. Like when I led music at a kids' Bible club in San Antonio. It was just a bunch of little kids, and they didn't bother me. But when I'm in front of people my own age or adults, I get nervous."

"Everyone gets nervous in front of a crowd. But the more you do it, the more comfortable you'll be. There is sincerity to your music—and in your voice—that will touch people. Don't hide that. Don't deny people the message that God has given you."

Elizabeth didn't know what to say. She had always been content to stay out of the spotlight, but everyone seemed to be pushing her into it. Bailey and Kristi, and now Mrs. Crenshaw. "I'll—do my best."

Mrs. Crenshaw patted her on the back. "That's all anyone can ask of you."

A sound at the back of the room interrupted their conversation. Elizabeth turned to see Bailey and Kristi waiting at the door.

"Friends of yours?"

"Yes, ma'am."

"Well, you don't want to keep them waiting. Think about what I said."

Elizabeth nodded. "Thank you. I will." When she got to the door, she saw the look on Bailey's face. She knew that look.

"What's going on?" she asked.

"Come with us," Bailey said.

Moments later the three girls stood on tiptoes in a snowbank next to the faculty lodge, trying to peer into a window.

"Are you sure this is the right room?" Elizabeth asked.

"No, but I'm pretty sure." Bailey hopped up and down, trying to see inside. It was no use. The more she hopped, the more she packed down the snow.

"And what makes you think this is his room?" Elizabeth gave up trying to be tall enough. The window was out of reach.

Kristi leaned against the wall. "During my last class, I remembered something I forgot to tell you all. When Robert dropped his things, he dropped a key with the number 117 on it. Since all of these buildings are similar, I figured out where room 117 would be in our lodge. First floor, east wall, second window from the back. I'm hoping this building has the same layout."

"Well, there's only one way to know for sure. One of us has to go inside and get a look at the room numbers," Elizabeth said.

"That's easier said than done. They've got a guard dog at the entrance." Bailey looked annoyed.

"A guard dog?"

"She means an attendant," Kristi clarified. "There's a woman at the front desk, and you have to show your faculty ID to get in. I guess they don't want us bothering the VIPs while they're resting."

Elizabeth leaned against the brick wall and thought about something she'd read in her schedule. She was starting to form a plan. But they might need help. . .from Mary-Lynn.

•—•—•

Later that evening, Elizabeth stood in front of the mirror in her room and tried not to laugh.

"Unbelievable," whispered Bailey.

"You're good," Kristi told Mary-Lynn.

Mary-Lynn gave a few finishing touches to Elizabeth's hair and make-up, then stood back and surveyed her handiwork. "Perfect. You look just like a Dolly Parton wannabe. I'm so glad you asked me to give you a makeover! I'm a little surprised, though. You don't really seem the Dolly Parton type to me."

Bailey giggled. "She's too tall to be Dolly Parton."

"She's too skinny. She needs more padding," Kristi commented.

Mary-Lynn looked Elizabeth over from head to toe, then opened Bailey's suitcase and began rummaging around. She pulled out some socks and tossed them to Elizabeth.

"I may be good at what I do, but I'm not a miracle worker. This is as good as it's gonna get."

Confused, Elizabeth began to put on the socks.

The other three burst into laughter. "Um, Beth? Those aren't for your feet!"

Elizabeth finally got the message when Bailey pointed to her chest.

A short time later, Elizabeth waited in the shadows by the faculty building, watching the various faculty members walk by in celebrity costumes as they left their lodge. There was a fake Carrie Underwood, a fake Johnny Cash, and a fake Reba McEntire. She held her laughter as she saw the dignified Mr. Forrest dressed as Willie Nelson.

I hate to miss their show tonight. The celebrity spoof should be hilarious! But this may be the only way to get into this building, she thought. She fingered the fake faculty ID Kristi had made and hoped the receptionist wouldn't ask to see it up close. It wasn't perfect, but would be fine at a distance.

Finally, when it seemed the coast was clear, she stepped out of the shadows. Taking a deep breath, she opened the door to the building and walked in, head held high, as if she belonged.

The receptionist gave her a puzzled look, then laughed. "Great outfit, Dolly," she said. "I didn't see you going out. Did you forget something?"

Elizabeth nodded, waved, and kept walking. The woman didn't try to stop her.

Rounding the corner, she walked down the long corridor to the second door from the end. Room 117, just as they had thought. With a quick look around to make sure no one was watching, she turned the knob. It was locked. They hadn't talked about her trying to get in Robert Kranfield's room, or she would have brought the key with her. But as long as she was here, she might as well try. When would they get another opportunity like this? And the building was empty, except for the receptionist.

She pulled a bobby pin from her oversprayed hair and unfolded it, thinking of the countless times her little brother, James, had locked her out of her own bedroom.

I never thought I'd be grateful for your stunts, little brother. But it's given me some good practice, she thought.

She poked it into the tiny keyhole and began wiggling. Soon she heard a click, and she pushed the door open.

With one last look around, she stepped into the room. Joshua Conrad posters covered the walls. *Why would he take the time to hang posters, when he'll only be here a few days?* Joshua Conrad flyers and magazine covers were scattered on the bed and dresser. *The guitar. Look for the guitar.*

Something in the closet caught her eye. She turned around and gasped.

Found and Lost?

There, leaning against the back wall of the wide-open closet, were three different guitars. Pretty fancy ones too. Could one of these be Kristi's?

Elizabeth moved closer, examining each guitar without touching it. One was shiny black with little flowers painted on the side. The middle one was a rich purple—an electric guitar. The final one was bright red with a lightning bolt on it.

But no, none of these seemed right. What was it Kristi had said about the guitar? It was very valuable. But hadn't she called it, "beat-up" looking? No, these guitars were in mint condition.

She abandoned them and continued looking. She hadn't planned to search the room—only to verify that this was the right room. She knew the others would be waiting for her report. They'd gone to the faculty show, in hopes no one would notice Elizabeth's absence. If anyone asked about her whereabouts, they could just point them to the ladies' room or something. But here she was, in Robert's room, going through his things.

What was that? Footsteps in the hall, followed by voices, caused her to freeze. She looked around for a hiding place, and then let out her breath as the voices passed by and continued down the hall. *I've got to get out of here before I get caught.* She started toward the door, opening it carefully and peering into the hallway. Clear.

As an afterthought, she rushed to the window and tried to unlock the latch. She struggled with it for a moment, but it was stuck. She finally gave up.

With one last look around the room, she stepped into the hallway. She was about to shut the door when something under the bed caught her eye. Was that a guitar head?

The very corner of a black head—the handle—stuck out from under the bedspread. She could see two of the tuning pegs. Then she heard more voices.

Do I go back in? Do I leave and come back later? Oh God, what should I do?

The voices came from the lobby. Was that Lori's voice? And Robert's? She quickly backed out of the room and shut the door. Keeping her head down, she walked quickly up the hallway, nearly bumping into Robert as she turned the corner.

Head down. Don't make eye contact. Oh God, please don't let them recognize me!

Robert said, "Oh, excuse me, ma'am. I didn't see you there."

With a laugh, Lori exclaimed, "Great Dolly Parton getup. You'd better hurry—they've already started the show."

Elizabeth nodded and kept walking. She pushed her way through the double glass doors, and then took off running. She had to find the others.

Her breath made little white clouds in the cold air, and the snow crunched under her feet. Her high heels slowed her some, and she nearly lost her balance more than once. *These boots were made for walking, not running!*

She was only a few feet from her destination when her foot caught on a patch of ice. She slipped, going down on her well-padded bottom, her hair falling in a teased mass over her eyes.

"Elizabeth. Is that you?"

Oh no. It can't be.

"Elizabeth, are you all right?"

Slowly, Elizabeth brushed her hair out her eyes. Sure enough, Mr. Forrest was standing over her, his fake Willie Nelson braid hanging over his shoulder. He reached out a hand to help her up.

"Oh, uh. . .hi, Mr. Forrest." She took his hand, and he pulled her to her feet. "You have to be careful on these icy sidewalks," he told her.

She brushed herself off and tried not to think about her throbbing backside. "Thank you," she said.

Mr. Forrest eyed her curiously. "That's quite a getup you're wearing. You look like you should be part of our show."

Elizabeth laughed nervously. "Yeah, it's the funniest thing! My friends. . .uh. . .they dressed me like this and, uh. . ."

"Say no more," the man said. "I can recognize a dare when I see one. You're a good sport. What, did you lose a bet? Oh, never mind. I don't even want to know. Are you sure you're okay?"

"Yes, sir."

"Well, you'd better get in there. Willie Nelson's on in about five minutes, and you wouldn't want to miss him!" He winked and headed around the building, toward what she assumed was the backstage entrance.

Dusting herself off, she entered the building and slipped into the auditorium, where she found Kristi and Bailey waiting for her in the back row. Mr. Forrest was just making his entrance onto the stage.

"What happened?" Bailey whispered.

"I think I may have found the guitar!"

"You went in his room?" Bailey exclaimed.

"What? Did you bring it with you?" Kristi asked a little too loudly.

The people in front of them turned. *"Shhhhh!"* they hissed.

"Sorry," Elizabeth whispered. Leaning closer to her friends, she said, "There wasn't time. Besides, what if it wasn't the right guitar? He had several guitars in his room."

Kristi leaned her head against the back wall. "Great. So close, yet so far."

Bailey said, "What are we gonna do now?"

Willie Nelson finished his song, and the audience roared with applause. Elizabeth joined them, and Bailey hooted and hollered. One of the "shushers" from the row in front of them turned, and this time, he caught sight of Elizabeth's costume.

"Hey, it's Dolly Parton!" he called out.

Several others turned and pointed. Before long, someone started chanting, "Dolly! Dolly!"

Elizabeth looked like a deer caught in the headlights. She had thought she would report to her friends, then slip back to her room to get out of the crazy getup.

Mr. Forrest was still on stage. A slow smile spread across his face, and he leaned into the microphone. "That's right, folks. We have a surprise visit from Ms. Dolly Parton! Come on up here, Dolly."

If ever she had wanted the floor to open up and swallow her whole, she wanted it now. *Oh God, no. . .please no. . .*she prayed.

Bailey gave her a gentle shove into the aisle, and the crowd roared its approval. *Breathe, Elizabeth. Breathe!*

Slowly, she put one foot in front of the other and began making her way to the front of the room. A voice whispered in her head, *Play the part.*

As the applause rang in her ears, she took a deep breath, then forced herself to relax, forced herself to smile. Mr. Forrest held his hand out to her and escorted her up the stairs to the stage.

"Hello, Dolly! We're so glad you could join us this evening. Are you going to sing us a song?"

Elizabeth let out a nervous, high-pitched laugh. *Play the part.* She spoke in the deepest Southern accent she could manage, and said, "Why Willie! I wouldn't want to sing right after you! You're a tough act to follow!"

Mr. Forrest placed an encouraging hand on her shoulder. "Oh, nonsense. You're a legend. These people want to hear you sing!"

She couldn't think of any easy way out of this situation. Phrases of country songs floated through her mind, but she couldn't think of a single Dolly Parton song. Not a single one! *Oh, why did I ever think this was a good idea? I'm going to blow my cover, right here in front of everyone.*

Then again, no one here knew it was really her. Well, almost no one. She realized that the costume—ridiculous as it was—gave her a certain freedom. She could hide, in a way, because the people weren't looking at Elizabeth. They were looking at some unknown person dressed as a country music legend.

Sing a hymn! Of course! Almost all country singers sang hymns at their concerts.

"Well Willie, I suppose I could sing just one little song before I have to be on my way. I wouldn't want to disappoint your audience, after all!"

Seating herself at the grand piano, she played a few warm-up chords.

"This is a song my Grandpa always loves for me to sing." She began playing "Amazing Grace," and the room grew quiet. In a quiet voice, she sang every word, every verse, allowing herself to get lost in the music. She pictured Grandpa sitting right there, listening to her. Just last week, she had sat in his living room and sung this very song for him.

As she finished the last notes of the song, she sat in silence, relishing the feel of the grand piano beneath her fingers, and she almost forgot she was singing in front of a room full of people. Dressed as Dolly Parton.

There was no sound in the room for several long seconds. Then, she heard one person's applause. Then another, and another, until the entire room was on its feet. *They're giving me a standing ovation!*

She stood and bowed.

No Lord, she prayed, *they're giving You a standing ovation.*

She realized, in a whole new way, that Mrs. Crenshaw's words were true. For a brief moment, Elizabeth had forgotten about herself. The costume had allowed her to leave her shyness, her insecurities behind, and she just worshipped God. And because of it, she led the entire room in worship. It didn't matter at all that no one knew it was Elizabeth under all that make-up and hair. What mattered was that they experienced God.

Mr. Forrest leaned forward and whispered, "Well done."

She smiled at him, and he directed her backstage, toward an exit. The other faculty members smiled and told her what a great job she'd done. As she passed by, she heard them whispering, "Who is that?"

"I have no idea. Must be a friend of Rick's."

She pushed open the heavy door and made her way around the building, to the sidewalk. Bailey and Kristi were waiting for her.

"That was amazing!" Bailey exclaimed.

"Honestly, Elizabeth. You belong on the stage!" Kristi told her.

Elizabeth could feel her heart pounding within her chest. "Thanks, y'all. Now, I've got to get out of this ridiculous getup!"

"Oh, I don't know," Bailey said with a sly grin. "I think it's a good look for you."

Elizabeth gathered up a handful of snow and tossed it in Bailey's direction, then took off running. Unfortunately, her boots slowed her down, and Bailey's aim was excellent. So was Kristi's. Before reaching her lodge, she was covered in snow and slush.

"Oh well. I needed a shower, anyway," she called from the building entrance. When Bailey and Kristi caught up with her, she stuffed a handful of the icy crystals down each of their coats, and then entered the building. She knew they wouldn't continue the snow war indoors.

A short while later, Elizabeth emerged from a nice, hot shower that wasn't nearly long enough. Wrapped in her fluffy robe, she found Bailey and Kristi waiting for her. Bailey held the phone in her hand.

"I've got the others on the line. Tell us again what you saw in Robert's room."

Elizabeth shared every detail.

"You've got to get back in that room," Sydney said.

"Yeah, but when? Robert will be sleeping there at night, so you can't go then. One of you will have to miss a class in the morning, and sneak back in," said Alex.

McKenzie let out a heavy sigh. "I hate that you'll have to do it in the daytime. Someone might see you. Do you think Robert goes out at night?"

"I don't know," Elizabeth replied.

"Hey, do you think Robert and Lori are dating? If they are, they may go on a long moonlight walk. . .or something," Bailey suggested.

"The conversation I heard didn't sound like they were in love," Elizabeth said.

"We may just have to wait until tomorrow morning, and go during his first class."

"We can't," said Kristi.

Elizabeth and Bailey looked at their friend. She'd remained silent up until that point.

Kristi pulled out her schedule. "You guys must have forgotten. Tomorrow, we're taking a field trip to one of the studios." She paused and looked at each of them. "And guess which studio it is?"

•—•—•

Later that night, Elizabeth lay wide awake, staring into the darkness. They had gone to bed early since they had to be at the buses at 8:00 a.m. If they wanted breakfast, they'd have to be at the dining hall by seven fifteen.

She was certain that had been Kristi's guitar under Robert's bed. *Why didn't I just grab it? But then again, I did run into Robert and Lori on the way out. They would have seen it. But I could have dropped it out the window. But no, it might have been damaged. And without knowing for sure it was the right guitar. . .*

Elizabeth continued to toss and turn, trying to figure out how to retrieve the stolen guitar. She sat up in bed. Was someone tapping on the door?

"Did you hear that?" Bailey whispered through the darkness.

"Yes. What time is it?"

"Eleven twenty-seven."

Elizabeth fumbled to find the lamp on the bedside table. Squinting, she made her way to the door, Bailey close behind her. It was Kristi. She was bundled up in her coat and scarf, and she held a flashlight.

"I can't sleep," she said. "I've decided to go spy on Robert's room. I know he's probably asleep, but I have to do something."

"Well, you're not going alone. Give us a minute to get dressed." Elizabeth held the door open for her friend to enter.

"I was hoping you'd say that," Kristi told her.

Within minutes, the three girls were crunching through the snow with only the dim light of Kristi's flashlight to guide them.

"I sure hope that thing doesn't run out of batteries," Bailey whispered.

Soon they were standing outside Robert's building. Counting the windows, they located Robert's room. There was a dim light.

They approached the window, walking carefully in the knee-high snow. "This is hard," Elizabeth whispered. "We don't get this kind of snow in Texas."

They stood back, not sure what to do next.

"Turn the flashlight off," Elizabeth whispered. "He'll see us."

Kristi switched off the light, then edged to the corner of the window. "It's no use. It's too high," she said. "I can't see in."

"We should have brought something to stand on," Bailey whispered.

Elizabeth looked at Bailey. She was the shortest. And the lightest. "I have an idea."

Together, Kristi and Elizabeth lifted Bailey to see in the window.

"There," whispered Bailey. "I can see. Wait, no. I can only see the top of his head. I need to go higher."

At the count of three, Kristi and Elizabeth lifted Bailey up even higher. For such a small girl, she was heavy!

"There! I can see him. He's sitting on his bed, facing the other way. And. . .he's strumming a guitar! It's an old guitar, black. . .and it looks like it has some scratches on it."

"That sounds like Dad's guitar!" Kristi exclaimed.

"Wait, he's getting up. Put me down—he's going to see me! Put me down!"

Bailey tried to duck, and the awkward movement threw Elizabeth and Kristi off balance. It seemed to happen in slow motion: Bailey tumbled down, down, down into the soft bank of snow, and she took the other two with her.

At any other time it would have been funny. But when they girls landed, they saw the outline of. . .someone. Standing over them. Watching them.

Star Adventure

Elizabeth gasped, and Bailey squealed. Kristi, on the bottom of the pile, must not have seen the person.

"Gt off mmmm!" Kristi mumbled. "Cnt brth!"

Elizabeth scooted to the side, but kept her eyes on the figure.

Kristi sat up, chuckling, but fell silent when she saw what her friends were looking at.

They sat there in silence for what felt like hours, but was really only a few moments. Elizabeth didn't know whether she should speak, or let the shadow speak first. She decided to go first.

"Hello," she squeaked. "Can we help you?"

"Can you help me? It looks like you're the ones who need help. What in the world are y'all doing?"

All three girls let out deep sighs of relief when they heard Mary-Lynn's voice.

"Mary-Lynn! What are you doing here?"

"I heard Kristi leave, so I got up to look for her. I left my room just as you all were turning the corner. I was curious, so I followed you."

The moon shifted, and the girls got a look at Mary-Lynn for the first time. She was in her robe and slippers.

"You must be freezing!" Elizabeth told her. Let's get out of here, and we'll tell you all about it."

The four girls trekked through the snow to the sidewalk.

"Hey, you guys, look!" Bailey whispered. Turning, they saw Robert's light had gone out.

Back at the room, the girls sipped hot cocoa from the vending machine down the hall. "So you really think you can prove Robert Kranfield stole your guitar?" Mary-Lynn asked.

"Elizabeth heard him talking about it with that Lori girl. I don't know if we can prove it or not, but we're positive he's the one who did it," Bailey told her.

Mary-Lynn shook her head. "Unbelievable. Does this have something to do with why you wanted a make-over today, Elizabeth?"

Elizabeth nodded.

Bailey paced the room. "Mary-Lynn, you can't tell anyone. *Anyone.* If Robert or Lori finds out that we suspect them, there's no telling what they'll do!"

"Oh, don't worry your pretty little head over me. I won't say a word. I may talk a lot, but I don't say much."

The other three laughed. It was an accurate description.

"And if there's one thing I'm not, it's a snitch!"

The girls finally went to bed and early the next morning, they shuffled out of their lodge. Elizabeth, still limping from her fall the previous day, squinted against the sun's glare on the white snow. "I feel as if I've been run over by a tractor."

"You and me both," agreed Bailey.

After a quiet breakfast, the girls climbed on one of three big Greyhound buses that would take them to Star Records. When the bus was loaded, Mr. Forrest stepped on board and commanded their attention. His eyes rested on Elizabeth for a moment. A smile hinted beneath his serious face, and he winked.

Bailey elbowed her.

"Maybe you'll meet the real Dolly Parton today, and you can offer to be her stand-in," she whispered.

Elizabeth stifled a giggle as Mr. Forrest spoke into the microphone.

"Star Records has graciously invited us for a tour. It's very important that we stay together as a group. The building is large, with some high-security areas. If you wander into the wrong area, you may end up in handcuffs. If that happens, I will pretend I've never seen you before. So stay with the group."

A few people chuckled. Most were too sleepy to appreciate the humor.

As Mr. Forrest exited the bus, Robert Kranfield boarded, carrying his briefcase in one hand and a guitar case in the other. He sat near the front.

All four girls nearly bored a hole in his back with their eyes. As if sensing their stares, he turned and scanned the bus. His gaze rested only briefly on Kristi, and then he turned back around and pulled a newspaper out of his briefcase.

"Do you think that's the guitar?" whispered Bailey.

Kristi stood up to get a better look at the case, as if she could tell what was inside. "Surely he wouldn't be that. . .bold," she said.

"He's not very sociable, is he?" whispered Mary-Lynn. "He sits by himself at meals, and I never see him talking to anyone, except Lori."

"Just another sign that he's guilty. He doesn't want anyone to get too close and figure out his little secret," Bailey replied.

"We've got to find out what's in that guitar case!" Elizabeth told her friends.

"How? We have a bus full of witnesses. There's no way we can sneak a peek without someone seeing us," Bailey said.

Elizabeth pulled out her phone and began texting. Maybe the other Camp Club Girls would have a suggestion. She pressed SEND, then held the phone in her hands and waited for a reply. She knew it would be awhile. It was too early on a Saturday for anyone but McKenzie to be awake, and McKenzie would be out tending to her horses.

She stared at the back of Robert's head, bent over his newspaper. She hadn't seen him smile much during the conference. He just seemed so. . .tortured. Then, she looked at Kristi.

Lord, please let Kristi get her guitar back. And Robert. . .he's done a really bad thing. But I can't help but think he let Lori talk him into it. I don't know what's going on in his heart. But he mentioned wanting to give the guitar back. Please help him to do the right thing, in the end.

The motor cranked, and soon the bus was rolling out of the snow-laden conference center and onto the Nashville highway.

"Do you think we'll meet some real stars?" Mary-Lynn asked from across the aisle.

"I hope so!" Bailey replied. "Does anyone know which stars record at this studio?"

Mary-Lynn's face lit up. "Paul Overstreet, Billy Ray Cyrus, Carrie Underwood. . .just to name a few!"

"You're kidding! Oh, I can't wait!" Bailey and Mary-Lynn continued their excited chatter. On the other side of Mary-Lynn, Kristi leaned her head against the window and said nothing.

Elizabeth couldn't imagine what Kristi was feeling. *Lord, please bring that guitar back to Kristi. She needs the money. Please make a way for her to go to Julliard.*

She leaned her head against the window and dozed. In no time, the bus was pulling off the interstate and into the parking lot of an impressive looking building. STAR RECORDS, the sign read. The bus drove to the back of the building and parked. The driver instructed everyone to stay seated, but Robert exited the bus as soon as the doors were open.

"What's his hurry?" Bailey asked.

Before Elizabeth could respond, her cell phone rang. "Hello?"

"Hi, Beth. It's Mac. I'm in the barn. What's up?"

"We're just pulling into Star Records for a tour. Robert's here, and he's carrying a guitar case. We need to find out if Kristi's guitar is in it, but there are too many people around. Any great ideas?"

"Hmmm. . .can't you tail him?"

"I suppose we could, but you should see the size of this place. It's huge!"

"Well, that's good. The bigger the building, the more places to hide. And if he catches you, you can just tell him you're lost. Which, knowing you, won't be very far from the truth." McKenzie chuckled.

"Ha, ha. Cute," Elizabeth told her.

"From what Kate said, Robert isn't the one you need to worry about. Did you read the email she sent late last night?"

"Email? What email?"

"Oh, I guess you didn't read it. Apparently, Lori is more than just mischievous. She's dangerous. She's gotten into some pretty serious trouble in the past."

Mr. Forrest stood at the front of the bus, waiting for everyone's attention.

"What do you mean?" Elizabeth whispered.

"What? I can't hear you. The cows are mooing."

"What did you mean that Lori is dang—" Elizabeth looked up to find many eyes on her. Including Mr. Forrest's.

"Gotta go," she said, and snapped her cell phone shut. She wanted to disappear into the seat cushion.

Mr. Forrest cleared his throat. "As I said before, you are expected to stay with the group. You've been a great bunch of kids so far, and I know you're going to enjoy yourselves today. Have a great time."

He exited, and the passengers began filing off the bus, row by row. When it was their turn, Elizabeth let Mary-Lynn, Bailey, and Kristi go in front of her. Kristi seemed agitated. No wonder.

Elizabeth knew that, at that very moment, the guitar could be changing hands. *We've got to find Robert. We've got to find out if he was carrying Kristi's guitar.*

As soon as the group entered the colossal building, Elizabeth realized it was more than she could have imagined. The bottom floor was occupied with a museum displaying portraits of various recording artists during their sessions, album covers, drum sets, old soundboards. . . even guitars. The tour guide gave a brief explanation of each piece.

Bailey and Mary-Lynn hung on every word the woman said, but Kristi kept looking around at the exits.

"What are you thinking about?" whispered Elizabeth.

"I've been at this studio dozens of times. Even though it's been a few years, I think I can remember my way around."

"Where do you want to go? Do you think you know where Robert went?"

"There's a good chance he's one of two places. He's either on the fourth floor, where they have a special studio and practice rooms for the writers—that's where Robert probably has an office, or at least a desk with his name on it. Or. . ."

"Or what?"

"Or he's on the sixth floor, in one of the recording rooms. Those rooms are soundproof, and so are the fourth floor practice rooms. He could easily meet with someone to sell dad's guitar, and no one would suspect a thing."

The guide led them through a door and down a hallway. Elizabeth wanted to enjoy the tour, but how could she? Somewhere in this building, a crime was taking place. Maybe. And she had to find out.

Bailey and Mary-Lynn pushed to the front of the crowd, hanging on the tour guide's every word. But Elizabeth and Kristi fell to the back of the crowd. Elizabeth noticed Kristi scanning the doors and exits.

Slowly, the two of them fell farther and farther behind the group. With her eyes, Kristi motioned toward a door up ahead, tucked into a corner.

When the group was led through another doorway, Kristi grabbed Elizabeth's arm. "Come on," she whispered.

Once inside the small passageway, Kristi led them up two flights of stairs. Elizabeth wanted to question her, but Kristi seemed in a hurry. Finally, they stopped on a landing just outside the third floor.

"We'll go into the hallway here. This is where the break room is, and there's a little coffee shop and burger joint. No one will suspect us—they'll just think we're trainees or something. One floor above us is the writers' studio. We'll have to be careful there."

Elizabeth tried to process the information. "Maybe we'd better split up. People might believe that a teenager has a job here. But two teenagers, walking the halls together? That would seem a little suspicious, don't you think?"

"Yeah, you're probably right. But you don't know your way around, and I'm still learning this detective stuff. I have to find that guitar, though. I don't have a good feeling about today."

Elizabeth took a deep breath. She wasn't sure she'd be able to find her way around this building. But she was willing to try. "Do you have your cell phone?" she asked.

Kristi nodded.

"Good. Put it on silent. You said the recording studio is on the sixth floor?"

"Yes."

"I'll go to the fourth floor and see what I can find. You check out the sixth floor. If either of us finds anything, we'll call the other right away."

Kristi looked hesitant. "Okay. But as I said, I don't have a good feeling about today."

"All the more reason for us to give this our best shot." Elizabeth cracked open the door to the third floor and squeezed out. Head held high, she walked down the hallway with more confidence than she felt. Up ahead, she saw a sign for a food court. She might as well try to blend in while she looked for the elevator to the fourth floor.

She stopped in front of a cart selling hot cocoa and muffins. "One large cocoa, please. And two chocolate chip muffins. In a bag."

The white-haired woman behind the cart smelled of peppermint, and made Elizabeth think of her grandma.

"There you go, dear." She handed Elizabeth the bag and took her money.

"Thank you," Elizabeth told her, and dropped the change into a tip jar. *Now I'll fit right in. Everyone will think I'm delivering these muffins to some important person. At least I hope that's what they'll think.*

•—•—•

Kristi stepped off the elevator onto the sixth floor. Memories came flooding back as she looked around. Not much had changed in the last decade since she'd been in the building. Oh, the paint and furniture had been spruced up—it still looked like a million bucks. But the layout was the same.

Checking to make sure she wasn't being watched, she caught a glimpse of the security camera in the corner. No use trying to sneak around. It would all be caught on tape.

A cleaning lady passed in front of her, pushing a cart with a vacuum cleaner, a broom, a mop, and various other cleaning supplies. She watched the woman go through the glass doors to her left, then punch a code inside. The woman then opened the inside door and went through, struggling with her cart.

She decided to follow the woman. *After all, what's the worst that can happen?*

"Here, let me help you," Kristi said and held the door open.

"Thank you," the woman told her.

•—•—•

Elizabeth watched people leaving the food court, and decided to follow the crowd. They'd probably lead her to the elevators.

She was right. She punched the button for the fourth floor and tried to fade into the woodwork. She wished she had paid closer attention to what Robert was wearing. Then again, she could always tell people she was looking for Robert Kranfield. The problem was, she had no idea what she would do when she found him.

We'll cross that bridge when we come to it.

Within no time, the door opened, and she stepped onto the fourth floor. It was unlike anything she'd ever seen.

She felt like she was walking into a giant music store. Every instrument imaginable was on display. To her left, a middle-aged man was alternately playing a drum set, then scribbling on a page. He was wearing headphones.

To her right, a woman hummed and played a keyboard. She too wore headphones.

Straight ahead was a row of rooms with windows in the doors. *Soundproof,* she bet. Some of the rooms had keyboards; others had various band instruments. She watched one man play a trombone, while another one appeared to write down the trombone player's notes.

Wow. Double wow. Imagine having a job like this, where you get paid to just sit around and write music all day! This would be the coolest job ever!

"Looking for someone?"

Elizabeth jumped when she realized the voice was speaking to her. A balding, middle-aged man with a pencil behind his ear looked at her quizzically.

"Oh! Um, yeah. I mean, yes sir. I'm looking for. . ." Did she dare tell the man? "I'm looking for Robert Kranfield."

The man chuckled. "Oh yeah. He was in a few minutes ago. Said he had an important meeting up on the sixth floor." He eyed the bag of muffins. "Did he order breakfast? I'm surprised he didn't tell you to go on up. Just take the elevator to the sixth floor, go through the double glass doors. The pass code is three, three, three. Once you're in, you're on your own."

Elizabeth couldn't believe her ears. "Thank you so much!" she told the man.

He waved her off and picked up a guitar.

She returned to the elevator and punched the six. She said the pass code over in her head. *Three, three, three. That should be easy enough.* She remembered Psalm 33:3 and smiled. *"Sing to him a new song; play skillfully, and shout for joy." What an appropriate verse for a music studio.*

A lady got on behind her and pressed the button for floor seven.

At the sixth floor, Elizabeth got out. There were two sets of glass doors. *Which ones should I choose? Did he say which doors?* Elizabeth tried to remember if the man said left or right, but couldn't recall anything except, "the double glass doors."

Elizabeth turned to her left. She nearly dropped her muffins, however, when the doors opened and Carrie Underwood walked through! The young woman smiled at her and kept walking.

She was still staring at the back of the star's head when she felt her cell phone vibrate.

Double Trouble!

"Hello?" she answered.

"Where are you?" Bailey whispered frantically.

"I'm on the sixth floor. Have you heard from Kristi?"

"No! You mean she's not with you?"

Elizabeth's other line beeped. "Hold on, Bales, I've gotta get this." She pressed the button. "Hello?"

"Elizabeth? It's Kristi. Meet me on the sixth floor as soon as you can. I'm on my way to the elevators to meet you." Kristi was gone before Elizabeth could say anything.

She punched back to Bailey. "Gotta go. I'll call you in a few minutes." She shoved the phone in her pocket.

"But—"

Elizabeth hated to cut Bailey off. But Kristi had sounded pretty urgent. Now where was she? At that instant, Kristi pushed through the double doors.

"Whoa. How did you get here so fast?"

"I was already here when you called."

Kristi grabbed Elizabeth's arm. "They're in recording room G! And they've got dad's guitar!"

"Who? Robert and Lori?"

"Yes! And some other man I've never seen before."

"Well, what are we waiting for?"

Kristi led Elizabeth through a long hallway, flanked on either side with soundproof recording rooms. Many of the rooms were empty, but a couple of them had people inside, some singing their hearts out into microphones, others working soundboards or playing instruments. Not a sound could be heard in the hallway.

They rounded a corner, and Kristi stopped. "They're in the next room. Should we stay out here and spy, or just barge right in?"

"Are you sure it's your dad's guitar?"

"Yes!"

Elizabeth peered through the window of studio G. Sure enough, Robert, Lori, and one other man were inside. Robert and Lori appeared to be arguing. The man was examining the guitar. He had a rocket-shaped tattoo on his right hand, and wore layers of gold and silver chains around his neck. His hair hung in waves past his shoulders.

They watched as the man stood, pulled out an envelope, laid it on the table, and said something.

Lori grabbed the envelope and pulled out a wad of cash. She shoved it back in the envelope, and then grabbed the curtain to pull it shut. Before the girls had a chance to move, she saw them. Her face registered something akin to shock.

A moment later, the door opened.

"Girls, what are you doing here? You're not supposed to separate from the group. Mr. Forrest isn't going to like this at all," Lori sneered.

"Cut the act, Lori. I know you have Dad's guitar. I saw it. Now give it back!" Kristi said, her voice getting louder with each word.

The man stepped into the hallway, guitar case in hand. "What's going on here?" he asked.

"Oh, nothing at all. These are just a couple of kids from the music camp. Robert and I will take care of it. Won't we, Robert?"

Robert glared at the woman.

"Well, you'd better," said the man. "I paid a lot of money for this guitar, and I don't want any problems."

"That's my dad's guitar!" yelled Kristi, and Lori grabbed her and shoved her in the room. Robert grabbed Elizabeth and did the same.

"You'd better get out of here," Lori told the man, and he left. With the guitar.

Elizabeth struggled against Robert's hold, but she was no match for him. "What do you think you're doing? You'll never get away with this!" she told him.

"Oh, be quiet!" Lori hissed. She pushed Kristi into a chair, and then began rummaging through the bottom drawer of a file cabinet. She pulled out cords, wires, and some duct tape.

"Here. Tie them up," she said, handing Robert the cords. She used the duct tape to secure Kristi's hands behind her back.

"This wasn't part of the deal, Lori. I agreed to take the guitar for you. You said you wanted it for your collection, and that I could play it anytime I wanted to, for inspiration. That was the deal. You weren't going to sell it! That guy doesn't appreciate the value of Joshua Conrad's guitar. He's just going to auction it on eBay. No telling who will end up with it!"

"You fool! Why would I want a stolen guitar in my collection? Do you know how many people see that collection? You don't think they'd figure it out?"

She jerked the cords from Robert and began to tie Elizabeth's wrists behind her back.

"But you said I could—oh, never mind. I should never have gotten mixed up in this." He looked at Kristi. "Your dad is my hero. I've been having writer's block, and my job is kind of on the line. When I read the letter that you sent to Lori's dad, asking him if he wanted to buy the guitar, I knew I had to get my hands on it. I knew if I could just hold it, I might somehow get the inspiration to write something worthwhile. But I knew I couldn't even begin to afford something like that."

Elizabeth flinched. The cords were cutting off the circulation in her hands. *Dear God, help us!*

"I don't understand," Kristi said to Lori. "Your dad could buy you that guitar. He could give you any amount of money you wanted. Why did you have to steal it?"

Lori ignored the question, using duct tape and cords to tie each girl's ankles together.

Robert laughed. "You're right, Kristi. Lori's dad has money. But what you don't know is that he's tired of bailing his little girl out of jail and paying for all her little fiascoes. He's cut off her allowance, and has made her go to work for the company just like anyone else. Why do you think she's a substitute teacher at a kids' music conference? It certainly isn't because she loves children and teenagers."

"You don't know when to keep your mouth shut, do you? I'm getting out of here, and I suggest you follow me," Lori said as she covered Elizabeth's, then Kristi's mouths with the duct tape. Finally, she yanked each girl's chair out from under them, leaving the girls bound and gagged on the floor. She drew the curtains, turned out the lights, and motioned for Robert to go ahead of her.

Elizabeth looked at him, wide-eyed, and prayed. His eyes held hers for just a moment, and then he turned and walked out the door. They heard it shut.

Click!

The lock was set.

Her heart pounded in her chest, and she prayed like she had never prayed before.

•—•—•

Bailey held the phone to her ear, straining to hear the conversation on the other end of the line. Elizabeth had failed to hang up her phone, and most of what Bailey could hear was a jumbled mess. But she heard enough to know that her friends were in trouble.

Keeping the phone close to her ear, she whispered to Mary-Lynn, "Elizabeth and Kristi need our help. I think I heard something about recording room G. . . . Which floor are the recording studios on?"

Mary-Lynn looked at her, then back at the tour guide. "She just told us—floor six. We're going there next."

The elevator doors opened, and Robert and Lori stepped out. Bailey hadn't heard any sound from the phone for several minutes. She didn't know whether to follow the two suspects or look for her friends.

Mary-Lynn saw them as well. "You go find Elizabeth and Kristi. Leave these two to me." She took off after them.

Bailey felt she had no choice but to trust Mary-Lynn. She had to make sure Elizabeth and Kristi were okay.

The tour guide smiled. "We'll stop for a short break on the fourth floor, where you can purchase a soda or a snack. Then you'll get to sit in on a real, live recording session with a mystery superstar! I can't tell you who it is, but trust me. You'll be thrilled!"

Spotting an emergency exit sign, Bailey decided to take the stairs. She pushed open the doorway and bounded up the steps two at a time, three flights up, and into the hallway on the sixth floor. Panting, she looked around. Two men carrying coffee were exiting a set of double glass doors, and one of them held it open for her.

"Thank you," she said. The long corridor held rooms on either side. Each door was labeled, Recording Room A, B, C, and on down the row.

God, please help me find them! And please let them be okay! She tapped her phone to make sure it was still working. Why hadn't she heard any sounds?

She was still tapping her phone as she rounded a corner and barreled right into a blond woman.

"Oh, excuse me," the woman said.

Bailey barely looked at the woman. "I'm sorry, ma'am. I was looking for my friend."

"Oh, maybe I can help you. Which room is your friend in?"

"I think she's in—" Bailey focused on the woman's face for the first time. She nearly dropped her phone.

There, smiling the friendliest smile, with the biggest blond hair she'd ever seen in real life, was Dolly Parton. The real Dolly Parton. The woman wasn't much taller than Bailey.

"I. . .uh. . ."

"I'll bet you're with that tour group, aren't you? Well, this is supposed to be a surprise, but I'm going to sing for you all. Are you lost? How did you get separated from your group?"

Bailey remembered her friends. This was no time to be starstruck. "I think my friends are in trouble. They said something about recording room G."

"In trouble? I hope not! Room G is right up ahead. Let's just take a look, shall we?"

Dolly led the way and tried to open the door. It was locked. "It doesn't look like there's anyone in there. The lights are off. Do you think they might be in a different room?"

"No, I'm pretty sure I heard them say room G. Look, I know this sounds crazy, but is there any way we can just check? Can we get a key?"

Dolly tossed her blond hair and said, "Of course we can, honey."

She pulled out a cell phone and punched a number. "Hi, Jim. I need to get into studio G, and it's locked. Could you send someone over here with a key?"

Closing the phone, she said, "You're in luck. Jim is right next door."

Jim turned out to be a security guard. He smiled at Bailey, and then unlocked the door. "There you go, Miss Parton."

Dolly turned the knob, pushed open the door, flicked on the lights, and gasped. "Oh my stars above!"

Bailey pushed past the superstar.

"Elizabeth! Kristi! What happened? Are you alright?"

Jim pulled out his walkie-talkie and called for backup.

•—•—•

"Lori! Robert! Wait up!" Mary-Lynn called. The two stopped just outside the lobby doors, turning to look at the young redhead. "Oh, forgive me.

I mean, Mr. Kranfield and Miss Miller. You're both so young, I keep forgetting you're teachers. Where are you going?"

Lori looked at Robert, then at Mary-Lynn. "You should really go find your group." She turned to go.

"No, wait!" Mary-Lynn grabbed the woman's arm. "I was actually wanting to know where you buy your clothes. You always look so. . . put-together."

Lori rolled her eyes. "I don't have time for this."

"No, seriously," Mary-Lynn said. "I want to be successful in life, like you are. And the first step is to know how to dress. I. . .um. . .am beginning to wonder if my clothes are a little too dramatic at this stage. I'm afraid they might be keeping people from taking me seriously."

"Well, you certainly look more theatrical than professional," Lori said. "But I have to go. Right now."

She pulled her arm away and turned toward the door. Suddenly, an alarm sounded, and several security guards rushed toward the entrance.

"We're sorry, Miss Miller, but we have a security issue. No one is allowed to leave the building until it's resolved," said one of the men.

"This is ridiculous! My father owns this studio. I demand to be let out of this building, immediately!"

Robert said nothing, just looked at his feet. Sirens sounded outside the building, and several police offers entered.

"We had a report of an assault," one of them said, and a security guard led the way to the elevators.

Lori glared at Mary-Lynn. "Now look what you've done!"

Mary-Lynn just smiled. Her work was done.

•—•—•

An hour later, Elizabeth repeated her story for the fourth time, as a uniformed police officer recorded her words on a yellow notepad. Kristi was in another room, telling the same story, she was sure.

"And you're sure it was Lori Miller who tied you up?"

"Yes, sir." She rubbed her wrists where the cords had been. Since becoming a Camp Club Girl, she'd found herself in some pretty sticky situations. But this one was the worst, by far.

"Thank you," the officer said, and then left the room.

Almost immediately, Bailey entered, nearly knocking Elizabeth out of her chair with a hug. "I'm so glad you're okay! I was so worried. Why did you sneak off like that without telling me?"

"I'm just glad you found us. I heard you telling the police officer you could hear us on the phone? I had no idea I didn't hang it up. I must have been so distracted, I accidentally put it in my pocket without shutting it."

"It wasn't an accident. God was looking out for you! If you hadn't done that, you might still be bound and gagged on the floor."

Elizabeth shuddered. That was an experience she'd just as soon forget.

Kristi entered the room, looking dejected. "They caught Robert and Lori. They have them handcuffed, downstairs. Unfortunately, they didn't catch the man with my dad's guitar. He's probably long gone by now."

"Maybe they'll find him. We gave his description to the police. With that tattoo on his hand, he should be easy to spot," Elizabeth reassured her.

"Unless he wears gloves," Kristi took the chair next to Elizabeth. "I can't believe we were so close to getting it back, and we failed. We caught the thieves, but we still don't have the guitar. This is going to break my dad's heart."

"He'll know it's not your fault. He won't blame you," said Bailey.

Kristi wiped a tear from her cheek. "Oh, he won't care about the guitar. But it will break his heart that now he'll never be able to send me to Julliard. We just can't afford it."

"Let's not worry about Julliard just yet," said a man's voice from behind them. The girls turned to find Mr. Forrest, leaning against the doorway. "Where there's a will, there's a way. I feel terrible that I had a couple of undesirable people on staff at the camp. Girls, I'm sorry. I'm going to make this up to you, I promise."

Just then, Dolly Parton pushed her way past Mr. Forrest. She had a tray in her hands, filled with burgers and sodas. "Excuse me, Rick. I thought these girls might be hungry after all they've been through. Here ya' go, girls."

Elizabeth was amazed. One of the biggest country music stars on the planet had just served her lunch, on a tray. Talk about humility.

"Thank you," she told her.

Dolly just laughed. "No need to thank me. I'm just glad that everybody's okay. And Kristi, don't you worry one bit about that guitar. I've made a few phone calls to my own security staff. With your description and Robert's confession, I think they may be able to track the guy down."

She pulled up a chair and helped herself to a french fry. "Mmmmm. These are good."

Elizabeth couldn't help but laugh. Dolly Parton was just a regular person. Just like she'd told Bailey—people are just people. She just hoped the woman's star-powered security team could track down that guitar.

The Song in Elizabeth's Heart

Back at the conference center, Elizabeth, Bailey, Kristi, and Mary-Lynn had taken on a celebrity status of their own. Everyone wanted them to tell their stories, over and over, until Elizabeth was downright weary of it all.

Mary-Lynn, on the other hand, thrived on the attention. "You should have seen Lori's face when the alarm went off. And Robert, well. . . he looked as guilty as could be. I almost felt sorry for him, standing there like a whipped puppy while Lori ranted and raved about her daddy and her lawyers and her money. I don't think her daddy or his money will be able to get her out of this mess, though."

•—•—•

The last day of the conference, Elizabeth awoke with a start. "Bailey! Today is the talent show!"

Bailey rolled over in bed and groaned.

"Bailey, I have to practice! I don't even know what I'm going to perform."

Silence.

"Bailey! Wake up! You have to help me. I can't perform on the stage of the Grand Ol' Opry if I'm not prepared." Elizabeth flicked the light on.

"Hey! Turn that off!" Bailey yelled.

Elizabeth chuckled. "It's payback time. Remember when you woke me up early at camp, just so I could help you practice for the talent show? Well, it's your turn. I need you."

Bailey pulled the covers over her head. "Go back to sleep, Elizabeth. Whatever you do, you'll be great. You'll probably win the thing without even practicing."

Elizabeth sat on the side of her bed. Obviously, begging wasn't going to work with Bailey this early in the morning. She needed to try another tactic. "You're probably right. I'll probably beat you."

That hit the mark. Bailey sat up in bed. "Beat me? Ha! Not without a fight, sister!"

Elizabeth laughed. She knew she could appeal to Bailey's competitive nature. "I'm just teasing. But I really do need your help. I don't know what to sing."

"I thought you were going to perform one of your originals," Bailey said around a yawn.

"I am. But I don't know which one. Kristi said she'd take a look at my stuff, but I haven't wanted to bother her. She has enough on her mind."

"All the more reason to bother her. She needs something to take her mind off the stolen guitar," Bailey said, rubbing the sleep from her eyes.

Elizabeth nodded. "Good point. I'll go ask her now." She started for the door.

"Um, Elizabeth?"

"Yeah?"

"You might want to wait until it's light out."

Elizabeth looked out the window. The stars were still bright. The clock read 5:47 a.m. "Another good point." She turned the light out, crawled back into her bed, and tried to relax her nerves.

•—•—•

"As soon as we finish eating, let's find an empty classroom, and I'll listen to your songs," Kristi told Elizabeth over breakfast.

"Finding an empty classroom shouldn't be a problem," said Bailey. "I just happen to know of a class that has lost its teacher!"

"Yeah, I wonder if we'll still have our songwriting class, or if they'll just cancel it." Elizabeth finished off her last bit of scrambled eggs just in time to see Mr. Forrest headed their way.

"Good morning, ladies. Did you sleep well?"

Elizabeth nodded, and Bailey shook her head. "Some of us have roommates who like to wake up before the roosters."

Mr. Forrest smiled. He pulled up a chair and looked at Kristi. "How would you feel about leading the songwriting class today?"

Kristi lifted her eyebrows and dropped her jaw. "Me? You want me to lead a class?"

"Why not?" Mr. Forrest asked her. "You probably know more about music than half of my staff. And I'll be in there with you. I thought you might want to tell the other students about your dad, about all his hit songs, who he's played for, how he gets his ideas. . .we could even listen to some of his music."

Kristi's face brightened. "I'd love to do that. I just wish Dad were here to teach the class himself."

Mr. Forrest looked thoughtful. "Maybe I'll ask him to be on staff at next year's conference, if he's feeling up to it."

"He would love that," Kristi said with a smile.

•—•—•

A short time later, Elizabeth sat at the keyboard in the empty classroom, playing and singing for Kristi. She had chosen three of her best songs. She'd let Kristi decide which one she should perform.

"I like them all," Kristi said. "But I think this one could be even better if you'd change this chord progression, and move the bridge to here." She pointed to Elizabeth's page. "May I try something?"

Elizabeth scooted over, and Kristi sat at the bench. She began playing, and soon she had turned Elizabeth's song into a masterpiece.

"How did you do that?" Elizabeth asked her.

"I don't know. I just hear the music. Some of it I inherited from my dad, but a lot of it is just practice. The more songs you write, and the more you experiment, the better you'll get at knowing what will work and what won't. It's just like anything else. Practice makes perfect."

"Maybe so, but you have a gift. You're like some kind of musical genius!" Elizabeth told her.

Kristi laughed. "Not really. I've just been around it all my life. It's become a part of me." She grew quiet. "That's why I wanted to go to Julliard. I want to keep learning from the very best musicians. But, I guess there's nothing I can do about that."

Elizabeth realized, for the first time, that Kristi *needed* to go to Julliard. Mr. Forrest had been right. Kristi knew more about music than most of the people on his staff. Here she was at a music conference, wanting to learn, and she was doing the teaching. Julliard was probably the only place Kristi would find musicians who knew more than she did.

Lord, please make a way for Kristi to go to Julliard.

•—•—•

"Elizabeth, you need lipstick," Mary-Lynn said as the girls got ready for the evening's talent show. "And if you'd just let me do something with your hair, I could make you look like a star. I've done it once already, you know."

Elizabeth laughed. "No thanks. One night as a superstar was enough for me. Tonight, I just want to be myself."

"Suit yourself," Mary-Lynn told her and leaned forward to apply mascara to her own lashes.

"I'll take some of that lipstick," Bailey said, and soon Mary-Lynn was giving Bailey a full-scale makeover.

Kristi sat on the bed watching them. "You all are going to be great."

Elizabeth plopped down next to her.

"I can't believe you're not going to be in the show. You're the most talented person here, and everyone knows it."

Kristi laughed. "I'm not so sure about that, but thanks for the compliment. No, I'd rather sit back and enjoy the show. Besides, without my guitar—dad's guitar—I'd just feel strange."

"But you were going to sell it anyway," said Bailey.

"I know. But I didn't want to."

"Don't you wonder what it will feel like, performing on the stage at the Grand Ol' Opry?" Elizabeth asked her.

Kristi grinned. "No. I've already done it."

"You *what*?" asked Elizabeth, Bailey, and Mary-Lynn in unison.

"When I was six years old, Dad had me come onstage with him and perform a song. I was too young to appreciate it then. I just sang, and everybody clapped. But now, I realize what a great moment that was."

The girls were speechless. "That is so cool," whispered Bailey.

Mary-Lynn stood back and surveyed her handiwork. "You look smashing, dahling."

Bailey spun around and showed off her new look. Elizabeth tried not to laugh. She looked like a miniature, dark-haired Mary-Lynn. Minus the freckles.

"Girls, you know I love you," Bailey told them. "But the minute we step out that door, it's game time. Don't think of me as your friend. Think of me as your fiercest competitor!"

Elizabeth laughed. "I'll remember that."

Soon, the girls gathered their things and headed for the buses, which were waiting to take them to the legendary music hall. It was nearly showtime.

Elizabeth was the last performer on the program that evening. She sat next to Kristi for most of the show, applauding loudly for both Mary-Lynn and Bailey. Either of them had a shot at the trophy, as did any of the other dozen or so performers. This was a talented group of people.

When it was almost her turn to take the stage, she stood to leave. Kristi grabbed her hand it squeezed it.

"You'll do great," she said. "Just remember. It's not about you. It's about what you can give to others."

Lord, that's why Kristi needs to go to Julliard. She has both the talent and the heart. Please make a way for her.

As the announcer called her name, Elizabeth walked onto the stage. She took a deep breath and tried to savor the moment. No matter what happened, she would have this memory. She was actually going to perform on the stage of the Grand Ol' Opry. Unbelievable.

"Go Elizabeth!" she heard Bailey yell from the audience. Elizabeth couldn't help but remember Bailey's words from earlier. *Fierce competitor, indeed.*

Elizabeth took her seat at the keyboard, adjusted the microphone, and said, "I'd like to dedicate this song to Kristi Conrad, who has taught me not only how to be a better musician, but how to use the gift of music to help others. Thanks, Kristi!"

She took a deep breath and let her fingers glide over the keys, playing the notes Kristi had suggested. Softly, she began to sing:

"Jesus, I long for Your Spirit,
I long to be made new.
Jesus, I know only You can change me.
Make me a mirror of you.

Make me a mirror of You, my Lord,
May each thought be pure and true.
May Your Spirit guide my footsteps
In all that I do,
And make me a mirror of You."

Elizabeth finished the song with Kristi's chord progression, softly fading away. The room was still for several long moments, until finally one person began to applaud. Then another and another, until Elizabeth looked out and saw the audience in a standing ovation. Here she was, getting a standing ovation at the Grand Ol' Opry! She smiled, for she knew they weren't applauding for her. They were applauding for her Lord.

She exited the stage, and Mr. Forrest patted her on the shoulder as she passed by. "Well done," he said to her before he took the microphone.

"Ladies and gentlemen, this has truly been one of the greatest displays of talent I've seen in a long time. Thank you to each of the contestants for making this evening such a pleasurable one for all. While the judges are tallying their scores, I have a special presentation to make. And there is someone special here to help me make it."

The audience gasped, then applauded as Dolly Parton walked onto the stage. "Thank you, Rick. It's a pleasure to be here. As many of you know, this has been a difficult week for one of your participants. Kristi Conrad came here expecting to sell her dad's guitar, to earn money for Julliard. Unfortunately, that guitar was stolen. Kristi, would you come up here, please?"

Elizabeth and Bailey nudged Kristi from either side. The poor girl was in shock. Slowly, she stood and made her way to the stage. Dolly put her arm around her and said, "Kristi, I understand that you are one talented young lady. I don't doubt it, if you're anything like your father. A group of your dad's old music buddies have put together the Joshua Conrad Music Scholarship fund, and we'd like for you to be our first recipient. This should be enough to get you through four years of Julliard, and then some." She handed Kristi an envelope.

Tears flooded unchecked down Kristi's face. "Thank you," she whispered. "I don't know what to say."

The room erupted in applause, and Elizabeth had to wipe tears from her own face. *Thank You, God. I knew You'd make a way for her!*

Suddenly, Dolly felt in her pocket and left the stage pulling a cell phone out of her pocket. The audience continued their applause, and a moment later the star returned, holding up her hands.

"Quiet down, folks! I've just had some wonderful news! They've caught the man who had Kristi's guitar. Kristi, your guitar will be returned to you as soon as the police have finished their investigation. And now, you won't have to sell it!"

Kristi covered her face with her hands, overcome with emotion. Elizabeth looked around the room, and saw many people wiping tears. The applause continued for many minutes.

Finally, Mr. Forrest directed people to take their seats, and a man in the front row handed him an envelope. "We have the results from our panel of judges. The grand prize winner of this year's talent show is. . . Miss Elizabeth Anderson!"

Bailey and Mary-Lynn jumped up from their seats, whooping and hollering. Elizabeth, however, was in shock.

"Elizabeth, go up there! You have to get your trophy!" Bailey urged her.

Standing to her feet, she walked to the front of the room as the audience continued their applause. Dolly held a hand out to her and helped her up the stairs. "I was backstage and heard your song. That was beautiful. You keep using that voice of yours to sing for the Lord, okay?"

Elizabeth smiled and accepted the trophy from Mr. Forrest. Kristi stepped forward and offered a big hug. It was almost more than Elizabeth's emotions could handle.

"It's funny how the Lord works," she whispered into Elizabeth's ear. "Bailey and Mary-Lynn came to the conference wanting to be discovered, but they're cheering for you more than anyone. You came to stay in the background, afraid no one would like your songs. But you placed your focus on God, and you won a trophy!"

"And just when you were about to give up hope, God provided money for Julliard and returned your guitar," Elizabeth whispered right back.

God is good, thought Elizabeth. *He really does put a song in my heart.*

Don't Miss the Rest of the Camp Club Girls Series!

Camp Club Girls: Bailey

Whether the Camp Club Girls are investigating the whereabouts of eccentric millionaire Marshall Gonzalez, encountering out-of-control elk stampedes in Estes Park, uncovering the rightful ownership to a valuable mine, or solving the case of frightening events in Mermaid Park, you'll encounter six charming, relatable characters who combine their mystery-solving skills to save the day.

Paperback / 978-1-68322-828-8 / $9.99 / February 2019

Camp Club Girls: Kate

Whether the Camp Club Girls are saving the day for a Philadelphia Phillies baseball player, investigating the sabotage of a Vermont cheese factory, going on a quest to uncover phony fossils in Wyoming, or solving the case of twisted treats in Hershey, Pennsylvania, you'll encounter six charming, relatable characters who combine their mystery-solving skills to save the day.

Paperback / 978-1-68322-854-7 / $9.99 / March 2019

Camp Club Girls: McKenzie

Whether the Camp Club Girls are in the middle of a Wild West whodunit, investigating a mysterious case of missing sea lion pups, uncovering the whereabouts of a teen girl's missing family member, or unearthing clues in an Iowa history mystery, you'll encounter six charming, relatable characters who combine their mystery-solving skills to save the day.

Paperback / 978-1-68322-879-0 / $9.99 / April 2019

Find These and More from Barbour Publishing at Your Favorite Bookstore or at www.barbourbooks.com

Check Out More Camp Club Girls!

Camp Club Girls: Sydney

Whether the Camp Club Girls are unraveling confusing clues that lead them through Washington, DC, and up to Fort McHenry, investigating peculiar tracks in the sand of the Outer Banks, uncovering the source of menacing sounds in the Wisconsin woods, or helping a young girl search for clues about her Cherokee heritage in North Carolina, you'll encounter six charming, relatable characters who combine their mystery-solving skills to save the day.

Paperback / 978-1-68322-942-1/ $9.99 / May 2019

Camp Club Girls: Alexis

Whether the Camp Club Girls are trying to save a Sacramento nature park, soaking up British history during the London Bridge festival in Lake Havasu, Arizona, witnessing odd incidents at a Lake Tahoe animal refuge, or filming a documentary for kids in Washington State, you'll encounter six charming, relatable characters who combine their mystery-solving skills to save the day.

Paperback / 978-1-68322-991-9 / $9.99 / June 2019